02/11/13
Largo Cultural Center

Copyright © 2008 by Carme Pitrello

All rights reserved. No part of this book may be reproduced or utilized in any form or by any means, electronic or mechanical, including photocopying, recording, or any other information storage retrieval system, without permission in writing from the Publisher except by a reviewer, who may quote brief passages for review.

Published by Pitrello Productions, LLC
P.O. Box 86102
Madeira Beach, FL 33738
(727) 459-2530

Pitrello, Carme, 1933-
  Sing Deadly
  ISBN 978-0-9823632-0-1

Printed in the United States of America
First Edition

Carme Pitrello

SING DEADLY

Carme Pitrello

Acknowledgments

When I started writing this book, two of my show biz friends gave me a lot of encouragement…

- Freddie Bell, whose name, Ferdinando Dominico Bello, I used as the main character. Freddie left us before the book was completed.
- Peter Anthony, a very funny comic, trumpet player and avid reader.

Carolyn Proctor, author, helped me enormously. But without the help of Sharon Newby and her son, Tim, the book would not have gotten off the ground. I can't thank them enough for their hard work and diligence in making this book readable.

Carme Pitrello

Author's Note:

This book is a work of fiction. All names and characters are invented or used fictitiously. I had to come up with lot of Italian names, and that's a lot of A, E, I, O and Us.

The names of the clubs and towns are real. I just added some unsavory characters along the way. If I've stepped on anybody's toes, it wasn't intentional, so don't call Guido or Nunzio.

Enjoy the book. Some of these things actually happened. You figure out which.

- Carme Pitrello

Carme Pitrello

***Dedicated to my best friend**
Freddie Bell*

Carme Pitrello

Chapter 1

This was to be an "in plain view" hit. The guy that hired him wanted the mark to know who had sent him. Danny had it all figured out. The ice pick was up his right sleeve and the point was resting on one finger tip. A slight move and the pick would drop into his hand, neat and clean.

It was a brisk afternoon in Chicago. The sun was out, but it was still overcoat weather. Danny DiBernardo sat on a bench humming softly to himself, a habit he had since he was a kid. He was watching the building down the street. He knew the man he was after would be coming out soon. Danny had been watching him for a week, so he knew his normal routine. Usually the guy would come out, light up a cigarette and walk to the garage where his car was parked. He always walked right past the bench where Danny was waiting.

Finally the mark came out, lit his cigarette and started walking toward him. Danny stood up and waited as the guy approached. The mark's coat was open. Good, that made it easier. As the man approached, Danny stood in front of him with a cigarette in his mouth and said, "Excuse me. Do you have a light?" The man said, "Sure." He reached for the lighter in his right front pocket. Danny stepped in, put his arm around him trapping the mark's right arm and gripping his left arm with his left hand. The pick slipped into Danny's right hand. In one motion, he slammed it up under the rib cage and said, "This is from Louie." He moved the pick from side to side shredding the man's heart. Danny looked into the man's eyes as the life went out of him. He eased him down on the park bench, keeping his arm around the man's shoulder like they were talking. He crossed his legs and buttoned his coat so it looked like old buddies having a smoke together. Danny checked the few people that were walking by. Nobody was paying any attention to them. He got up, smiled, and started walking down the street singing to himself. "So long, it's been good to know you."

******

Danny parked his car in front of the Italian restaurant and went inside. He sat at the bar and acknowledged the hello's from wise guys and wanna-be wise guys. He ordered wine and looked at the pictures on the wall behind the bar. His picture was there.

It seemed like a long time since he had been a Marine. His thoughts drifted back to when he was a kid. At age seven his father was killed during a shootout in a speakeasy. His mother couldn't handle it and went over the rainbow. Danny was left on the streets. He fought his way up, rolling drunks, stealing, and always in trouble with the law. When he was 14, they sent him to reform school for two years. On his first day, the bully of his block tried to roust him. Danny beat him senseless and had to be dragged off by the guards.

A boxing coach at the reform school saw what happened, realized his natural talents and convinced the warden that he had the potential to be a fighter. So he took Danny, trained him to be a boxer, and channeled all that anger and hate into a formidable fighting machine. Danny never lost a fight in the two years he was there. He pounded everybody they put up against him. When he left reform school, the boxing coach gave him the name of a trainer that could take him to the next level.

Danny would have contacted him too, but the need for fast cash was stronger. So, he started running numbers for Don Angelo. Then, fate stepped in. One day, on his way back to the drugstore to turn in the money and the slips, a punk tried to rob him. Danny punched him so hard, he killed him. That's when Danny came to the attention of Don Angelo. The Don figured that anybody fighting that hard for his money deserved a break. So, he took Danny under his wing and made him a collector. He was ruthless. If they didn't pay he would break bones or punch their teeth out.

He started moving up in the organization. The Don finally made Danny a "made man" after having him kill a local official who had been nosing around his business. Danny caught the guy as he was waiting for an elevator in the underground garage of his apartment building. He pumped two shots into his heart and one into the guy's head for good measure. The cops never found out who did it.

Things went fine for a couple of years until one night, in a local hang out, three guys from a rival gang jumped Danny. He was arrested after putting one in intensive care and beating the other two senseless. With the Korean War going on, the judge gave this nineteen year old a choice. He could enlist in the military or go to jail.

Danny chose the Marines. The bad thing about it was that Danny wasn't use to taking orders while being yelled at. During the night, on more than one occasion, he waited for a particular noncom to come walking by. With a blanket thrown over the guy's head, Danny's fists did the rest. His buddies covered for him, so no one could ever prove anything. He finished boot camp and was sent to Korea. There he could take out his anger on the North Koreans and the Chinese. He became a killing machine and the marines gave him medals for it.

Now, he was killing for the Don. Danny looked at his face in the restaurant mirror. Looking back was a face that had been through it all. With scars around his eyes from countless fights, a broken nose and knife scar on his right cheek, he was still, what you might call, ruggedly handsome. Standing six foot tall, with 200 pounds of solid muscle, Danny had no trouble getting broads.

He felt a hand on his shoulder and turned to see Don Angelo standing beside him. Danny loved the Don like a father. Don Angelo leaned in and asked, "Did everything go OK?"

"Like clockwork. No problems. He's probably still sitting on the bench in the park where I left him."

The Don patted him on the cheek. "You're a good boy, Danny. Say, we're having a big party tonight at the Italian

American Club with lots of food, broads and good music. Starts at eight. I want you to come and sit with me."

"Sounds good. I'll go home and change. See you there."
They hugged, then Danny finished his wine, got up and left.

*****

When he got to the Italian-American club, the party was already in full swing. Four hundred people were drinking and dancing. It took him awhile to get to Don Angelo's table. He had to stop and hug guys and girls alike. Lots of back slapping and friendly insults were the rule. When he finally got there, the Don stood up, hugged him and kissed him on both cheeks. Danny bent down and kissed momma Angelo and she smiled up at him.

The Don introduced him to the man and woman at his table. Danny didn't know them. They were from Buffalo. Sitting at the end of the table was a beautiful black haired girl with hazel eyes. Even sitting down Danny could see she was built. The Don said, "Danny, I want you to meet Ritchie Regerio and Carmen. She's Ritchie's daughter. Go sit next to her." Danny shook hands with Ritchie, walked around the table and sat next to Carmen. He took her hand and said, "I'm glad to meet you."

She looked into his eyes. "I'm glad to meet you, too. The Don has been telling me about you. He thinks a lot of you."

"I hope he hasn't made me out to be a choir boy."

"On the contrary, he said you are hard, tough, efficient and extremely loyal. What else could a person ask for?"

"Well, I could ask you to dance."

Carmen smiled, "I'd like that." She stood up and Danny almost fell out of his chair. She had a body most men would kill for. He got up, offered her his arm, and headed for the dance floor. On the way, she got some whistles and a few remarks which stopped immediately when Danny glared in the direction of their source. When they got to the floor, she literally melted into his arms as they moved together. Danny had trouble keeping an erection from being discovered. She made a move and pushed her pelvis against him.

Abruptly, she leaned back and said, "My, my, you're hard all over aren't you?"

"What did you expect? I'm human and one hundred percent Italian." He pulled her closer and started to sing softly. They were playing "Arrivaderci Roma." He was singing it in Italian. She leaned back and looked at him with amazement. "You really have a beautiful voice. How come you're not up there singing with the band?"

"Me? You got to be kidding. I couldn't do that. I sing along with my albums at home. I could never sing with a band."

"I don't see why not." She grabbed his hand, and started pulling him up to the bandstand. Reluctantly, Danny followed. She was very persistent. Carmen motioned to the bandleader. He leaned over to her as the band was playing. Carmen said, "Take it from the top. He has agreed to sing for us."

The band came back around to the beginning. Danny hesitated, shook his head, then stepped up to the microphone and reluctantly, started to sing. The whole room stopped and the dancers all came to the front of the bandstand to listen. Danny's voice was velvet. You would never think a sound like that could come out of a guy who was big, mean and killed people. When he got through, there was generous applause and shouts of, "More, more." Danny smiled and started to step down.

Carmen looked up at him and said, "Please, do another one for me. Do Al Di La."

He didn't want to disappoint her, and everyone was encouraging him, so he nodded to the bandleader and went into the song. He sang it in English and Italian.

As Danny sang, Carmen thought to herself, *"Wow, I can't believe this. He is an absolute natural. Not bad looking either."* She glanced around the room. He had the complete attention of everyone, even the men. *"He evidently has never had any singing lessons, but I don't think anybody recording today has a better voice. Incredible! He just needs a little polish and someone to advise him. Just listen to that voice! I'm going to convince my father to let me make this my own project. With the people that we* know, there is a possibility to make some serious money with this guy."

Danny looked down at this beautiful creature and smiled. He felt like he was floating. He never had this feeling before. Once again, when he was through, there were shouts of, "More, more."

Danny waved and stepped off the bandstand into Carmen's arms. She pulled his head down and kissed him. "You are absolutely beautiful."

"I must admit, it was kinda fun." "

"Come on, we have to talk to the Don."

They walked back to the Don's table. Don Angelo and everyone at his table stood up. He came over and hugged Danny. "You never told me you could sing like that. Momma and I couldn't believe it. That was absolutely beautiful."

"I never sang in front of a live band before. It made me a little nervous. I usually just sing along with records at home."

Carmen said to the Don, "Don Angelo, this guy has all the makings of a real star. Did you see how people reacted to his singing? You could do this for him. I'd like to discuss this with you at length. I think that there is a real opportunity here."

The Don nodded his head in agreement. "You know, you may have something there. Danny, I want you and Carmen to come to the office tomorrow at one o'clock. We got to talk this out. Now go have fun you two."

Carmen got him out on the floor again. She loved to dance. "So, what do you think of that?"

Danny looked down at her. "I don't know. I don't know anything about show business. And look at this face. How can I be a star with a kisser like this?"

"That can be taken care of. I have a guy in Buffalo that can make you look like anybody you want. I'll be at the meeting tomorrow with you, and we can hash it all out. But tonight, you're mine." She moved in again, shifting her pelvis back and forth against him. He couldn't help but moan as he became aroused. "Oh don't worry, Danny. I know what to do with it."

He looked into her eyes and said, "I'll bet you do."

Chapter 2

They woke up at eleven o'clock in each others arms. She looked at him and said, "For the first time in my life I have been completely and thoroughly fucked. I've never had anybody like you. That thing you have has to be ten inches long. It's almost like a weapon lying there."

Danny smiled, reached over and cupped her breast. "I'm glad you like it. His name is Ninja." At the mention of the name Carmen screamed with laughter. "Boy, you sure named him right."

"How about another round before we have to go?" He reached down and put his hand between her legs and stroked her. She started to shiver as he rolled her on top of him. She sat there with her eyes closed as he slid deep inside. She had never had one this big and it filled her completely. She started to move, slowly at first. He looked up at her and those beautiful breasts swinging gently above him.

He said softly, "Come on Carmen, do it for me." She started to buck and ride him hard until her climax started. "Come with me, please come with me." She felt him grow larger as she climaxed. She kept going until she fell on his chest exhausted. They lay there panting and sweating, waiting for their hearts to slow down. He rolled her off to the left. They looked into each other's eyes. He smiled at her. "Now, that sweetheart, is best way to start a day."

She stretched like a cat and said, "It's better than Wheaties. That's for sure."

After a few moments she sat up and said, "Time to get up. We have to be at the Don's in less than two hours. Go get ready and I'll meet you there."

He got up, gathered his clothes and went into the bathroom to dress. When he came out she was waiting for him. She came into his arms and kissed him. "Danny Boy, today could be the best day of your life. Now, get out of here so I can get ready."

He kissed her lightly and headed for the door. As he opened it, he turned to her. "It's already started out to be just that." He smiled at her and left.

******

When they walked into Don Angelo's office together, the Don was sitting at his desk talking to four gentlemen. One was Carmen's father, Richey. They all looked up and smiled. The Don said, "Danny, you and Carmen come over here and sit down. We have things to discuss." He introduced his friends. "This is Tomasso from Pittsburgh, Carlo from Cleveland and of course you know Carmen's father. This guy here, is Patsy from New Jersey."

They went over and sat down. The Don got up and walked around. "We've been discussing what we have to do to get you into show business. Now, we can make you a star. That's easy, but we have to do something about your past. You weren't exactly a saint growing up and you've got a rap sheet a mile long. The feds know you work for me and what you do for me. So, we have to figure out a way to do away with Danny DiBernardo and come up with somebody else."

Carmen's father spoke up. "Don Angelo, don't you have a nephew in Italy about Danny's age? As I remember, a good looking boy, got paralyzed in a car accident about a year ago?"

"Yeah, that's my sister's boy. He's in a convalescent home. He'll never be the same and will probably spend the rest of his life there. What are you thinking?"

"I'm thinking we can make Danny Di your nephew! I know he was born here and your sister took him to Italy to live a number of years ago. It's simple. He comes back here and becomes a singer. He already has a birth certificate and a social security number. All we have to do is upgrade his passport. We have people that can do that with out any questions. And who would check a small town in Italy for somebody that got hurt in a car wreck?"

Carmen spoke up. "Don Angelo, I have a plastic surgeon in Buffalo that can work miracles. I'm relatively sure he can make Danny look like your nephew. All we need is a recent picture."

The Don thought for a moment. "It could work, but what do we do about Danny DiBernardo?"

Carlo from Cleveland spoke up. "We kill him!" All heads turned towards him. "We blow him up in his car so there's nothing left but some ID."

"But, who are you going to get to blow up in the car? There's got to be a body!" The three men looked at each other and smiled. Big Tomasso from Pittsburgh said, "Hey, don't worry about it. We can handle that. In the mean time, we all have a piece of the boy, right?"

Don Angelo looked at the four friends. "Of course, he belongs to the five of us. We run interference for him, set him up in the best clubs, and get a recording contract for him when he's ready."

Danny finally spoke up. "Don Angelo, I thank you and these gentlemen for doing this, but I don't know anything about show business. I wouldn't know where to start."

Carmen spoke up. "I can help him with all of that. I know arrangers and choreographers and people who can stage him. We take him to Buffalo and do everything there. And when he's ready we can bring him back to Chicago. This way nobody is the wiser. There's something else. We have to have a name for him. What's your nephew's name?"

"Ferdinando Dominico Bello."

Carmen laughed. "That's a mouthful! Since he belongs to the Angelo family, why don't we name him Danny Angel?"

They all looked at one another. The Don thought awhile, smiled and finally said, "I like it. It has a nice ring to it. What do you guys think?"

They all nodded in unison and "Danny Di" became Danny Angel. The Don asked his friends, "So, when do we start?"

Carmen's father said, "Now. We take him back to Buffalo with us. I need a picture of your nephew. Then Tomasso and Carlo can do what they have to do about getting rid of Danny DiBernardo. Wait, what about his family?"

"He has no family. I'm his family." The Don reached over and patted Danny on the cheek. "So, we have nothing to worry about there."

Carmen's father looked at Danny and said, "You leave everything at your place. You take nothing with you. Whatever you need we'll get for you. You're starting a new life and, like your old one, you start naked. Capisci?"

Danny nodded his head. "Capisci."

The Don hugged Danny. "You go on now, and when you come back we'll celebrate your new life. Richie will keep me informed of what's going on. I promise you, I'll give you a nice funeral. The best."

Danny hugged him. Carmen took his arm and walked him out the door. She leaned in and said, "Now, I have you and Ninja for a long time. Don't get me wrong, you're going to work hard and long, but the rewards will be well worth it."

He smiled at her, "And I intend to give you a workout personally, every chance I get."

She grabbed him and felt herself getting excited.

*****

When they got off the plane in Buffalo, it was snowing and bitter cold. Danny felt like he was back in Korea. The wind went right through him. He shivered. Carmen put her arm round him and guided him into the terminal. The heat was a welcome relief. "Is it always this cold here?"

"Well, this is winter and it's like this until April. You'll get used to it."

"I didn't in Korea and I bet I won't here."

They walked to the front entrance. There was a big black limo waiting. The driver was loading the luggage into the trunk.

Two big body guards were standing by the car looking around. One came up to the door and motioned them out. They got in the limo and started for the house. The driver was excellent on the snowy, icy streets.

They came to a mansion with big wrought iron gates guarding the front. The gates opened and they drove in. Danny had never seen a house as big as this. Not even Don Angelo's house was this big. They pulled up to the front door, got out and walked quickly into the house. It was absolutely beautiful. Inlaid marble was on the floor. Statues and fountains lined the foyer. Mrs. Regerio came out of a room that must have been the kitchen. The smell of sauce was delightful. She came over and hugged and kissed her husband and Carmen. She looked at Danny. "And who is this young man?"

Carmen took her mother's hand. "Momma, this is Danny Angel. He'll be staying with us for a while."

Momma looked at her husband and raised her eyebrows in that all-questioning Italian way. Richie smiled at her. "He's Don Angelo's nephew and, if everything goes according to plan, we're going to make him a singing star. He'll live in the guest house out back. Consider him part of the family."

Momma smiled at Danny. "Good, I always wanted a son. Maybe he can sing to me at night. But come, you must be hungry after that long flight." She turned and headed back into the kitchen with the three of them following her. The kitchen looked more like a restaurant kitchen. They sat down and were served by the kitchen staff. The food and wine were perfect and Danny ate his fill.

Momma smiled at him. "See, he eats like a real Italian. Not like Carmen who picks at her food." She looked at her daughter and smiled.

"Ma, if I ate like Danny I would be like a balloon. I've got to keep my girlish figure."

Momma rolled her eyes and sighed. Carmen said, "I'll take Danny out back and get him settled. We have to go shopping tomorrow for clothes and make some appointments to get other things done."

She got up and motioned Danny to follow her. He thanked momma for the meal and said he would see her later. They put on their coats and went out back to the guest house. It was complete with a workout room, sauna, Jacuzzi, and a well-stocked kitchen. Carmen showed him through the house. They ended up in the master bedroom. It was bigger than his apartment. The bed was king size and three feet off the floor. Carmen looked at him and smiled, "Our play ground."

Danny sat on the bed and said, "What about your mother and father? Won't they mind? I mean, I am a guest here."

Carmen came over and sat next to him. "They have long ago given up trying to figure me out. I do what I please and never embarrass them. So, this is where you, me and that anaconda of yours will spend many happy days. Does that scare you?"

He reached for her and pulled her down on the bed. "Nothing scares me, sweetheart. I can handle anything that comes my way. Would you like a sample now?"

She wiggled out from under him. "I would like nothing better, but I have to go back inside and get things rolling. We have all night for that."

They reluctantly got off the bed, put their coats on and returned to the main house. Ritchie was in his study talking on the phone. He motioned them in and pointed to the chairs in front of the desk. They sat down and waited until he had finished his conversation.

"That was Tomasso. Everything is set for next week. They got Danny's car and are wiring it up. There's a guy in Pittsburgh about Danny's size that has been opening his mouth to the wrong people. So, he'll be in Danny's car when it goes boom. There's enough plastic and gas to completely disintegrate every trace of the body. So Danny, you get to watch your own funeral."

Danny smiled and looked down at his hands. "Everything is happening so fast. It's hard to believe that only two days ago, I was doing a job for the Don. Now I'm going to be somebody else, and the only way I'll be killing people, is from a stage."

That drew a laugh from Carmen and Ritchie. Carmen patted

his knee. "You're going to be just fine. With that voice and your new good looks you'll be a star in no time. I'm going to make an appointment tomorrow with my plastic surgeon. The sooner we get it done the better. We don't want any of your friends accidentally seeing you when you should be dead."

Danny looked at her. "Are you sure he can make me look like that picture? I mean, look at this face. It's been through a lot, and there's a little matter of the knife scar on my cheek."

Carmen took his hand. "Danny, trust me. You are going to be gorgeous. Even the Don will have to look twice to see that it's really you. Now, you go back to your house and settle in. Take a sauna or Jacuzzi to relax. I'll be over later after I make some calls and talk to my father."

Danny got up and took his leave. Her father looked at her. "You like him don't you? Listen, don't let that get in the way of what we're trying to do here. Keep your sex life separate from the business of making this kid a star. There's going to be a lot of hard work ahead."

She came around the desk and sat on his lap like she used to do as a kid. "Daddy, I know how important this is, and I won't let my emotions get in the way. But, I do like him. He's the first real man I have ever known. All the other boyfriends were wimps. They were either trying to impress you or were afraid of you. I'll be careful." She kissed him, got up and went to make her calls.

Her father shook his head and watched her go. Under his breath he said, "Yes, she's her father's daughter alright."

*****

She came to him in the night. They made love like two desperate people. They couldn't get enough of each other. Finally, sleep overtook them. At 10am they got up, showered together, fooled around, got dressed and went into the main house for breakfast. Momma gave her an all knowing look, but said nothing. They finished breakfast and planned their day. The doctor's appointment was set for four o'clock. That gave them time to get a new wardrobe, from the socks up. Carmen took charge.

They got in the limo and headed for downtown Buffalo. She knew the tailors and all the best shops. Danny just sat back and let her do her thing. For the next four hours he was measured, tried on countless coats, suits, shirts and shoes. Carmen bought shirts and sweaters right off the rack because he was easy to fit. His suits and tuxedos were being made by the best tailors in the area.

Finally, it was time to go see the doctor. Danny was nervous. Carmen had to hold his hand and assure him everything was going to be all right. She thought to herself. *"He may be a killer and a tough guy, but under it all, he's still a little boy."*

The doctor brought them into his office and sat them down. He came over and looked at Danny's face, then poked, prodded and measured. "So, what do you want done to this face?"

Carmen handed him the picture. He studied it for awhile. He would look at the picture, then at Danny's face. "I can do this. I'll have to re-break the nose and trim it down, get rid of the scar tissue around the eyes and do some restructuring. But, it can be done. He has a good face for it."

"So, Paul, when can you get to it? But, before you answer, I have to tell you something. Once we start this, and it's done, it never happened. Do you understand?"

Paul looked at her with a smile on his face. "Carmen, I've known you all your life. Your father and I grew up together. He was responsible for me going to medical school. If you say it never happened, it never happened. But, I'll have to do the operation in my office. I have all the equipment here and a nurse who can keep her mouth shut. I gather you want this done in a hurry, so how about tomorrow night? Can you have him here at seven o'clock?"

"He'll be here, and thanks Paul." She got up, walked around the desk and kissed him on the cheek. "See you tomorrow night." She motioned for Danny to follow her out of the office.

*****

Don Angelo sat across from Tomasso, Patsy and Carlo. As

they drank wine from Don Angelo's cellar, they were discussing Danny and the details of what had to be done. Tomasso leaned back in his chair. "So, Don Angelo, we're going to make this kid a star. Is he really that good?"

The Don sipped his wine. "Yes, he is. Surprised the hell out of me and I thought I knew all about him. Now, it's going to cost us some money to get it off the ground, but it will come back ten fold. Have you ever known me to do anything that doesn't make money?"

Carlo chuckled. "Not you, Don. That's what I admire about you. You're always one step ahead of other people. Now getting back to Danny, I had my guys wire the car up and it's ready to go. I figure, maybe in three days. Tomasso's guys will have the fink by then. They're going to drive him up here so nobody will suspect anything. He'll just disappear from Pittsburgh. He's a smalltime hood with a big mouth and a police record, so I don't think anybody will make a stink."

Tomasso spoke up. "You're right, Carlo. Neat and clean."

The Don stood up. "Now, we got to start him small. He has to pay some dues, so he can learn the business. Ritchie has New York sewn up. Buffalo, Syracuse, Utica, Rochester, and when he's ready, New York City. Tomasso, you have Pennsylvania and I know you own interest in clubs in Philadelphia and Pittsburgh. Carlo has Ohio. Youngstown, Toledo, Cleveland and he has Detroit through the Purple Gang. Patsy has New Jersey and Atlantic City. As you know, we'll have the whole country at our feet when we get ready to make the big move. So, we wheel him through the east. Then, we record him and put him on every juke box on the east coast. We get Dick Clark to put him on that show he has.

I can handle him when I bring him to Chicago. Now, it's going to take awhile to make him a big star, but when he is, we get our money from his records, movies, TV and any other thing he does. But, that's not where the big money comes in. I have a plan I've been kicking around with some people in Europe and our own government here. Remember when the C.I.A. came to us to kill Castro? There were numerous other times they wanted something done by us that they couldn't be involved in.

Well, Danny is a killing machine. He's smart, fearless and who would suspect a superstar of killing people? Not just ordinary people. I mean heads of state, ambassadors, and people like that. That's where the real money comes in. Millions. They'll pay millions for it." He stopped and looked at his friends. They were looking at him in awe.

Tomasso finally said, "Don, that's fucking brilliant. But will Danny go along with this?"

"Danny will do what we tell him to do. He's like a son to me, but you know our code. Nothing personal. Strictly business."

Carlo spoke up. "Don, what kind of time frame are we looking at here, before we start this thing?"

"I figure maybe a year to get him started and maybe two as a major superstar. That should do it."

Patsy looked at the Don and said, "So, this is going to be worldwide, not just here in America?"

"Right. We send him all over the world and he'll take care of business. We don't tell him about it until he's ready. Then we'll work out the details. So, what do you think?"

They all nodded their heads, yes. The Don smiled at them. "This has never been done before. It should be interesting."

Chapter 3

Danny stood before the big mirror in the bathroom staring at his face. He leaned in and looked at the scars around his eyes. He remembered the countless punches he took and the pain when a guy he was fighting, head butted him and flattened his nose. How many times did he break it? It was hard to tell. His finger felt the knife scar on his face. Danny could still picture the face of the North Korean soldier that put it there. His training in hand to hand combat saved his life. He had taken the knife away from the Korean and forced it into his heart. Staring into the man's startled eyes, he watched the life go out of his body. He remembered saying to the soldier, "Too bad the last thing you're ever going to see, is this fucked up face."

He leaned back from the mirror and laughed. "It's the same thing all over again. This is the last time I'll see this fucked up face. By next month or so I'll be looking at a new face. It will be the same body, but a new kisser."

Carmen came up behind him in the bathroom naked. She put her arms around his waist and pressed her body against his back. "What are you laughing at?"

He reached back, grabbed her ass with both hands and pulled her closer. "I was just saying to myself that this is the last time I'll see this fucked up face. It's going to be strange looking into a mirror and seeing somebody else."

"Does that make you sad?"

"I don't know. It's going to take me awhile to get adjusted to this whole thing."

"Don't worry. I'll be here to help you."

"You'd better be. I'm not used to being in a straight world. I don't know how to act around those people."

"We'll have plenty of time to teach you while you're healing. We'll talk about that over breakfast." She reached around and grabbed Ninja, turned him around and led him into the shower. Danny laughed and said, "I feel like a pull toy."

They showered, got dressed and went into the kitchen of the main house. Mrs. Regerio and Ritchie were sitting at the table. She gave them a look that said she knew what they had been doing. Carmen went over and kissed her on the forehead. She did the same to her father. Ritchie looked up from his morning paper. "Sit down you two and have some breakfast. We got a lot to discuss today."

They sat down and started to eat. Carmen looked at her father. "I'm taking Danny out to pick up the clothes we ordered yesterday. The tuxes can wait until he has healed from the surgery. I want to go by a music store and get a few song books of all the great songs, so he can start learning the words. Then, we get Tony Odie over when he's healed to start putting the act together. We can use McVan's nightclub to stage him in the afternoons. I know Harry at The Town Casino would let us use his place, but when Danny plays there, it will be as a headliner. We don't want to tip our hand.

Her father put down his fork. "Good thinking. I see you're really into this. That's good. You handle that end and I'll do the rest."

They left and went to downtown Buffalo to get the things for Danny. They drove the Mercedes. Ritchie didn't send any bodyguards with them because he knew Danny would look after his daughter. They got all their things done and Carmen took him to the Chez-A-Me for a late lunch.

They were enjoying the meal and each other when a wanna-be wise guy came to the table and started talking to Carmen. He ignored Danny completely and was hanging over Carmen like he owned her. He made a move to sit down. Danny leaned forward in his chair and said in a flat voice, "I wouldn't do that if I were you."

The guy turned toward him and was going to make a smart

remark but, when he saw Danny's eyes, he froze. It was like looking into hell. He said a hasty goodbye and practically ran out the door. Carmen was beside herself with laughter. "I'll bet he has to change his shorts when he gets home. He's been trying to date me for a long time, but he's a jerk. I'm glad you were here to scare the hell out of him. Do you usually have that affect on people?"

Danny turned to her. His eyes softened. "I don't like guys like that with no respect for women." He stood up, threw some money down on the table to cover the tab and tip. He helped Carmen to her feet. As they walked out, all the men in the room were looking at Carmen. Danny smiled and said to himself. *"Look all you want, but she's mine."*

They got in the car and she drove over to the Doctor's office. Danny was nervous and it showed. He kept thinking.. *This would be the last time he would be looking like his old self. He would be walking out of here wearing another man's face. And, no more killing. From now on he would have, a new life without violence and bloodshed. It's going to take awhile to get used to this.*

The doctor came out of the back wearing his scrubs. He sat Danny down and explained what he was going to do. He handed him a hospital gown and showed him where to change. Danny undressed and put on the gown. He stood in front of the mirror and said, "Good bye Danny Di. Hello Danny Angel."

He walked out. Carmen was talking to the doctor. She smiled at him, came over and gave him a hug and a kiss. "I'll be here when he's finished with you. Don't worry." She held his face, looking at it so she could remember. The doctor took him by the arm and went into the operating room. Carmen sat down, picked up a magazine and started to read.

Six hours later, the doctor came out and sat next to her. "Well, he's done. I must say I did a magnificent job. He should look just like the picture of the Don's nephew, but a little older and more mature. He's going to be sore for awhile, so I'm giving you some pain pills and sleeping pills. You have to ice him down to keep the swelling at a minimum. With no complications, I'll see him in two weeks to see how he's doing. I put a bed in his room so you can be close to him. You can take him home in the morning. I'll check on him in awhile. My nurse will be monitoring him the rest of the night."

Carmen leaned over and hugged him. "I can't thank you enough, Paul. Just send the bill to my father and he'll take care of it. He insists. It's a joint effort so don't hold back. Charge what you would charge those fat clients of yours."

The doctor laughed and patted her hand. "OK, I promise. You can go in now. He'll be asleep for awhile. If you need anything, call my nurse."

"Thanks Paul, I will. I have to call my dad and let him know what's going on. Then I'll go to Danny." She walked over to the phone on his desk and dialed.

******

They were coming, hundreds of them, screaming, flares going off, bugles blowing, gunfire all around him. He was standing in his stocking feet in the bitter cold. His M1 rifle blazing as he cut down the first Chinese to attack his position. His buddy lay wounded at his feet, loading for him. He reached down and took a newly loaded M1 and started shooting again.

They were falling and screaming in front of him. The barrel of the rifle was getting hot. But he kept up a murderous stream of fire. He felt a hot burning in his leg where a bullet creased him. He took a bullet in his left shoulder, but he kept on. Then help came. He fell to the ground, feet frozen and blood coming out of his leg and chest.

He was lying in his fox hole. The fog so thick you could cut it with a knife. The Chinese soldier pouncing on top of him... The desperate struggle to kill him seemed to go on forever. Then the frantic need to push the body off.

Now came the pain in his face. He was in the ring with Joe Louis and taking a beating. He tried desperately to hit him, kill him, but he couldn't do it. Everything was moving in slow motion.

He saw the faces of the people he had killed. They were

staring at him. He beat at them with his hands to smash their faces. There was the North Korean soldier coming at him with a bayonet. He felt the sting as the bayonet cut his face. In rage, he took the bayonet away from the soldier and slammed it into his heart over and over, and watched as the life went out of his eyes. Then, he was in the bedroom with Carmen and they were making love.

He felt her cool hand in his and her voice saying, "It's all right. You're going to be all right." He tried to sit up, but a hand pushed him back down. "No, just lay still. I'm here." He relaxed and dropped off again.

More weird dreams... more killing and fighting. Bodies blown to pieces were everywhere. The smell of blood and fear were unmistakable. The Chinese soldier firing down on his buddies had turned towards him and fired. The enemy bullet went through his sleeve as he fired his Thompson sub-machine gun.

Fifteen forty-five caliber slugs ripping into the soldier's body... the hat flying off... the long black hair falling down her back. He ran down the hill and cradled her in his arms, begging her not to die as bullets snapped and whipped around him.

Then, he was trapped in a halftrack under water. He couldn't breathe. He fought to get out...He freed himself then headed for the surface. His lungs were bursting, as he broke through and gasped for air. Danny woke up. His heart was pounding as he lay there sweating and breathing hard.

He felt a cool hand on his arm. Carmen's voice was reassuring. "It's all right Danny. I'm right here. I'll take good care of you. Just relax."

He lay back and felt the pain in his face. He couldn't see because his eyes were bandaged. The pain was bad, but he had suffered worse. He tried to talk, but only a croak came out. He felt a straw in his mouth and sucked a mouthful of cool water. He never knew water tasted so good. The nurse was talking to the doctor about pain medication.

He squeezed Carmen's hand and whispered to her. She got up and leaned over him to hear what he was saying. He could feel her face close to his. He reached up and squeezed her left breast, which caused her to laugh out loud. The doctor and nurse looked at her.

"He's going to be all right. He just told me so."

Chapter 4

The blast broke windows a block away. The car was an inferno. By the time the fire department got there, there was nothing but smoldering wreckage. The only way they knew who owned the car, was by the license plate, which they found half a block away. Chief of detectives, John O'Malley was talking to the fire chief. "So, they had gasoline in the car before they blew it?"

The fire chief wiped his head with a rag, "Yep, enough to burn everything to cinders. They must have really had it in for the poor bastard. Who was he?"

"We just ran the plates. Belonged to a hood who worked for Don Angelo. Danny DiBernardo. A tough cookie. We tried to pin some murders on him, but couldn't get passed the Don's influence. I wonder what he thinks of his boy now? Serves him right. These Dagos all end up in the same place sooner or later. Is there anything left of the body for identification?"

"Not a hell of a lot. That fire burned hot. They must have added some extra high octane stuff."

"Well, the crime lab boys will let us know." He walked over to his partner. "Hey Louie, have we got an address on this guy?"

Louie looked in his note book, "Yeah, he lived across the street. Apartment 22A."

"Come on, we'll go toss it and see if we can find anything that can help us. He may have something on the Don we can use."

"I doubt it. These guys are closed mouthed, but it's worth a try."

They headed for the super's apartment. They were a strange

pair. John was 5'10, 170 pounds and Louie was a big mick, 250 pounds on a six foot five frame. They had gone through the police academy together and had worked their way up through the ranks to detective. They got to 1A, the superintendent's apartment, and rapped on the door. It was opened, to the length of the chain, by a little man wearing big glasses. "Yes, can I help you?"

John showed him his shield. "Lieutenants O'Malley and Johnson. Chicago police department. We need the key to 22A."

The Super blinked behind those big glasses, "That's Danny DiBernardo's apartment. Why do you want the key?"

"Danny isn't with us anymore. Didn't you hear the explosion across the street?"

"Yes, but it wasn't any of my business. You mean Danny was blown up?"

"Yes, he was, so we need to check out his place to find out who to notify of his death. So, give me the key or come with us. Either way makes no difference to us."

The super closed the door to unlatch the chain and reopened it holding a key in his hand. "Please make sure I get this back when you're done."

"Will do, and thank you." He turned to his partner. "Let's go up and see what a made man's apartment looks like."

They got in the elevator and started up. When they got to the twenty second floor they got out and headed for 22A. John unlocked the door and stood aside. He turned the handle and pushed the door open. Nothing happened so he peeked around the door jamb. The apartment was empty. He drew his pistol and entered with Louie right behind him. A quick search and they relaxed.

The apartment was neat and clean. On one wall were records and albums of all the great singers, plus albums of Italian songs. John took out one of Sinatra's albums and looked at it. "Well, at least he had good taste in music. Louie, you check in here and I'll take the bedroom." John walked into the bedroom. It was as neat as the rest of the place. He checked the drawers and the bed finding nothing of interest. He went over and opened the closet and looked in. The suits were neatly arranged with a two inch space between each hanger. But hanging on the end was something that made him yell. "Holy shit, Louie, you got to come see this."

Louie came running into the room and stopped next to John. John pointed to the object hanging on the end. It was a Marine Corps dress uniform with a chest full of decorations. But the thing that stood out was the Congressional Medal of Honor hanging around the neck of the uniform.

Louie whistled. "Holy shit, he was a Medal of Honor winner. Who would have ever thought that a hood could win that?"

"You could if you were a killer before you went in. He was a tough cookie. His rap sheet is as long as your arm. He was Don Angelo's number one enforcer. The Don's not going to like this. I hope this doesn't trigger some reprisals."

He stepped back and closed the door. "Let's get back and check in with the chief. I'll have to let the Don know, and see what he wants to do about the remains and all this stuff." They went down to the super's apartment and gave him back the key with instructions that no one go in there, except the police. They went outside. It was like a movie scene. People were gawking, the firemen cleaning up the mess. The medical examiner was picking up pieces of body parts and bagging them.

John and Louie walked over to the M.E. "Hey, Alex. Do you think there's enough left to get a make on who was in the car?"

The M.E looked at him. "I was never good at puzzles, John. This guy is all over the place. Who ever did this, didn't want a lot left behind. I'll know more when I get all these pieces back at the morgue. One thing is strange though. I can't seem to find any teeth. Usually there are some left around, but I can't find any! What do you make of that?"

John thought for a minute. "Maybe they wanted to make it hard to identify him or they worked him over before they blew him to hell. It's happened before." He grabbed a cop going by and said, "I want you to go over to that apartment building and put up a crime scene tape on Apartment 22A. Seal it up and keep an eye on it."

The cop nodded and headed off. They walked to their car and got in. John started the engine and before they took off he glanced at what was left of the car. "That's a hell of a way to check out of this world. But whoever said, 'Live by the sword, die by the sword' knew what he was talking about." He put the car into gear and headed for the station house.

******

Don Angelo was in his study smoking one of his expensive cigars when the phone rang. He picked it up and said, "Hello." The voice on the other end said, "Don Angelo, this is Detective John O'Malley. Do you remember me?"

Don Angelo smiled. "Sure I remember you. You've been trying to put me away for years. What can I do for Chicago's finest?"

"It's what I can do for you, Don. I hate to tell you this, but your number one boy got himself blown up tonight. Danny DiBernardo is splattered all over a parking lot."

The Don sat back and smiled to himself. Now's the time to set the hook. He leaned back up and said in a hard flat voice, "You had better be kidding me. Nobody blows up my boys. Especially Danny."

"Well, somebody did, and I hope this doesn't start some kind of gang war. My boss is jumpy as it is. I wanted to know what you want done with the remains and Danny's stuff inside his apartment. I have to tell you there's not much left of the body. The coroner will release what there is, in a few days. You can have somebody pick him up."

"I'll take care of it. Now, you tell me something. Are you going to find out who did this, or sweep it under the rug like always, because he's a dago and worked for me?"

"No, Don. We have men canvassing the neighborhood trying to find out if anybody saw anything. But, you know how it is. They clam up if it doesn't concern them. We'll stay on it and work it like any other murder investigation."

"Sure you will. But I have my own resources who can also find out things. Maybe we can compare notes. Somebody killed a man that was like a son to me. I loved that boy and it angers me to have lost him. And you don't want to see me angry."

John could feel the heat over the phone. "Look Don Angelo, we'll do the best we can. Give us some time. Don't do anything foolish."

"Who, me? I'm not a foolish man. You just keep me informed." He hung up the phone and sat back and laughed. He picked up the phone on his private line and dialed a number. It rang three times and a man answered.

"Hello, Joe Vespia here."

"Joe, this is me. Somebody blew up my right hand tonight. Danny is dead. I want you to call down to police headquarters and find out what's going on. You have to make arrangements to get the body and Danny's things out of his apartment. You handle this for me. I'm too broke up to think straight. Keep me informed on what's happening. I'm counting on you Joe."

"Have I ever let you down? I'm sorry about Danny. I liked that kid. I'll handle everything. Just don't worry. I'll call you tomorrow and fill you in on what's going down."

"You're a good boy, Joe. Thanks." He hung up the phone, sat back in his leather chair and puffed on his cigar.

******

Danny was sitting on the couch with Carmen when the news broke on TV. The camera showed Danny's car in the back ground smoldering. A newscaster was standing off to one side and was saying, "This is all that's left of a car belonging to a suspected gangster named Danny DiBernardo, otherwise known on the streets as Danny Di. It is rumored that he worked for one of the crime bosses here in Chicago. At 8:30 tonight he met his untimely death when his car exploded and caught fire. The flames were so hot that, by the time the fire department got here, there was not much left of the car or its occupant, as you can see over my left shoulder. Police are searching the neighborhood trying to find anybody who saw anything. This is the first mob related killing in some time. Let's hope this doesn't start a gang war. I'm sending you back to the studio now for an update. This is Roger Clark, WGN News, here in Chicago."

The camera switched to the newsroom of WGN. A newscaster sat behind a desk with papers in his hand. A picture of Danny was on a screen behind him. He said, "This is Jimmy Fellows. Tonight at around eight thirty a car was blown up in a parking lot on Chicago's south side. The blast broke windows a block away and caused some minor injuries. The car belonged to a Danny DiBernardo, a known member of the Don Angelo crime family. The police believe Mr. DiBernardo was in the car at the time. We'll have more as information comes in."

Richie turned off the TV and turned to Danny. "Well, looks like you're gone. The boys did a good job on the car. Now, all we have to do is wait until the police release what's left of the body for the funeral."

Danny turned towards Ritchie until he could see him through the bandages. "I liked that car. I wonder if the insurance company will give me a new one?" That brought laughter from everybody in the room.

Carmen squeezed his hand. "Don't you worry, Danny. Your next car will be a Mercedes. Do you want me to get some ice for your face? The pain medication should be wearing off about now. I'll get you some more and some ice packs." She got up and went into the kitchen.

Danny had been home three days and the pain was still bad. He could live with that. He had lived with pain before. Ice helped with the scars that had started to itch. He was fidgety because he couldn't scratch them. When he looked in the mirror, he laughed. He looked like the invisible man or the mummy from horror pictures.

Tomorrow he would start learning songs. Carmen had a record player put in the guest house. She had bought all kinds of albums so he could learn the songs and listen to the arrangements. She had also contacted a song writer friend of hers to write some original tunes for him. The girl was amazing. He woke up in the morning with a big hard on. Carmen had used her mouth and the feeling was awesome. The pain in his face and the intense climax was like two forces fighting each other, good and evil. His thoughts were interrupted when Carmen returned.

"Here, take these pills and I'll put the ice packs on your face." She gave him the pills and a glass of water.

Danny took them and said, "You're a real Clara Barton. You know that?"

Carmen smiled at him. "You don't think I know who she is, but I do smart guy. And yes, I am your nurse. Or maybe you want Paul to send that two hundred pound ex-army nurse back to take care of you?"

"Oh no, you'll do just fine."

Ritchie broke in on their conversation. "I'll call the Don and give him my condolences on your death. I'll use my regular phone which is tapped to make it more official. Now, when you're healed, we'll take some photos for your passport. The Don said it was coming up for renewal. We'll get one of our guys coming in from Italy to get it stamped. We have connections in the immigration department. This way, they'll know you're back in the states. So, from now on, your name is Ferdinando Dominico Bello A.K.A., Danny Angel. The Don is sending his nephew's signature so you can practice it. As long as it's close, it'll do. His driver's license is expired, but we can fix that. He's also sending all the information on his nephew, so you'll know where he was born and all the things you should know about his past. If you're going to become a star, these are the things you should know for interviews."

"Boy, the Don thinks of everything. Looks like I'm going to be a busy boy for awhile. I'll have a new past, new songs, new life, and a new face. I'll be like a caterpillar coming out of a cocoon as a butterfly."

Carmen laughed at that. "You're the biggest damn butterfly I've ever seen. Come on, we'll go to the guest house and start going through songs." She got up and pulled Danny to his feet. "Come on Ferdinando Dominico Bello. Time to go get some work done."

Danny looked at Richie and said, "She's worse than some of

the drill sergeants I had in the Marines."

Richie looked up at his daughter, and then at Danny. "Believe me, she's tougher."

Chapter 5

Sergeant John O'Malley sat in the police chief's office. The chief was pacing up and down in front of him. He stopped in front of John and said, "Let me get this straight. Danny Di was in the car as far as we know. When the coroner turns the remains over to Don Angelo for burial, there has to be a full military funeral with all the brass there, because that murdering dago bastard was a Medal of Honor winner?"

"That's about the size of it, I guess. The Mayor, City Council, Police Commissioner, some brass from the Marine Corps, and even the Governor will be there. Believe me Chief, there's no way around it."

"The commissioner is going to shit a brick when I tell him."

"Better you than me. Well, I've got work to do. I gotta go. Good luck with the commissioner." O'Malley got up and left.

The chief sighed, picked up the phone, and dialed the commissioner's number. His secretary answered. When he came on the line the chief said, "Bill, it's Harry. You're not going to like what I have to tell you, but here it is. That hood that got blown up in his car a few days ago was a Medal of Honor winner. They will be having a full military funeral for him with all the dignitaries there. This means, you have to be there in full dress uniform, white gloves and all." He held the phone away from his ear as he knew what was coming. It did.

"You have got to be fucking shitting me. You think I'm going to dress up and stand around with all those goombas on television and pay tribute to a fucking hood?"

"Bill, calm down. I don't like this anymore than you do, but it's protocol. You have to be there, hood or no hood. What will the Mayor or the Governor think if you're not there?"

"God damn it, Harry. Normally I would tell both of them to kiss my ass. But, I'll tell you one thing. If I go, you go. You're going to be standing right next to me. So, you'd better get your uniform cleaned and pressed and make sure it still fits."

"Wait a minute. How did I get roped into this?"

"I told you, I'm not going alone. You'll be there to represent your precinct. After all, it happened on your turf."

"Yeah I guess you're right. I'll let you know the time and place. The Mayor will probably be calling you about this, so you can set his mind at ease. Tell him we'll be there, reluctantly."

"That little piss ant will be in his glory. If they were honoring Jack the fucking Ripper, he'd be there with that shit eating grin on his face."

Harry started to laugh. "You do have a way with words, Bill. I'll be in touch." He hung up the phone.

******

The Don was sitting in his study listening to his lawyer. Sitting around the room were some of the Don's wise guys. The lawyer was trying to explain to the Don about Danny's funeral. The wise guys were trying to talk to the Don about who did this and who they should whack for it. The Don held up his hand for silence. When it got quiet he said, "One thing at a time. Larry, you're trying to tell me that my boy was a war hero? I knew he got some medals, but he never talked about them. Now, you're telling me he won the Congressional Medal of Honor!"

"Yes, and that calls for a full military funeral. As I understand it, there will be a General from the Marine Corps along with some lesser brass. The Mayor, Governor and local officials will be in attendance. There's also a Marine Corps color guard that will be there to give him a gun salute, plus a bugler, who will play taps at the end of the ceremony. Don Angelo, this is big stuff."

"Hey listen, my Danny deserves the best and that's what

he's getting. The very best. What makes me laugh is that the Mayor and the Governor and all those other big shots, are going to have to be there and kiss my ass because my boy won a medal."

The lawyer continued, "Now, as I understand it, Danny is going to be buried in your family crypt."

"That's right," replied the Don. "I have asked The Hayden Funeral Home to handle everything. When is all this supposed to take place?"

"On Saturday. Four days from now. I've already got the church and the mass scheduled at St. Mary of the Lake, 4200 N. Sheridan. The mass will be at eleven o'clock in the morning. The Monsignor wants to do the mass himself, out of respect for you."

"Good. I want you to notify the other families and let them know. Meantime, keep me informed. Now, leave us. I have to talk to my boys."

Larry gathered up his papers and left. The Don waited a second, and then turned to his guys. "I want to know who did this to Danny. I already got calls from all the families telling me they had nothing to do with this. The Mick's said the same thing. The Jews and the Titsonis swear they didn't do it. But, I don't believe them. I want you to check out everybody and find out who's responsible for Danny's death. Somebody has got to know something. Lean on them. Do what you have to do, but bring me something. Now, get out and do what I pay you to do."

They got up and left. The Don sat down and smiled. They'd find some poor bastard who had nothing to do with anything, whack him, and tell me that he was the one. His mind drifted to Danny. It's typical of him to not tell me that he won that medal. He knew Danny had been decorated, but not this. It made him proud. He'd tell Danny how he felt the next time he saw him. Meantime, he would get ready for the big ceremony.

******

Danny had been working steadily on music and getting to know all about his past as Ferdinando. The Don even sent some school albums of his nephew and some of his friends, in case Danny ran into one of them. Hell, he could fake it if he had to. He was just finishing up when Carmen came in. She dropped her coat on the couch and came over and sat across from him. She had this funny look on her face. Danny looked at her and said, "You look like the cat that swallowed the canary. What's up?"

Carmen leaned forward and said, "I just got a call from Don Angelo informing me that there is going to be a big ceremony Saturday for you at St. Mary's of the Lake Catholic Church. There will be all kinds of Marine Corps brass and dignitaries there including the Governor and the Mayor of Chicago. It will be televised, so we can watch it here. Seems you neglected to tell anyone you were a Medal of Honor winner."

"I didn't think it was anybody's business. I did what I had to do, that's all. Did the Don seem mad?"

"Hell no, he's proud of you and can't wait till Saturday to stick it to the molindrinos, as he put it. He said to tell you that you will be getting the best funeral Chicago has ever seen. The Monsignor himself is performing the mass. Now, that's clout. How are you coming with the songs and the life story of the Don's nephew?"

"Fine. The kid didn't do much. Not like my childhood. The songs are coming along. I made a list of the ones I like, and can do without a lot of trouble." He handed her the list.

She read it and said, "These are great songs. I like the selection." She was interrupted by a buzzer on the two way intercom from the house. She walked over and hit the button. "Yes Dad, what is it?"

"Turn on the TV. There's a newscast from Chicago you gotta see."

Danny walked over and switched on the TV. The same newscaster was talking. Behind him, this time, was a picture of Danny in full dress blues with all the decorations and the Medal of Honor around his neck. "As it turns out, Danny DiBernardo who was killed when his car was blown up last week was a Medal of Honor winner. DiBernardo was alleged to have ties to the Don

Angelo crime family. We have a film clip from Paris Island, South Carolina, the Marine Corps training grounds. Our reporter, Rick Warren, had this interview with General Harrison, Commandant of Paris Island."

They were standing in front of a statue of the flag raising on Iwo Jima. "This is Rick Warren from station WGN Chicago, here at Paris Island, where DiBernardo went through boot camp before being sent to Korea. With me is General Larry Harrison, Commandant of this post. General, as you know, one of your Marines, Sgt. Danny DiBernardo was killed last week in Chicago. Being a Medal of Honor winner, he is entitled to a full military funeral with all the trimmings. My question to you is this. Does the Marine Corps, knowing that he had ties to a crime family and was known to be an enforcer for the mob, have any qualms about giving him a military funeral?"

The General gave him a look that would melt a brick. "Let me tell you something, young man. See that statue behind me? Those are fighting Marines. I don't give a damn what they were in civilian life. They were Marines. As far as Sgt. DiBernardo goes, I don't care if he had ties to Tinker Bell or the tooth fairy. He was a Marine, a hero, a Medal of Honor recipient, not a winner! He didn't win it in a lottery or a box of cracker jacks, he won it fighting, defending his position, and he will be given full military rights. And, one more thing. I knew the Sgt. He served under me, and a tougher Marine you'd never find. I'm coming to Chicago to do the honors myself. And son, nobody better be standing in my way. Do I make myself clear?"

"Yes, sir." He backed up a step like he was afraid the General was going to slap him. He turned to the camera. "This is Rick Warren, WGN news in the Carolinas."

The announcer from the studio came on. "Well, it looks like it's going to be an interesting weekend. We'll keep you advised."

Carmen was beside herself with laughter. "Now, that's what I call a tough marine." She turned to Danny who was sitting on a chair with his head down. "Hey, what's the matter?"

Danny looked up at her through the bandages. "If I had

known that my getting killed was going to cause all this confusion and bull shit I would have never gone for it."

Carmen came over and kneeled in front of him. She took his head in her hands and raised it so she could see his eyes through the bandages. "Look, it had to come out sometime. If you died of old age it would still be the same. Let the Don have his moment, and let's get on with your new life."

Danny reached out and touched her face. "You're some kind of smart girl. You know that? Now, I want to take a break and make love to you for awhile."

She laughed and pulled him to his feet. "What are you waiting for big boy, an engraved invitation?" As they started for the bedroom the buzzer rang again. They looked at each other. Carmen sighed and said, "We may have to postpone it for awhile. The master calls." They put on their coats and went to the main house.

Chapter 6

Saturday dawned bright and clear with a slight breeze and a nip in the air. It was overcoat weather. North Sheridan Street was lined with polished, black limos for a solid block. The drivers were standing along side them talking to each other. The F.B.I. guys were sneaking around taking pictures of all the license plates and the occupants. The inside of the church was packed with people. On the left side down front was the Governor, the Mayor and other city officials. Across from them were Don Angelo and the rest of the crime bosses with their families and friends. The Catholic Church was packed full of Italians.

The Marine Corps General was sitting next to the Don, which pissed off the police commissioner. The lesser brass was seated a few rows behind. The Marine Corps color guard was standing next to the altar where a picture of Danny had been placed on an easel amid sprays of seasonal flowers. A beautiful urn with the Medal of Honor hanging around it was prominently placed on the altar.

The organist was sitting on the bench in front of the huge European pipe organ, waiting for the signal to start. When he got the nod from the priest, he hit the first big chord and started to play. The noise made everybody jump, and every hood in the church reached for his piece. The choir started to sing as the Monsignor came down the aisle from the back of the church. The alter boys led followed by priests dispensing incense. The Monsignor climbed up to the pulpit and started the Mass. It was a beautiful sermon. He had stayed up late to prepare the psalms that he would use to praise Danny, who he knew shit about and could care less about.

He was thinking of the money the Don would give him for the church, but would probably end up in his own pocket. The Mass ended and the people started to leave the sanctuary for the procession to the cemetery. The other Dons left by the side door, in order to avoid the TV news cameras that they knew were out front. Don Angelo and General Harrison walked out together through the narthex. The hearse was waiting for the urn, which the other Marine Corps brass were bringing out together with the color guard. The Don and the General got in the lead car and waited for the rest of the people to get in line.

The Police Commissioner and the Police Chief were standing with the Governor and the Mayor. The commissioner turned to the Governor. "You know George. This is a bunch of crap. I don't see why we have to honor that son-of-a-bitch. He was a hood. A fucking killer. You know it and I know it. And here we stand, surrounded by the same fucking crime families we've been trying to put in prison for years. It just don't make any God damned sense to me."

The Governor nodded. "Sense or not Bill, it's something we have to do. I don't like it anymore than you do, but there it is. So, I don't need to hear any more. You and the Chief, go get into your little police car and get in line."

The Commissioner's face turned red. He came up to the Governor and looked him straight in the eye. "If we weren't standing here with all these TV cameras and people around, I'd knock you right on your ass, you pompous son-of-a-bitch. Who the fuck do you think you're talking to?"

The Police Chief got between them. "Come on Bill, it's not worth it." He pulled Harry away from the Governor, whose face had turned white.

As they went away the Mayor said, "George, that was close. Bill can be a very violent man at times. He didn't get to be Police Commissioner by chance you know. He came up the hard way. Come on, here's our car." They got in and followed the procession to the cemetery.

The gravesite looked like a scene from a B movie. All of

the Dons were seated with their bodyguards behind them. The Governor and the Mayor were seated with them. All the rest of the crowd stood. The urn was on a pedestal with the American flag on one side and the Marine Corps flag on the other.

General Harrison read the citation that awarded the Medal of Honor to Danny. The Marine Corps rifle squad, from the Marine Corps Reserve in Chicago, fired the required amount of volleys while the officers and the Commissioner and Chief saluted the urn, much to their dismay. A Marine lieutenant folded the American flag and gave it to the General. He, in turn, took the flag with the medal resting on it and presented it to the Don.

There were actually tears in his eyes as he accepted it. Then from a hill not far from the gravesite, a Marine bugler played taps. The sound was eerie and haunting as it flowed over the people standing there. They stood transfixed until the last note faded away. At last, it was over. As they started to leave, the press was all over the Governor and his party. The Don and the General stood there and accepted the condolences of the people passing by. On the way to the car, the Don said to the General, "I'm having a little reception at my house for some close friends. I would like you to join us. But, if you feel uncomfortable with it, I'll understand."

The General smiled at him. "I would love to join you, and as for understanding, there's something you should know about me that not many people do. I'm married to Vito Genovici's daughter, Pietra."

The Don stopped, threw back his head and laughed. "Son-of-a-bitch. That's beautiful. Just fucking beautiful."

******

Danny had been jumpy all day. They got a call from Chicago and a rundown of all the day's activities. They said there would be a special broadcast on the six o'clock news. When the time came, they were all sitting in the living room watching TV. "First, the local news." Then announcer said, "We are now going to Chicago for a special newscast." When it came up, the picture was in front of the church with all he families and the local officials in the back ground.

The announcer was saying, "Today, they are burying a local hero who was the recipient of the Medal of Honor. What makes it more interesting, is that Danny DiBernardo was a suspected criminal who, according to sources, was a hit man for the mob and worked for one of the most powerful crime families in Chicago. We are going to follow the procession to the cemetery and we'll see if we can get some interviews with the Governor and the Mayor."

The scene switched to the cemetery. The camera was set up on a slight rise so it could take in the whole panorama. The camera zoomed in on the General as he was reading the citation. "And Sergeant DiBernardo, though wounded twice, stood his ground and laid down a withering fire, holding off the Chinese advance until help arrived." The camera panned over to the Don. There were actually tears in his eyes as he listened to the general.

The camera panned over to the Governor, the Mayor and lastly on the Police Commissioner, who had a look of disgust on his face. The camera came back to the General as the Marine Corps rifle squad fired the volleys. The General came over and presented the Don with the American flag displaying the Medal of Honor. The bugler played taps while everybody saluted. The scene switched to the announcer talking to the Governor, Mayor and the Police Commissioner. The announcer was saying, "So Governor, how do you feel about having to honor a known member of the syndicate?"

The Governor looked perplexed like he didn't know how to answer. He was saved by the Police Commissioner. "I don't know about the Governor, but I'll tell you what I think. I think it stinks. The man may have been a hero in Korea, but he was just a hood here. It would have just been a matter of time before we put him away. And that's all we have to say about it." He pushed past the announcer with the Governor and the Chief right behind him. The announcer looked into the camera. "Well, I guess that about says it all. Rick Warren, station WGN, here in Chicago."

The weather came on and Richie went over and turned off

the TV. "Well, you're officially dead. Now, we start on your new life." Before anybody could say anything, Ritchie's wife cut in. "Excuse me, but I'm confused. We watched Danny getting buried, but he's here. How can that be?"

"Angelina, it's OK. I'll explain it to you later. Right now, it's time to toast Danny Angel."

He went to the bar and opened an expensive bottle of wine and poured four drinks. He brought them to the coffee table in front of the couch and set the tray down. Everybody took a glass and held it up. Richie offered a toast. "To Danny Angel, the next superstar." They clinked glasses and drank.

Chapter 7

The next few weeks went by fast. The doctor checked him a number of times, changed the bandages, and pronounced that he was doing fine. The scars itched, and his face itched from not shaving, which made him want to scratch all the more. Of course, that was a no, no. He worked everyday on songs and sang along with the records. His voice was getting stronger and richer as he went along. Carmen was his constant companion and when he wasn't singing, he was making love to her.

Along with the singing, he was working out on the weights and keeping fit and lean. Richie had a punching bag brought in and a speed bag so he could punch and do footwork. For a guy his size, he was light on his feet and could move like a dancer. Carmen would sit and watch him work out. When he punched the bag, he would grunt. The sound of the grunt and the noise made by the gloves striking the bag would turn her on. Violence, she loved violence. She would get up and come over to Danny and grab him. She loved the smell of sweat gleaming on his rippling muscles.

She would grab Ninja through Danny's shorts and start to rub him. He would throw off the gloves, grab her, and lay her on the matt and make hard, brutal love to her. No finesse. No foreplay, just raw sex.

Meanwhile, Don Angelo was busy getting things organized. He had one of his goombas in Italy get fingerprints of his nephew. He would need them if Danny had to be fingerprinted. There were ways to get around that. All he needed was a recent picture of Danny for the passport which would be taken once his face had healed. He missed Danny. He was used to having him around. It's going to seem strange looking at the face of his nephew with Danny's voice coming out of him. He thought to himself, *I love my nephew and I love Danny. Now I got both in one. I can live with that.*

The day came when the bandages were to be taken off. Danny woke up, rolled over and pulled Carmen close to him. He whispered in her ear, "After today you'll be making love to the Don's nephew."

She smiled at him. "The face may be new, but that thing is still the same. Hey, for the last six weeks I've been making love to Lon Chaney, as the mummy. So, tell me, are you nervous?"

"Yeah, I am. But, I'll be glad to get these bandages off and shave. I probably look like Bluto from Popeye."

Carmen laughed. "All in good time. Now, I want you to make love to me for the last time as Danny DiBernardo."

He did. It was a gentle, wonderful, a loving kind of sex, as though it was to be the last time. When it was over, Carmen had tears in her eyes as she asked, "God that was wonderful. Can Ferdinando Dominico Bello do that?"

Danny smiled down at her. "Everytime baby."

They showered and went into the house for breakfast. Ritchie was at the table reading the paper over coffee. He looked up. "So, today's the big day. The limo will take you down and back. It's going to snow and the streets are going to be bad. Gino is an excellent driver, so I don't see any problems."

Carmen got herself a cup of coffee and came over and kissed her father. "Thanks, dad. Danny's sort of anxious to get the bandages off so he can shave and see what his new face looks like. I'm sort of anxious too."

"OK, have the car brought around. See me when you get back."

Carmen came around and got Danny. They said their goodbyes and headed for the front door. The limo was waiting with Gino holding open the back door. They got in and headed for the doctor's office. As predicted, the weather got bad. Gino wove in and out of traffic avoiding the accidents. Cars were stuck in mounds of snow piled along the curbs from the snow plows.

They got to the doctor's office and went inside. Paul was waiting for them and took them into a small back room. He sat Danny on a stool, came around in front of him and said, "I'm going to take the bandages off now. You're still going to be a little swollen and you'll look like you went ten rounds with Tony Galento, but it will pass. Just don't let that bother you. It will be fine in a couple of weeks. You can shave, but be careful of the scars until they heal all the way. Now, are you ready?"

Danny nodded and the doctor started cutting the bandages away. He got to the last layer and slowly pealed it off his face. Carmen sat there with her eyes wide open. Even with the swelling and the beard he looked like the Don's nephew. The doctor got a mirror and handed it to Danny.

"Now remember, the swelling will go down and you will look exactly like Don Angelo's nephew.

Danny took the mirror and looked at his new face. The shock of seeing his face swollen and bruised almost made him swear. But, through the bruises, he could see the face of the Don's nephew with the straight nose, the high cheek bones and the eyebrows with no scars. The scar on his cheek was stitched with tiny stitches. The doctor saw him looking at it. "Those stitches will come out in a few days. When it's healed, it will be a little thin line barely noticeable. We'll take the other stitches out at the same time. I want to see you in two weeks. Meanwhile, you can shave and shower, but like I said, be careful of the stitches. Now, do you want me to put a light bandage on your face or just leave it as it is?"

Danny looked at Carmen. "Do you think you can look at this face the way it is?"

"I can stand it, if you can. If you let the air get at it, you'll heal faster. Nobody's going to care around the house."

"OK. Is that all we need doctor?"

"That's it. See you in two weeks." He shook Danny's hand and gave Carmen a hug. "Give my best to your father."

"I will and thanks, Paul."

They got their coats on and Carmen turned Danny's collar

up to protect his face against the cold and prying eyes. They got back in the limo and started back to the house. The weather had turned nasty with blowing snow and ice. Gino was driving extra careful to keep the limo from skidding. They came to a stop light and Gino was tapping the brakes to slow down. A guy came off the curb and Gino had to swerve to miss him. The guy started yelling and pounded on the hood.

"Why don't you watch where the fuck you're going, buddy? Just because you got a limo you think you're king shit."

Before Gino could react, Danny was out the back door, had grabbed the guy and pulled him up so they were face to face. The guy looked at Danny's face and turned white. It was like looking at the face of Frankenstein's monster. While he was gawking, Danny hit him twice and threw him into a snow bank along side the limo. He got back in and Gino pulled away.

Carmen sat there stunned by the brutality she had just seen, but found herself turned on by the violence. When Danny was seated again, she got close to him, reached under his coat and started to massage him. Danny whispered to her. "When we get home I'm going to tear up that thing you're sitting on."

Carmen shut her eyes and squeezed her legs together in anticipation.

******

The next morning, Ritchie called Danny into his study. When he was seated, Ritchie said, "Gino tells me you got out of the limo and smacked a guy and threw him into a snow bank."

Danny started to say something, but Ritchie held up his hand. "That was Gino's job. He's there to take care of you. Now, I know you've been taking care of yourself for a long time. But, it's different now. If you're going to become a star, you have to cool it. Now, I'm not saying that if some asshole comes at you and threatens to do you bodily harm, you just stand there and take it. No, you knock the shit out of him. I'm just saying that you have to be careful and control that Italian temper.

When you're ready, we're going to send you to some clubs in downstate New York so you can break in your act. These are strip joints run by friends. You've got to learn to handle crowds that are there to see the broads, and not you. There are a lot of wise guys around there, and they will be in to see you from time to time. Be nice to them but don't take any shit off of them.

With your new face, you're going to be a target for every jealous husband and boyfriend that comes to the club with his lady. They'll want to challenge you to a fight. Talk your way out of it, if you can. If you can't, take them out in a hurry. You can't afford to mess up that face. The word will get around that you're pretty, but nobody to fuck with. Any questions?"

Danny thought for a second. "What if I run across guys I know from Chicago or any place else?"

"You act like you just met them. The best thing is, you know what they do and all about them. So you got the edge over them and you can avoid any situations that may come up. Remember, you'll look entirely different to them. Just make sure you don't do anything you use to do, to make them suspicious. If you should slip up, talk your way out of it. You were in Italy a long time, so switch to Italian. That will throw them off. Besides, being Don Angelo's nephew, they won't push the point."

"Yeah, Carmen has been brushing me up on my Italian. The Don's nephew spoke a different dialect, but I'm handling it."

"That's my girl. So, how's the face coming along?"

"Good. The doctor said I can shave and he'll take out the stitches in two weeks. He said the scars should be barely visible. I just have to get use to looking at a face that's not mine."

"You'll get use to it, but just remember what I said. Be careful and be on guard. Carmen is waiting for you in the living room so have fun."

Danny got up and shook Ritchie's hand. "I'll try hard to remember that I'm the Don's nephew and not Danny Di anymore. It's going to take a bit of getting use to, but I'll do it." He turned and left to find Carmen. Ritchie smiled and said to himself, *"I know you will."*

Chapter 8

Danny stood in front of the mirror and admired the face looking back at him. The stitches were gone and so was the swelling. What was left was a ruggedly, handsome face. Carmen came in and stood next to him. She looked in the mirror and said, "You're fucking gorgeous. You're going to drive the women crazy. I'll have to get a whip, chair, and a gun to keep them off of you."

He turned toward her, put his hands around her waist and pulled her close. "You'll just be protecting your interest. One thing baby. When we make love, you'll be looking at the face of the Don's nephew, but it will be Danny Di's cock that'll be making you crazy."

"You do have a way with words. I'd take you up on that right now, but we have to go into the house and meet Tony Odie. He's going to start putting your act together. You think I worked you hard. You ain't seen nothing yet. He's the best at what he does. So, get dressed before I change my mind and jump on that pogo stick hanging there." She flicked it with her finger and slipped out of the bathroom. Danny smiled and shook his head. He shaved, showered, got dressed and went to the main house. Carmen and her mother were in the kitchen having coffee. Carmen's mother looked up at him. "What a handsome boy you are. But I think I liked the other face better. It had character. It showed who you really are."

Danny walked over and kissed her on the cheek. "I liked it too mama, but to you, I'll always be Danny Di." He sat down across from Carmen. "OK, where's this boy wonder who's going to make me a star?"

"He'll be here in fifteen minutes, so you had better have

some coffee and biscotti. It's going to be a long day."

Danny was standing in the front parlor when Carmen came in with Tony. Danny almost swore out loud. Tony was a slim, nattily dressed, effeminate man. Carmen brought him over. Tony took one look at Danny and his eyes lit up like a Christmas tree. Danny shook hands with him and it was like shaking hands with a limp noodle. Danny said to him, "It's nice to meet you. Could you excuse us for just one minute?"

He grabbed Carmen and went into the next room. "What the hell are you doing? He's a fenoikia, a fag. You want me to take lessons from a fag? You're out of your fucking mind."

Carmen stood her ground. "Listen to me. He is the best there is. You don't have to fuck him, just learn from him. He's really a sweet guy. He can teach you all you have to know. We're lucky to get him. He doesn't come cheap and he's worth every penny. So, let's get back in there and get started."

Danny gave her a look. "OK, but if he makes one pass at me, I'll twist him into a pretzel and stick his head up his ass."

Carmen gave out a laugh. "Like I said before, you do have a way with words. Come on tough guy, let's get started." They walked back into the big parlor and Tony was at the piano noodling. He called Danny over. "Let's see what kind of range you have. I'll play some scales and you sing them for me. This will give me your top and bottom notes.

For the next half hour Danny sang all kinds of scales and notes that Tony played. Half way through, Tony looked at Carmen and smiled. Carmen knew then that they had a winner. When the scales were done, Tony asked Danny to sing a song for him. Danny chose "Mala Femmina." Tony played the intro and Danny sang like a bird. When he hit the E-flat note at the end, Tony stood up from the piano and yelled. "Bellissimo. That was beautiful."

For the next three hours he had Danny sing a multitude of songs and wrote down the keys and how he wanted the song to go. He stopped Danny from time to time to correct a phrase or gave him an alternate note. When they were done he said to Danny, "You have a wonderful voice. It's strong, yet can be gentle and smooth.

I'm going to give you a list of songs that we will put into your first show. Learn them and then I'll be back. I'll get with the arrangers to get the songs written the way we want you to sing them. Then I'll choreograph and stage you so every move is a picture." He turned to Carmen. "Can he move?"

Carmen said, "Oh yeah, he can move. He use to be a boxer and he can dance too. So, I'm sure he can do anything you want him to."

Tony clapped his hands. "Good, then we can really do some good stuff." He turned to Danny. "You really have great potential and I'm sure we'll get the most out of you." He shook hands again and said his goodbyes. Carmen walked him to the door. He handed her a sheet of paper. "Get these songs for him and make sure he learns them. I'll be back in a week to get started." He kissed her on the cheek and left. Carmen walked back into the parlor. "Well Danny, what do you think?"

Danny smiled at her. "He knows his stuff, that's for sure. But, what's with this moving stuff? I'm not going to prance around the stage like a fairy."

"No, of course not. He'll give you moves to match the song you're doing. Subtle moves. Sexy moves to drive the ladies wild. Not like Elvis. More like Sinatra or Dean."

"That's pretty heavy company. But, I can do it. I want the Don to be proud of me."

"Oh, he will be. We'll give him a call later and find out when you're coming to America. I want you to be ready to work, so we can get you back here. We'll start working small clubs to get you ready for the big time. But right now, it's lunch time and mama made you cavatelli as a special treat.

"How did she know that it's my favorite pasta dish?"

Carmen smiled at him. "Maybe a little bird told her."

Danny looked her in the eye. "The only bird I know is a black-headed, double-breasted, mattress thrasher. Sound like anybody you know?"

Carmen started to walk away. She turned her head and over her shoulder said, "Tweet, tweet."

*****

The Don hung up the phone and smiled. He always liked talking to Danny.

Things were moving right along. He thought about his sister in Italy. It took some persuading, but he made her see that her son would be famous as if he were here. He would be living in Danny's body. Don Angelo had never mentioned the fact that he was footing the bills for all her son's care in the rest home. The Don also had to tell his wife because she would have seen right through the whole thing. He didn't want to shock her. He had to work on getting his nephew back in the U.S.A. The photo would be taken in a day or two, and then he would get it to Heime.

Now, it was simply a matter of getting one of the boys to bring the passport in and get it stamped. He had already taken care of the official who would do it. It was simple. All the messenger coming from Italy needed to do was get in his line at the immigration check in, and come on through. Then, shortly afterwards, the official would meet with an unfortunate accident. Danny would then get on a plane in New York and fly to Chicago for a family reunion.

It was going to be interesting to watch Danny's friends to see if they could identify the imposter. They had never met his nephew from Italy, so they had nothing to use as a comparison. Also, Danny knew all of the Don's family, their names and what they did. Consequently, he had the edge on them. He wouldn't be in town long enough for people to get suspicious and start asking questions. The next time he came to Chicago, it would be as a singing sensation. The Don would roll out the red carpet for him and invite everybody to his opening at the Chez Paree. Hell, he might even invite that candy ass Governor and his entourage, and really shove it up his ass. Don Angelo's phone rang and he answered it. It was Tomasso. "Hey, how's everything in Pittsburg?"

"Everything is fine. I just called to see how things are going over at you know where."

"Everything is coming along fine and it won't be long before my nephew comes home."

"Now that's good to hear. Let me know and maybe I can be there to toast him with a glass of vino."

"You will be the first to know my friend. If I need anything I'll call you."

"You do that. Give my best to your lovely wife." He hung up. The Don sat there and thought about the next phase of the plan. Things are going to start happening fast, and soon.

******

Everything was ready. Danny had been working with Tony for two weeks and it was coming together. The passport was on its way back from Italy as planned, and Danny was packed and ready for the drive to the airport. He would then fly to New York and on to Chicago. They did it this way to avoid suspicion in case anybody started checking on him. The guy flying from Italy was using Danny's name on the ticket. They had thought of everything.

Carmen had made all the arrangements for his flight from New York to Chicago and his return flight to Buffalo when the time was right. Danny was looking forward to seeing Don Angelo again. He missed him. He was the only father Danny had ever known. Carmen came into the living room, walked over and put her arms around him. "You look nervous. Don't be. I'm coming to New York with you. We'll get a nice hotel and wait for the word that your passport is here. They'll deliver it to the hotel. Then I'll take you to the airport and put you on the plane for Chicago. At that point, you're on your own big boy"

Danny hugged and kissed her. "You're only coming to New York to get laid. I know you. But I'm glad you're coming. When do we leave?"

"Tomorrow morning. We'll have plenty of time to get there and get settled in at the hotel. Oh, by the way, tomorrow night a friend of my father and the Don is having a dinner party for us. So, you can try out your new identity. You will probably know some of the people there, so be careful. Remember, if you get in trouble, switch to Italian. You just came from Italy remember?"

"Yeah, I'll be careful."

The next morning they were taken to the airport by limo. They checked in and went to the gate. Carmen was smiling. Danny asked her what was so funny. She answered. "Don't you see the women looking at you? If I wasn't here they would probably attack."

Danny looked around and sure enough the women were looking at him with that look women get when they see something they like. He also noticed the men staring at Carmen. They did make a handsome couple. It came time to board and they got on the plane. The flight attendant couldn't do enough for them. She fawned over Danny and kept bending over him so her blouse would fall away, giving him a clear view of her breast. Carmen had to giggle. She leaned over and whispered in his ear. "You'd better get use to this. This is what's going to happen wherever you go, especially when you become a superstar."

He took her hand and looked at her. "It's going to take some getting use to. Danny Di never had this to worry about."

"Yes, but you're Danny Angel now, so enjoy it."

The plane touched down in New York. They gathered up their stuff and got off, but not before the flight attendant slipped a note in his hand. He read it on the way to get the luggage, laughed and handed it to Carmen. It was a number where the fight attendant would be staying that night. Carmen smiled, wadded it up and threw it in a trash container. They got to the luggage area and found a guy holding up a sign with Danny's name on it. They went over and introduced themselves. He took the luggage tickets, got their bags and carried them out to the waiting limo.

They got in and headed for the hotel. Sitting next to the driver was a very large man who was silent the whole way. Danny knew who he was. He was sent to take care of them. They got to the hotel, checked in and found their suite ready. The driver announced that he would pick them up at seven o'clock.

They undressed, got comfortable and made love on a luxurious feather bed. Afterwards they took a short nap, and then ordered room service. When it was time to get ready, they showered and got dressed.

At seven o'clock they were standing outside the hotel as the limo pulled up. The muscle bound man got out and opened the back door. He gave Danny a look like, I know you from somewhere. He got back in the front seat and the four took off. They drove for a half hour and finally came to an impressive house with a circular drive, huge front gates and a guard house. The guard came out, looked in the car and the electronic gates slowly opened. The limo pulled up to the front door and the two got out. Danny took Carmen's hand and squeezed it. As they walked down a long hallway, Danny could hear a live band playing, with laughter and talking. Arm in arm, Carmen and Danny entered an immense living room. Danny recognized the host, Vito Cadenza. He had met him before, after doing a job in Long Island for the Don. They walked over. Vito saw them and put out his arms.

"Ferdinando. What a pleasure to meet Don Angelo's nephew." He grabbed Danny, then hugged and kissed him on the cheek. He turned to Carmen, "And you my dear, you get lovelier every time I see you." He hugged and kissed her too.

Vito escorted them to a dance floor in front of the band. Taking the microphone, Vito called for silence. He then introduced Danny and Carmen to his guests. They all came up to pay their respects to the Don's nephew. After they had all hugged and kissed him, Vito took them over to his table and offered them a seat. "So Ferdinando, the Don tells me you're going to become a singer."

"That's Don Angelo's plan. I've been singing in Italy and he decided I should come home and try it here. So, here I am. He also changed my name to Danny Angel."

"That's wonderful. I was wondering if you would maybe do a couple of songs for my guests. I would really appreciate it."

Danny knew what he meant. It wasn't a request, it was a quiet order. "I'd love to. What would you like to hear?"

Vito replied, "Anything you want to sing."

Danny got up and went up to the bandstand and talked to the leader. They agreed on a song and the band went into "Sorrento." The whole room went quiet as Danny sang the song. He ended to enthusiastic applause. The cries of "more, more" came up from the guests. He picked another song and they began dancing to the ballad he was singing. He noticed a wanna-be talking to Carmen. He was trying to get her to dance and she was shaking her head no. He grabbed her arm and she shook him off. Danny's blood began to boil. He finished the song and left the bandstand with cries of more ringing in his ears.

He returned to the table and accepted sincere praise from his host. Danny looked at Carmen who was still trying to wrestle away from the half drunk hood. Danny walked over, taking him by the arm. "Hey Paison, let's take a walk." He almost lifted the guy off the floor as he walked him to the foyer. Slamming his head against the wall, Danny knocked him senseless. He sat him in a chair, and then went back to Carmen. She looked at him. He just smiled at her and said, "How did I do? The band was good."

She replied, "You did great. Did you see the reaction you got from the crowd? They loved you."

Danny sat back and smiled. People started making their way to Danny's table, congratulating him and fawning over him. Vito smiled, hugged him and said, "The Don's right. You're going to be a star. When you're ready, you'll play my club here in New York. I'll lay out the red carpet for you."

Danny took his hand. "You've got a deal. It will be my pleasure."

The rest of the night went by quickly and soon they were in the limo on their way back to the hotel. Carmen was fidgeting. Finally, she spoke up, "OK. I can't stand it anymore. What did you do to that jerk that was pestering me?"

Danny smiled at her. "He developed a headache and had to leave."

Chapter 9

They stood at the entrance to the plane. The passport had arrived that morning. Carmen had her arm around his waist. "You know I'm going to miss you. Don't you?"

Danny looked at her and kissed her lightly on the nose. "I know what you're going to miss, but I'll be back before you know it. If it gets too bad, you can fly to Chicago."

She smiled at him. "I might just do that, big boy. But right now, you have to get on the plane."

He kissed her, walked on board, sat down in first class and accepted a drink from the flight attendant. She gave him a knowing look which left nothing to the imagination. The plane took off and he settled back to relax and enjoy it. The meal came and the flight attendant made a fuss over him. She couldn't do enough.

They landed in Chicago and Danny was getting a bit nervous. He had the flight attendant's name in his pocket. He may need some calming down later. He got off the plane and there stood Don Angelo with his bodyguards. The Don saw him and held out his arms. Danny came over and hugged him. The Don said in his ear, "I missed you, Danny. The doctor did a good job. You look like Ferdinando. It's good to have you home." He turned to his bodyguards who Danny knew. "This is my nephew Ferdinando. But you can call him Danny."

The two came over and hugged him. They picked up the luggage and got in the limo for the ride home. The Don was talking a mile a minute in his ear trying to get him caught up on what was going on and what he had planned for Danny while he was in Chicago. They got to the house and went inside leaving the two guards by the limo. The Don walked him into the kitchen where his wife was cooking cavatelli. She turned around and her jaw dropped. "Madonna, you look just like Ferdinando. Now, I've got the best of everything. I got my nephew and my son all in one. Come here and give me a hug."

Danny walked over, hugged her and said in her ear, "Momma, I missed you so much. I'm glad it's all over. Now I can be with you more often."

She backed off and looked up at him. "It's going to take some getting use to, but it's wonderful. You must be hungry. Sit down. I made your favorite pasta." They sat and had a great meal with wine and lots of laughs. Don Angelo said to him, "Tomorrow night we will have a nice party for the family and you can try out your new face on them. If you can fool them, you can fool anyone. I have some guests coming in from out of town to see you. You know them. They want to see how you look."

"It's still very strange looking in a mirror and seeing this face looking back at me. But, it's better than the one I had."

Momma came over and hugged him. "I don't know. I liked Danny's face. It had character."

Danny hugged her back. "You're right, but this face will carry me a long way. And the local police force has nothing on Ferdinando Bello. He's like a choir boy to them."

The Don smiled, "You're right. It's going to drive them crazy trying to figure out what's going on. Oh, they'll check on you all the way back to Italy, but they'll run into a stone wall. I have everything covered. But right now, why don't you go upstairs and unpack. Rest, and later we'll have some vino and talk."

Danny got up, gave them a hug and went upstairs.

******

The whole family and many friends were downstairs eating and drinking. Danny stood in front of the mirror and admired himself. He was wearing an Italian suit, tailor made and Italian loafers. The shirt and tie matched perfectly. He took a last look, and then went out the bedroom door to the top of the stairs. There, below him, was the family. He took a deep breath and started down the stairs. The Don saw him approaching and called for attention. "Hey, say hello to Ferdinando." All eyes turned toward Danny as he made his way down the stairs. They all crowded around to greet him. It was a good thing he knew them, because he was able to call them all by name.

They fawned all over him. Danny carried it off beautifully. He spoke Italian to the old ladies and men, hugged and kissed all the cousins, while laughing inside. He had made love to half of them! He knew he couldn't do that now. They would remember the scars on his body and Ninja. Nobody seemed suspicious or noticed anything different about him. Ferdinando had been gone a long time, so it was natural for him to have aged somewhat. A couple of the Don's bodyguards looked a little puzzled, as if they were trying to place him. He could change the face, but the body and the actions were Danny Di's.

The Don came over, rescued him from the throng and led him into the den. There sat the boys from Pittsburgh, Cleveland and New Jersey. They came over and greeted him. Tomasso held him at arms length. "Jesus. What a difference. That doc did a great job. I would have never believed he could do this good." The other two agreed.

The Don asked them to sit and said, "Now that everything is done, we need to figure out what's next. Ritchie wants to send him to Utica to work a club and get him use to being on stage. It's a rough joint but he has to be able to handle himself. Then, he'll move him to a better club in Syracuse, opening for somebody. Tomasso, I want you to put him in Philly at the Latin Casino or Palumbo's. Find a star he can open for. Then wheel him around Pittsburgh. Carlos will play him around Ohio. And Patsy will put him in some clubs in New Jersey. That covers a lot of ground. Danny, how long before you're ready to go?"

"I need three weeks. The music is done and the act is coming together. I've been working with the guy from McVan's and he's good. So, tell Ritchie to book me in Utica in three weeks.

Then, you can take it from there. Oh, by the way. I want to thank you for the nice funeral."

They roared with laughter. Tomasso wiped his eyes. "Every time I think about that I have to laugh. Some punk, know nothing, small town hood, gets the funeral of a lifetime and didn't even know it." He laughed again. The Don got up. "I guess we should go back to our guests. Danny is doing a good job and nobody seems the wiser." They all went back to the party.

Danny saw this good looking girl he hadn't seen before going into the den. She came over with one of the Don's nieces. "Ferdinando, I want you to meet a friend of mine from work. This is Sheila." Danny took her hand and kissed it while looking into her eyes. "I'm glad to make your acquaintance my dear." She looked right back at him and said, "I've heard a lot about you. You've been living in Italy for a long time. What brings you back here to Chicago?"

Danny let go of her hand and said, "My uncle wants to make me into a singer. I sang around Italy and other countries. Now he wants to see what I can do here."

"I think that's great. Will you be starting here in Chicago?"

"No. I'll be on the east coast for a while, and then back here when I'm ready."

"Chicago has changed a lot since you've been gone. I'd like to show you around if you have time."

Danny replied, "That sounds interesting and I do have time.

"How about tomorrow?"

"Sounds good. I'll call you here and we can set a time for me to pick you up."

"By the way. What's your last name? You look Irish to me."

"It's O'Bannion. And it's not the family you're thinking of. My father is a brick layer and my mother stays home and takes care of him."

"I never even thought about that. So Sheila, I'll see you tomorrow." He kissed her hand again and went to find the Don. He found him talking to Carlo. He walked up and said to the Don, "I just met a friend of your niece named Sheila O'Bannion. She wants to show me around Chicago tomorrow. Can you check her out for me? Something's not right. I can feel it."

The Don wrote her name down and called one of his body guards over. He handed him the paper with the name on it. "I want you to call you know who and check this girl out. Tell him it's important. I want it by morning." The bodyguard took off. "You think there's something fishy about the broad?"

"I don't know. Just a hunch. Usually when broads hit on me, they smile and act coy. This girl smiled, but her eyes didn't. I just want to be on the safe side."

"Good boy. We'll check her out." Danny left and went back to the party. Around one am the party broke up and Danny said his good nights to everyone.

Sheila got into her car and drove to a parking lot two miles from the Don's house. There was a lone car parked there. She came up to it and rolled down her window. Sitting in the other car was Detective John O'Malley. "Well, what did you find out?"

"Not a whole hell of a lot. He is the Don's nephew. Looks like the picture you showed me but older and more mature. He's a handsome son-of-a-bitch, and charming. I'm taking him out tomorrow to see the sights. I'll get more information on what he's been doing and what he plans to do. Did you run a make on him?"

"Yeah, he's like a fucking choir boy. We checked all the way back to Italy and the guy is clean. Too clean. Find out what you can and keep me informed." He rolled up his window and left the parking lot. Sheila sat there for a minute. Clean or no clean she meant to have him anyway.

Chapter 10

Danny came down to breakfast and sat down with the Don and his wife. The Don handed him a sheet of paper. Danny read it. The Don said, "Your instincts are still good. She's working undercover for the police department."

Danny put the paper down. "You know she's Carla's best friend. She's probably trying to get something on you too. Keep an eye on her. I'll see what she's up to when we go out today."

"Son-of-a-bitch. I never suspected that. She's been here a number of times with Carla. I'll have the boys keep an eye on her. She may have an accident if she gets too close."

"Don't do anything until I find out what she's up to. She must not have found out anything or they would have been down on you by now. And now that you are aware of her it will be easy to fool her. It'll drive them crazy downtown."

The Don laughed. "You're right. I can keep them guessing and running around chasing shadows. By the way, I got all your money out of the bank and your apartment. I sent it to your Swiss account. I had it changed to Dominico Bello so you can draw on it. It's nice to have friends in foreign places." The door bell rang and Danny answered it. There stood Sheila. "Well, you're on time. Would you like some coffee before we go?"

"I just had some. Let's just go and we can have lunch later."

Danny got his coat. They got into her car and headed out. She drove toward the loop and Danny got a good look at her as she drove. She was beautiful and from what he could see she was built. She was the first to speak. "So, what part of Italy were you in. I love Italy. I've been there a couple of times."

"My mother has a villa outside of Perusia in Umbria. That's near Rome. I spent most of my time there and went to school in Perusia."

"It must have been nice growing up there. Why did your mother leave Chicago?"

Danny smiled to himself. She's digging. "She left because my father was gunned down on the street. There was crime and violence all around Chicago. She wanted me to grow up in a peaceful calm setting away from all the killing and mobs. Does that answer your question?"

Sheila looked over at him. "I'm sorry, I didn't mean to pry. It's just that your uncle is head of the most powerful crime family in Chicago. I was just curious as to why he brought you here."

"What my uncle does is his business. I came home to sing. He wants to make me a star, so I can be somebody to respect. That's why he changed my name to Danny Angel. No ties to the Angelo family. It's an uncle helping his nephew. That's all. Now are we through with the twenty questions or do you want to know the size of my cock?"

Sheila actually blushed at the last question. She finally regained her composure. "No, not really. I can find that out for myself."

Danny leaned back and laughed. "You're quite a girl. I tried to embarrass you and you came back at me like a champ. I like that. Shows you got moxie. Now, let's just have some fun and forget about everything else. What do you say?"

"I say that's a good idea." They drove all around Chicago and stopped for lunch at a nice Italian trattoria in Cicero. She dropped Danny off at his uncle's house. She would pick him up at eight o'clock to go to dinner and a show. Danny went inside. The Don was in the den talking to someone on the phone. He waved Danny in and pointed to the chair in front of the desk. The Don finished his conversation and hung up. "That was Ritchie. You're going to open at The Plush Horse in Utica in three weeks. He wants you back in Buffalo by Sunday so you have two weeks to get ready. Carmen said you were doing great with that Tony guy. By the way, what did you find out about the broad?"

"She asked a lot of questions but I stopped her. She's picking me up tonight, so I'll know more later. I figure that the boys downtown have checked on me and came up with nothing. So they sent her to dig a little deeper. They probably want to find out if I'm connected to your side of the family. She's going to run into a stone wall, but it will be nice to play with her for awhile."

The Don laughed. "You're a devil. You just be careful. Now, go kiss your aunt and have some coffee and biscotti. She made them special for you."

"Thanks, Don. See you later." He got up and left the den. On the way to the kitchen he ran across one of the Don's bodyguards. He knew him well. He had been looking at Danny strangely since his arrival. Danny suspected he wanted to know something. He stopped and said, "Hello, you're John aren't you?"

John stopped and came over. "Yeah, I'm John. You know, you remind me of somebody I used to know. You have the same walk and mannerisms that he had. Did you ever know Danny Di?"

"No, I never did. Was he somebody I should know?"

"He was the Don's favorite. Almost like a son to him. Got blown up in his own car not long ago. It's uncanny the resemblance. Except for the face, you could be him."

Danny was treading on real thin ice here. "I take that as a compliment. He must have been something special."

"Oh, he was. Well, I'll see you around." John turned and went into the den. Danny went into the kitchen.

*****

The night went exceedingly well with dinner and dancing. Sheila leaned back in the middle of a slow dance and said, "Do you always get this hard dancing?"

Danny chuckled, "Only if I'm dancing with somebody that really appeals to me." He pulled her closer so she could feel Ninja. She leaned into him so their bodies were moving as one.

"Why don't we make this a short night and go to my place

for a drink?"

"Suits me fine. But, if you don't mind, I would appreciate you walking in front of me so I don't shock anybody with this hard on."

She laughed and turned to walk off the dance floor in front of Danny. They got the car and headed for her house. Once inside she turned and kissed him while grinding her hips against his. She stepped back and with one move, released a clasp behind her neck. She was standing in front of him in her lace bra and panties. She had a great little body. Danny reached around her, undid her bra and let it fall to the floor. Her breasts were large and firm. He ran his hand over her nipples and she shuddered.

"You seem to be a woman of few words."

She smiled, then grabbed his hand and pulled him toward the bedroom.

Once inside, she stepped out of her panties and was completely naked. Danny shed his clothes revealing a huge erection. She couldn't wait. He carried her to the bed and laid her down. He played with her, giving her just a little until, frantically, she begged for it all. Then without warning, he rammed it all the way inside, causing her to gasp and squeal with delight.

He went in and out in a steady rhythm. She arched up to meet his thrust and cried out as the first of her climaxes hit her. She couldn't stop. It was so good. Then she squealed as an even bigger climax followed the first. She begged for him to come with her. Danny was waiting for her desperate plea. He bore down and increased his stroke. She cried out in pure ecstasy as they both came together.

She stroked his face gently. "I knew it was going to be good, but I had no idea it would be that good. Can we do it again?"

Danny looked at her. "I have to be in Buffalo on Sunday."

"Good. That gives us five days. That's if it's all right with you." She looked down then asked, "Where did you get all those scars?"

"Playing soccer and lacrosse in school. They're rough sports." That seemed to satisfy her curiosity. They went into the bathroom and got dressed. She wanted to drive him home, but he insisted on taking a cab. He kissed her goodnight with the promise that they would continue the next night.

Danny went down stairs, got in the cab and told the driver to take him to the Don's restaurant. As he walked in, all the wise guys gave him the once over as he went to the bar. Danny had to smile. He knew them all and they didn't recognize him with the new face. He saw his picture behind the bar and felt a moment of remorse. After a short time, it passed. He ordered wine from the bartender. "Excuse me. Is my uncle here?" The bartender said, "And who would your uncle be?"

"Don Angelo." The bartender jumped like he had been slapped. "Madonna, you must be Ferdinando. Geez, I'm sorry. Hold on. I'll let him know you're here." He ran to the phone and called the office. The Don came out with a smile. He walked over to Danny and hugged him. He called out, "Hey, say hello to my nephew Ferdinando." They came up and greeted him. Some shook hands and some hugged in the Italian way. The old guys greeted him in Italian and he answered them the same way. Finally, the Don took him away and they went into his office. When they were seated, the Don said, "So, what about the girl? Did you find out anything?"

Danny smiled. "I found out that she loves to fuck like a mink. She quizzed me on a lot of things, but I gave her all the right answers."

"Wait until I bring you back here as a star to the Chez Paree. I'll invite her bosses to your opening and put them down front. Really stick it in their ass." He leaned back and laughed.

Danny laughed with him. "Well, I guess I'll go home. Got to get my rest. It's going to be a wild week."

The Don laughed again. "I'll go with you. We can have a glass of vino together." They got up and left the club for home.

It was a wild week. He spent the days with the family and the nights with Sheila. She was insatiable. When she wasn't jumping on it, she was sucking it. He didn't mind at all. Then it was the last night. They were lying in bed after a marathon ball.

She was crying softly. He reached over and pulled her close and put her head on his chest. "Don't cry. I'll be back before you know it. I have to go out and break in my act. I'm not use to American audiences. Have to make sure everything works before I come back here. You don't want me to look bad do you?"

She looked up at him. "No, of course not. I want you to be absolutely wonderful. It's just that I'll miss you."

"Hey, I'll call you and let you know what's going on. There's one thing you have to do for me though."

She sat up and looked down at him. "Anything you want. Just name it."

"I want you to stop being a cop."

She sat there and turned white. She just stared at him with a shocked look. "I really don't… I mean who said… I would never."

He reached up and put his finger on her lips. "Do you honestly think that the Don would let me go out with you before checking you out? He has friends in the department that can find out anything. Sheila, get out while the getting's good. You're in way over your head. Your cover's blown, so tell whoever you're working for to reassign you to something else. When I come back I want to make sure you're here."

She sat there and cried softly. "You're right. It started out as an assignment, but I didn't think I'd care this much for you. I'll do that. I do want to be here when you get back."

"Good. Now let's just have another go at it and forget the whole thing." They did, and with everything out in the open, it was even better than before.

When Danny got back to the Don's house he went into the den and talked to the Don. He explained everything to him and the Don agreed that he'd done the right thing. Danny went up to pack and the next morning he flew back to Buffalo.

Chapter 11

Carmen met him at the airport with the limo and he was truly glad to see her. She kept squeezing Ninja all the way home. They got to the house and she took him out back. The minute they got inside she was all over him. They threw off their clothes and made love for awhile. She was wild and Danny had to laugh. "Boy, you sure are horny. Leave you alone for a week and you turn into a nympho."

She laughed that deep laugh she had and said, "It's your fault. You made me this way. But don't get too comfortable. We have a lot of work to do over the next two weeks. You open at the Plush Horse in Utica two weeks from tomorrow and you have to be ready. Tony will be here this afternoon and line up your shows for you. We figure four weeks in that place should toughen you up. Your next job is in Syracuse at The Three Rivers Club. You're opening for Don Rickles. No strippers. This is a class supper club with a nice ten piece band. You'll do thirty minutes in front of him, twice a night. We'll be there for that opening to make sure nothing goes wrong. You just go out there and sing your heart out and we will handle the rest. You're on your way baby."

Danny smiled at her. "Seems you got it pretty well handled. I'll do my part. What time is Tony getting here?"

"He'll be here at three. That gives us time for some more fun and games."

At three o'clock Tony showed up and they got started. He lined up Danny's shows in order so he could practice them. He told him that after the second show he could repeat the first one. He should have a turn over crowd by then. He walked him through the moves for each song. Nothing flashy, just subtle, sexy moves that would drive the ladies wild. He gave him some patter to say between songs if he needed it. They worked until eight o'clock when Tony had to go to work. He told Danny he would be back tomorrow. That's the way it went for the next two weeks. Everyday he sang, moved, and worked on patter and one-liners. He had a book on heckler squelchers.

Then came the day he had to leave. They packed all his stuff in a new Buick Electra that Ritchie had bought for him. He had all his music and wardrobe in the trunk. She told him that the band was just three pieces (piano, sax and drums). He would be doing twenty minutes between each girl, from eight o'clock at night until around two in the morning. There would be six girls and the feature. Carmen said the girls would do around fifteen minutes apiece and the feature would do forty-five or fifty. That left the rest of the time for him to fill. He had Bob Orbin's joke books and had been learning jokes and one-liner's to use. Carmen had been coaching him between bouts of sex. He already new a lot of Italian jokes from the comics around Chicago.

He got on the New York throughway heading toward Syracuse. His mind was all over the place. How the hell had he been talked into this? He was a hit man, a killer. Now he had to forget that and be a pretty boy singer and wear a tux with a frilly shirt. Tony had suggested wearing a clip on bow tie, so if he got into a beef they couldn't strangle him with it. It was an old mafia trick. Tony had done a good job of putting his show together and filling in the cracks. He took him to McVan's one night and had him do a guest spot. It went over good. He felt right at home on stage.

Now, he had to do it all alone. Introduce the girls and keep things moving. He had that feeling in the pit of his stomach, like the first time he went out on a hit for the Don. Tony said that would pass when he got on stage. He hoped so. Carmen chose to stay home for a couple of weeks to let him do his thing and not have to worry about her. She would come down to see him later. She was looking for a special song to have him record. Richie said that they would put the song on every juke box in New York and the surrounding areas. The first thing they would see on the song list would be his. They would line up TV shows for him to appear and plug it. Dick Clark's American Bandstand was available through the boys in Philly. Things were moving fast.

******

The miles flew by and he sang along with the radio. Five hours later he pulled off the turnpike and headed for Utica. After arriving he looked for the Plush Horse, a club on Main Street. Half way down the block he saw the marquee. There it was, in big letters. Starting tonight, Danny Angel, The exotic Flame Fury and six strippers live on stage.

He parked the car across from the club and just looked at the marquee. It gave him a bit of a lift to see his name up in lights. He got out of the car, locked it and went across the street. He entered the club and stood there taking it all in. It was a big room with the stage against the right wall in the front half of the room. To the back of the room was a raised area with a railing. A plush velvet curtain was against the back wall. Opposite the stage, in the front half of the room, was a twenty foot bar with seating all the way around it. The stage had no curtain and was bare, except for a piano, a set of drums, and a Shure microphone, back where the band would be set up. A doorway curtain restricted view to the hallway leading to the backstage area.

He looked over to the bar and a man was checking the stock. He walked over and sat on a stool. "Excuse me. I'm Danny Angel. Is Cheech here?" The man looked up. He was built like a fire plug. "I'm Cheech. Welcome to the Plush Horse. Richie said to expect you." He held out his hammy-looking hand and shook hands with Danny. It was like shaking hands with a gorilla. He smiled when Danny matched him pressure for pressure. "You got a room across the street at the hotel. Go check in and be back by five. The band will be here to rehearse you and Flame. She'll be here about that time. I'll fill you in then about the other girls and what you're expected to do."

Danny got up, thanked him and walked out and to his car. He got his suitcase and hanging bag out and went into the hotel. The desk clerk was a good looking brunette with a great pair of tits. Her name-tag read "Lois." She gave him the once over and turned on the charm. "Hey good lookin.' How can I help you?"

Danny smiled at her. "I'm Danny Angel. I'm told you have a room for me here."

"We sure do. I've been expecting you. Here, fill this out and I'll get your key."

Danny filled out the card and handed it to her. When she took it, her hand brushed his and she gave him a coy smile. "Now if there's anything you want, you call me. Anything at all."

Danny gave her his best smile and said, "You can count on that sweetheart." He said to himself, *"sooner than you think."* He took his key, went over to the elevator and pushed the button. As he entered the elevator he looked over at her. She was smiling and leaning forward so her blouse hung down, giving him a clear look at her tits. Yep, he thought to himself, *"Much sooner than you think."*

He got to his room and unpacked. He hung his clothes neatly in the closet with hangers two inches apart. It was a habit he had left over from his Marine Corps days. He laid out his shaving things in the bathroom and, out of habit, put his gun under the mattress where he could get it in a hurry. Some habits were hard to break. He stretched out on the bed and took a short nap.

At four o'clock he freshened up and headed across the street for rehearsal. He passed the desk and gave wonder-lungs his best smile. Cheech was behind the bar having a cup of coffee. He waved Danny over to a bar stool and poured him a cup of coffee. "The band will be here in a half an hour. Let me hip you to some facts. I have two bouncers, Louie and Salvador. Any trouble you can't handle, they will. You got charge of back stage. Nobody gets back there. Capisci? There's a set of brass knuckles in the top drawer of your table. Use them if you have to. We don't want to mess up that pretty face. Ritchie tells me that you can handle yourself pretty good."

"I get by. What about wise guys? Do I stop them too?"

"They know better. The Don has the word out. If they try, knock their teeth out. He turned and looked at the clock behind the bar. "I'm expecting the feature any time now. I hope she's good looking. What I do is, I send them upstairs to undress. Then, I go up and give them a shot. If they're any good, I know what goombas to give them to. Works out fine, I get a free piece of ass and they get extra money from the guys."

Danny thought to himself, *"That's the only way this guy could get laid. Who'd want to fuck a hairy bowling ball with arms?"*

The door opened up and Danny turned and saw one of the most beautiful girls he had ever seen. She had red hair hanging down to her ass. At five foot three, she had a perfect body and a beautiful face with sparking green eyes. She walked over to the bar. She gave Danny the once over and turned to Cheech. "I'm Flame Fury. I'm looking for Cheech."

Cheech stood there with his mouth open. "Ah, I'm Cheech." He looked her over and liked what he saw. "Listen, Flame. I want you to go upstairs, first door on the right. Get undressed and I'll be right up."

She gave him a look that would stop a train. She reached into her shoulder bag and came out with a silver plated Berretta and pointed it at him. "And I'll blow your balls off, you Dago prick. You put one little greasy finger on me and I'll break it off and shove it up your ass. I came here to dance and that's it. I know about you from other dancers that worked here. I don't get passed around like a football."

Cheech looked to Danny for support. Danny smiled at him. "I do believe the lady is serious. Anybody with a face and body like hers, and a set of wise guys balls, I'd keep around."

Flame looked at him and laughed. "Yeah, that's me, beauty and balls." She turned towards Cheech who was still standing like a statue.

"What about it, Cheech? Do we start even or do I walk out the door?"

Cheech looked at both of them. "Miss Fury, you stay and I guarantee nobody will bother you as long as you're here."

She nodded and put the gun back in her shoulder bag. She turned to Danny. "You must be Danny Angel. I'm Flame. Nice to meet you." She held out her hand and Danny took it. She looked into his eyes and liked what she saw. She gave his hand a squeeze and said, "Be nice working with you. I have my intro written out so you can make an off stage announcement. I'll let you know what my closing number is so you can be ready to take me off."

Danny smiled down at her. "It will be my pleasure. I'm sort of new at this so you may have to bear with me for a bit."

"No problem. How would you like to help me bring in my wardrobe and stuff?"

Danny nodded and they went out to her car. She opened the trunk and leaned over to get her music. Danny saw that nice ass and immediately got a hard on. She handed him the music case and he quickly put it in front to hide his erection. Her gowns were laid out in the trunk on hangers. He grabbed the hangers and pulled the gowns out and followed her into the club. They went backstage and found her dressing room, right across the hall from his. His room was closest to the stage so he could block anybody coming back there. He hung up the gowns and put her case on the dressing room table.

"I'd better go out and get my music. The band should be here any moment." He went out past the bandstand where the drummer and piano player were standing talking to each other. He walked over and introduced himself.

"Hi, I'm Danny Angel." He shook hands with both of them.

The piano player said, "I'm John and this is Buddy. Louie will be here in a second. You got your music?"

"I'm on my way to get it. Flame is in the dressing room with her music. Maybe you want to do her first."

"Yeah we can do that. I'll go back and get her charts."

As the piano player went back stage Danny went out to his car to get his music. He opened the case and just took out the three books he would need. When he went back into the club, Flame was on stage talking to John about her music. Louie showed up, got his horn out and blew a few riffs to set the reed.

Danny sat there and watched Flame rehearse the band. She knew her music and would stop them from time to time to explain what she was doing at that time. Danny was impressed. He was learning just watching her. She had a habit of standing spread legged which pulled her skirt tight across her ass and legs outlining every curve. He was going nuts just watching her. When she was done, she turned to him.

"OK, handsome, your turn." She came off stage and sat where he was. Danny went up and gave the guys their charts. They looked over the book and John nodded in approval. "Nice charts. Johnny Lawrence wrote these, huh? You must know somebody 'cause he don't write for just anybody."

"Let's just say he's a friend." They went through the charts. Flame was beside herself, wriggling and clapping. Even Cheech stopped what he was doing and listened. When they were done John said, "Man, what a set of pipes you got. What the hell are you doing here?"

"I'm learning the ropes, and according to my manager, paying some dues."

"I can dig that. We'll line up the shows tonight before we go on."

"Good. Now I'm going to take Flame over and get her checked in. That OK with you little lady?"

"Sounds good to me." Danny walked her out of the club and across the street to the hotel.

The same girl was behind the counter. She took one look at Flame and Danny and knew her chances were getting slim. She checked her in and gave her a room key. It was right down the hall from Danny's. Flame went over to the bell captain to have her luggage taken up to her room. The girl behind the desk looked at Danny. "I guess this means no hanky panky for us, huh?"

Danny leaned over the counter so he was close to her. "Tell me that tonight, when you're naked in my bed. You know what time I get off. You got a pass key. Use it." He brushed her breast lightly as he leaned back and went over to help Flame. They went up together and she went into her room to get her things hung up. Danny said he would escort her to work at 7:30pm. She kissed him on the check and closed the door.

Danny went to his room and called Carmen. He told her about the club and the rehearsal. He said he would call her when he was done and tell her how it went. He lay down and took a short nap.

Chapter 12

They arrived at the club at 7:30 and it was filling up. The band was laying down some nice jazz. Danny walked Flame back stage and then went up to the bar to talk to Cheech. Cheech came over and told Danny what he wanted. "Listen. Those six other broads backstage are all a pain in the ass. They all think they are stars. Your job is to keep them off each other and schmooze them. I don't care how you do it. The order they go on and their intros are written on the wall next to your dressing room. You can use them or make up your own. Remember, nobody gets up on stage or back stage. In case of big trouble, you got Louie and Salvador out front. Keep it moving and with that voice of yours you should do OK. Any questions?"

"Not at the moment. I'd better go meet the other girls." He turned and went back stage. On the other side of Flame's dressing room were six small rooms with six girls in them. Danny called out and asked them to step out of the rooms for a minute. They came out in all stages of dress or undress. He looked them over and they looked him over. They were all sizes and shapes. Some had big tits that hung down. Others had small perky tits and no bellies. "Hi, I'm Danny Angel and I'll be introducing you. I'm new at this, so I'll do my best to do a good job on your intros. I see the list on the wall and I guess I'll go by that. When you get dressed, could you stop by my dressing room and let me know your closing number so I can be there to take you off?"

The girls all nodded and thanked him and went back to their rooms to get ready. Danny went to his dressing room and changed into a tux with the frilly shirt. He stood in front of the mirror admiring how he looked. A voice cut in, "You look good enough to eat and boy am I hungry."

He turned and Flame was standing in his doorway wearing just a silk robe.

"The diner's open twenty-four hours a day, my dear. No reservations needed." She laughed. "I just came to wish you luck. Knock 'em dead." She came over and kissed him on the mouth. As she backed away his hands brushed her breast and she shuddered. "This should be an interesting two weeks." She turned and went back to her dressing room.

John came in at that time with the music and they lined up the shows. John said, "If there are any songs you want to sing and you don't have charts, let me know. We know all the standards and then some. So, don't worry about calling out what you want."

"Thanks, John. I'll do that. There are some Italian songs that might be requested which I don't have charts for."

"Don't worry about that, I've done enough Italian weddings in my time, so I know all the songs. You just call them out."

"Thanks. I guess we're about ready, huh? I have to get the closing numbers from the girls. Ten minutes to show time. I'll be ready." He sat down and studied the list of girls. First up was Peggy O'Neil, then Monica, Crystal Chandelier, Sabrina, Cashmere Bouquet and Tawny Angel. The girls came by and gave him their closing numbers. Some of them lingered and flirted.

Danny was too wound up to notice. Then came the drum roll and the show was about to start. He heard John giving him an intro, the music started and he stepped out on stage. Danny took the mike and went into his opening number. As he sang he looked around the room. There were hookers and pimps, gays, transvestites and some good looking women with wise guys.

The rest were square johns looking to see titties. He was singing Bobby Darin's, "River Stay Away From my Door." The band was smoking and at the end, he got a good round of applause. He had their attention. He went into some light jokes and got some laughs. Then he brought out the first girl. "Ladies and gentlemen, direct from Ireland, here she is, a pretty little colleen, Peggy

O'Neil."

She stepped out on stage as an Irish lass dressed all in green and shamrocks. She was tall with black hair and blue eyes and a descent figure. She winked at Danny as she took the stage. Danny went off stage and stood there with his head bowed.

Flame saw him and said, "Hey, you did great. Keep up the good work and don't worry. You'll be just fine."

He smiled at her and said, "Thanks. I just have to get used to this. It did feel good though. I have to get this night under my belt and I'll be fine." He took Peggy off. He went into another song, then jokes. He did ad-libs off the crowd and then brought on the girls.

Then it came time for Flame. He gave her a big intro and stood just off stage so he could watch her. She was sex personified. She moved like a gazelle. Every movement was in perfect sync with the band. It took her two numbers to get her gloves and hat off. When she took off the hat, her hair cascaded down her back and drew a gasp from the audience. Red hair caught in the lights appeared like a red flame caressing her body. Her gown seemed to just melt away as she moved to the music. One minute she was clothed and the next she was in pasties and panels.

As she glided through the red lights on stage, the hair and panels flowed behind her. She passed by the curtain where Danny was standing and her panels dropped at his feet. She was now standing in just a sparkly G string and pasties. Flame closed her show with a flourish and let the G string fall as she exited the stage. She brushed Danny's crotch as she passed. He went out to thunderous applause. Danny brought her back. She was wearing a beautiful robe with flames on it. She took her bows and left.

Danny continued the night with everything running together. Girls coming out followed by songs, jokes and finally Flame to close out the night. She was magnificent. After the show, Cheech came backstage overjoyed. He thanked Danny and then went to see Flame. He asked her to come out, say hello and have a drink with some friends. She agreed and he left. She came into Danny's dressing room. "You don't mind standing by in case I have to split do you? Sometimes friends get too touchy feely for me."

Danny agreed and they went out into the club. The bouncers escorted her to a table with some well dressed men who stood up to greet her. Danny knew they weren't wise guys. They were just men out looking to get laid. He went over to the bar and was immediately surrounded by hookers, gays and some straight chicks. They were all complimenting him on his voice and looks. He had a couple of drinks and some laughs all the time keeping an eye on Flame. The guys were getting a little carried away as men do trying to impress Flame. Each one was thinking he would be the lucky one. She looked over at Danny giving him a knowing look. He excused himself and walked over to the table.

"Hi, sweetheart. Ready to go? I just called the babysitter and the kids are fine. You gentlemen don't mind if I steal my wife do you?"

They all stood up not knowing what to say. Danny took her arm and walked her out of the club. When they got outside she burst into laughter.

"Where in the hell did you come up with that? Babysitters! Kids! That was a real hoot."

"It worked didn't it? Come on. I'll walk you home."

They crossed the street, entered the hotel, and took the elevator to their floor. Danny walked her to her room, opened the door and said good night. She looked at him a little funny, but went inside.

Danny went to his room and opened the door. He knew Lois was there. He could smell her perfume. She was sitting up in his bed naked from the waist up. Her large breasts were hanging down and swinging gently as she breathed. Danny walked over and reached down and stroked her breast. She shuddered.

"I'm going to take a quick shower and will be right back." He went in to the bathroom, stripped and got in the hot water and let it beat down on him. He lathered himself with soap and rinsed off. After drying off he came out of the bathroom naked. She took one look at Ninja and said, "My God, bring that over here." He did and she grabbed it with both hands. She said, "I've never had one this big. I don't know if I can take it all."

Danny smiled down at her. "Let's just see how much you can take." He laid her on her back. She was more than ready. He slowly pushed down.

She yelled into his ear. "Give it all to me. I want it all." He shifted a bit and plunged it deep inside her. She came hard, scratching and moaning. Her climax seemed to go on forever. Danny came with her. He lay on top of her breathing heavily, and then rolled to the side as she tried to regain her composure.

Finally she said, "I'll say one thing. I've never had that happen before. When you pushed it in, I saw stars."

Danny replied, "I'm going to be here for a month. We'll do it again sometime soon. Now, let's take a shower and you can go home. I need to get some sleep." They got up and showered. She got dressed, and kissed him good night.

Danny went over and phoned Carmen and told her about his first evening at the Plush Horse. He hung up and his phone rang. It was Flame. "I see you had some extra curricular activity tonight. I could hear her all the way down here. You must be good."

"There's only one way to find out, my dear."

"That's an interesting thought. I'll sleep on it. See you tomorrow."

Chapter 13

Danny met Flame for an early dinner and then on to the club. It was packed. Danny noticed there were more women in the club than the night before. He walked Flame backstage and then went to the bar to talk to Cheech. Before he had a chance, three women came up to tell him that they were at the club the previous night and that they had brought some lady friends to see him. He turned on the charm and had them salivating. He promised to sing one of their favorite songs. Cheech was busy so he went backstage to his dressing room.

He was sitting there when Peggy came in complaining that she didn't like going on first because she was a better dancer than the other girls. Danny sat her down. "That's the reason I need you to go on first. I need a strong opener and you are strong. You set the pace for the whole night. So, do it for me."

"Gee, I never thought about it that way. I'll do it for you." She kissed him lightly on the lips and left. Danny was just about to get undressed when Monica came in. She was complaining about having to go on second. Danny sat her down.

"Monica, I need a strong second dancer. You know Peggy can't dance that good, so I need someone to pick up the show, and that's you. You're my life saver."

"You really think so? Yeah, I can do that for you and thanks." She too kissed him and left. He did this three more times before he got dressed. After the fifth one left, Flame came over to his dressing room. "You sure have a way with women. To con five girls into thinking that they're the best is quite a feat. My hat's off to you."

"It's called keeping peace. House rules say keep the girls from killing each other and nobody gets back stage."

"Well you're the man for the job. Have a good show." She turned and went back to her dressing room.

The night went very well. Every time Danny got on stage the women and the gays would cheer and holler. He sang, did his moves and ad-libbed his way through the night. The girls danced and Flame was awesome. The girls and the gays loved her. At the end of the evening, Danny was standing at the bar having a glass of vino. Women came up to him and fawned over him. Cheech was happy. Even the bouncers came over and thanked him. All the time, he kept his eyes on the entrance to backstage. From experience, he knew this was the time. The drunks would make their move when they thought nobody was paying attention. The girls came out and hit the bar to mix with the customers. Flame was still backstage.

When she finally came out Danny waved her over. He sat her down and bought her a drink. Guys kept coming over and thanking her for the wonderful shows all the time thinking that maybe they would get lucky. She handled it all with cool efficiency, smiling that beautiful smile and tossing that red hair around.

Danny looked over and saw one of the wanna-be wise guys looking in her direction and talking to his buddies. He kept pointing at Flame and making gestures. Danny knew he would come over. As soon as the guy started toward Flame, Danny got up to intercept him. He met him half way. "Hey, paison. You don't want to go over and bother the lady. She's had a tough night and just wants to relax. Why don't you go back over and sit with your buddies?"

The guy looked Danny over, sizing him up. He saw the handsome face, but also the muscular body. However, he hesitated when he looked into Danny's cold and penetrating eyes. He noticed the way Danny was standing too. He was ready for what ever came along. Louie saw this and came over. "We got a problem here?"

The wanna-be looked at the both of them. "Hell, no. I was just going back to my friends." He turned and almost ran back to his buddies. Louie looked at Danny. "Trying to take my job?"

Danny laughed. "No, I just wanted to block trouble before it started. The guy's a jerk. I've seen that kind in every bar and juke joint I've been in."

Louie looked down at him. "You move like a fighter, and looking at your hands, I believe you've banged a few people around in your time."

"Well, when I was in Italy, I did box for my school. Plus you know how guys are with broads. Look at them the wrong way and they want to fight. So yeah, I've banged a few heads in my time."

"I thought so." Louie started to walk away.

Danny said, "Hey, Louie," and the bouncer turned around. "I got your back." Louie smiled and walked back to the bar. Danny went back to Flame. He sat down and sipped his wine. She looked at him with a curious look. "I take it you weren't always a pretty boy singer. That was a classic bouncer move you just made."

"Let's just say, I've hung out in some rough clubs in my time. I don't like jerks and wanna-be tough guys. Let's go to the hotel and have a drink in the bar. It'll be quieter and we can relax." They got up, said their goodbyes and headed across the street. Once in the bar, they sat and ordered a drink.

Flame said, "After this drink I want to find out what that girl last night was screaming about."

"We can do that. It'll be my pleasure."

They finished their drinks and went up the elevator to his room. He opened the door and was relieved to find it empty. Flame suggested a shower would be nice after doing her shows. He agreed. She went into the bathroom and undressed. She called out to him to join her in the shower. He had already shed his clothes and was standing there naked. When he walked into the bathroom, she turned and exclaimed, "Now I know what the screaming was all about. Get in here and let me wash that thing." He got into the shower. She was small but her body was perfection. She looked like a doll with long red hair. She only came up to his chest.

He got the soap and started lathering her. He washed her

breasts and watched the nipples get hard. He moved his fingers between her legs and started to massage her clitoris. Flame leaned into him and held on. As he massaged her, she stroked Ninja causing it to stand up.

He picked her up and held her against the shower wall. She wrapped her legs around him. He slowly let her down. She was tight. She raised herself up and came down on it getting a little more each time. She was kissing him and moaning. Up and down until she had it all. He could feel her insides squeezing him.

She said in his ear, "Take me to bed." He walked out of the shower with Flame wrapped around him, and Ninja completely inside. Then holding her tightly, he lowered her onto the bed and started to move. She matched his thrust with a side to side motion that was driving him wild. It was like a hand inside her was squeezing him. Her muscles were squeezing him and pulsing. He couldn't hold it and came hard. She kept squeezing and loosening her muscles until he fell on her exhausted.

She laughed. "Bet you never had that before. But then, I never had one that big to work on before. You're amazing."

Danny rolled off her and pulled her close. "You're the one who's amazing. Where did you learn that trick?"

"From bellydancers. They have great control over their muscles."

"I'll say. Let's get cleaned up and play some more." They got up, showered again and dried off. He took her to bed and laid her on her back. He started to kiss her mouth, then her neck. He moved to her breast and sucked on the nipples. She moaned and moved her pelvis. He worked his way down to her patch of red hair. He parted the hair with his tongue and found her clit. She gasped and started to move. He sucked and licked it until she came hard. He kept it up until she came a third time. She was begging him to stop. He looked up and said, "I thought you wanted to find out what that screaming was all about?"

She looked at him and smiled. "Now I know. Come up here and kiss me." He slid up her body and put Ninja between her legs.

They lay there side by side enjoying each other until they

fell asleep.

*****

The week seemed to fly by. Every night was packed and every night more women came to the club to see Danny. Cheech loved it. More women meant more guys buying them drinks and trying to score. Danny had to add to his show. Cheech cut the stripper's shows down giving Danny more time, except for Flame. The women loved her. The other dancers didn't care. They were getting the same money for less dancing. He had it made. Do shows and make love to Flame every night, all night.

Now it was Saturday. Danny walked over to the window and looked across the street at the club. It was 7:00pm and the line of women waiting to get in the club stretched all the way down the block. He heard a knock on the door and Flame came in carrying her makeup case. She walked over to him and looked out the window. "Those are your groupies, Danny boy. You're getting a following."

"Seems that way. Does make it easier than working to all men. I think we'd better use the backstage door tonight to save a lot of confusion. Let's go downstairs and grab a snack before we go to the club." They went downstairs and into the restaurant. After having a bite they entered the club through the back door, passing the girls in their dressing rooms. They all called greetings and he answered them. He put Flame's makeup case in her dressing room and went to look out the curtain into the club. It was packed. There were four guys sitting ringside. Danny thought they must have tipped real good to get that table.

John came backstage and they lined up the first show. He went into his dressing room. He was clipping on his bow tie when Flame came in. As usual she was wearing her silk robe open down the front showing him his play ground. She kissed him and wished him luck. He fondled her until she broke away, running to her dressing room. He heard the drum roll and John made his announcement.

Upon hearing Danny's name, there was a roar from the crowd. He stepped through the curtain and went into his opening number. You could hardly hear it over the screams and clapping from the women. He sang and kibitzed with them, then brought on the first girl. He was standing watching her through the curtain to make sure nobody got on stage, when Flame came up to him and put her arm around his waist. "You killed them. You're way too good for this place. You know that?"

"This is just a stepping stone. I'm learning and, as they say, getting my chops up. By the time I leave here, I'll know what the hell I'm doing. This is a great proving ground."

"Well, you're proving it all right. Keep it up Tiger." She went back to her dressing room. Danny went out and took Peggy off and went into Bobby Darin's, "River Stay Away From my Door." As he was singing, the front door opened and in walked a natty little man about five foot three. He was wearing a blue pinstriped suit complete with a boutonniere. He sported a gray fedora and matching gloves. Three bodyguards with a combined weight of somewhere around twelve hundred pounds were with him.

Cheech came running over to greet him while the three bodyguards physically moved the four guys sitting at the ringside table. Cheech came down with a waiter and cleaned off the table. He put a bottle of wine down and one glass, then motioned for the natty man to come and sit down. Danny knew a Don when he saw one. The man took off his hat and gloves. He sat back, crossed his legs, then snapped his fingers at Danny. Danny stopped the band and asked, "Something I can do for you?"

The mobster replied, "Sing for me, Melancholy Baby."

Danny looked down at him and said, "No." A hush fell over the room. Cheech was at the bar waving frantically at Danny. The bodyguards started forward, but the natty little man raised his hand and they stopped. Danny said, "I don't like that song. How can I sing a song about a girl with a head like a melon and the face of a collie?"

Danny went back to singing his song. The little man wrote a note and signaled for the waitress. He handed her the note and pointed at Danny. She approached the stage, handing the note up to Danny. He stopped the band and read the note, as the room got very quiet. It said, "Please sing Melancholy Baby." Wrapped up in the note was a thirty-eight bullet!

Danny got so tickled, he laughed out loud. He turned to John and said, "Give me a G-7." John gave him the chord and Danny went into the song but in a solid four beat. The people started clapping in time to the song. Danny finished with a flourish. There were cries of, "One more time." He went back to the bridge and kicked the hell out of the song ending to a standing ovation.

Even the little Don was standing. He motioned Danny over. Danny came ringside and leaned down to shake his hand. The Don slipped a hundred dollar bill into the top pocket of his tux. He had scored. The rest of the evening was like a dream. The Don stayed until after Flame's show, then left. The four guys rushed back to get their table. At the end of the evening, Danny came out into the club and was mobbed by the ladies waiting to see him. He signed autographs on napkins, deposit slips and even on one young lady's breast. He made it to the bar where Flame was sitting with Louie.

Cheech came over and gave him a hug. "You scared the hell out of me. Nobody ever said no to Don Bannacci before. I thought you were a dead man but, you pulled it off beautifully. He has invited you and Flame to a private party. He's sending his limo for you around two o'clock in the afternoon. I have to tell you that it's a great honor. He doesn't invite just anybody to his home."

"It'll be our pleasure. Does he know Ritchie?"

"Yes, they have dealings together, but I don't think he knows that you're his boy."

"He probably knows everybody I know. It'll be fun. Thanks, Cheech." He went over to Flame. "Well, are you ready for some fun and games?"

"I thought you would never ask. Come on stud, let's go rehearse for the Olympic balling team." That brought a laugh. They said their goodbyes and left.

******

It was Sunday morning and Danny was lying in bed talking to Carmen. Flame had gone to her room to shower and freshen up for the party. Danny phoned Carmen and mentioned the natty little Don. "His name is Pietro Bannacci. He controls the towns around Utica all the way to Syracuse". Carmen said, "Don't let his size fool you. He used to be in your former profession. He does things for my father. I don't think he knows that my father is your sponsor. He also knows your uncle. So you'll be well taken care of. Oh, by the way. I found the perfect song for you to record. It's called, 'Somebody Loves You.' It'll go platinum. I'm sure of it."

"When can I hear it? If it's that good, I should be learning it."

"In due time. I'll have it for you before you open in Syracuse. Be a nice place to break it in and see how it goes. I'm getting the arrangement done now. I've got to find a song for the flip side of the record. Oh, Tony is sending some more charts he had written for you. There are some really good songs."

"Good. Thank him for me. The way things are going I'll need them. I've got to shower and shave. They'll be picking us up in an hour."

"Us? Oh, the dancer. She's going with you?"

"Yes, the Don said to bring her. She's arm candy. Do I detect a note of jealousy?"

"Me? Never. You just be careful and have a good time. Let me know what happens. I'll be with you soon enough to take care of your plumbing."

"Yeah, I bet you will. I'll call you later." He hung up and went to get ready.

Precisely at two, the limo pulled up in front of the hotel. The Don's house was a short drive on the outskirts of town. When they got close, Danny could see the house set way back from the road surrounded by an electric fence and a guard shack next to the big gate. There were horses running free in the cold, nippy air with frosty breath coming from their nostrils. The car pulled up in front of a big English Tudor. They gave their coats to the butler standing at the front door. One of the bodyguards came over and greeted them and, at the same time, patted Danny down.

He turned to Flame and paused because he didn't know what to do. She spread her legs, held her arms out to the side and said, "The only weapons I carry are these two thirty eights under my blouse."

They heard a laugh and turned to see the Don standing there. He came over and took her hand. They were both the same height. "I never saw a better pair my dear." He turned to Danny. "You, and I gotta talk. Bruno, take Flame into the party for me. I'll be right in."

He took Danny's arm and led him into his study. When they were seated he said, "So, a thirty eight bullet doesn't scare you?"

"A couple of years ago, I was in Korea being shot at with big bullets. A little thirty-eight would have been a welcome addition. Besides, I liked the look on your face when I said, no."

"You took a hell of a chance. My boys were ready to rip your head off."

"I knew you wouldn't let them do that. You remind me of my uncle."

"And who is your uncle?"

"Don Angelo from Chicago. I'm his nephew from Italy."

"Madonna Mia. No wonder you got balls. How is my dear friend?"

He's fine. He sent me to Ritchie in Buffalo to get my career started."

"Son-of-a-bitch. Ritchie didn't tell me anything about this."

"He wanted to see how I'd do on my own without his protection. Only Cheech knew and he was sworn to secrecy."

"Well, now that I know, you have my blessing and my protection. You got one hell of a voice and I can see you going a long way. Anything I can do to help, just ask."

"Thanks Don Bannacci, I'll do that. By the way, Carmen says to tell you hello."

"What a sweet girl. No dummy either."

"That's for sure. She's masterminding my career. I don't know anything about show business. She's doing it all for me.

Ritchie gave her a free hand."

"From what I saw last night she's doing a good job. Come on, let's go out and meet some of my guests." They walked out of the den and into the beautifully furnished, oversized living room. Marble statues, bronzes, and French porcelains were strategically located by the French doors, mirrors and fireplace. A wide terrace wrapped around the living room, with stairs going down to an expansive lawn. There were twenty or thirty people chatting while a trio played softly in a corner near a well stocked buffet. Two butlers were busy offering drinks to the select group of guests. Flame was surrounded by five or six guys. She looked like a little doll next to these big goombas. The Don took him around and introduced him to his guests. Most of them were made men. The women fawned over Danny and flirted.

Then the Don took him over to a guy who looked like a fire plug. He was short, squat and ugly.

"Danny, this is Joey DiGeorgio from Toledo." Danny shook hands with him. His hand was like a rock. He knew this guy. He was called, the dentist. He was an enforcer for the Ohio syndicate. When he hit you, he would knockout most of your teeth. He was a real bad ass.

"So, you're Don Angelo's nephew. What are you doing here?"

"I'm singing at the Plush Horse."

The Don spoke up. "Ritchie from Buffalo is handling his career for Don Angelo. The kid can sing. He's going to go a long way."

"Tell Ritchie to put him in Toledo. We got a nice place called The Akuakua room. It's in the Town House Motel. Hottest joint in Toledo. You come there and we'll treat you right."

"Thanks, I'll tell Ritchie to do that." They shook hands again and the Don took him around and introduced him to the rest of the people. As they passed the trio the Don said, "The kid playing piano is my nephew, Johnny. He graduated from that music school in New York City, Juilliard. Not bad, huh?"

"He's great. Plays better than the one I got playing for me at the Plush Horse. I'd like to meet him."

The Don walked over and told the band to take a break. He walked his nephew over to meet Danny. They shook hands. "You play a lot of piano, Johnny. Be nice if you were backing me. The guy backing me at The Plush Horse is good, but not in your league. You got a nice touch."

"Thanks. Would you like to do a few numbers with us next set?"

"I'd love to. We can do a couple of Italian songs and go from there."

"You call it. We know them all. Be up in about fifteen minutes. Union rules, the band gets a break." He put his arm around his uncle's shoulder. "Right, Uncle Pete?"

The Don laughed. "I think you make up your own rules. But go ahead."

Johnny left and the Don turned to Danny. "That's a real good kid. No booze or drugs. Spends most of his time writing music. He's doing a thing now for some big orchestra in Rochester."

"That's nice to know." Danny felt a presence near his left arm and looked down. Flame was standing there. "Are you two going to ignore me the whole day? I've been hit on by every broken nose guy in this joint, except for you Don. You don't like little girls with big tits?"

The Don threw back his head and roared with laughter. He put his arm around her shoulders and said, "For a little lady, you got more balls than half the guys in this room. Most people are afraid to say anything that might offend me. But not you. You shoot straight from the shoulder. You know, if I was thirty years younger, I'd take a shot at you myself."

"Hey, I can make you feel thirty years younger. But your wife might not go for it. I imagine she's tougher than anybody in this room."

"You got that right. Come on, Danny's going to sing and I want to get everybody over here." As he left with Flame, she turned her head and winked at him.

Danny went over to the trio and told them what he wanted to sing. He chose "Al Di La" for an opener. The trio was wonderful. They followed his every move and it was like they had been together for years. He sang for twenty minutes and had to beg off as they wanted more. He invited them to come down to The Plush Horse. He introduced Flame and told them not to miss her act. The Don was pleased. "You're going to get a lot of people in to see you. I'll be sending some people in that you should know. Now, come on. Let's go eat." He took Flame's arm and they went into the dining room.

Chapter 14

Danny was lying naked on his bed talking to Carmen. Flame was in her room making some calls and would be down later. He was telling Carmen about Joey. "He thought he knew me. I met him when he came to Chicago for a meeting. He said there's a great club in Toledo I should work. It's in the Town House Motel."

"I know the place. That's Slicks club. It's run by the Jews. They're tied in with The Purple Gang. That's Patsy's territory. He'll put you in there and some clubs in Detroit when you're ready.

"Good. By the way, there was a trio at the Don's party that just played their asses off. The piano player's the Don's nephew. They backed me for some songs and I have to tell you they were great. The kid also writes charts. Be nice to keep them in mind if I need some backing."

"I'll call the Don and find out about it. I think I'll come down to Utica for your last week and get everything ready for Syracuse. Right now, I have to get dressed. My father is taking us out to dinner. Call me tomorrow."

******

Monday night the club was packed, mostly by women. Danny peeked out the curtain. There were some people from the Don's party sitting ringside. Their bodyguards were at the end of the bar so they could keep an eye on everything. The gays and hookers were on the other side of the bar facing the stage. Danny saw Cheech coming and stepped aside so he could get backstage. Cheech went into his dressing room and motioned him in. "Danny, you got to do me a favor. I want you to do a forty-five or fifty minute first show. More if they want it. Then you can bring on the girls. The people sitting ringside came to see you not the broads. So did all those women out there."

"What ever you want Cheech. I'll get John to line up the show. Those people ringside were at Don Bannacci's party yesterday. They're going to want to see Flame. I don't think they'll stay all the way through the girls until she comes on. Why don't I bring her on after me and then we can go from there."

"That's a good idea. They're from New York City. Heavyhitters."

"I figured as much. Don't worry. I know how to handle them. Would you send John in on your way out?"

"Yeah, good luck."

He went out through the curtain and in a minute John came back with his piano book. "There's been a change of plans. I'm going to do about an hour the first show, then bring Flame out. So, let's set my book up."

When John left Danny walked over to Flame's dressing room. "I'm going to open and do about an hour. Then bring you on. The people from the Don's party are sitting ringside and they want to see you. So my sexy little nymph, you be ready when I call you. Now, I have to go tell the other ladies what's going on."

"I'll be ready, willing and able my Italian lover." She rose up and kissed him. Danny told the other ladies what was up and they were pleased. They got paid one way or the other so they didn't care.

The show started as John made his introduction. At the mention of Danny's name, a roar went up from the crowd. He stepped on stage and the ladies went wild. He could hardly hear the music. He sang, did comedy, moved just like Tony taught him and the ladies loved it. He closed to a standing ovation with cries of, "more, more." The people from New York were standing. One motioned him over and put some bills in his top pocket.

Danny introduced Flame. She came out and wowed them. The women loved her and gave her a standing ovation too. The club was alive. The people from New York left shortly after Flame's performance.

The rest of the night flew by. Danny came out after the end of the evening and was mobbed by the remaining women. They wanted pictures with him and autographs. Some gave him their phone numbers and hotel keys. He was gracious and charming to all of them. Then Flame came out and they went to the bar to get a drink. The hookers and the gays applauded them and fawned over them.

Cheech came over and said, "That was the best night we ever had in here. I liked the way the show ran. Just you and Flame. I'm going to send the other girls down to my club in Albany and just use the two of you. You do an hour, then let the band take a fifteen minute break. Then Flame does her forty five and the band takes a break. This way we can do three shows a night and get a turn over. Plus it will give me time to put a big ad in the paper and some radio spots on the air. What do you think?"

Danny looked at Flame then at Cheech. "I think that's a great idea, but one thing Cheech. Could we add to the band? A bass, trumpet and trombone would make it so much better musically. You're saving money by sending the girls to your other club. And the three extra musicians won't cost that much."

"Yeah, we can do that. I'll tell John. He knows the players around here. We'll start this on Wednesday. You can rehearse Wednesday afternoon. Oh, by the way. Carmen called. She has a photographer coming to town tomorrow. She said you need some eight by tens to give away and something for the marquee. He'll put a rush on them. She'll call you at the hotel and give you the time and directions."

"Thanks Cheech. I really appreciate this." He felt a hand on his leg under the table playing with the head of his cock. He looked down and Flame was smiling up at him. "Looks like you're on your way. By Wednesday, this place will be a night club not a strip joint. I think we should go over to the hotel and celebrate." She squeezed his cock. "What do you think?"

"I thought you'd never ask." They said their goodbyes and

left.

*****

Danny lay in bed and smiled to himself. Things were going along fine.

He was getting laid on a regular basis, and his shows were getting better by the day. Carmen was happy to hear that he would be doing regular shows. She gave him the appointment time and directions to get his pictures taken. It was a photo studio four blocks from the hotel. He grabbed a tux out of the closet along with a shirt and tie. The patent leather shoes went into a shoe bag. He called Flame and they walked the four blocks to the studio. There was a sign on the door, Bruno of Hollywood. Flame said, "You must have clout. He's the best there is. If you don't have your pictures taken by him, you're not very good."

They walked in and there stood Bruno. You'd think with a name like Bruno he would be big and beefy. He was just the opposite. He was around five foot five, slim and impeccably dressed. He walked over and introduced himself. "I'm Bruno and you must be Danny. And this lovely lady must be Flame." He took her hand and kissed it. He turned to Danny. "The dressing room is over there. You change and I'll set up the lights and talk to this lovely lady."

Danny nodded and went to change. He got dressed and came back out. Bruno had the lights and the cameras ready. He looked at Danny and said, "My, what a handsome man you are. I just hope my lenses do you justice."

He came over and looked closely at Danny's face. "We need just a little makeup to take away the sheen. He turned to get his makeup case and Danny shot Flame a look like "I'm not going for this."

She smiled and mouthed, "Just do it." Bruno came back and sat him on a stool and added a light coat of make up. Next, he did the eyes with a liner. Standing back from Danny he said, "You're perfect. Now starts the fun."

For over an hour he took pictures of Danny in numerous positions. Finally it was done. He stood back and said, "I think that's enough. Oh, Flame, I want to take a picture of you with Danny for my collection." She came over and he posed her with Danny. He took several shots. "I'll have these later this afternoon. I'll call you at the hotel and you can come pick out the ones you like. I'll make up a few for Cheech for the marquee board. Also, Carmen said for me to send the negatives to New York to get a thousand pictures made for you. You must be something special for her to fly me in from Kansas City to do this."

"Let's just say she's a good manager. She thinks of everything. Can I get out of this tux now?"

"Sure. There's cold cream back there so you can take off the makeup." Danny nodded and went back to change. He came out ten minutes later and they said their goodbyes. They went back and dropped off the clothes at the hotel. The rest of the day they just knocked around until it was time to select the photos. Danny was amazed at how good he looked. It was like picking out someone else's pictures. Bruno was delighted and offered to drop some eight by tens off at the club later that night.

They went back to the hotel. By seven o'clock the line of women stretched all the way down the block. After getting into the club through the back way, Danny peeked out the curtain. The place was filling up fast. Sitting ringside were two of Don Bannacci's wise guys, one with his back to the stage. With them were two very buxom ladies, probably hookers. Both guys were a little drunk. John came backstage and they lined up the first show.

Like the night before, when John announced his name, a roar went up through the club. The ladies jumped up to greet him. He sang, he moved, he ad-libbed. The wise guys never looked up or turned around. Their dates were having a hell of a time, flirting with him, and shaking their boobs at him. He closed the first set to a standing ovation. He introduced Flame and she hit the stage like a bomb. The wise guys actually turned around to watch her. She was wonderful and the ladies loved her. Danny came back on and took her off.

The ladies were hollering for an Italian song so Danny went into "Al-Di-La." As he was singing, the wise guys got into an argument. The guy with his back to Danny reached over the table and slapped the other guy in the face. As the other guy recoiled from the slap, he reached inside his jacket and came out with a thirty-two pistol and fired it at the guy who slapped him. The bullet missed, and hit Danny's microphone. It knocked Danny's hand back before ricocheting into the ceiling.

Everything happened at once. Screaming…people hitting the floor…the band crouching behind the piano… and John continuing to try to play. In an instant, Danny tore the cord out of the two pound microphone and threw it at the hood that fired the shot. The mic hit him in the breast bone breaking ribs. Danny was over the rail, taking the one hood down who was trying to get up. He slammed into the shooter. He knocked him off his feet, and then Danny hit him, breaking his jaw and sending teeth flying.

He felt himself being lifted up and set aside like a baby. Louie and Salvador were there. Louie smiled at him. "We got it from here Champ." Louie grabbed one, leaving Salvador to lift the other one clean off the floor.

Salvador looked like Primo Canero at six foot seven and three hundred pounds. The two guys were taken to the office at the back of the club. Cheech was there calming everybody down. The band was still playing his song. Danny got up on stage. Holding his hands up, he got their attention.

"Ladies and gentlemen, please be seated. Sorry for the interruption. I guess they didn't like the song. If they had just told me, I would have sung something else." That got a laugh from the crowd. "Now, I would like to bring out a lovely lady to dance for you. Here she is, direct from Ireland, Peggy O'Neil." Peggy came out and Danny went backstage picking up the mic on his way.

Cheech came backstage with a soldering kit. He took the mic, stripped the wires and soldered them back to the mic. "It happens all the time. You did a good job out there. Are you all right?"

"I've been shot at before. What's going to happen to the

wise guys?"

"Don Bannacci is on his way down. It's out of my hands." He slapped Danny on the back and left. Danny knew what that meant. They broke a rule and would pay dearly for it. Flame came in and wanted to know if he was all right. She hugged him and kissed him before going back to her dressing room. He stood in front of the mirror and looked at himself. He was a bit messed up. The adrenalin was still pumping through his veins. For a moment he was back in his old world. He loved the violence and hitting that hood was pure pleasure. He cleaned himself up and went out to take Peggy off.

The rest of the night was uneventful. Danny was singing the last set when the Don came in with three bodyguards. He waved to Danny on his way back to the office with Cheech on his heels.

After the last song, Danny came down from the stage into a crowd of women. He was gracious and charming and had them all salivating. He signed autographs and kissed cheeks and the hands of the ladies. The two bimbo's that were with the wise guys came up and hugged him and offered to do a three way if he wanted it. He declined politely. The Don and Cheech came out of the office and the Don waved him over. They went to a table in back of the bar and sat down. Cheech brought a bottle of wine and two glasses. The Don looked at him and smiled. "So, you're still not afraid of little bullets. You did a good job on the shooter. He won't be around to bother you anymore. They're both going on a long trip straight to hell."

"I guess hell is a long way from here."

The Don laughed and slapped him on the knee. "Cheech tells me that, starting tomorrow, it will be just you and Flame. I like that. I'll be bringing in some good people to see you." Danny looked up as Louie brought Flame over to the table. She sat down and crossed her legs. Cheech brought another glass to the table and the Don poured her some wine. She thanked him and took a sip. She put the glass down and looked at Danny.

"You're some kind of guy. You know that? I mean you get shot at, go over the rail like a full back, knock the hell out of the guy, and get back up on stage like nothing happened. You either got ice water in your veins or you're crazy." She turned to the Don. "If he ever gives up singing, I'd use him as a bodyguard."

The Don chuckled. "Bodyguards I got but, not with a voice like Danny's. Believe me, it won't happen again. Now, a toast." He raised his glass. "To the next superstar." They touched glasses and he rose to go. "I'll see you in a couple of days." He kissed Flame's hand and walked over to the bar toward his bodyguards.

They left. Within minutes Bruno came in carrying an eight by ten envelope. He saw Danny and sat down at the table. Danny signaled the bartender for another glass. Bruno took the pictures out of the envelope and spread them on the table. They were beautiful. Danny's name was across the bottom and in the right hand corner was a little sign that said, "Bruno of Hollywood." Bruno sat back and sipped his wine. "If it's all right with you, I'd like to use one of your pictures for my brochure and on the wall of my office."

"It's fine with me. You do beautiful work. Carmen will be real happy with these. From now on you will be my man." Danny put out his hand and Bruno shook it. They chatted for a few minutes before he left. Cheech came over and picked out a couple photos for the marquee board and the paper.

Louie and Salvador came to the table. Louie was smiling. He put out his hand for Danny to shake. "If you ever want to give up singing and become a bouncer, you let me know. Sal and I aren't use to coming over and picking up the pieces. You made our job easy. I'm glad you're all right."

Danny got up and gave him a hug. He turned to Salvador who was standing there like a big statue. He put out his arms and Salvador sheepishly gave him a hug. "I think this calls for a real drink. Come on, sit down. Cheech is buying. Right, Cheech?"

"Hey, anything you guys want up to a buck and a quarter is fine with me." That got a big laugh. They had some drinks, then Danny whispered in Flame's ear. "How about we go home and I tear up that red haired goody of yours."

"You'd better bring a seat belt fella. You're going to need it."

Chapter 15

The phone was ringing as Danny entered his room. Flame had gone to her room to change and shower. It was Carmen. "I just got a call from Don Bannacci. He tells me you had quite a night. Are you all right?"

"Yeah, I'm fine. For a minute there I was back in my old world. I have to tell you, it felt good."

"Well, I'm just glad that it turned out all right. I don't want to lose you just yet. I have plans for you."

"I bet you do. You must be hornier than a two-peckered billy goat by now." He heard her low laugh coming over the phone line.

"You know me too well, but I can wait one more week. By the way, how did the pictures turn out?"

"They're wonderful. The guy knows his business. He brought some into the club tonight. Cheech took a couple to put in the paper tomorrow. He's also changing the marquee. Gonna put "Starring Danny Angel" in big letters. Things are moving fast, babe."

"Glad to hear it, but I knew they would. These next three weeks will be a great break-in period. You keep up the good work. Now, get some sleep and I'll call you tomorrow."

"You got it. Sleep well." He hung up the phone as Flame knocked lightly on the door and came in. She was wearing one of her silk robes and he knew she was naked under it. She came around the bed and stood in front of him. Danny pulled the sash and the robe fell open. He pulled her close and those wonderful tits were right in front of his mouth. He kissed and sucked on her nipples until they were hard.

He leaned back and pulled her on top of him. She sat straddling him. He reached down and put his hands under her legs and around her waist. He lifted her up and brought her right above his mouth. He started to lick and suck on her. She began to move against his mouth. He rolled her over keeping his mouth on her and started to lick slowly and lightly.

He waited until she was right at the point of climax and took his tongue away. She was arched like a bow. She begged him. "Please, don't stop." He leaned in and blew warm air on her clit and she went off like a rocket. He put his mouth back on it and sucked it until she went limp. She lay there quivering and breathing hard. He came up and lay along side her.

She looked at him and said in a breathless voice, "Where in the hell did you learn that little trick? I thought I would never stop coming. That was the best ever, and believe me, I've had a lot of good ones."

Danny smiled at her. "A little Korean girl taught me that in a hooch in Taigoo. She liked to teach me things."

"Well, I can't wait to find out what else she taught you. If they're as good as that one, I'll be like a limp dish rag by the end of the week. But I'll be smiling."

"I bet you will. Now, you lay here and relax while I take a shower. He kissed her and got up. He took off his clothes and went in the bathroom. The shower felt good. He let the hot water beat on his neck and shoulders. The tension was still there from the club as he thought how close he came to being shot. It made his blood boil. Go through a war, come home and get killed by a pansy assed hood with a pop gun.

He got out and dried off. He wrapped a towel around his waist and went back into the bedroom. Flame was curled up in a little ball sound asleep. Danny came around the bed and lay down next to her. He covered her with a blanket and fell asleep with his arm around her.

******

They got to the club at four o'clock. The band was set up and waiting. Flame went first. It sounded so much better with the horns and bass. When she was done, Danny went up and gave them his books. John conducted them and they played their asses off. Danny was pleased and after rehearsal he bought them all drinks. It was going to be a good night. They walked outside and watched the guys changing the marquee. It gave him a feeling of pride watching them put his name up in big letters. Flame gave him a hug around the waist and said, "You earned it big boy. From now on your name will always be in big letters."

Danny smiled down at her. "I'll say one thing little girl. No matter how big the letters get or how big I get, I'll always remember these two weeks. It is the start of a new life and a new career. And you're part of it."

Flame looked up at him and her eyes filled with tears. "That's one of the nicest things anybody has ever said to me. I'm glad I was here to share it with you." She reached up and kissed him lightly on the mouth. Now come on, buy me an ice cream cone and then we'll get ready for tonight."

Danny stood at the window and watched the line of people waiting to get into the club. The line, mostly women, stretched all the way down the block. He felt a twinge of excitement go through him like waiting for a hit. He couldn't wait to sing with the horns. There was a soft knock on the door and Flame came in carrying her make up case. She walked over to Danny and looked down at the crowd gathering for the show. "They're coming to see you, you know. You got that magic touch my boy."

Danny put his arm around her. "If anybody would have told me four months ago that I would be standing here with a beautiful girl waiting to go on stage and sing, I would have told them they were nuts. This was the furthest thing from my mind."

"Well I'm glad somebody recognized that voice and the charisma you have. Otherwise you'd be doing what ever you did that gave you all those scars on your body." She looked up at him and smiled. "You're no choir boy Danny. I never thought you were. I don't care what you did before. This is what you were put here to do."

He looked down at her. "You're right. I was wondering when you'd get around to asking me. Let's just say I graduated from the college of hard knocks and let it go at that."

"Deal, now let's get over to the club and get ready to wow them."

They went through the ally to the back door of the club. Flame went into her dressing room and Danny checked the crowd out through the hole in the curtain. It was strangely quiet back stage with the other girls gone. The place was packed. The whole ringside was nothing but ladies.

The hookers and the gays were at the bar along with the transvestites. They were chatting and laughing and having fun. Danny saw John coming with the music and backed up to let him in. They set the books for both shows and some alternate songs if needed. John went out to the bandstand and Danny got dressed.

Then it was show time. The lights came down and John made the announcement. As soon as he said Danny's name, a roar went up in the club. Danny stepped on stage and started his show. The ladies were going crazy along with the gay guys at the bar. For an hour he sang, danced, did shtick and the people loved him. He begged off after two encores and brought Flame on. She was wonderful. The crowd loved her. The band took a break and they did it all over again. Nobody left. The people coming in for the second show had to stand at the back of the bar to enjoy the show.

Then it was over and Danny came out to the applause of the many ladies who were waiting for him. He worked his way to the bar, sat on a stool and greeted all comers, men and women alike. The blonde bimbo's were there. They came up and flanked him. Both put their huge tits against him while someone took a picture. The one on his right slipped a note in the top pocket of his tux. She whispered in his ear, "Call anytime lover. The three of us will have good time." She kissed his cheek and they left. Finally, it thinned out. Flame came out of the dressing room and headed for the bar where Danny was seated. She sat down and Danny ordered her a drink.

There was a noise at the end of the bar. The hookers were arguing with the gays. They were arguing who was better with men. The hookers said they were, because they had all the equipment men wanted. The gays argued that they gave better blow jobs, because they knew what they were working with. One of the little gay guys got mad and yelled at one of the hookers. "You're nothing but a prostitute." She yelled back, "You're nothing but a substitute," and the fight was on. There was hair pulling and slapping and screeching. Somehow the transvestites got into it. There were wigs flying all over the place. Nobody was really getting hurt, so they let them go at it. The lesbians decided to join in and that's when Louie and Sal put an end to it.

Danny, Flame and Cheech were exhausted from laughing. The transvestites and hookers were trying to find their wigs. The gay guys were consoling each other. The Lesbians got disgusted and left. Cheech told Louie to lock the door. He called for attention. "I want you all to sit down at the tables. I'm buying drinks for everybody. Come on, move."

They all sat down at tables and chatted like magpies. There were apologies and tears as they made up. Danny and Flame sat at a table with two hookers. One hooker by the name of Velvet, a knockout with a little too much to drink, was telling Danny how she pulled the wig off a transvestite and messed him up.

Danny looked at her and said, "You're just jealous because he looks better in women's clothes than you do." Velvet's eyes hardened. She took her Tom Collins glass, broke it on the edge of the table and came straight for Danny's face with the broken edge. Danny saw it coming and moved his head to the right, grabbing her wrist, twisting it and making her drop the glass.

Before Danny could do anything, he heard Cheech yell, "You son-of-a-bitch." He came around the table, grabbed her by the hair, and with that big fist of his, slammed her straight in the face. He broke her nose, cheek bones and loosened all her front teeth. He was going to hit her again but Danny, Louie and Sal grabbed him and pulled him away. He screamed at Louie, "Get that mother fucker out of here." Sal picked her up and headed for the back room. Louie tried to calm him down. Cheech looked around the club. Everybody sat frozen in place.

"Nobody fucks with my people. You got that? You come in to my club and I welcome you. But nobody tries to hurt one of my people. That's a one way ticket to hell, and I'm the engineer."

Danny came over and put his arm around Cheech's shoulder. "Thanks Cheech, I owe you. I had Flame call an ambulance. They'll pick the broad up in the ally. No sirens or lights. She's going to need a lot of medical attention."

Cheech looked up at him. "I should have killed the mother fucker. Then she wouldn't need any medical attention."

"That's one way of looking at it. Come on, sit down and have a glass of vino with me." They sat down and drank some wine. Flame came over and told them that the girl was on her way to the hospital. She sat down next to Cheech. She put her hand on his face and said, "Thanks for taking care of my boy. Be a shame to mar that handsome face." She leaned in and kissed him on the cheek. He actually blushed. The party lasted another half hour. Then Danny and Flame went to the hotel and made love until dawn.

Chapter 16

The phone rang at eleven o'clock. It was Don Angelo. "Ritchie tells me you're doing fantastic. How come you don't tell me that when you call?"

"You know I've never liked to blow my own horn, but I'm doing OK. Getting better all the time."

"That's my boy. After Syracuse you're going back to Buffalo and record the song. While you're there you'll be playing the Town Casino and the Glenn Park Casino. When you're through with the recording, we'll take it from there. You're going to be A-1 on every juke box in the country. Carmen is setting up your personal appearance tour. We're calling in some favors from some of the families in New York, Philly and the whole east coast. When the time is right, you'll come back here and open the Chez. It will be the biggest opening this town has ever seen."

Danny responded, "I miss you and the town. Be nice to come home with nobody breathing down my neck to put me away."

"That's for sure. You take care of yourself and if you need anything you call me."

"I will. Kiss mamma for me," and he was gone. Danny lay there and thought about all the things that were happening. It was coming fast and he wanted to be ready. He had to admit to himself that he liked singing and being on stage. As much as he liked killing, he liked this better.

He thought about the hooker from last night. Nineteen years old and her career as a hooker was gone. She had a dynamite body, but no longer a face to go with it.

The phone rang. It was Lois from the front desk. "Danny,

there's a guy here who wants to talk to you. He said it's urgent."

"Yeah, ask him what he wants."

He could hear her talking to the guy. Finally, she came back on the line. "He says it has to do with last night at the club. One of his girls got hurt."

Danny sat up. He felt the anger starting to build. "You tell him to meet me in the lounge. I'll be there as fast as I can." He heard her relay the message and hung up. He thought to himself, *"It has to be her pimp."* He dressed in a hurry, went downstairs and into the lounge. The bar was empty except for the bartender. Sitting at the end of the bar was a sleazy looking guy. He had pimp written all over him. Danny motioned him over to a table. They sat down and the pimp started to whine about how Cheech had ruined his best hooker.

Danny said, "So what do you want from me?"

The pimp looked at him and said, "Well, my other girls tell me that it was your fault that Cheech hit her. I think I should be compensated from you two for taking money out of my pocket."

"Your girl tried to slash me with a broken glass. She's lucky to be alive. And, if you try to get money out of Cheech or me, you'll be in the hospital bed next to her."

The pimp bristled at that. "Oh, yeah? I have friends here too, you know. They may just have to mess up that pretty face of yours."

Danny's hand came at him with the speed of a rattler and grabbed him by the throat. He lifted him off the chair and pushed through the door of the men's room that was next to the table. Once inside he really lost is temper.

"Mess up my face. You low life cock sucker." He slammed him against the wall and started to hit him with punishing blows to the face and body. The rage was uncontrollable. Even when the pimp was out he kept hitting him. Danny finally stopped and let him slump to the floor. He stood over his body, breathing deeply. He needed to calm down. Bending over, he checked to see if the pimp was still alive. He was, but in very bad shape.

Danny opened the narrow bathroom window. He picked the

pimp up and pushed him out. He landed in some bushes about seven feet below. Danny closed the window and went back into the bar. The bartender was washing glasses and looked up and smiled as Danny approached.

"Hey, Danny. I see you had a little talk with Ron. I hope you messed him up good. He's a wanna-be tough guy. Beats his girls just for fun."

"He won't be beating anybody for a long time. You never saw me in here today. Did you?"

"Me? Hell no. Place don't open for two hours yet. I'm here all alone just getting ready for the day."

"Thanks Jimmy. I owe you one." Danny walked out of the bar, got in his car and drove around to the back of the hotel by the bathroom window. He opened the trunk, lifted the pimp inside, then drove across the street and parked in front of the club. Cheech was behind the bar counting money. Danny went over to him. "Cheech, we've got a little problem."

Cheech stopped counting and looked up. "And what kind of problem would we be having?"

"I just had a run in with that hooker's pimp, Ron. The one you put in the hospital. He thinks we owe him for ruining his girl from working and he wants us to compensate him for it."

Cheech let out a laugh. "You got to be shitting me. Where is that little prick?"

"At the moment, he is in the trunk of my car outside. He's in pretty bad shape. He pissed me off. I don't like to be extorted. Now, the problem. What do we do with him?"

"That's no problem at all." He picked up the phone and made a call. "Hello Georgie, Cheech here. I need you to come down to the club and handle something for me. No. Right now. OK, see ya." He hung up the phone.

"He'll be right down. Here, have a cup of coffee and relax."

Ten minutes later Georgie arrived. He was a natty little guy wearing slacks and a nice shirt. He looked like the boy next door. Cheech greeted him and introduced him to Danny. "Listen, Georgie. I want you to take Danny's car, the Buick out front, and get rid of what's in the trunk. I don't care how you do it, but get rid of it. Then come back here."

Georgie put his hand out for the keys to Danny's car. He nodded to Cheech and left. Danny watched him go. "Hey Cheech, he looks like a college kid."

"Don't let that fool you. He's a stone killer. He works for Don Bannacci. Don't worry. He'll take care of our problem."

"Good. I'm going back over to the hotel and make some calls. When he gets back just keep the keys here. I'll get them tonight."

Cheech nodded and Danny left. He said to himself, *"No more pimp. The girls will have to get some one else."* He walked into the hotel and Lois called him over. "Flame was looking for you. She's in the restaurant having some lunch. You also had two calls. Here are the messages." She handed him the two pieces of paper. He thanked her and winked at her as he went into the restaurant to meet Flame. She was sitting by the window and waved him over. He sat down across from her and smiled at her.

She said, "Who was that driving away in your car?

"He's from the car wash. Going to wash and detail the car."

"Oh, that's nice. How about some lunch?"

"I could eat something." He looked into her eyes and she blushed.

"I know what you're thinking. Later, big boy. Right now you need some food. Try the meat loaf."

"That's one thing I never do. Let my meat loaf."

*****

The rest of the week flew by. The club was packed every night. There was a picture of the pimp in the paper under missing persons. His hookers were having a field day making money and not having to split it with him.

Saturday night was the night that the Don brought some friends in from New York City. There was a Senator and his wife, an agent, a nightclub owner plus some wise guys and their comares.

They had the ringside tables. The shows went great and after the second show Cheech politely ushered the people out and locked the doors. They had a going away party for Flame. She was touched by the love and respect that was shown her. The Don got Danny aside.

"I want you to come to the house tomorrow afternoon. I'll send a car for you. I'm having a little get together for the Senator. He's doing me a favor and I want to repay him. He can do you a lot of good down the road."

"Sounds good. Flame is leaving around noon, so anytime after that is good for me."

"OK. By the way, my nephew will be there with his guys playing. Maybe you can do a couple of songs for my guests."

Danny knew that it was not a request. "I'd be happy to. I like the way your nephew plays."

"It's settled then. Let's get back to the party."

They went back and sat down at the table. Danny was sitting across from the Senator's wife. She kept giving him the eye when her husband wasn't looking. Danny smiled politely and turned to talk to the nightclub owner. "I hear you have a club in the city?"

"Yes I do. It's one of the biggest. We run all the big names through there. That's why the Don invited me here tonight, just to see you. He tells me you're going to be a big star soon, and when you are, I want to use you."

"That's great, but I think Vito Cadenzo has the first dibs."

"Why not, he's my partner. He's the one the Don called suggesting that I come to come see you."

"Small world isn't it. I take it that this is your agent for the club." He shook hands with the agent sitting next to the owner. "Yes, this Chuck Eddie from A.B.C. Agency. They're the biggest in the country."

"Nice to meet you, Chuck. When I'm ready, I'll have my people contact your people. Isn't that some kind of show biz talk?" That got a laugh. They saluted with their wine glasses and drank.

The party broke up around three in the morning. Danny and Flame went to the hotel. She went to her room to shower and get ready for him. He did the same and was laying naked on the bed when she came into the room. She looked lovely. Her hair was shinning and hung down her back. She came to the bed and stood there looking at Ninja. "I want to remember this picture." She reached down and began to caress him. "And I want to remember this magnificent trophy."

Danny pulled her down on top of him and for the next three hours they made love every possible way. They fell asleep exhausted. When Danny woke up she was gone. He called her room but there was no answer. He called the front desk and asked Lois if she had seen Flame.

"She checked out an hour ago. She left a letter for you. I can bring it up if you like."

"No, I'll come down." He got up and went into the shower. He thought to himself, *"She didn't want a long good bye. Just like her to think of that."* He dressed and went down stairs. He picked up the letter at the front desk and went into the coffee shop to read it and get some breakfast. The letter was sweet. She left him all her numbers and asked him to call every now and then. He read it again, folded it and put it in his pocket. He finished breakfast and went to his room to call Carmen. She picked up the phone on the second ring. "I thought it was you. Who else would call me this early in the morning?"

"It's noon Babe and about time you got up. I'm going to the Don's house this afternoon. He's got some big shots in from New York City and wants me to schmooze them a little. The shows at the club are getting better by the day. Tomorrow I go it alone. This is the test. Nobody else but me. Don Angelo filled me in on everything after Syracuse. I like that. I'll be able to spend time with you while I'm having fun."

"You're going to be a busy boy. I've got everything lined up for the recording sessions and the night clubs. I sent you the songs and tapes of how they go. I want you to go over and over them and sing them until you feel good about them. You can do them in Syracuse to see what kind of reaction you get."

"Good, I can get the Don's nephew to come by the club in

the afternoon and run them down with me. By the time you get here next Monday, I should have them down perfectly."

"Good, 'cause I have some plans for you that will keep you busy for awhile."

"I knew you weren't coming to see me. You're coming to visit your cock. You dago broads are all the same."

"Oh, no. This one knows what she wants and gets it. So brace yourself."

Danny laughed, "I'll be braced. I'll let you know how it goes tomorrow night. I'll call you after the show." They said their goodbyes and hung up. Danny glanced out the window at the club. There was a lot of activity. Guys were unloading boxes on dollies and running them into the club. There was a guy up on a ladder changing the marquee. Danny decided to go to the lounge and wait for the limo. He rode the elevator down and walked into the lounge. There were people having drinks and talking. Danny sat at the end of the bar. The bartender came over and took his order. When he set his order down in front of Danny he said, "Did you hear about our friend Ron, the pimp? He's missing. Now ain't that some kind of shame?"

"He probably took a vacation somewhere. Climate maybe got too hot for him around here."

"That was my thinking too. Good riddance." He smiled and went to get a drink for a customer. Lois came in from the front desk and sat next to him. "You had a call. They said the limo is on the way. Do you think maybe we could get together tonight?"

Danny looked at her. "I don't know when I'll be back. How about a rain check for tomorrow? Come up on your break and you can have this for an hour." He took her hand and placed it on his cock. She grabbed it and gave it a squeeze. "I'll be there." She smiled and went back to the front desk.

Danny finished his drink and walked across the street to see what was going on. He walked into the club and over to Cheech who was behind the bar. "Hey Cheech, what's going on?"

"We're making this place into a night club with table cloths, candles on the tables and the waitresses dressed in uniforms that show some skin. First class for you. We're even taking reservations for the shows. Tables are all numbered and we have a seating chart. It was the Don's idea. He believes that when you have a first class act, you should have a first class club. So that's what we're doing. The Don also had that Bruno guy make a big picture of you for the marquee. Wait till you see it. I had my printer make table tents with your picture, and a short bio so you can sign them. Then your fans can take 'em home. It's going to be a great two weeks."

"I'll say. I'm going to the Don's in a little while and will thank him personally."

"I'll be there later after I get this place organized."

"Good, we can have a drink together." He looked out the window as the limo pulled up to the hotel. "Gotta go. My ride is here." He walked across the street and got into the limo. It didn't take them long to get to the Don's house. He walked into the big living room and was greeted with lots of back slapping and hugging. The Senator's wife gave him a hug and pushed her crotch into his. It was a real subtle move, one that women do when they're interested. Danny smiled at her. He stepped back and kissed her hand. "We didn't get a chance to talk last night due to all the excitement. I'm Danny."

She smiled up at him. "I'm Dolores, but you can call me Dee. You are a marvelous singer. And the way you move. You had those ladies all hot and bothered last night, including me." She looked him straight in the eye.

He knew what she was after. "I guess that means my choreographer did a good job. I'll have to tell him. He'll be thrilled." He smiled at her. The Don came over and grabbed him. "Excuse me, Dee, I have to borrow my boy." He didn't wait for an answer. He just led Danny over to the Senator and the two guys from New York. "Here he is."

The Senator shook his hand. "I really enjoyed your shows last night. We're going to have to get you down to Washington. There's a couple of great clubs where you would do well."

"That's great. I have Chuck's card. I'll have my manager

call him and they can go over the openings in my schedule."

The trio started to play. Danny excused himself and went over to listen and talk to Johnny. He did a half hour of songs and patter that he didn't do in the show the night before. The boys followed his every move. He broke in an Italian routine that Tony had written for him, and had the guests howling. When he finished, the Don came over with tears in his eyes. "That was a funny thing you did on Italians. I loved it."

"I'm putting that into the show this week. Your nephew and the boys are really great. I'd love for them to back me at the club."

"Done. If you want them, you've got them."

"What about John and the drummer? I'd hate to see them lose their jobs."

"No problem. I'll put them in my other club. A real classy place. I'll even give them a raise. Cheech will be here in a while and I'll have him set it up. Let's go tell my nephew he's employed."

They went over to the bandstand as the trio was finishing a set. The Don said to his nephew, "Starting tomorrow, you and your boys are going to be playing for Danny at the Plush Horse. Now I can tell my sister that you're no longer a bum. You're working."

"You're not kidding Uncle Pete? That's just great." He hugged his Uncle and Danny. "What about rehearsals?"

Danny spoke up. "We can rehearse tomorrow. I'll have Cheech contact the horn players. It's gonna be a great two weeks." They shook hands all around and Danny went back to the party.

Chapter 17

He stood looking out the hotel window at the marquee. There was Bruno's big picture of him that took up most of the marquee, with big letters saying, "Starring the newest singing sensation, Danny Angel."

Danny was at the club early. John was packing up his stuff. He saw Danny and came over and shook his hand. "I can't thank you enough for getting me the job at the Elegant Lounge. I've been trying to get that gig for years."

"Glad I could be of help. You deserve it."

John grabbed his stuff and was gone. Danny went over to the bar. Cheech was counting money. He looked up as Danny approached. "The band will be here at four. The phone's been ringing all day in the office for reservations. The Don's sending me the captain from his other club to help out with the seating. According to Madge, we're completely sold out."

"That's great Cheech. I'm looking forward to tonight. I'm going backstage and set up my books for both shows. By that time, the guys should be here." He headed for the dressing room. A half hour later, the band arrived and Danny rehearsed both shows and some ad-lib tunes, just in case. They were great and they were ready. Danny went back to the hotel to get ready for the evening. Two hours later he was standing at the window watching the long lines waiting to get in. He saw cars going down the ally to the back door of the club. Those would be the wise guys and special guests. He got dressed and went down the ally and into the club to his dressing room.

When he opened the door, he was shocked. It was full of

flowers. There was a stack of telegrams on the dressing table. He opened them. They all wished him good luck on his opening. Well, he wouldn't disappoint them. They wished each other luck. Danny got his tux on and waited behind the curtain for his introduction. The lights came down, he heard a drum roll, and then the intro. As soon as Danny's name was mentioned, a roar went up. He stepped through the curtain and walked to the microphone. It was hard to hear his opening number with so much cheering. He picked the mic off the stand and started to sing. The crowd got quiet and he sang his heart out. When he finished his number, he looked over the room. It was packed. All the wise guys were ringside along with the Don and his party. Sal and Louie were dressed in tuxes with white turtle necks.

Danny smiled and said, "I want to thank you all for coming. Now I would like to sing a song for a special person in the audience."

He turned to Johnny. "Hit it." Johnny counted the song in with a driving tempo in four. Danny went into "Melancholy Baby." The Don started to laugh and clap. When the song was over, he called Danny over to his table and put a hundred dollar bill in his pocket. The crowd loved it. For an hour and fifteen minutes Danny had them in the palm of his hand. When the show was over, Danny came out front to the delight of all the ladies. He signed the placemats and table tents for them and was extra charming.

He sat with the Don's party for a while until Louie walked over. There was someone at the bar who wanted to talk to him. It was important. He excused himself and went to the bar. Sitting at the end was the hooker who was with the one Cheech smashed in the face. Danny came over and sat next to her.

"What can I do for you?"

"My name is Clarise. I was at the table when my girlfriend tried to change your face with that glass. Her name is Velvet. She's really a sweet person, but she was drinking that night and lost her head. She's in the hospital in really bad shape. The worst thing is, she has no insurance. Our pimp handled all the money, but he disappeared and the money with him. Not that it's a great loss. He was a real bastard. The point is, the hospital wants to be paid and will only keep her for a few more days. If you could talk to them, and maybe go see her, it would mean an awful lot."

Danny looked her in the eye. "Give me the name of the hospital and her room number. I'll go by tomorrow and straighten it all out."

Clarise took out her trick book and tore out a page. After writing it all down, she handed it to him. "Thanks Danny. You're the best."

Danny took the paper and put it in his pocket. "By the way, who's going to be handling you girls now?"

"We didn't want a pimp, but Georgie Boy, Ron's friend, decided to take over. We have no say in the matter. You know how it is."

"You tell him I want to talk to him tomorrow. Have him meet me at the hotel in the bar around three o'clock. Tell him that he shouldn't be late."

"I'll tell him and thanks again." She leaned in and kissed Danny on the cheek and left.

The second show was better than the first. Danny put the Italian bit in the show and had the audience rolling in the aisles. The band was cooking on all burners. After the show, it was party time. Danny left and went to the hotel.

Chapter 18

He was up early. He called Carmen and filled her in on last night. He went down to the coffee shop to get some breakfast. He ate and got directions to the hospital. When he got there, he asked for the head of hospital finances. He was directed to an office down the hall. Behind the desk sat a man who looked like Mr. Peepers wearing big glasses on his small head. He looked like a bug. Danny sat down across from him.

Mr. Peepers had a wooden name plate on the desk in front of him. Mr. Bruce Grey had been routed out on it. He blinked his eyes and said, "How may I be of assistance to you?"

"You have a girl in room 1523 named Velvet. She came in a few nights ago all beat up. I hear that the hospital wants to be paid when she is released. She has no insurance. I'm here to put your mind at ease. I'll pay her bill and whatever else you need." He reached into his pocket and pulled out a roll of money. He counted out a thousand dollars in hundreds and laid it in front of Bruce. Bruce blinked his eyes again.

"Let me get her file." He went to a cabinet and came back with a folder. "Let's see. Oh, yes. Well, she doesn't owe that much yet."

"Give me a receipt and if it's more, you can call me and I'll make it good."

Bruce got the receipt book and said, "Who should I make it out to?"

"Danny Angel."

At the mention of his name, Bruce almost dropped the pen. "The Danny Angel from the Plush Horse?"

"The same."

Bruce started to babble about how wonderful he was, and on and on. Danny stopped him with a wave of his hand. "Come to the club tonight as my guest. Your name will be at the front door. Now, how about my receipt, so I can go visit Velvet?"

Bruce wrote out the receipt and thanked Danny for the comp. Danny left the office and found Velvet's room. He walked in. She was propped up on pillows and her face was covered with bandages. She looked like The Mummy's Bride. She saw Danny and tried to talk, but nothing intelligible was coming out. Her jaws were wired shut.

Danny came to her bedside and pulled up a chair. He sat down, took her hand and said, "Don't try to talk. Just listen. I'm sorry about what happened. I had it handled but Cheech gets a little crazy. I don't want you to worry about anything while you're here. Your bills have been taken care of. Just get well and let me handle it. If you need anything, you have them call me. I'll leave my numbers at the nurse's station on my way out. The main thing is that you get better. When you get out of here, I'll take care of everything. OK?"

She grabbed his hand and squeezed it. Danny could see tears in her swollen eyes. He got up, kissed her hand and told her he would drop by tomorrow. He left his numbers at the nurse's station with instructions to give her anything she wanted. The nurses knew him and fawned over him. He charmed them and left. On his way back to the hotel he stopped at a florist and had them deliver three nice floral arrangements to Velvet's room.

At two forty-five he was in the bar sitting at the table closest to the men's room. At three o'clock the would-be pimp showed up. He saw Danny sitting there. Danny waved him over. Georgie Boy was six foot tall, around one eighty. He had this mean look on his face. He came to the table, leaned over and said, "I don't like to be told when to be some place from a pretty boy singer."

Danny reached up, grabbed his hair and slammed his head on the table breaking his nose. He stood up, pushed him into the men's room. Georgie Boy was blubbering and crying. Danny stood him up against the wall. "Listen to me you prick. You lay off the girls. Leave them alone. Ron wouldn't listen and he's gone. You'll join him if you fuck with me. Now to make my point clear... Danny hit him four or five hard shots to the head and body. Georgie Boy slumped to the floor. Danny went over and opened the window. He picked Georgie up and pushed him out the window. He went back into the bar. The bartender waved him over. "Danny, have a drink on me. I like your style. They go in the men's room and never come out."

"I guess it's haunted." He drank his drink, put some tip money on the bar and left. He went to his room and called Carmen. He explained what happened at the club and how Cheech wasted Velvet's face. "She was a beautiful girl, Carmen. Now she has a body with no face to go with it. I want your boy in Buffalo to fix it for her. I feel responsible and I'll pay him."

Carmen chuckled. "Is this the same Danny that used to put people away? Sweetheart, I love you for it. You do have a soft spot in that armor. I'll handle it. And don't worry about the money."

"You're the best baby. I'll make it up to you."

"Yes you will. I'm taking it out in trade."

"Animal."

She laughed, "By the way, you should have the music and tapes by now."

"I'll check downstairs. The band was smoking last night. Johnny really knows his stuff."

"Good. Let me know about tonight. Gotta go. My father is calling me. Later, darling." And she was gone.

******

Danny was up early. He called the Don and told him he wanted one of the Don's lesser lawyers to take care of the girls. The Don was glad to do it. Danny asked him if he could have a couple of the boys toss Ron's apartment and see if he had any cash stashed there. Also, Danny asked him to have his man check the banks and see if he had any money there, and get it out. He wanted to set up an account for the girls.

The Don asked him, "Why are you taking such an interest in those hookers?"

"Let's just say, I owe them a favor."

"That's good enough for me. I'll see to it," and he was gone.

Danny drove to the hospital to see Velvet. When he walked into her room it looked like a florist shop. She was sitting up in bed. When she saw him she held out her arms for him to come over to her. He went over and she gave him a big hug. She had a pad to write with, so she wrote "thanks for the flowers and everything."

He sat down and took her hand. "I want you to listen to what I'm saying. You can nod yes or no when I'm done. OK?" She nodded. "There's a plastic surgeon in Buffalo that is excellent. He can make you look just like you did before. I've made arrangements for him to take care of you. I have to go to Syracuse for two weeks after I finish here. I'll come back and pick you up and drive you to Buffalo. Is that all right with you?"

She sat there looking at him through swollen eyes. She grabbed her pad and wrote, "Why are you doing this for me?"

He read it and said, "It's my fault you got hit. I was being funny and you took the heat for it." She wrote, "I'll never be able to repay you."

"You don't have to. Let's just say I'm doing my good deed for the year. Well, is it a deal?"

She squeezed his hand and nodded yes.

"Good, I was hoping you'd say that. I have to go now and get ready. I'll drop in tomorrow." He waved goodbye and went back to the hotel.

The club was packed again and Danny was at his best. Sitting ringside were three couples. One of the girls was just adorable. She looked like a college cheerleader. Blonde hair, blue eyes, and when she smiled she had deep dimples. From what he could see from the stage, she was built solid. Her boyfriend was a typical jock with a crew cut. He was arrogant, and had a loud mouth. He kept trying to keep her attention off Danny.

Danny came over and sang half a song to her, just to piss him off. After the show Danny came out front. The three couples were leaving but the jock turned around and said, "I didn't like the way you sang to my girl friend, Darlene. You think you're something special. Well, to me you're just another greasy wop."

Danny shifted to his right so he could crack this guy in the mouth. Sal caught the move came over and grabbed the jock and almost lifted him off his feet.

"I think it's time you went home fella." He almost carried him out the door. The blonde followed him out. Sal came back and put his arm around Danny's shoulder.

"I hated to spoil your fun, but you have another show to do. Wouldn't want you to muss your hair." He smiled and went to the bar. The next show was like the rest. Danny went out to mix after the show. He changed and went out the back door into the ally to go back to the hotel. He got almost to the street when three guys stepped out of the shadows and blocked his way. It was the jock and his buddies.

Danny stopped. He said to himself, *"There is a God."* The jock said, "You haven't got your boys to protect you now, asshole. We're going to show you what happens when you fuck with somebody's girl friend."

Danny slid his belt off and wrapped it around his right hand letting the buckle hang down. The buckle was extra heavy and sewn on so it wouldn't come off. The jock had a short sap in his hand. The other two had nothing.

Danny said, "You have just made the biggest mistake of your life. Come on loud mouth."

The jock moved in swinging the sap. Danny was standing in darkness and the jock didn't see the belt until it was too late. Danny swung the belt and caught him on the side of his head opening a big gash. The jock stumbled. Danny came in fast and smashed him in the face with his left hand. He turned and whacked the closest guy with the belt and he went down. The third guy tried to run but Danny caught him and beat him senseless. The jock was on his hands and knees. Danny dropped the belt, lifted him up and pushed him against the wall. The blood was flowing through his veins and the adrenalin pumping. He was Danny Di again.

"I'm going to teach you never to fuck with an Italian again." He slammed him with lefts and rights in the face and body. Each punch was like a sledge hammer. The jock fell to the ground. Danny picked up his belt and left them where they lay. He went to the hotel and up to his room.

He called the Don. "Don Bannacci, I've got a little problem."

"It must be a big problem to call me this late at night. What is it?"

"Three guys jumped me in the ally next to the club. I really hurt them bad. They're going to need a lot of medical help. I can't afford to be taken in and fingerprinted, and I don't want Don Angelo's name to be linked to this."

"I'll handle it. Are you all right?"

"Yeah. They never laid a hand on me."

"Good. You just relax and let me handle everything. I'll call you later."

"Thanks Don. I really appreciate this."

"It's nothing." He hung up.

Danny went to the window and looked across the street into the ally. They were still out. He heard sirens coming. A police car and ambulance arrived at the same time. The medics were busy trying to revive the guys, while the cop was trying to ask them questions.

The watch commander arrived and took charge. The medics got the three into the ambulance and hurried off. The watch commander talked briefly to the cops and they left.

Danny smiled. The Don had a lot of people in his pocket. He went into the bathroom and washed the blood off his belt buckle.

Chapter 19

Danny had just left Velvet's room after spending some time with her. Her spirits were up and she was able to talk a little. As he was turning a corner in the hospital hallway, he literally ran into the jock's cute blonde, Darlene, from the night before. He grabbed her before she fell.

"I'm sorry. I didn't look where I was going."

Darlene looked up at him. She'd been crying. "No, it's my fault. I never expected to see you here. I thought you'd be in a hospital room somewhere."

"If your jock boyfriend and his buddies were any good, I would be. The three of them came at me."

"I know. He's always been that way. The morning papers said that they were attacked by a gang of hoodlums."

"Yeah. Let's let it stay that way for his sake. How would you like to have lunch with me so we can talk?"

She stood back and looked at him. She was thinking, *"God he's handsome."* "I'd like that."

"Good, we'll go in my car and I'll bring you back when we're done." He took Darlene's arm and walked her out to his car. He was thinking. *"She's just beautiful. Five two and built. The all American girl."*

They went to a small Italian place that advertised home cooked Italian food. Danny and Darlene sat at a table in the corner and talked.

She asked him, "How come you don't have a mark on you? Dick, David and Larry look like they went through a meat grinder."

He took her hand in his. "Sweetheart, I haven't always been

a choir boy. I used to box. Besides, they made me angry."

"Remind me to never do that." The touch of his hand made her feel weak. She actually felt herself tingling all over. She was wondering what it would feel like to make love to him. They finished the meal. She was sorry to see it come to an end. He walked her out and opened her car door. As she got in, she brushed up against him and a shiver shot through her. They drove back to the hospital.

She asked him, "You're staying at the hotel across from the club?"

"Yeah, it's convenient for me. I just have to walk across the street and I'm there." He walked around the car, opened her door, and escorted her to her car.

"Thanks for the lunch and the conversation. I'm just sorry that Dick tried to hurt you. Maybe this will teach him a well deserved lesson. God knows he needed one." She got in her car and left. Danny drove back to the hotel. He was going over some songs when there was a knock on the door.

He opened it and there she stood. He stepped aside as Darlene entered the room. He closed the door and turned to her. Darlene stood there for a second, and then walked into his arms. Her lips found his. He put his arms around her. Then lifting her up, they were face to face. She wrapped her legs around him and hung on. He felt himself getting aroused. He walked the cute little blonde over to the bed and eased her down under him, their lips still locked together. He ran his hand under her sweater and released her bra strap. He moved his hand around the front and cupped her right breast, causing her to moan. It was firm and smooth. The nipple was hard to his touch.

She sat up and in one motion pulled her sweater and bra over her head. There she sat with long blonde curls cascading down, almost to her nipples. She was beautiful. Danny got up and started to get undressed. She never took her eyes off of him. When he dropped his pants, her eyes grew wide. She eagerly moved to her hands and knees, and crawled to the edge of the bed.

Looking into his eyes she said, "I know there is a lot to

learn, and I want you to teach me everything.

He lowered himself down and slid inside her. She was really tight. Darlene gasped as he began to push. She started to rise up to meet him, a little at a time. She was thrashing and moaning and saying over and over, "I want it. I want it all."

Danny let her exhaust herself with absolute pleasure. Then he exploded. She hung on as he groaned and thrust uncontrollably. They found themselves lying on their sides looking at each other. He was still inside her.

She finally said, "I don't know about you, but for the first time in my life I am totally and completely satisfied. I hate to say this, but, I'm glad you put Dickey in the hospital. I would have never known this. Can I have more?"

"You can have as much as you want this week."

"Wonderful, I can't wait. How about after your show tonight? I'm coming to the show with some girlfriends. I can get rid of them."

"Great. I'll give you a key and you can meet me here after the show. You can even spend the night if you want to. It gives us more time to explore all the possibilities."

"I'd like that." They got up and she went to clean up and get dressed. He kissed her good bye. Danny went over to the window and watched her cross the street to her car. He smiled.

******

The rest of the week flew by. The shows were outstanding and the club packed. Danny made love to Darlene every night and sometimes in the afternoon. He visited Velvet and worked on his songs. Then it was Saturday. As usual the club was packed. He did two shows to standing ovations. He mixed and was mobbed by the ladies. When it was over, he took Darlene back to the hotel.

Since it was her last night, she was all over him. She wanted him to do everything to her. He accommodated her every desire, and in the morning she left sore and teary eyed. Danny showered and got ready to drive to Syracuse to pick up Carmen. He stopped at the front desk. Lois was on duty. He said, "Can you have the maid do a special cleaning job on my room today? I'm expecting company."

"I guess the blonde is history, right?"

"Right, the number one team is coming to stay with me for the week. I'm on my way to pick her up."

"It shall be done master." She winked at him and put in a call to housekeeping.

Danny made it to Syracuse in record time. He was waiting for her as she came through the door into the terminal. Carmen saw him and ran over and kissed him hard on the mouth. He grabbed her and they stood there with lips and bodies locked. People getting off the plane looked on with envy. They were two beautiful people.

When she finally pulled back she said, "I've waited a long time for that. Come on, let's get my luggage and get out of here." On the way back to Utica she sat close to him with her hand on Ninja. They talked about the shows and what was coming up for him. When they got to the hotel, Danny got her luggage out of the trunk and they walked into the lobby. Lois took one look at Carmen and smiled. As they passed by her desk, she gave Danny the OK sign with her fingers. Once in the room she wasted no time getting him in bed. She was wonderful, just like he remembered. They did it all afternoon. Finally, they lay side by side to cool off.

She turned her head to look at him. "Was it good for you?" Danny burst out laughing. When he finally got control, he said, "No, not really." She jumped on him and the tussle was on. They were laughing and rolling around the bed just having fun. The phone rang. Carmen said, "Were you expecting a call?"

"No." He picked up the phone. It was Clarise. "Danny I hate to bother you, but a problem has come up that I think you should know about. One of Velvet's old boyfriends showed up and is hassling her about money he thinks she owes him. She really doesn't because he lived off her for quite awhile. He told her that since she has the money to pay the hospital, she can pay him. He's making a real stink about it."

"OK, I'll be right over." He hung up the phone. Carmen

looked at him as if to say, *"What's up?"* He explained the problem.

She said, "Let's go."

"Hey, you don't have to go. I can handle it."

"Yeah I know, but I want to meet this girl. Plus, I'd like to see you handle this jerk."

They dressed in a hurry and headed to the hospital. Danny walked into Velvet's room with Carmen at his heels. Clarise was sitting in a chair. Velvet was sitting up in bed crying. The old boyfriend was standing over her.

He turned when Carmen and Danny came into the room. "What the hell do you two want?"

Danny walked over to him. "I would like to talk to you outside if you don't mind.

"What the hell for?"

Danny's right hand shot out and grabbed him by the throat. He put pressure on it and the guy's eyes started to bulge. He almost lifted him off the floor as he walked him out of the room and into the stairwell. Once inside, he let him go. The guy was gagging and rubbing his throat.

Danny came in close. "I want you to listen to me, because I'm only going to say this once. You leave Velvet alone. You get your ass out of here and don't ever come back or bother her again. If you don't, your own mother won't recognize you. I'll break every bone in your body, starting with your face. Now, just so you know I mean it." He slammed him in the jaw and the guy went down like he had been pole axed. Danny pushed him with his foot to the edge of the stairs and watched as the guy rolled down to the landing.

Danny went back into Velvet's room. Carmen was sitting by Velvet's bed holding her hand. "I see you two have met?" Carmen smiled up at him. "And I see you handled the problem in your own diplomatic way. I was just telling Velvet how much fun we're going to have when she comes to Buffalo."

"Oh, I see. Now I'll have two of you to contend with." He looked out the window and saw the old boyfriend limping to his car holding his shirttail to his mouth to stop the bleeding. He got into the car and peeled rubber all the way out of the lot.

Danny said to Velvet, "He won't bother you any more." He turned to Clarise. "Can I talk to you out side for a minute? The girls can get along without us for that long." They walked out into the hall.

"Thanks for calling me. Now, listen. I'm having the guys go through Ron's place. He has money stashed away someplace. I never knew a pimp who didn't. Also, he must have a bank account in town. We'll find it. I want you to take the money and open an account for you and the girls. You can form a company. Call it *"Temporarily Yours."* This way, if you get busted you'll have bail money. Also, you'll have money to pay medical bills. You run it like a business."

Clarise looked up at him with tears in her eyes. "Why are you doing this for us? We're hookers. Working girls. Most people couldn't care less about us."

"I came off the streets of Chicago. I grew up around working girls. They were always nice to me. Took me under their wings, so to speak. They taught me a lot about women. Actually we're not that much different. I sell my self on stage. You sell your self off stage."

Clarise reached up and kissed him on the cheek. "Thanks, Danny."

They went back inside. Carmen was talking and laughing with Velvet. "Well, I see you ladies are still at it."

"Yes we are. I talk and she mumbles." That started them laughing again.

"I hate to break this up, but let's let Velvet get some rest now. We can come back tomorrow."

They said their goodbye's and left. On the way back to the hotel, Danny told Carmen about the plan to set up an account for the girls. She loved the idea and said she would help. They got to the hotel, had dinner, and then went up to the room for more fun and games.

Chapter 20

Danny and Carmen stood at the window of the hotel watching the line form across the street for his show. He called Cheech earlier to reserve a table for Carmen and the Don's party. Carmen had called the Don earlier to pay her respects. Don Bannacci said he would be delighted if she would sit with him for the show. Danny glanced over at her. He thought, *"She's just beautiful"*. She was wearing a dress that showed off her curves with out being ostentatious.

Danny kissed her on the cheek. "Well my love, shall we join the masses?"

Carmen turned towards him. "I don't know about you, but I'm excited. I finally get to see the fruits of my labor come to life."

"Well, I hope you're not disappointed. I must say you and Tony did good job on me." He put his arm around her waist and they went downstairs to the lobby. Danny decided to go through the ally to avoid the front of the club which was mobbed. He took Carmen's hand. They got to the back door and went inside. Danny took her through the curtain to the reserved table out front. Cheech came running over and gave her a big bear hug.

"You look absolutely beautiful. Your boy's been doing a bang up job for me." He sat her down and hustled off to the bar.

The Don's party arrived. There were hugs and kisses all around. Danny walked around the room schmoozing the ladies. Then it was show time. He told Johnny to put the new song, "Somebody Loves You," in as a surprise for Carmen. He had written a beautiful arrangement and was anxious to try it.

The show started and he was at his best. He sang his heart

out. Carmen sat there with tears in her eyes. He did some jokes, and worked off the crowd getting laughs along the way. When it was time for the new song, he gave Johnny a signal to lower the lights.

"Ladies and gentlemen, in a few weeks I will be recording my first song. So tonight, I thought it would be nice to sing it for you in appreciation for the way you took me into your hearts. He had to stop and wait for the crowd to quite down from clapping and cheering. He looked at Carmen. "For you." Johnny started the introduction.

Danny sat on a stool and sang "Somebody Loves You." You could have heard a pin drop. The whole crowd was completely mesmerized. They hung on every word. Tears were coming down Carmen's face. Danny hit the last note and held it sweet and pure.

The song ended and there was complete silence in the room. Danny stood up and opened his arms. Like a clap of thunder, the crowd exploded into applause. They were on their feet cheering, crying, reaching their arms towards him. He stood there looking down at the crowd. He looked at Carmen and the Don's party. They were all on their feet, with tears coming down their faces.

Danny felt something wet on his cheeks. Then he realized what it was. For the first time in a very long time, tears were falling from his eyes. The song had done something nobody could do. It made him cry. Here he was, a hit man, a killer, a bone breaker, standing in front of a crowd crying. This was so foreign to his nature. Strangely enough, he didn't care. He put the microphone on the stand and walked off the stage into the crowd. They were all over him. The women were hugging him and kissing him on the cheeks. The men slapped him on the back. He worked his way over to the Don's table. Carmen rushed into Danny's open arms and hugged him tightly.

"My God Danny, that's your song. That's your ticket to stardom. I expected you to be good, but you are way beyond good." Danny kissed her. The Don came over and hugged him. "That song is platinum. I'll do everything I can to see that it is number one. You let me know when it's ready."

Danny thanked him. "By the way Don, Johnny wrote that arrangement for me."

"He did? I guess I can't call him a bum anymore." That brought a laugh from his party.

The rest of the night was like dream. The second show went off without a hitch. Danny sang to them, made them laugh, and even danced a little. Then it was over and the club emptied out. All that was left was the band, the help and the Don's party. Cheech had sent out for Italian food. He had a spread set up behind the bar. For two hours they ate, drank wine and laughed. When it was finally over, they said their goodbyes and returned to the hotel.

Carmen undressed and lay naked on the bed. Danny looked at this beautiful woman. He got undressed and lay next to her.

She turned towards him. "Tonight you were absolutely wonderful. The song is going to be a big hit. I have to tell you something that I have never told any one else in my life except family. I love you Danny Di. I tried to keep it on a business basis, but it didn't work. My father warned me about this, but I can't help my feelings. I've never felt this way about anything in my life. All I know is, I love you and..." He silenced her with his lips on hers. He kissed her long and tenderly. He pulled her on top of him so their faces were inches apart.

"You talk too much." She could feel him getting hard against her stomach. She eased forwards so her breasts were at his mouth. He started to lick and suck on her nipples. She reached back and put the head of Ninja inside her. While he worked on her breast she slid down taking it deep inside her. She sat up and looked down at him.

"You're right. No more talk, just action." She started to move slowly at first, then gradually picking up speed. Her large breasts were swinging above him. He reached up and grabbed them and squeezed her rigid nipples. Carmen let out a gasp and shuddered as she climaxed. Putting her hands on his chest she pushed herself backwards allowing Ninja to rest along side his leg. Gently, she started to move again. This time it was rubbing against her clitoris. The feeling was overwhelming. She increased the rate and pressure, riding it hard.

She said, "Come with me, please come with me." He did. In a frenzy of kisses and moaning, they came together. She collapsed on his chest gasping for breath. He held her close while running his hands over her silky body.

"If it's any consolation, I love you too. I have since the beginning. You have to understand Carmen. I have never loved anything in my life. Never wanted to get that close to anybody. I'm used to violent, tough ways. Hell, a few months ago, I stuck an ice pick in a guy's heart. Now, I go on stage and kill them in a different way. I may be wearing the face of Don Angelo's nephew, but underneath it all I'm still Danny Di. I just don't want to disappoint you and Don Angelo. Am I making any sense, or am I worrying too much over nothing?"

She rose up so she was looking at him. "My darling, you don't have to worry about anything. I'll take good care of you. You just love me and leave everything to me. This dago broad has everything under control." She kissed him and rolled on her side. They held each other and fell asleep.

Chapter 22

They got to the club early. When they opened the dressing room door, it looked like a florist shop inside. There were flowers all over the place. On the dressing room table were a stack of telegrams. Danny was speechless. Carmen got the cards from the flowers and read them to Danny. They were from the Don and friends. The telegrams were from Velvet and the girls, Flame, Sheila, and even the blonde Bimbos.

Don came walking in. He looked around and said, "Who died? I haven't seen this many flowers since the Kentucky Derby and they were on the neck of a horse. Who's opening for who here? You got flowers and I got nothing but a bar in my dressing room. But it's stocked with the best booze. Carmen, you can come over anytime but leave Mr. Adonis home."

Carmen giggled. "Don, if I came over, you'd need a seat belt, riding crop and spurs. Tell you what. If you can stay on for eight seconds, I'm yours."

"That's what I've always wanted… a nymphomaniac with a sense of humor."

They talked and joked for awhile until it was time to get dressed. Carmen went out front to get seated, as Johnny came in to go over the song list. Danny got dressed and waited back stage. The house band was playing a dance set. People were dancing and having fun. When the set ended, Johnny, Gus and Vinnie went out and set up. The band got back on the stand, the lights came down and there was a drum roll.

The announcer said, "Ladies and Gentlemen, tonight the Three Rivers Night Club proudly presents the comedy of Don

Rickles, and the latest singing sensation, Danny Angel. Now, put your hands together and welcome to the stage, Danny Angel."

The band went into its opening number as the curtain came up. Danny stepped out on stage and walked to the microphone. The spotlight was hitting him right in the eyes. He had never worked with a spot before. He couldn't see anybody, but he figured they could see him. He went into his opening song, "Day In, Day Out." The band was smoking and he drove the song home. The applause was deafening. Shouts of more and whistles came at him from beyond the lights. He settled in and did his show.

There were laughs with the jokes, and sighs with the ballads. After the last number, the lights came up and he was looking at a standing ovation. They wanted more. Danny checked the clock hanging on the wall above the curtain. He had time. He chose for his encore, "Somebody Loves You." The lights came down and he went into the number.

The crowd was enthralled. They were on their feet before the last note was sung. They clapped, shouted, and whistled, while Danny stood there with his arms out. He seemed to be embracing the whole audience. He left the stage amid shouts for more.

Rickles was standing in the wings. He walked over to Danny. "That was beautiful. They loved you. Now I have to go out there and try to make them laugh. It's like throwing this little Jew boy to the lions."

Danny looked down at him. "I just warmed them up for you. You'll kill them." And he did. He destroyed them. He worked them for almost an hour and left the stage to thunderous applause.

Danny was sitting in his dressing room as Don came off stage. He walked over to Danny's dressing room and stuck his head in. "You were right, but I knew it all along. Come on over and have a drink when you get changed."

He went into his dressing room. Danny got up as Carmen came in. She threw her arms around him. "You were magnificent. You had them eating out of the palm of your hand. I brought some people backstage that want to say hello." She stepped aside as Don

Angelo came into the room. Danny was stunned. He let out a holler and hugged Don Angelo. "I never expected you'd be here."

The Don looked up at him. "Did you think we'd miss your opening at this wonderful club? Not on your life. Oh, there's more people that came to see you." He motioned to his bodyguard and Ritchie came in followed by Thamaso, Carlo, Patsy and all their bodyguards along with Don Bannacci. It was a party. Everybody was talking, laughing and congratulating Danny.

In the middle of all this commotion, Rickles came out of his dressing room and shouted. "What's going on out here?" He was immediately lifted off his feet by two big bodyguards. He looked up at one and then the other. Danny walked out of the dressing room and stood in front of Don.

Don smiled and said, "I hope these are friends of yours. Could you tell them to put me down? I'm afraid of heights."

Danny signaled and the bodyguards put Don back on the floor. "Don, I want you to meet some friends of mine." He introduced him to all the people in the room. Rickles was at his best. He had them laughing right off the bat. He finally said, "Hey, let's go to my dressing room. I have a bar stocked with booze and nobody to drink it."

Don's dressing room started to fill up and the party was on. People started to come in from the showroom. Danny was surprised to see the two blonde bimbo's with Mike. He had his arms around their waists. Their boobs were even with his head. Every time they would turn to talk to each other, his head would disappear. Mike was in heaven. He saw Danny and came over still holding on to the girls.

"You were right. You're the best. Stay as long as you like." He looked around and seeing all the Dons, his mouth dropped open. He started to sweat. "I didn't know you knew these people. Jesus, Danny, you're not going to tell them about our little talk today are you?"

"No, Mike. That was between you and me. So, what do you think of my girls here?"

"I love 'em. They told me they were friends of yours, so I

brought them with me."

Danny hugged each one and told them he was glad they came. He whispered in their ears, "Take Mike out and do a job on him. I think he needs it." They smiled and gave him the OK signal.

Danny went back to Don Angelo. "I'm glad you came. So, what do you think?

"I think we made the right decision. You're going to be a big star. The boys all agreed. I never thought Danny Di could do this. You made me real proud tonight. I can't wait to get you back to Chicago and show those ass holes some real talent."

Danny was about to answer when Johnny came in with Gus and Vinnie. He saw his uncle, went over and got a hug. Don Bannacci came over to Danny. "The kid did all right. And you were magnificent. What a difference from The Plush Horse. Here you had everything, lights, sound and a great band. You're going to go a long way Danny. Always remember, we're right behind you."

"I'll remember."

"Good, I booked a suite at the hotel. Let's get everybody and go over there. I got food coming and good wine. We can finish off the night there."

"Great." Danny called for attention and told them what Don Bannacci wanted to do. They all agreed. They brought the limos to the back door and left for the hotel. Carmen was sitting next to him with her arm through his. "You were great tonight, Danny. And the song went over like gangbusters. I told you it was your song. Now, I can't wait to get back to Buffalo and record it. The sooner we get it out, the sooner you'll be on your way to the big time."

Danny leaned in and kissed her. "The only big time I want tonight is you."

"Oh, I'm ready big boy. As soon as we dump this crowd, it's you and me."

When they pulled up to the hotel, it looked like an Italian wedding or a Mafia movie with all the limos, bodyguards and everyone in top coats and hats. They went up to Don Bannacci's suite and the party began.

******

The party lasted until three in the morning. Everybody was up early and down to breakfast because they had planes to catch. Don Angelo and Ritchie were the last to leave. Danny gave them both a hug. "I can't thank you enough for coming. It means a lot to me."

"I wouldn't have missed it for the world. I was telling Ritchie that Carmen did a bang up job on you. If anybody would have told me that my number one made guy could sing like that, I would have told them they were pots, stunad."

Ritchie gave Danny a hug. "You've come a long way in a short time. Carmen knew that she had a diamond in the rough. Oh, she told me about Velvet. You bring her to Buffalo, and we'll take care of her. Now, I've got to get Don Angelo to the airport. Take care of my daughter for me."

Once again there were hugs all around and they were gone. Carmen stood next to him and watched them go. "If there were any doubts in their minds about you or what you could do, they're gone now. By the time we get back to Buffalo you'll be ready to record and get out on the road to do the big clubs. These two weeks are going to be great."

And they were. The club was packed every night. Danny was improving with every performance. The women loved him and showed it by the things they threw on stage. He got flowers, hotel keys, car keys, bras, panties and dozens of slips of paper with ladies numbers on them, asking him to come to their rooms or homes. He got propositioned every night. He could have fucked his way into the Guinness book of world records, but once they saw Carmen, they knew they didn't stand a chance. Many of them tried anyway.

The blonde bimbo's were there almost every night. They were staying with Mike and he looked like death warmed over. The girls were really doing a number on him. They still tried to get Danny to do a threesome.

His song "Somebody Loves You" stopped the show every night. Everybody wanted it. Danny told them it would be out soon.

The local wise guys came in and invited Danny and Carmen to their homes for dinner. They had great food, good wine and lots of laughs. Carmen called Velvet everyday to check on her. She was doing fine and couldn't wait for them to come and get her. The girls were doing great with *Temporarily Yours*. No pimps would come anywhere near them. The word was out on the street to leave them alone or else.

Closing night Mike threw a big party for Don and Danny. Booze flowed like water. The cooks laid out a wonderful buffet. The party lasted until the wee hours of the morning. Danny and Carmen slipped out around two. They went back to the hotel and made love. They got up at noon to have breakfast and pack the car. Johnny and the boys were all hung over, so they decided to stay until evening. They would be in Buffalo in a week for the record session.

Danny and Carmen got in the car and headed for Utica. They got there and found Velvet at Clarisse's house. Danny blew the horn and the girls came running out. There were kisses and hugs all around. Velvet came out and stood on the porch. She was wearing a dress that left nothing to the imagination. Her body was perfection. The bandages remained, and her face was still a bit swollen. Carmen gave her a big hug and walked her over to Danny. Danny gave her a hug and a kiss on the forehead.

"Well sweet thing, you ready to go get a new face and a new life?"

"You bet I am. I'm tired of sounding like a cartoon character with a head cold."

"Then let's get out of here." They said their goodbyes, got in the car and headed for Buffalo. The girls chattered like magpies all the way there. Every once in a while they would include Danny in their conversation. He had his mind elsewhere, so he really didn't mind. He was thinking about the recording session and what followed.

The job in Syracuse really went well. He knew he was ready for bigger things. Being on stage was becoming natural, just like when he was doing hits for the Don. He also knew he still had some rough edges that Tony would have to smooth out. He was thinking about Chicago and going back there among all his old friends, even though they didn't know it was him.

They stopped for gas and food. The girls went inside while Danny had the car serviced. He paid the bill and followed them inside. Carmen and Velvet were sitting in a booth. Leaning over them, with his hands on the table, was a big farm-boy. He was trying to get Carmen to dance with him to the music coming out of a beat up juke box. She was politely trying to decline, but he was having none of it. His buddies were sitting at a table down the way egging him on.

Danny walked up and said, "Excuse me, but that's my lady you're pestering." The farm boy straightened up. He was probably six foot four and two hundred ninety pounds. He looked down at Danny.

"Well, look at the pretty boy. I was just going to show her what a real man is."

"Well, if you find one let me know, and I'll introduce him to her. Now, sonny boy, why don't you go back to your friends and let us eat in peace?"

The farm boy turned red in the face. "You know something. I'm going to change that face of yours so your own mother won't recognize you. Then, me and the boys are going to show these girls some good ole country fun."

He never saw the move. Danny slammed him in the throat with the edge of his hand. The farm boy grabbed his neck and was choking. Danny grabbed him, spun him around and launched him at the table where his buddies sat. They couldn't get out of the way fast enough. He plowed into them like a bowling ball, knocking them all over the place. Carmen grabbed Velvet and made for the door. Danny walked over to the guys. They were trying to get untangled to stand up.

He stood over them. "If you get up, I'm going to break every bone in your heads. He had it coming. Maybe this will teach him not to fuck with somebody else's lady. Now I'm leaving. If any of you want to get in on this, I'll be outside. But, if you come out, you'd better be ready. I don't fight fair. I fight to win."

He turned on his heel and walked out to the car. He stood there watching the door. Nobody came out. He got in and headed north. Carmen looked at Velvet and started to laugh. "Does this mean we aren't going to eat anything?"

Danny looked at her and Velvet. "We'll stop in the next town and find a nice place to eat with no interruptions." He found a nice mom and pop Italian restaurant that served home made pastas. Carmen called her father and told him their expected arrival time. They got to Buffalo just as the sun was setting. Momma had dinner ready for them. Carmen introduced Velvet to her mother and explained what they were going to do.

Her mother looked at Velvet. "With a body like that, who needs a face?" She came over and hugged Velvet. "You're more than welcome here. You stay as long as you like." She turned to her daughter. "Take Velvet up and show her to her room. It's the one next to yours. Then come down and we'll have supper." She came over and hugged Danny. "Ritchie tells me you're a wonderful singer. I told him I would find out for myself when you work here."

"I'll have ringside seats for you. I want you right down front."

Ritchie walked over to Danny. "Let's go into the den. I have something to talk to you about." They excused themselves and walked into the den. Danny sat in the big leather seat in front of the desk. Ritchie lit up a stogie and sat back. "I talked to Mrs. McVan and Tony. They want you to work McVan's while you're here recording. That way Tony can do some more songs for you. He's thinking of putting some girls with you as back up singers. He'll choreograph them and teach you some moves. Should make it a more professional looking show."

"I like that. It will add to the stage. Like decorating the formica."

"Once the record hits we'll move you to the Town Casino or the Glenn Park Casino. That's where the big boys play." They heard the girls coming down the stairs. Ritchie got up and motioned Danny to follow him. They met the girls in the foyer and went into

Chapter 21

The week flew by. Carmen visited Velvet every day helping her and Clarise set up the new company, *Temporarily Yours*. The Don's boys found Ron's stash and safety deposit box, containing over eighty thousand dollars. Carmen laughingly commented when hearing about the money that was found. "That's a lot of money for pussy."

The shows were getting better and the song, "Somebody Loves You" was an instant hit. Darlene and her friends were there almost every night along with the two bimbos. Danny was charming and they loved it. Carmen suggested Danny take the trio with him to Syracuse, because Johnny worked so well with him and could write any charts he might need. Danny agreed. Johnny was all for it and the Don loved the idea, so it was all settled.

Saturday night the club was packed to the rafters. People were waiting outside hoping somebody would leave, so they could get in. The Don had all his friends there for two dynamite shows. When they were over Danny mixed with the crowd, hugging and kissing all the ladies. Cheech shooed everybody out so they could have a going away party. He made an announcement that the club would stay the way it was. He would be hiring acts to work the club and do away with strippers. Chuck Eddy was sending him acts from New York City. Everybody applauded. The party lasted until four in the morning. Carmen and Danny said their goodbyes and went back to the hotel.

They got up early, packed the car, had breakfast and said goodbye to Velvet. Danny assured her they would be back in two weeks. They met Johnny and the guys in front of the club and headed for Syracuse. When they got there, they drove by the club. There on the marquee, in big letters, they read "Starring the Comedy of Don Rickles" and beneath it, in the same big letters, "Featuring, Danny Angel."

They checked into the hotel, had lunch and talked about the show. Rehearsal was at four o'clock. Johnny had the books already lined up for both shows. He would handle the rehearsal while Danny settled into the dressing room.

They went up to their room. Carmen ordered a bottle of wine from room service. When it came, she pored two glasses. She sat next to Danny on the couch, handed him a glass of wine and said, "You've been awfully quiet. What's on your mind?"

"I was just thinking. This is a class supper club not a strip joint. I guess I'm a little nervous. If it was a hit I'd be fine."

"You're going to be fine anyway. Strip joint or no you're still going to knock 'em dead. The only difference here is that it's an established club that runs stars. Before long, you'll be the star and have an act opening for you."

"I guess you're right." He raised his glass towards her. "Here's to a successful opening." They clinked glasses.

******

They got to the club at three o'clock. The boys went to set up on stage. The house band had already arrived. Johnny introduced himself and the boys to the house band members. Danny and Carmen went to his dressing room and hung up the tuxes and shirts. Don Rickles' dressing room was right across the hall. Carmen left Danny to find the lighting technician. He would need a light cue sheet for Danny's show.

There was a knock on his door. Standing there was a short neatly dressed Italian man. He put out his hand. "I'm Mike Molinaro. I own this joint."

Danny took his hand. "Good to meet you Mike. Thanks for having me here."

"If you want to know the truth, I didn't have much say so in the matter. They asked me for a favor, and you know what that means. I don't even know what the fuck you do."

Danny stepped back. Mike was getting a little hostile and Danny didn't want to get sucker punched by this miniature mobster. "I'm a singer Mike. I sing songs, English and Italian. I'm sorry about the guys putting the muscle on you. Tell you what. If you don't like what I do, after the show I'll be out of here and you don't owe me a dime. And you don't have to worry, 'cause I'll square it with the boys."

Mike stood there with his mouth open. "Now, there's an offer I can't refuse. You must be pretty sure of yourself."

"I know what I'm working with, you don't. Now, how much time do you want me to do?"

"Thirty five minutes, no more than forty. Can you do that?"

"Standing on my head. I'll see you after the show."

"Yeah, I'll be here." He turned and walked down the hall. He passed Carmen coming the other way and gave her the once over. He liked what he saw and smiled at her. She gave him her dazzling smile. She had to turn a bit sideways as the hall was narrow. He walked under her big tits. Danny had all he could do to keep from busting out laughing. Carmen came into the dressing room and closed the door. Danny fell on the couch holding his stomach and laughing.

"That has to be the funniest thing I've ever seen."

Carmen let him laugh. "OK, who was the midget?"

Danny composed himself. "That's the owner of the club, Mike Molinaro. Mike is not too happy that I'm here. So I made him an offer." He told her what went down.

"Well, once he sees you on stage, he'll be kissing your ass from here to Buffalo. The next time you play here, it will be for big money."

There was a knock on the door. Carmen opened it. There stood Don Rickles. He took a good look at Carmen. "I thought I would come over and say hello. I didn't expect Miss Universe to be here." He kissed her hand.

"Well aren't you sweet. Don, this is Danny Angel."

Don stared at Danny. "You're beautiful. What a handsome guy. Hey, if you can attract ladies like this, I'm sticking with you."

Carmen put her arm around his shoulders. "Tell you what Don, I'm the first string. What ever else comes in is yours."

"Gee that's great." He turned to Danny. "So, you're opening for me. Once they get a look at that kisser, they'll throw rocks at me."

Danny smiled at him. "Don't worry Don. If anything happens, I'll send Carmen out to take care of you."

"Hell, they get one look at her and I'll really be in the toilet. Hey, have you met Mike?"

"Yes, we had a few words."

"He's really a case, huh? He thinks he's Napoleon. He's just mad 'cause he's so short. He's tired of going up on broads. If he had one like Carmen, he'd have to make two trips." He was on a roll. He had them laughing for fifteen minutes. "Well, gotta go. See you tonight." He left for his dressing room.

Danny could hear the band going over his songs with the big band. What a difference! He grabbed Carmen and went out on stage to listen. The sound man came over and gave him a microphone, so he could get a sound check. Danny sang some of the songs they were playing, and got an OK from the sound man.

He turned to Carmen. "Did you hear that sound? It's crystal clear. I can hear what I'm doing. It's not like the Plush Horse."

"From now on, you'll have the best, Danny boy. I can't wait until they hear you tonight."

They stayed through the rest of the rehearsal. Johnny was great with the band. The light man came down and they went over the lights for the show. When the rehearsal was finished, Danny took them all out to eat. Afterwards, it was back to the hotel to get ready for opening night.

Chapter 22

They got to the club early. When they opened the dressing room door, it looked like a florist shop inside. There were flowers all over the place. On the dressing room table were a stack of telegrams. Danny was speechless. Carmen got the cards from the flowers and read them to Danny. They were from the Don and friends. The telegrams were from Velvet and the girls, Flame, Sheila, and even the blonde Bimbos.

Don came walking in. He looked around and said, "Who died? I haven't seen this many flowers since the Kentucky Derby and they were on the neck of a horse. Who's opening for who here? You got flowers and I got nothing but a bar in my dressing room. But it's stocked with the best booze. Carmen, you can come over anytime but leave Mr. Adonis home."

Carmen giggled. "Don, if I came over, you'd need a seat belt, riding crop and spurs. Tell you what. If you can stay on for eight seconds, I'm yours."

"That's what I've always wanted... a nymphomaniac with a sense of humor."

They talked and joked for awhile until it was time to get dressed. Carmen went out front to get seated, as Johnny came in to go over the song list. Danny got dressed and waited back stage. The house band was playing a dance set. People were dancing and having fun. When the set ended, Johnny, Gus and Vinnie went out and set up. The band got back on the stand, the lights came down and there was a drum roll.

The announcer said, "Ladies and Gentlemen, tonight the Three Rivers Night Club proudly presents the comedy of Don

Rickles, and the latest singing sensation, Danny Angel. Now, put your hands together and welcome to the stage, Danny Angel."

The band went into its opening number as the curtain came up. Danny stepped out on stage and walked to the microphone. The spotlight was hitting him right in the eyes. He had never worked with a spot before. He couldn't see anybody, but he figured they could see him. He went into his opening song, "Day In, Day Out." The band was smoking and he drove the song home. The applause was deafening. Shouts of more and whistles came at him from beyond the lights. He settled in and did his show.

There were laughs with the jokes, and sighs with the ballads. After the last number, the lights came up and he was looking at a standing ovation. They wanted more. Danny checked the clock hanging on the wall above the curtain. He had time. He chose for his encore, "Somebody Loves You." The lights came down and he went into the number.

The crowd was enthralled. They were on their feet before the last note was sung. They clapped, shouted, and whistled, while Danny stood there with his arms out. He seemed to be embracing the whole audience. He left the stage amid shouts for more.

Rickles was standing in the wings. He walked over to Danny. "That was beautiful. They loved you. Now I have to go out there and try to make them laugh. It's like throwing this little Jew boy to the lions."

Danny looked down at him. "I just warmed them up for you. You'll kill them." And he did. He destroyed them. He worked them for almost an hour and left the stage to thunderous applause.

Danny was sitting in his dressing room as Don came off stage. He walked over to Danny's dressing room and stuck his head in. "You were right, but I knew it all along. Come on over and have a drink when you get changed."

He went into his dressing room. Danny got up as Carmen came in. She threw her arms around him. "You were magnificent. You had them eating out of the palm of your hand. I brought some people backstage that want to say hello." She stepped aside as Don

Angelo came into the room. Danny was stunned. He let out a holler and hugged Don Angelo. "I never expected you'd be here."

The Don looked up at him. "Did you think we'd miss your opening at this wonderful club? Not on your life. Oh, there's more people that came to see you." He motioned to his bodyguard and Ritchie came in folowed by Thamaso, Carlo, Patsy and all their bodyguards along with Don Bannacci. It was a party. Everybody was talking, laughing and congratulating Danny.

In the middle of all this commotion, Rickles came out of his dressing room and shouted. "What's going on out here?" He was immediately lifted off his feet by two big bodyguards. He looked up at one and then the other. Danny walked out of the dressing room and stood in front of Don.

Don smiled and said, "I hope these are friends of yours. Could you tell them to put me down? I'm afraid of heights."

Danny signaled and the bodyguards put Don back on the floor. "Don, I want you to meet some friends of mine." He introduced him to all the people in the room. Rickles was at his best. He had them laughing right off the bat. He finally said, "Hey, let's go to my dressing room. I have a bar stocked with booze and nobody to drink it."

Don's dressing room started to fill up and the party was on. People started to come in from the showroom. Danny was surprised to see the two blonde bimbo's with Mike. He had his arms around their waists. Their boobs were even with his head. Every time they would turn to talk to each other, his head would disappear. Mike was in heaven. He saw Danny and came over still holding on to the girls.

"You were right. You're the best. Stay as long as you like." He looked around and seeing all the Dons, his mouth dropped open. He started to sweat. "I didn't know you knew these people. Jesus, Danny, you're not going to tell them about our little talk today are you?"

"No, Mike. That was between you and me. So, what do you think of my girls here?"

"I love 'em. They told me they were friends of yours, so I

brought them with me."

Danny hugged each one and told them he was glad they came. He whispered in their ears, "Take Mike out and do a job on him. I think he needs it." They smiled and gave him the OK signal.

Danny went back to Don Angelo. "I'm glad you came. So, what do you think?

"I think we made the right decision. You're going to be a big star. The boys all agreed. I never thought Danny Di could do this. You made me real proud tonight. I can't wait to get you back to Chicago and show those ass holes some real talent."

Danny was about to answer when Johnny came in with Gus and Vinnie. He saw his uncle, went over and got a hug. Don Bannacci came over to Danny. "The kid did all right. And you were magnificent. What a difference from The Plush Horse. Here you had everything, lights, sound and a great band. You're going to go a long way Danny. Always remember, we're right behind you."

"I'll remember."

"Good, I booked a suite at the hotel. Let's get everybody and go over there. I got food coming and good wine. We can finish off the night there."

"Great." Danny called for attention and told them what Don Bannacci wanted to do. They all agreed. They brought the limos to the back door and left for the hotel. Carmen was sitting next to him with her arm through his. "You were great tonight, Danny. And the song went over like gangbusters. I told you it was your song. Now, I can't wait to get back to Buffalo and record it. The sooner we get it out, the sooner you'll be on your way to the big time."

Danny leaned in and kissed her. "The only big time I want tonight is you."

"Oh, I'm ready big boy. As soon as we dump this crowd, it's you and me."

When they pulled up to the hotel, it looked like an Italian wedding or a Mafia movie with all the limos, bodyguards and everyone in top coats and hats. They went up to Don Bannacci's suite and the party began.

******

The party lasted until three in the morning. Everybody was up early and down to breakfast because they had planes to catch. Don Angelo and Ritchie were the last to leave. Danny gave them both a hug. "I can't thank you enough for coming. It means a lot to me."

"I wouldn't have missed it for the world. I was telling Ritchie that Carmen did a bang up job on you. If anybody would have told me that my number one made guy could sing like that, I would have told them they were pots, stunad."

Ritchie gave Danny a hug. "You've come a long way in a short time. Carmen knew that she had a diamond in the rough. Oh, she told me about Velvet. You bring her to Buffalo, and we'll take care of her. Now, I've got to get Don Angelo to the airport. Take care of my daughter for me."

Once again there were hugs all around and they were gone. Carmen stood next to him and watched them go. "If there were any doubts in their minds about you or what you could do, they're gone now. By the time we get back to Buffalo you'll be ready to record and get out on the road to do the big clubs. These two weeks are going to be great."

And they were. The club was packed every night. Danny was improving with every performance. The women loved him and showed it by the things they threw on stage. He got flowers, hotel keys, car keys, bras, panties and dozens of slips of paper with ladies numbers on them, asking him to come to their rooms or homes. He got propositioned every night. He could have fucked his way into the Guinness book of world records, but once they saw Carmen, they knew they didn't stand a chance. Many of them tried anyway.

The blonde bimbo's were there almost every night. They were staying with Mike and he looked like death warmed over. The girls were really doing a number on him. They still tried to get Danny to do a threesome.

His song "Somebody Loves You" stopped the show every night. Everybody wanted it. Danny told them it would be out soon.

The local wise guys came in and invited Danny and Carmen to their homes for dinner. They had great food, good wine and lots of laughs. Carmen called Velvet everyday to check on her. She was doing fine and couldn't wait for them to come and get her. The girls were doing great with *Temporarily Yours*. No pimps would come anywhere near them. The word was out on the street to leave them alone or else.

Closing night Mike threw a big party for Don and Danny. Booze flowed like water. The cooks laid out a wonderful buffet. The party lasted until the wee hours of the morning. Danny and Carmen slipped out around two. They went back to the hotel and made love. They got up at noon to have breakfast and pack the car. Johnny and the boys were all hung over, so they decided to stay until evening. They would be in Buffalo in a week for the record session.

Danny and Carmen got in the car and headed for Utica. They got there and found Velvet at Clarisse's house. Danny blew the horn and the girls came running out. There were kisses and hugs all around. Velvet came out and stood on the porch. She was wearing a dress that left nothing to the imagination. Her body was perfection. The bandages remained, and her face was still a bit swollen. Carmen gave her a big hug and walked her over to Danny. Danny gave her a hug and a kiss on the forehead.

"Well sweet thing, you ready to go get a new face and a new life?"

"You bet I am. I'm tired of sounding like a cartoon character with a head cold."

"Then let's get out of here." They said their goodbyes, got in the car and headed for Buffalo. The girls chattered like magpies all the way there. Every once in a while they would include Danny in their conversation. He had his mind elsewhere, so he really didn't mind. He was thinking about the recording session and what followed.

The job in Syracuse really went well. He knew he was ready for bigger things. Being on stage was becoming natural, just like when he was doing hits for the Don. He also knew he still had the kitchen for some of momma's pasta.

Chapter 23

The next few weeks flew by. Danny worked nights at McVan's and spent his days in the recording studio laying down the tracks for "Somebody Loves You" and "What Would I Do Without My Music." Tony had him singing and dancing with the chorus line. Danny was getting better and the club was packed every night with ladies who fawned over him. He was becoming Buffalo's heartthrob. Tony got him three good looking backup singers and dancers. He worked with them every night after the second show. Since they were the first chapter in his new act he called them Chapter One.

Carmen took Velvet to the plastic surgeon and he redid her face. The bandages would be coming off soon. She was excited. Momma had adopted her and was overjoyed to have two daughters and a son. They were surprised to find out that Velvet had graduated from college with a master's degree in finance.

It happened one day in Ritchie's study. He was going over the books and having trouble with some figures. Carmen and Velvet just happened to be there. Velvet asked him if she could help. He asked her if she knew anything about bookkeeping, knowing that she was a hooker. Velvet came around the desk, took the books, sat down and went through them. She made notations on a piece of paper.

Ritchie and Carmen just watched her. She finally looked up and told Ritchie that he was being cheated. She showed him how it was being done. The bookkeeper was skimming money and doctoring the figures. Ritchie hired her on the spot. The bookkeeper, got into a terrible accident and died, but not before he gave Ritchie back most of the money he took. He had it squirreled away in shoe boxes in his closet.

Carmen was busy setting up the people who would be putting Danny's record on every juke box on the east coast. They would put it on A-1, the first place people looked when they made a selection. She also had some good clubs lined up for him with great money. She contacted Bruno to come to Buffalo and take pictures of Danny with and without the girls. She ordered a whole photo shoot of Danny in different places and in casual surroundings. She had him set up to do some benefits in and around up state New York and Canada. He was getting some good T.V. exposure.

Johnny, Gus and Vinnie were working with Danny at the club and the recording studio. Johnny had taken over the orchestra. He rewrote most of the parts for the songs and they were working out beautifully. He had a natural gift with music. He recorded each section separately starting with the rhythm section, then the brass, strings, and vocal background. It took the A and R guy a week to mix it to Johnny's satisfaction. He called Carmen. "Hey, it's Johnny. The tracks are done. Danny can come in and lay down his voice. I think you're going to like what you hear."

"Good. How about the day after tomorrow, after the second show? His voice will be warmed up. He works better at night."

"Great, I'll set it up. See you then."

Carmen walked into the bedroom. Danny was sitting up having breakfast in bed. "Johnny just called. The tracks are done. We'll record day after tomorrow after your second show. I can't wait to hear the music."

"Hey, that's great. I'm ready. I've sung that song every way possible and finally have it down the way I want it." He motioned for her to sit on the bed. "You know I couldn't have done this without you. I don't know how I can ever repay you."

Carmen reached under the covers and grabbed him. "Oh, I can think of a few ways. Trust me"

******

Danny, Carmen and Johnny walked into the recording studio. The only person there was the sound engineer. The studio was dark except for the glass booth where Danny would record. The headset and microphone were waiting for him. Johnny told them, "I've set the mood. All you have to do is go in there and sing the song the way you like it. We can do as many takes as you want until you're satisfied."

Danny went into the glass booth and shut the door. He put the headphones on and tested the microphone. Johnny's voice came into his headset, "Listen to the track first so you know what it sounds like. We can play it as many times as you like until you feel comfortable with it." Danny nodded and his headset was filled with music. He listened in wonder as the song played, mentally singing it in his head. He asked to hear it two more times. Then he was ready.

Johnny lowered the lights in the booth to give it a romantic touch. Danny sang the song like he had never sung it before. The music swelled around him and the voice came out pure and simple. He was singing a love song. Halfway through the song he was surprised to feel tears rolling down his cheeks. He finished the song on a clear high note as the music ended. He stood there with his head bowed and was surprised at the emotion the song had brought out in him. It wasn't like him to cry.

Then a voice in his ear said, "That was the greatest damn thing I've ever heard. You sang the shit out of it. I don't think we could get it any better than that. I'm going to play it back for you. Hold on." Danny stayed in the booth with his head bowed. The music started and his voice came on. He stood there in wonder as he heard himself sing the song. His voice was like velvet. He had never heard it this clear. He almost shed another tear.

When the song ended Carmen came into the booth and hugged him. She had tears in her eyes. "My darling, that song is platinum. The whole thing is magic. Music, back up singers, the whole works is perfect."

Johnny came into the booth. "Danny, I don't think we could get it any better than that. When it's mixed it will be dynamite. Are you happy with it?"

Danny smiled at him. "Yeah, I'm happy with it. That arrangement of yours is just beautiful. Your uncle will be proud. Let's take five then do the other song."

They came out of the booth and sat talking. When Danny was ready, he went back into the booth to record his second song, "What Would I do With out My Music." He listened to the song a couple of times then sang it. He was right on and they took that cut also. The sound man was overjoyed. Usually he would have been there for hours until it was right. Now all he had to do was mix the voice with the music and he was done. Danny suggested they go out and celebrate. The only place open at that time of the night was The Blue Moon, a colored night club. When they got there, the place was jumping.

The show had just started as they sat down at a table. The emcee came out dressed in a matching green chartreuse outfit. Even the shoes were green. He sang and danced. Then he brought out the other acts. First was a colored comedian who had them in stitches. Following was a ventriloquist with a colored dummy named Amos, who insulted the whole crowd to the delight of the people. The last act was a colored stripper named Ebony. She was absolutely beautiful and moved with the grace of a gazelle. She was perfection. When she was through, Danny and Carmen stood up cheering and applauding.

The emcee came back on stage and asked for quiet. "Ladies and gentlemen, it has come to my attention that we have in the room, a singer who works at McVan's. Since they are the only white folks in the room, it was easy to spot him. Would you give a nice round of applause for Danny Angel?"

Danny stood up to the ovation they gave him. The emcee motioned him to come up on the stage. Danny walked up and they shook hands. The emcee turned to the crowd. "Would you like to hear the white boy sing?" There was a thunderous round of applause followed by shouts of yes, yes.

Danny motioned for Johnny to come up and take over the piano. Danny asked for a G7 chord. He started softly, singing rubato just him and Johnny. "Swing low, sweet chariot. Comin' forth to carry me home. Swing low, sweet chariot. Comin' forth to carry me home." He went into tempo and the rest of the band joined in. The crowd was clapping along to the song and swaying to the beat of the music. He finished to the sound of thundering applause and shouts of more. He did two more songs and got a standing ovation after the last one.

He sat down at the table and people rushed over to thank him and shake his hand. The emcee came over and had them put another table along side so he and the other acts could join them. Ebony came out and sat at Danny's right. Danny ordered a round of drinks for the tables. She told him, "You have a marvelous voice. I could listen to you all night." He looked at Ebony. "Thank you. I'd like to sing to you all night." She smiled, got up, made her apologies and left to go backstage. The party lasted for another hour. Finally they left and went home. Carmen got undressed and came to bed. When she was lying next to Danny she leaned over him and said, "I didn't know you sang gospel."

He kissed on her nose. "Neither did I. Some colored guy used to sing it all the time at a club where I used to hang out in Chicago. I just thought I'd try it out on that crowd."

"Well, it worked. You were great. Now I have a reward for you for doing so good at the recording session." She disappeared under the sheets.

Danny lay back smiling. "I do love the way you reward me."

Chapter 24

It was the day that Velvet's bandages were to come off. Paul had come to the house to do it, so everybody could see her new face. She was as nervous as a cat in a room full of rocking chairs. She sat in a chair in the kitchen holding Carmen's hand. Momma and Ritchie were there to give her moral support. Paul started to unwrap the bandages. He got down to the last layer and said, "Now Velvet, there will be a little swelling so don't get excited. It will all go away in time. Are you ready?"

Velvet nodded yes and squeezed Carmen's hand tighter. He undid the last bandage and stood back. Everybody stared at her face. It was beautiful even though it was a little swollen. Carmen picked up a big mirror she had in her right hand. "Are you ready to see the new you?" Velvet nodded and reached for the mirror. She brought it up to the front of her face. Looking back at her was the face of a movie star.

It was better than her original face, which was beautiful. He had made some nice improvements. Tears came to her eyes and she said through them, "I don't know how to thank you. I'm me again. I never thought I could ever show my face again in public." She got up and hugged Danny and kissed him on the cheek. "You made all this possible. You gave me a new life, a family, and now a new face. I promise you I won't ever let you down."

He held her at arms length. "You just be happy. Now, that you are no longer a mummy, you can come to the show tomorrow night and show off that beautiful face."

She hugged him again. Carmen got up and said to her, "Now that you have a new face, you should have some new clothes to match. Come on, I have something upstairs to show you." They ran up the stairs and in a few moments they heard squeals coming from the bedroom. They all smiled, sat down, and had coffee and home made biscotti.

The songs were ready. Carmen had contacted a recording company that her father said was waiting for the demo. Carmen and Danny got on a plane and hand delivered it to New York City. The head of the recording company met them at the airport and took them to dinner. He liked what he saw in Danny and knew if he sang as good as he looked, he had star on his hands.

After dinner they went to the studio and played the tape. He couldn't believe it. The songs were beautiful and the voice was pure velvet. He signed Danny to a recording contract on the spot. He told them that, within a month, those songs would be in every juke box on the east coast and mid west. He would set up a tour for Danny to promote the songs, do radio interviews, and public appearances. There would be posters, flyers, magazine articles, Billboard, and Variety. He would cover all the bases.

They left and went back to the hotel. Carmen called her father and told him all that went on. He told her that everything was being set up for Danny once the record hit. After she hung up, Danny called Don Angelo to fill him in. He was delighted. He couldn't wait to get Danny back to Chicago to open the Chez Paris.

Vito Cadenzo was called out of courtesy. He was delighted and wanted them to come over for dinner tomorrow. He would send a limo for them. That settled, they got naked, made love until they were exhausted and slept.

They were up early and out on the town. Carmen wanted to shop, and Danny wanted to go to Little Italy and look round. They decided to meet for lunch at Alfonzo's at one o'clock. Danny took a cab to Little Italy. He knew where he was going. A bar and grill with pool tables was a local wise guy hangout. There was a secret room in the back used for a horse book and numbers. Behind that room was a plush room with it's own bar. This was where he was heading. That room was headquarters for Murder, Inc.

There were some local toughs lounging around the front of

Sing Deadly

the place. Danny walked up and turned to go into the bar. One of the guys grabbed his arm. "Where the fuck you going, pretty boy?"

In one swift motion, Danny whirled around breaking the guys hold, and with the heel of his hand, slammed him in the breast bone. The guy folded up like an accordion. Danny stepped back. "Anybody else want to stop me?"

The other toughs just raised their hands and shook their heads no. Danny went inside. He went to the back of the bar. A bad looking bodyguard was guarding the door to the back room. Danny walked up to him. "I came to see Alberto. Tell him that Chianti is best served chilled."

The bodyguard looked him over real careful. He reached for a phone and made a call. Before long a guy came out and looked at Danny. He didn't recognize him. The guy on the door whispered in his ear. He motioned for Danny to put his arms up. He padded him down for weapons, then motioned for Danny to follow him. The race book was in full swing. They walked through to the other room. Once the door was shut, it was quiet. Alberto was behind the desk. His bodyguards were standing behind him. He looked up at Danny. "I don't know who the fuck you are, or how you got the password. You tell me and it better be good."

Danny smiled at him. "Still the same old hard ass, I see. And speaking of that, did you ever tell your boys here, how you shot yourself in the ass with your own gun?"

Alberto shot out of the chair. "There's only one guy in the world who knew that and he's dead. So how the hell do you know that?" Alberto took a closer look at Danny.

"Because Bert, I was with you on that job. I took you to the sawbones to get you patched up."

Alberto came around the desk and looked into Danny's eyes. "It can't be. You got somebody else's face but you got Danny Di's eyes and voice. And Danny Di is the only one that calls me Bert."

Danny gave him a hug. "You're right. Tell your boys to take a break. I've got lots to tell you."

Alberto dismissed the bodyguards. He poured wine for them. Danny told him everything. Alberto sat there with his mouth open. "I don't fucking believe this. You're a singer?"

"Yep, and a good one. I've got a record coming out this month that will make me a star. The reason I came to see you is, I'm going to need bodyguards. You know how that works. Like Frank and Dean. I don't want just anybody. I want the best. You know I can take care of myself. But, I don't want anybody getting suspicious by having to defend myself."

"That can be arranged. You tell me when you need them. You know, it's really weird having Danny Di's voice coming out of that face. I got to say it's a real improvement over the other one."

"Your ass. Now listen, Bert, only a few people know that I'm really Danny Di. You know all of them. To everyone else, I'm Don Angelo's nephew, Ferdinando. Vito is having us over for dinner tonight. Call him and invite yourself."

"I'll do it. So, what are your plans now?"

"Nothing until I meet my lady at Alfonzo's at one o'clock."

"Good, I'll join you. Wait." He picked up the phone and called Alfonzo's and made reservations for them. When he hung up he said, "The best table in the joint. Nothing's too good for my old paison. Who's the lady friend?"

She's Ritchie Regerio's daughter, Carmen. She's the one doing all this for me."

"I know Ritchie. He's a Buffalo guy. I've done some business with him. Come on, let me show you around."

He took Danny out and showed him his operation. Danny placed a few bets on some horses and won on one of them. Then it was time to go. They walked outside. The toughs were still there. The one Danny slammed was sitting on the ground with his back against the wall rubbing his chest. Alberto looked down at him. "What the hell's wrong with you?"

Danny answered for him. "I had to give him a lesson in manners."

Alberto broke into laughter. He looked down at the tough. "You're lucky he left you alive." He took Danny's arm and they walked the two blocks to the restaurant. They were seated at the back table facing the street. One bodyguard was at the front door the other was at an adjoining table. When Carmen walked in, Alberto gave a nod to the bodyguard at the door. He took her arm and walked her to the table. They stood up. "Carmen, I want you to meet one of my old friends. This is Alberto."

Carmen gave him an inquisitive look, but put out her hand so Alberto could kiss it. "I'm glad to meet you." She sat down. She looked at Danny. "Is there something here I should know about?"

Danny smiled at her. "Yes, Alberto and I go back a long way. I have no secrets from him. He's going to supply the security guys I'll need. I'll fill you in later."

Alberto took her hand. "You have nothing to worry about. His secret is safe with me. I do business with your father from time to time. As for Danny, I'll protect his sorry ass. Now, the food here is excellent. It's time to eat and drink a little vino."

Chapter 25

The limo picked them up and took them to Vito's house. The driveway was full of cars. The drivers were lounging around smoking. Danny and Carmen were led into the house and the main living room. Out of the fifteen people there, Danny recognized three men who were heads of crime families. Everybody there had at least two bodyguards. They were all in an adjoining room. Alberto and his date were at the bar. Vito saw them and hurried over. "I'm so glad you could come. Let me introduce you around." He called for quiet.

When it calmed down he said, "This is Danny Angel, Don Angelo's nephew from Italy. He's a singer. And this lovely lady is Carmen Regerio, Ritchie's daughter from Buffalo." He escorted them around the room introducing them to his guests. He spoke Italian to the old mustache Pete's. They all asked about Don Angelo's health. Danny told them he was still on this side of the grass which got a big laugh. Vito took them over to meet Alberto. They hugged and exchanged small talk. Carmen noticed that all the men gave Alberto respect, even the heads of the families. Later she would ask Danny why he let Alberto know his true identity.

Dinner was a magnificent affair. The food was outstanding and the talk was about Danny's business in New York. He explained about the record and his plans. They all pledged their support. After dinner, the ladies went into the parlor to chat, while the men went into the den to smoke cigars, drink Cognac and talk a little business. The party lasted until close to midnight.

The limo took them back to the hotel. Once in the room, Carmen came over and stood in front of him as he sat on the bed.

"OK buster. Let's have it. Who is Alberto?"

Danny pulled her down on his lap. "Alberto is the head of Murder, Inc. We used to do some jobs together before he formed the company. He's the only hit man that ever shot himself."

Carmen started to laugh. "You're kidding. How did he do that?"

"We were out on a job and he had his pistol in his right back pocket. The mark we were after saw us and started to run. Alberto tried to get the gun out of his pocket and accidentally pulled the trigger shooting himself in the ass. I had to chase the guy down and finish the job, which wasn't easy, 'cause I was laughing so hard, I almost choked. He swore me to secrecy. I had to take him to a mob doctor and make up a story. I may need him down the road, so I let him in on everything. Believe me he's the best. Next to me, of course."

She hit him on the arm. "Oh, Mr. Modest. Just remember, you're not in that business anymore. From now on, the only killing you're going to be doing is on stage. You got that, big boy?"

He kissed her. "Whatever you say. Now let's get naked and do nice things to each other."

They were up early and at the airport. Gino picked them up in Buffalo and drove them home. When they got in the house Ritchie came out of his den followed by Velvet. She was wearing a business suit which still showed off that magnificent body. She had a pencil behind her ear and a handful of papers. Her face had lost the swelling and was flawless. There were hugs all around and then they headed for the kitchen for coffee and Italian cookies. Momma was glad they were home.

Ritchie asked, "How did it go?" Carmen filled him in on all the goings on and the party at Vito's.

"The record will be out by the end of the month. It should fly."

And fly it did. The record came out in three weeks and was in every juke box on the east coast and mid west. Disc jockeys played it over and over. The record went on sale and was sold out the first week. Everybody wanted it, and everybody wanted Danny.

Offers came rolling in. Chuck Eddy was swamped with calls wanting Danny. They decided to put him in south Philadelphia in Palumbo's. That way he could do the Dick Clark show. He sold out the club every night.

The Dick Clark show went over big and every teeny bopper wanted to be the one he took to bed. On any given night the place was filled with goombas and wise guys. It was like a Who's Who in gangster land. Then, it was the Copa in New York City. The families all came out to see him and the wine flowed like water. Danny spent his days in the recording studio making an album of the best songs of the day. Carmen picked them and he sang them. Alberto came through with two of his best men to take care of Danny. Tommy "the Ox" Shavetti, and Willie "the Weasel" Quomo looked like Mutt and Jeff, but both guys were stone killers.

The show was better than ever. The girls sang and danced around him. Women threw themselves at him. Carmen had to come to his rescue a few times. Danny loved it.

From there, it was The Lake Club, a mob gambling joint in Springfield, Illinois. When the cops were spotted in the parking lot, a red light would flash in the bass drum. Hugo, one of the owners would push a button and the walls would reverse hiding the black jack tables and the slots. It looked like a supper club. The cops knew what was going on, but they had to make a show of it. When they left, Hugo would slip the Chief an envelope. He left there a few thousand dollars richer. Danny would just keep on with the show like nothing happened. He was doing a landslide business.

Don Angelo called him and told him he was coming home to Chicago to do The Chez Paree, after he finished Sutmillers in Dayton, Ohio. It was going to be the biggest opening since Frank played there. Danny was looking forward to that. He was going to be singing for, and hobnobbing with, the same people who for years tried to put him in prison and the electric chair.

He got a call from Chuck Eddy telling him that Sutmillers was completely sold out for the two weeks he would be there. The boys from Toledo and Youngstown would be there to see him. They wanted him for their clubs.

Carmen would be going home to Buffalo after Ohio. She had things to do for him and wouldn't be needed for the opening in Chicago. She would come up the second week. She was also worried about her father. There was bad blood between the rival families from Buffalo and Toronto Canada. It had been brewing for a long time.

The opening at Sutmillers was like New Year's Eve. The place was jammed. He did his shows to standing ovation after standing ovation. They couldn't get enough of him. He managed to make the Mayor's wife and daughter all in the same day. The two weeks flew by, and then it was time to go home to Chicago.

******

Don Angelo was beside himself. Danny was coming home to open the Chez. He had invitations out all over Chicago. Parties, press conferences, and TV talk shows were planned. He was doing it up, big time, for his boy. He had invited the Governor, Chief of Police, the Police Commissioner, the head of the detective bureau and the Mayor. Engraved invitations were sent out to the heads of all the families including the O'Bannon's, the Irish mob from the north end.

He reserved four suites at The Palmer House. One was for Danny with an adjoining suite for his bodyguards, one for Johnny, Gus, and Vinnie. The fourth suite was for "after the show" parties. He had a piano sent up, so Danny could sing if he wanted to. Danny's back up singers were down the hall in regular rooms. He wanted everything to be perfect.

The day arrived. The Don arrived at the airport with his bodyguards. Rick Warren from WGN TV was there with a camera crew to film Danny's arrival for the 6 o'clock news. They watched the plane land and taxi to the terminal. The ground crew pushed the steps to the plane. The door opened and Danny stepped out on to the platform. He looked wonderful. The Don almost cried. He came down the steps with his bodyguards close behind. Following was Johnny, Gus, Vinnie and his back up singers. Once on the ground, they flanked him as he walked into the terminal.

The cameras were recording as he walked up to the Don. Danny hugged and kissed him on both cheeks. Then there was a lot of hugging and back slapping from the Don's bodyguards.

Rick Warren came over with his microphone. "This is Rick Warren from station WGN here in Chicago. We're here welcoming the nation's newest singing sensation, Danny Angel." He walked over to Danny. The Don and his guys faded away from the camera. "Danny, welcome home."

Danny smiled at the camera. "It's good to be home. I've been looking forward to coming back. It's going to be a great opening at the Chez."

"Your record went platinum in a very short time. The whole country is playing it."

"Yeah, I got lucky. It's a beautiful song. I've just recorded an album that will be out soon. That song is on it plus a lot of other great songs."

"The whole town is looking forward to your opening at the Chez Paree on Monday. It isn't often that one of our own becomes a big star."

"Like I said Rick, I got lucky. I just want to say to the people here in Chicago, I'm still a hometown boy. I'll see you at the Chez." He shook Rick's hand and walked over to the Don.

Rick signed off, packed up and left. The Don watched them go. "Not bad, huh? Come on, mamma has cavatelli waiting on the stove." He took Danny's arm as they left the terminal and got into the limos. On the way back to the house Danny filled the Don in on all the happenings. He told him about Albert. The Don said it was the right thing to do. He knew Albert would go to his grave before he told anyone. They talked and laughed the rest of he way to the house.

When they got there, Danny got out as momma was coming out the front door. She saw Danny and hurried over with tears in her eyes. She hugged him and kissed him on both cheeks. She leaned back and said, "My boy has come home." That brought on more tears. The Don came over and put his arm around her. "Come on momma, it's time to feed your boy and his friends."

They went into the house. Momma had already set the dining room table. The meal was delicious and the talk was wonderfully Italian filled with laughs, jokes, and ribbing each other. Danny told Momma all that happened since he left. She screamed with laughter when he told her about his first meeting with Tony. When dinner was over they all went into the living room for coffee and drinks.

The Don motioned to Danny to follow him into the den. He got a bottle of good wine from his wine cooler. "I got to tell you Danny, you're making me proud. I get calls every day from my goombas wanting to know when they can have you in their clubs. I got a call two days ago from Sammy Two Fingers. You remember him. He's the Hollywood guy you did a job for. He wants to put you in pictures. Things are moving fast."

Danny took a glass of wine the Don handed him. "I'll say. Chuck calls me every day and tells me where I'm going next. The money is getting real good. They're paying a small fortune for me. But one thing I don't understand. Chuck is taking his commission but you're not. Why?"

The Don smiled at him. "I had a talk with the boys and we decided that we wouldn't take any money now. You'll pay them back by working their clubs for a little less money. That way they make a lot of money off you and you still get a taste." What he didn't tell Danny was that they decided to let the money ride until the real big money came along later. Let him have his fun before they called in the markers.

Danny didn't know what to say. "I really didn't expect that. You know I always pay my debts."

"I know that, but this is different. You're going to be a big star. You're going to be making so much money you won't know what to do with it. So, instead of giving it to Uncle Sam, you give it to us. Capisci?"

"Capisci. And thank you. They raised their glasses in a toast to one another.

"By the way, who's working with me on the show?"

The Don reached in the desk drawer and pulled out an eight by ten envelope. He took out some pictures and laid them in front of Danny. "You know the Chez has a chorus line. Well, seeing that you have your own singers and dancers, we decided to give them the time off and bring in a group that's one of Chicago's favorites. They're from Philly. They go by the name Freddie Bell and the Bell Boys. It's a high energy and funny group and will be a good opener. They should get the crowd up on their feet."

"Good. I know them. They came to see me when I worked Palumbos. It'll be a good show."

The Don stood up. "I know. That's what we thought. Now, come on, let's join the party. We'll talk some more tomorrow." He took Danny's arm and they went into the living room.

*****

The week was a whirlwind of TV appearances, radio interviews, record store signings, parties and rehearsing.

Carmen called every day. Things were still nasty in Buffalo, with killings on both sides of the border. Velvet was doing well taking care of the books.

Then it was opening night. The front of the club looked like London during the Second World War. Klieg lights were crisscrossing the sky. The limos started to arrive. Bosses and bodyguards were everywhere. The Governor and his entourage didn't look too happy having to mingle with the heads of the Chicago mobs. The Don's family was right up front. It was standing room only. They even tried to squeeze tables in along the back wall.

Showtime arrived. The lights went down, a drum roll started, and an announcer's voice came out of the darkness. "Ladies and gentlemen, the Chez Paree proudly presents America's newest singing sensation, Danny Angel." A roar went up from the crowd. "And now to open our show, Chicago's favorite Rock and Roll band, direct from Philadelphia, Freddie Bell and the Bell Boys."

They hit the stage like a bomb with high energy, singing,

playing, and comedy. For forty-five minutes they had the crowd rocking. They went off to a standing ovation. It was time. The lights went down and the announcer's voice began, "And now the moment you have been waiting for. The Chez Paree proudly presents Chicago's own, Danny Angel."

The orchestra started his opening number and Danny stepped on stage. The crowd went wild. He walked to the front of the stage. He acknowledged the crowd and started to sing. It was magic. The band, the crowd, the songs were total perfection. The hour and twenty minutes flew by. Then for his last song, he sang his hit record to standing ovations and cheers. He had to do two encore numbers. Then it was over. The crowd was wild.

Danny stood backstage and took it all in. Who would have ever thought that the Governor and his crowd would be giving him a standing ovation? He went to his dressing room to await the special people that were coming backstage for a small party. The families went to the hotel to wait for them. They didn't want to mix with the press or the Governor and his bunch.

The Don and his family were the first to arrive backstage. Momma was so excited. She kept kissing him and telling him how good he was. Sheila was all over him with kisses and body rubs. The dressing room filled up fast. The Governor's party came back and was all smiles. The Police commissioner and the police chief acted like they didn't want to be there. The head of the detective bureau begged off. Booze flowed like water. Every body was having a good time. Danny told his back up girls to go schmoose the Governor's party.

They were all over the Commissioner and the Police Chief. Even the governor got into the act. It was time to go to the hotel for the real party. Danny thanked everybody for coming. They went out the back door and into the limos.

When they arrived at the hotel, it looked like an armed camp. Bodyguards were everywhere. The whole top floor was one big party. Johnny and the boys had gotten there early and music was coming down the hall. When Danny walked into the main suite, he was greeted with hugs and kisses from all the Dons and their families. He saw the O'Bannon mob in the corner watching the goings on. Danny excused himself and walked over to Mike O'Bannon. "Mike, I'm glad you could make it."

"Your uncle told me you were good, but I never expected you to be that good. I got a big club in Boston I think you would do good at."

"Great. I'll have my agent get a hold of you, and we'll set the date. I'd love to do it for you. Oh, come on. I want to show you something." Danny took his arm and walked him into the adjoining suite where the food was. You could smell the garlic blocks way. He took Mike over to a table set aside from the big Italian buffet. On it was all Irish food, Corn beef and cabbage and the works along with a keg of beer. Mike smiled and put his arm around Danny's shoulder. "Your uncle has class."

"He didn't want you have to eat all this Italian food. The garlic would stay with you for days."

Mike laughed and motioned his boys over. "Help yourselves, but don't drink too much." It was an order not to be disobeyed. Danny took him around and introduced him to Mary Ann. He could see that Mike was interested in her so he hugged her and whispered in her ear. She nodded and he left them alone and went back to the Don. The party heated up. Danny was asked by momma to do a couple of Italian songs. He did. He told Italian jokes and had them screaming. He did a beautiful Irish song that made them cry. Mike was tearing up too.

The party broke up around five am. Mary Ann came over and whispered in his ear. He nodded yes. She went over to Mike, took him by the hand, and led him to one of the bedrooms in Danny's suite. His bodyguards didn't know what to do. Danny took them into the suite and let them have the couches. He told them there were drinks at the bar, and to help themselves. Danny retired to the master bedroom. It had been a long day.

Chapter 26

The week flew by. Every night was like New Year's Eve. The crowds were coming out of the woodwork. He had standing ovations all through the shows. Mike O'Bannon came in and gave him a Rolex to thank him for turning him on to Mary Ann. They spent every night together and some afternoons. He was looking tired but happy. Chuck Eddy called and gave him his schedule. He had talked to Mike and they set a date for Blinstrums in Boston. He said he had to move some things around to do it. Danny knew Mike had put some pressure on him.

Carmen called every day. She was worried about her father. Things were heating up with the Canadian faction. Danny told her to be careful. He had talked to Don Angelo about it and the Don was looking into it.

Saturday night the Chez was packed to the rafters. Danny did two shows to get all the people in. After the second show, they were in the dressing room having a party. Lots of people, including a congressman and the state Senator with their entourages, were mixing with the Don's people. They wanted to give Danny a plaque and the key to the city. They were setting up a luncheon with him as the guest of honor. Danny agreed and the Don was overjoyed. His boy was going to get the key to the city that, for years, had tried to put him away. The party broke up. Danny, the Don and all the bodyguards went out the back door to the limo that was parked in the lot.

The bodyguards spread out looking around. There were a few employee cars still parked in the lot. As they got to the limo, Danny caught a movement out of the corner of his eye. A guy stood up and came around the back of one of the cars. He had a silenced pistol in his hand. The bodyguards were facing the wrong direction to see him. As he raised the pistol, Danny took the Don down with a cross body block. He heard the bullet pass his ear like an angry bee. He rolled off the Don, did a long forward dive roll and came up under the shooters hand. He grabbed the wrist and twisted. At the same time, he slammed the guy in the nose with the heel of his hand, driving the bones into the brain killing him instantly. He dropped like a stone. Danny was up and came over to the Don who was being helped up by one of his bodyguards. The other ones were scouring the parking lot looking for more trouble. Danny grabbed the Don. "Are you OK?"

The Don looked at his bodyguards, and then at Danny. "Thanks to you I am. How the hell did he get that close?"

"He was in their blind spot. I just happened to catch the movement. Better have the guys put him in the trunk and see if they recognize him." They didn't. They put the body in the trunk and left the parking lot for the Don's house. When they got there, Danny, John and the Don went into the house followed by Danny's guys. The other two guys drove away to get rid of the body. John motioned Danny over. They walked a little way away from the Don and Danny's guys.

"I don't know what the hell is going on, but there is only one guy I know who could do what you did tonight. You may have the Don's nephew's face but you have all the moves of Danny Di. Look at me." Danny looked at him and smiled. John grabbed him by both arms and looked into Danny's eyes. "You son-of-a-bitch. It is you. The face is different, but those are Danny's eyes."

Danny laughed. "Guilty, but keep it to yourself. The Don went through a lot of trouble to make Danny Di disappear."

"You know I'll do that. What do you think about that shooter? I didn't recognize him. Never saw him before."

"He's from out of town. Did the guys find anything on him that might tell us where he's from?"

"Nothing but cigarettes and matches." He gave Danny the matchbook.

Danny read the cover and said, "Son of a bitch." The matches were from a night club in Toronto Canada.

"What's up?"

"John, get the Don and meet me in the study."

John went to get the Don. Danny went to the study and put a call through to Ritchie. He was talking to him when the Don came into the study. Danny motioned him to sit. He finished talking to Ritchie and hung up. He turned to the Don. "That shooter was from Toronto. Ritchie tells me you've been trying to help him get some things straightened out. Obviously somebody doesn't want you to succeed."

The Don shook his head. "Well, thanks to you, I'm still here." He looked at John. "What the hell were you guys doing? What do I pay you for? To protect me. If it wasn't for Danny, I'd be laying in the morgue right now."

John shifted his weight from one foot to the other. "It's my fault Don Angelo. We checked the lot and didn't see anything suspicious, so we had our backs to the cars to watch you. It's a good thing Danny Di caught the movement."

The Don jumped like the chair was hot. Before he could say anything Danny said, "He knows Don, but it's OK. You know he won't say anything. Right now we have a problem. Did the shooter come alone or did he have a back up? John, get a hold of our guy at the airport in immigration, see how many Canadians flew here in the last week from Toronto. Get the names. Then check the outgoing flights, and see who's flying back and when. Look for two guys flying together. That should narrow it down some. He's going to know something's wrong when the first shooter doesn't show up. That may force the second one to try."

The Don smiled up at him. "You're always looking out for me. But you don't have to do this. We can handle it."

Danny put his hand on the Don's shoulder. "Somebody tried to kill you. That makes me angry. They'll try again. If we can find the other shooter we may be able to squeeze him and find out who sent him and why."

The Don nodded then turned to John. "Do it. Use any

means you have to, but find out. Keep me informed." John left.

Danny sat down next to the Don. "I'm going to have my guys guard you. They're the best next to me. I'll take John and a couple your guys to watch out for me while I'm here. I think you should stay close to home until we find out something."

"Good idea. I can do everything I have to from here. Danny, it's like old times, huh?"

"Yes it is. And I have to tell you, I miss it."

******

It didn't take John long to find out what they needed to know. In the last week, mostly families and some college kids came through the airport. Of all the people that came in from Toronto, two guys stood out. They were staying at the Majestic Hotel. That's what they told immigration. John checked and they were registered. Danny told them to get him in a hurry, before he split or made an attempt on the Don again. John took Louie and Georgio, two tough guys from the west side. They got to the hotel and John asked the desk clerk if Mr. Gibbons and Mr. Shaffer were in.

The desk clerk informed them that Mr. Gibbons had just gone up to his room. John got the number and they took the elevator to the sixth floor. The maid was cleaning rooms. John asked her if she had done room 618 yet. She said she hadn't.

"I want you to go to the door and knock. Tell him it's the maid. Then, get lost." He slipped a hundred dollar bill in her hand. She was smart enough to know what was coming down. She knocked on the door. A voice answered her. "Who is it.?" She said, "It's the maid. I've come to clean your room."

"OK, give me a minute," said the voice inside. John motioned her to leave and she needed no encouragement. Louie and Georgio stood in front of the door and watched the handle. As soon as they saw it turn, they slammed into the door, driving the guy behind it into the room and over a chair. They were on him in a flash. Louie twisted a gun out of his hand. Now, they knew they had the right guy.

John came into the room and shut the door. "Put him in the chair and tie him up. Use the cord from the drapes but don't gag him." When it was done they tossed the room and found two more pistols with silencers. John stood in front of the shooter. He was a natty, slim guy that could pass as a school teacher. "You want to tell me who sent you, or do you want the boys to help you remember?"

He looked at John. "Go fuck yourself."

John laughed. "Of course, you know your partner isn't coming back. He made a mistake. The same one you made by coming to Chicago. Now you're going to go to sleep for awhile and when you wake up you're going to talk your head off."

He nodded to Louie. Louie smacked him in the head with a leather sap knocking him cold. They gagged him, wrapped him in a sheet and carried him to the service elevator and down to the basement.

They waited until Georgio brought the car around. The shooter was put in the trunk and the car headed for Cicero. They went to a meat packing plant that was owned by the mob. It was after hours. They took the shooter out of the trunk, stripped him, tied his hands tight and hung him on a meet hook with his feet off the ground. Louie threw some water on him waking him up. The guy started to squirm and twist, only making the ropes on his wrists tighten and cause him pain. He looked down and saw he was naked.

John stood in front of him. "Welcome back. I told you that you would talk to us. Now I'm going to ask you again. Who sent you?"

The guy looked at him with hate in his eyes. "And I told you to go fuck yourself." He didn't see Georgio and Louie behind him with two cattle prods. They both touched him at the same time, causing his body to jerk and a scream come out of his mouth. He twisted and turned, but to no avail. They hit him again. Louie walked around in front of him. He touched the prod to his balls and pushed the button. The jolt made the guy scream louder. He looked like a puppet on a string.

John said, "I want to know who sent you. We can keep this

up for hours. Now make it easy on yourself and tell me." The guy said through clenched teeth, "Go...fuck...yourself." John nodded and Georgio put the prod behind the guy's ear at the same time Louie put his prod on his cock. The guy screamed and passed out from the pain. John said to Louie and Georgio, "Tough little mother fucker, isn't he? Let's see how good he does with heat. Louie, go get the acetylene torch and the tanks."

Louie went into the maintenance shop and came out with the torch and the tanks on a cart. He turned the tanks on and lit the torch with the flint lighter. The torched popped and a blue flame shot out of the end. Louie adjusted the flame so it was white hot. They woke up the shooter so he could see what was going to happen to him. His eyes saw the torch and he started to squirm. Louie came closer.

John asked him again. "I want to know who sent you. You tell me and you limp out of here. If you don't, then Louie is going to start by burning your cock and balls to a cinder. Believe me, that's going to hurt real bad."

The shooter kept his eyes on the torch. "Who are you shitting here? I tell you and I'm dead. You know that as well as I do."

Louie moved the torch closer and burned some pubic hair. The shooter let out a yell. John stepped in closer. "You got something to tell me?"

The shooter was sweating now. "All right, all right, I'll tell you. It was Big Louie Lacatta. He wants to take over Buffalo and Niagara Falls. Ritchie is in his way. He didn't like the fact that Don Angelo was going to help Ritchie. He thought with him dead, Ritchie would come around."

John motioned to Paulie to shut off the torch and step back. "Keep an eye on him, I'll be right back." He left and went into one of the offices and called Danny at the club. When he came on, John said, "It was Big Louie from Toronto. He wanted to stop the Don from helping Ritchie. He wants Buffalo and Niagara Falls."

Danny thought for a second. "If those shooters fail to show up in Toronto, Big Louie will know that they failed and maybe one of them talked. What's the second shooters name?"

"The name on the air line reservation is Gibbons. I don't know if that's his real name or not."

"What's he look like?"

"Around five ten, 180 pounds. Nice looking' guy. He's got a scar from a bullet on his left shoulder."

"Does it look like a sun burst?"

"Yeah, yeah, it does. You know this guy?"

I know him. His name is Tony Gracci. I was with him in Korea when he got that scar. He was with the Canadian Special Forces. He got hit with a tracer round. Burned worse than a garlic rubbed bullet. How bad did you mess him up before he told you?"

"Not bad. The cattle prods didn't work but the blow torch did the trick. Just burned off some pubic hair."

"Get him dressed and meet me at the Don's restaurant in the back room after my second show. Go in the back way."

"OK, will do." The line went dead. John walked back to where the shooter was still hanging. He looked at John. "I guess this is when you tell me how sorry you are and shoot me."

John smiled at him. "You must have an angel on your shoulder. We're going for a little ride. Friend of mine wants to talk to you." He motioned to Louie to cut him down.

Chapter 27

They were in the car driving to the Don's place. Danny asked the Ox and Weasel, "Do either of you know Tony Gracci from Toronto?"

They looked at each other and back at Danny. The Weasel answered for both of them. "Yeah, we know him. Why do you ask?"

"He's the second shooter that was sent to hit the Don. We're going to see him at the Don's place."

"You want us to take care of him for you?"

"We'll see. Depends on what he has to say. He already told John who sent him. It was Big Louie from Toronto."

Both guys jumped at the mention of his name. Tommy said in a flat cold voice, "That mother fucker is a piece of shit. He needs to be whacked. We wanted to hit him a couple of years ago, but Albert said not to."

The Weasel looked back at Danny. "Remember a couple of years ago in Toronto when a whole family was wiped out with a car bomb? Father, mother and four kids were executed. Big Louie ordered that. You know why? Because he couldn't fuck the guy's wife. She fluffed him off. He couldn't stand it. So a whole family died because she wouldn't let him dip his wick. That's the lowest. Tommy wanted to rip his cock off and stuff it down his throat. We're paid to kill people, but not women and kids."

Danny leaned forward. "You may still get the chance. If he makes another try at the Don, you have Carte Blanche. Take him out, any way you want." That got a smile out of both of them.

They arrived at the Don's place and went in the back way.

Tony was sitting in a chair. John and Louie were sitting on both sides of him. Tommy and Willie walked into the light and stood in front of Tony. Tony had to shade his eyes to see. He recognized the Ox. Before he could say anything, the Ox said, "Hey Tony. Looks like you got yourself in a world of shit, huh?"

Tony shrugged, "I guess so. You guys here to do the job on me?"

Danny answered from the shadows. "That all depends on what you have to say. I want to know why you thought you could come here and take the Don out. You know he has good protection."

Tony tried to see who was talking. "We thought with Danny Di gone it would be easy. But I guess we were wrong."

Danny smiled to himself. "I guess so. Did you know Danny Di?"

"Yeah, we served in Korea together. When I got shot he patched me up then carried me to an aide station. He was a tough mother fucker."

"Now, getting back to you. The question is, what do we do with you? You can't go back to Toronto. They'll kill you for not doing the job. So, I'll tell you what we're going to do. You're going to call Big Louie and tell him that your buddy fucked up and missed the Don and he's dead. You have to get lost for awhile, because we know who you are. You tell him you'll let him know where you are when things cool down. You'll come back to Toronto. Now, being you knew Danny Di, I'm going to give you a break. I'm going to send you to Freeport in the Grand Bahamas. We have interest in a couple of casinos there. You can be a bodyguard to one of the owners. The island is British owned, so you won't have any fear of anybody coming to hassle you. You have a family?"

"None that I care to hang around. I do have a girlfriend. We've been together a long time."

"OK, we'll see that she gets to Freeport to join you. Give John all the details. He'll see that she gets to you. One thing, Tony. Now you owe us a favor. One day we may collect on it."

Tony tried to see who was talking. "Why are you really doing this? We all know that our lives can be snuffed out at any time. That's the chance we take being in this business."

"Let's just say it's professional courtesy. Now you're going to go with John and the boys to a hotel while I make all the necessary arrangements. One more thing, Tony. Don't ever cross us, or you'll never leave that island."

He left Tony with John, walked around to the front of the restaurant and went in. The Don was sitting at the bar talking to some people. When they saw Danny, they came running over and started to pump his hand and slap his back. Danny was gracious and charming to the ladies. He wanted to talk to the Don, so he made his excuses, and went over to where the Don was sitting.

"Can we go to your office? I have something to discuss with you." Once in the office Danny told him what was going down. When the Don learned that it was Big Louie who ordered the hit, he was furious.

"That son-of-a-bitch! That big fat dago bastard. I'm the one who helped him out when he was having trouble with the Frenchies from Quebec. I'm the one who had the sit down, and got everything straightened out. And this is how he repays me! I want him dead."

Danny calmed him down. He told him about the shooter and what he wanted done with him. The Don looked at him like he was demented. "What the hell's the matter with you? The guy came to kill me, and you want me to put him in Freeport and protect him. What are you, stunad?"

"No, he knows everything about Big Louie. We do him this favor, then if we want Big Louie dead, we have him do it. He knows all about him and his habits."

"OK, but I didn't want you involved in any of this. You're a star now. I don't want anything to get in the way of that."

"I know, but I've been looking after you for so long, it's hard to stop. I'll stay in the background just in case."

The Don came around the desk and hugged him and kissed him on the cheek. "That's my boy. Come on, let's go to the house and have some pasta and a nice glass of wine." They gathered the bodyguards and left.

*****

The show closed at the Chez Paree to record breaking crowds. The party after the last show was the talk of the town. The Don rented an Italian restaurant for the night. There had to be two or three hundred people there including the Governor and his entourage. The wine and liquor flowed like water. Mike was there with Mary Ann. They were holding hands and talking.

Danny knew they wanted to talk to him and why. He walked over to where they were standing. "Mike, there's something I'd like you to do for me if you will."

Mike looked at him. "Anything, just ask."

"Good. I want you to take Mary Ann off my hands. She sings flat and she's driving me crazy."

Mary Ann looked at him and tears came into her eyes. She grabbed Danny and hugged him. "Oh Danny, that's the nicest thing anybody has ever said to me. How did you know?"

"Believe me it wasn't hard. Anybody looking at you two together would know you're in love."

Mike took his hand. "Thanks, Danny. We've been trying to figure out how to ask you. From now on, anything you want from me you got."

"Just take care of this girl and sort of keep an eye on the Don for me."

"That's easy and thanks again."

Mary Ann said to him, "I hate to leave you stuck with out a backup singer. I feel awful."

"Don't worry. I knew this was coming, so I got a replacement. You just have fun." He left the two of them hugging each other and walked over to where Johnny was standing. "When does that backup singer get here from Rochester?"

"She'll be in tomorrow afternoon. I'm going to be working with the girls until we leave for Detroit. You'll love this one. She has chops and looks. She'll do fine."

Danny slapped him on the back. "Great. Get the boys together and let's do some songs for these people." Johnny left to find Vinnie and Gus. Danny walked up to the small stage. He took the mic. "Hello. Is everybody having a good time?"

There were shouts and cheers. "I thought I would do a couple numbers for you, if that's alright." There were more cheers and encouragement from the crowd. Danny did an hour of songs and requests. The party lasted until four in the morning.

On the way back to the hotel Danny was thinking to himself, *"How lucky can one guy get? I got a hit record, I'm booked in the best night clubs in the country, and I'm getting more ass than a toilet seat. Yeah, life is good. All Danny Di had to look forward to was a bullet behind the ear or prison time. Thanks to Carmen I'm going to be a big star!"*

Danny slept in until one o'clock in the afternoon. He ordered room service, showered and shaved. Johnny called and told him he was on his way to the airport to pick up Rosalie, the back up singer. Danny told him to bring her by when he got back. He called Carmen to fill her in on what was happening. "I think you should come to Detroit with me. Be good for you to get out of Buffalo and good for me too."

There was a chuckle from the other end of the phone line. "Does this mean you miss me? I'll have to check my calendar and see if I can make it."

Danny laughed. "You know what I'll do with that calendar. I'll pick you up at the airport when you get there. The place I'm working is called The Rooster Tail. It has something to do with boats."

"OK, I'll make reservations. What day do you want me to get there?"

"Three days from now. Let me know the time you're arriving and the flight number."

"Will do. Gotta run. My father is taking Velvet and me to lunch. I'll call you soon." And she was gone.

Danny called the Don and talked to him for awhile. The Don was setting things up for him in Detroit through the Purple

Gang. He was to be wined and dined. The club was adding musicians for him, plus billboards and TV spots were going to be running. Danny told him he would drop by later and have dinner with the two of them. He called down to the desk to get his messages. There were quite a few so he sent John down to get them. When he came back Danny went through the messages. One was from Flame.

He called her right away. She answered the phone and when she heard his voice she broke into tears and sobbed. Danny asked her, "What's wrong? Why are you crying?"

She calmed herself down to talk to him. "I'm in Peoria working the Stage Door. The owner and his goons are passing me around like a football. I'm trapped. I can't get out. They lock me up during the day. I'm fed food from the kitchen. I do my shows and have to mix, and they're making me fuck their friends and anybody that wants me. Oh, Danny. I don't know what to do."

Danny felt a cold rage working its way inside him. "You just hang on sweetheart. I'll handle it. Just go on like nothing's wrong. Can you do that?"

"Yes, as long as I know you're coming."

"I'll be there. Bye for now." He hung up and stormed around the suite. He called John in. "I want you to get the limo ready. I'm going to need some muscle. Bad boys. We'll take your guys along with my bodyguards."

"What's up?"

"Do you know a place in Peoria called the Stage Door?"

"Yeah, a high end strip joint. The owner is a piece of shit. Why?"

"He's got a good friend of mine hooking for him against her will. I want to bust his ass and put him out of business. Get the boys ready and meet me down stairs in half an hour." John left and Danny called the Don. "I have to take care of something, so I'll miss dinner. I'll tell you about it tomorrow."

"No, you'll tell me now."

"OK, a friend of mine is working in Peoria at the Stage Door. She's in trouble. I have to go help her."

"I got people there that can take care of it for you. Why do you have to go?"

"It's a personal thing."

"OK, I'll call some friends of mine there and have them meet you. You be careful. Call me when you get there and tell me where to send the boys. I take it you want muscle?"

"Yeah, I'll call you." He hung up and changed clothes. He put on an old jacket and a slouched hat. Once downstairs, he got the guys together outside next to the limo. "We're going to Peoria to take a joint apart. I want the owner. He's mine. The rest you can have. Let's go."

They got in and headed for Peoria. It was a four hour drive and the closer they got, the angrier Danny became. John knew where the club was, so they stopped two blocks away. Danny called the Don and told him where they were. Danny was told to wait and the toughs would be sent to him. Ten minutes later a car pulled up and five rough looking guys got out. Danny motioned them over. "We're going to take the Stage Door apart. I want you guys to go in the back door, and knock the hell out of anybody you see. We'll go in the front door. I want the owner. Bust the joint apart and leave nothing standing. You got that?"

The meanest looking tough said, "It'll be a pleasure. He's had it coming for a long time. The telephone wires are in a box by the back door. We'll rip them out before we go in. He's probably got five or six wanna-be wise guys in there with him. They play cards, drink, and ball the strippers during the day before the club opens."

Danny's eyes got hard. He wanted to kill. "Give us ten minutes and come in." They got in the limo and headed for the club. They parked across the street and got out. Danny looked the place over. He motioned for them to cross the street. Once in front of the door he tried the handle. It was locked. He motioned for Tommy, the Ox, to kick it in.

Tommy stood back and raised his big leg. On Danny's signal he hit the door and it flew inwards. They were all inside in a second. There were six guys seated around a table playing cards.

The bartender was washing glasses. They froze when they saw Danny and his crew. Before they could say anything, the back door flew in and the five toughs came in. Danny looked at the six guys. "Which one of you is the owner?"

The guys looked at each other and didn't respond. Danny signaled his nearest, tough guy. With one motion, he slapped one of the six guys in the head hard enough to knock him off the chair.

"I'll ask you just one more time. Which one of you is the owner?"

The guy got up off the floor. "He's upstairs in room 22." Danny was up the stairs in a flash. Tommy and the Weasel had to run to keep up with him. Danny got to the door of room 22 and hit it with his shoulder. The door broke apart and he was in the room. There was a guy on top of Flame. She was naked and her hands were tied to the bed post. The guy was banging her and calling her filthy names.

When he heard the door give way he looked up. Danny was right there. He grabbed him by the hair and jerked him off of Flame. He hit him hard in the jaw, again and again. The guy started to sag. Danny wouldn't let him. He pushed him against the wall and held him with one hand while the right hand smashed his face into oblivion. He stepped back and kicked him hard between the legs. Once. Twice. He was ruthless. Tommy came around and grabbed him.

"Easy, Danny. We got him. You take care of the girl. We got this son-of-a-bitch."

Danny came out of his fog. He ran over to Flame and untied her. She was sobbing and holding on to him for all she was worth. She couldn't talk. Danny held her and soothed her. He motioned to Tommy. "Throw that bastard over the railing. Then, tear this place apart, starting with those assholes downstairs. I want nothing standing." Tommy did as he was told.

All the guys down stairs saw was the owner flying out the door and over the railing. He hit the floor with a sickening thud. Tommy and the Weasel came out. "Tear this fucking place apart."

Danny was rocking Flame and talking to her. "It's over

sweetheart. Nobody is ever going to hurt you again. I promise. We're getting out of here and I'm taking you back to Chicago. You'll be safe there. He could hear screams and things smashing. He covered her ears. He looked up and three girls were standing there. They were huddled together with fear written on their faces. Danny smiled at them. "It's all right girls. The cavalry has come to your rescue. Get your things together. You're going with us." They squealed and ran down the hall to get their things. Danny stood Flame up. "Let's get you dressed sweetheart. Where are your things?"

She took a deep breath. "I'll get ready, but you stay right here. I don't want to wake up and find this was all a dream."

She got dressed and threw her things in a suitcase. When she was ready, Danny took her hand and they went out the door. He looked down. The place was a shambles. The six guys were lying on the floor. There was blood everywhere. The owner was still lying where he landed. Danny took the girls down the stairs. He motioned for John to come over.

"Take the girls out to the limo. We'll be out in a minute." Flame didn't want to leave him, but he made her go. Once they were out side Danny turned to the five toughs. "You did a good job. I see you left the bartender standing"

The mean one said, "He had nothing to do with all this. He's just a working stiff. We figured maybe you would want him around to tell the law what happened here. You know... the motorcycle gang that came in and wrecked the place."

Danny smiled, "Good thinking." He motioned the bartender over. "Here's a grand. You know what to say. Now get lost and forget you ever saw us. These guys know you, so you won't be hard to find. Understand?"

"Yes, sir. I understand." He ran out the back door. Danny walked over to where the owner was lying. He was barely breathing. He rolled him on his back with his foot. He reached in his pocket and took out a pocket knife and opened it. "So, you like to fuck girls against their wills. This time my friend, you fucked the wrong girl."

He grabbed his cock and balls in his hand and cut them off with the knife. "You'll never do that again you son-of-a-bitch." He threw the cock and balls over the bar. They stuck to the bar mirror leaving a bloody trail as they slid down.

The bodyguards looked at him with new respect. Danny walked out the door and over to the limo. They all got in and headed back for Chicago. Flame wouldn't let go of him. The other girls were talking it up with the bodyguards. Danny said, "When we get back to Chicago, you'll stay with me at the hotel. I'll make arrangements for the girls to stay in rooms on the same floor. The Don has some good clubs you girls can work and you'll be under his protection. Nobody will ever mess with you again."

Flame looked up at him. "I have to tell you something. When you came through that door, it was the greatest moment of my life. Now, I know how the fairy princess felt when her knight in shining armor saved her." She reached up and pulled his head down and gave him a kiss.

Chapter 28

They were sitting up in bed watching the news. It was showing pictures of the Stage Door. The announcer was saying, "Yesterday, a gang of motorcyclists came into this club. According to the bartender, they didn't like the service they were given or the way they were treated. They decided to break up the place. They put six men, who were in the club at the time, in the hospital in critical condition. The owner of the club, Joseph Bonarro, is in the intensive care unit at the hospital. His condition is listed as very serious. The police are investigating, but so far have not come up with anything. We will keep you posted on this story as it breaks."

Danny turned the TV off. The phone rang. It was the Don. "I see you got done what you went there for. How did the local guys turn out?"

"Just fine Don. They were very professional. Now I have to ask a favor. The reason I went to Peoria was to rescue one of the best exotic dancers in the country. I have her here with me. She's special to me and I want you to book her in your clubs and take care of her for me."

He heard the Don chuckle. "I change your face, make you a star, but you still have Danny Di's sense of values. Help the little guy. That's what I always loved about you. When can I meet this charming lady?"

"How about lunch today here at the hotel? Say one o'clock."

"I'll be there. I'll make a couple of calls in the meantime."

"Thanks Don, see you at one." Danny turned to Flame. "Little lady, you're going to meet my uncle. So, get yourself dressed and be ready to go at one. I have to go down the hall to check the new back up singer. I'll be back shortly." He kissed her and left. He knocked on Johnny's door and it was opened by a tall beautiful black haired lady. She just stood there and looked at him. Her eyes were jet black. Danny looked right back at her running his eyes up and down her body. She actually blushed. "You must be Danny."

"And you must be Rosalie. Nice to meet you. Has Johnny gone over the songs and dance routines with you?"

"Yes. I've got most of the songs down and the other girls are helping me out with the dance routines."

Danny stepped into the room. Johnny was at the piano. "She's doing great Danny. She catches on real fast. I thought the next couple of days we could run through them with you. Let her get the feel."

"I don't see why not. We got the time. How about you doing a number for me, so I can hear you?"

"Sure, pick one Johnny." Johnny picked a torch song. She sang the hell out of it. Danny was impressed. "You got some good chops. You'll do just fine." He turned to Johnny. "I have some business today. Let's get together tonight and go over a few things. Have the other girls in my suite by eight o'clock. See you both then."

He turned and left. Roslalie stood looking at the door. "He sure is a handsome son of a gun." Johnny just smiled.

Danny picked Flame up and they went down to the hotel restaurant. They sat at table in the corner so Danny could take in the whole room….a habit from the old days. The Don arrived promptly at one. John walked in first. He saw Danny and waved behind him. The Don entered and headed for Danny's table. Danny stood up and gave him a hug.

The Don stood back and looked at Flame. "I can see why you went to get her." He took Flame's hand and kissed it. "Welcome to Chicago." He sat next to her, but kept his eyes on her. "If you can dance half as good as you look, I'll make you a star, my dear."

Flame gave him a look that would make most guys come in their pants. "If you're half as good as Danny says you are, I'll make you a fortune. I'll bet my tits on it."

The Don threw back his head and laughed. He turned to Danny. "I like this girl. I'll take good care of her, don't you worry. I've made some calls and I have her booked in Toledo at the Akuaku room. She's working with a great comedy team, Carme and Paul. She'll do real good there. It's a class club. She flies out tomorrow morning and opens on Monday. I'll have John pick her up and take her to the airport."

Danny reached out and laid a hand on his shoulder. "I can't thank you enough. She's just been through a rough time."

The Don nodded. "Flame, will you excuse Danny and me for just a minute?"

"OK, but don't go too far." She gave him her dazzling smile. The Don motioned Danny aside. When they were out of ear shot he said, "You took a hell of a chance going to Peoria and wrecking that joint. What if somebody recognized you? You could have blown a hell of a thing."

"I wore a slouched hat so nobody could see my face. The guy I beat the shit out of, never saw anything but my fist, and he won't be around long enough to identify me. The bartender was so scared that he never looked at anybody. Besides, the guys there know where he lives so he won't be doing any talking. And who would suspect a nice looking guy like me with a hit record to do something like that?"

The Don smiled and thought to himself. "*Yeah, who?*"

They went back to the table and had lunch. After lunch Danny and Flame went upstairs and, for two hours, made love. Danny couldn't get enough of her. They finally fell asleep from exhaustion. After waking at six, they ordered room service, and had a nice leisurely dinner. At seven o'clock Johnny arrived with the girls. He introduced everyone to Flame and got to work. Flame was amazed at how Danny handled the rehearsal. It was a far cry from the Plush Horse. He had come a long way. The girls were wonderful. They sang and danced and once in a while stopped to show Rosalie a step or a vocal part.

After two hard hours, Danny called a halt. "You girls are great. Roz is catching on quick. By the time we get to Detroit we'll have it nailed down. Now, how about a snack?"

The girls were hungry. Danny called room service and ordered a bunch of stuff. When it arrived they had an impromptu party. It broke up at midnight. Danny and Flame stood on the balcony looking out at Chicago. She had her arm around Danny's waist. "I'm going to miss you. You know that, don't you?"

"I know, but think of it this way. Don Angelo is going to make you a star. That means you'll work the top supper clubs in the country. We'll be crossing paths lots of times. And sometimes when you're not working, you can come with me."

"I like the way you think my man. Now come inside. I want to have a night to remember.

Chapter 29

Flame left in the morning. The Don sent the other girls to a club in Joliette. Danny went to the Don's house. Today was the day he would get the key to the city. The Mayor and City Council would be there to present it to him. Every time the Don thought about it, he would laugh to himself. *If they only knew. Danny was the one who killed the Mayor's business partner.* He always thought that the Mayor had something to do with it. He stepped into a real sweet deal with his partner gone. The Don was overjoyed. There he would be, the biggest crime boss in Chicago and surrounding areas hobnobbing with the Mayor.

The Don was waiting for him. "We got to be at city hall at two o'clock. They're having lunch, then the award. Dress up, look nice, and get one of your girls to go with you as arm candy. This is a big day. I never thought it would happen. Not in my lifetime. My Danny is getting the key to the city, and I didn't have to pay for it or call in any markers. It's totally legit."

Danny smiled at him. This was his day, not mine, he thought. But what the hell. He owed a lot to the Don. Let him enjoy it. "You're right. Trust me, I'll be adorable." He put his arm around the Don's shoulder and walked him into the kitchen. Momma was making espresso coffee and had fresh biscotti on the table. She hugged him and kissed him on the cheek.

"You make me so proud. Sit. Have some biscotti and espresso. I made them special for you."

They chatted and laughed for an hour. Finally, the Don said, "You better go to the hotel and get ready. I'll pick you up at one fifteen."

Danny said his goodbyes and left. When he got to the hotel he stopped at Rosalie's door and knocked. She opened the door and was surprised to see Danny standing there. "Well, this is a surprise."

Danny laughed. "Yeah I guess it is. The reason I'm here is, I'm getting the key to the city today and I thought you would enjoy it. Would you like to go with me?"

"I would love to. What time should I be ready?"

"We leave at one fifteen. Wear something you think would fit the occasion."

"You got it. I'll be in your suite at one o'clock."

"Good, see you then." Danny went to his room to get ready.

At one o'clock sharp there was a knock on the door. Danny opened it and there stood Rosalie. She was wearing a black outfit that showed off her body without being suggestive. He thought to himself, *"Who's going to be watching me with her standing there?"* He regained his composure. "You look great. The Don will be here in fifteen minutes. We'll go down to the bar and wait for him. Maybe have a little taste."

Tommy and the Weasel were waiting in the hall. They went to the bar and had a quick drink. At exactly one fifteen the Don's limo pulled up. They got in. Rosalie was on one side of the Don and Danny on the other.

He looked at Rosalie. "My Danny always finds the most beautiful girls around. I haven't seen you before, my dear." He turned to Danny. "Where have you been hiding this lady?'

"This is Rosalie. She's my new backup singer from Rochester."

The Don took her hand and kissed it. "Welcome to our little family. When we get to city hall, you sit next to me. The Mr. Key to the City Guy will be up on the podium, with all the big city ass holes." He roared with laughter. In fact everybody did. When they got to city hall, they went inside. The meeting hall was decorated with flags and streamers. The Don's table was right up front. He sat down with Rosalie and both their bodyguards.

Danny was called up to the dais by the Mayor who shook

hands and was babbling like an idiot. The Mayor was so excited, Danny thought he was going to wet himself like a puppy does when it gets excited. He sat Danny down next to him. It was the usual format with the benediction, the pledge of allegiance, and the Mayor's welcoming speech followed by lunch.

Before the dessert came, the back of the room started to fill up with TV cameras. The Mayor stood up and tapped his knife on his water glass for attention. The room quieted down. He walked around the dais to the microphone in front.

"Ladies and gentlemen, as you know, we are here to honor one of Chicago's sons, who has brought fame to this city. It is my pleasure to present to you a man, who is not only a big star but a man who loves this city the way we all do. Danny Angel."

There was a thunderous round of applause as Danny came around the dais and stood next to the Mayor. The Mayor picked up a big gold key with red white and blue ribbons hanging from it. He turned to Danny. "It is with great honor I give you the key to this great city of Chicago." He handed Danny the key. Danny took it and held it up for all to see. The applause was deafening. Danny stepped to the microphone. The crowd grew quite.

"Ladies and gentlemen, thank you for honoring me with this wonderful key to the city. The honor does not belong to me alone. I had someone who believed in me, and through his hard work and diligence, made me a star. Without him, I would still be singing on street corners and working Italian weddings. My uncle, Guiseppe Angelo."

The Don sat straight up in his chair with his mouth open. Tears formed in his eyes. Danny continued. "So if you don't mind, I'd like to share it with him."

The crowd went wild. Danny came down the steps and handed the key to the Don. The Don took it and hugged Danny and kissed him on both cheeks. There were tears all around. Danny looked down at Rosalie, she had tears running down her face. She looked at Danny and mouthed, "That was wonderful."

It took a good hour before they were back in the limo heading for the Don's house. The Don had a surprise for Danny when they got there. The whole family was there plus friends to help him celebrate. The Don had catered the food from his restaurant. Momma was mumbling that she could have done better. Johnny, Gus, and Vinnie were set up in a corner playing Italian music. Rosalie felt right at home. She was speaking Italian to the old ladies and the mustache Pete's. She helped momma set things up. Momma was jabbering to her in Italian, they laughed and carried on. The food, the wine, the pastries, the music and the laughter were everything a true Italian could have wanted.

Danny walked over to the band, took the microphone and started singing in Italian. Everybody gathered around. He was having fun. Rosalie came over and stood next to him and was singing harmony to the song he was singing. Their voices were beautiful together. The family went wild. Danny backed off and let Rosalie sing a couple songs on her own. She had a great quality to her voice and she moved like a dream. They did a couple more songs together then danced to a few songs. The party lasted until eleven o'clock.

Danny, Rosalie, Tommy, and the Weasel took the Don's limo back to the hotel. They went up to Danny's suite. The boys went to their rooms leaving Danny and Rosalie alone. She sat on the couch and crossed her legs.

"I like your family. Reminds me of mine back in Rochester."

Danny got two glasses of wine, gave her one and sat across from her. "I didn't know you spoke Italian. What's your family's name?"

She sipped her wine then said, "Torrano. My uncle is Pat Torrano."

Danny knew the family. Pat was the Capo of Rochester. Danny Di knew him, but not Danny Angel. He played dumb. "I don't think I know your family, but I've been away in Italy for a long time. I liked the way you sang with me. Our voices sound good together. How would you like to do a couple numbers with me in the show?"

She sat up straight. "You mean it? I'd love to."

"Good. I'll get with Johnny and have him write something for us. He knows our ranges so I'll just let him do his thing." He got up and came over and sat next to her.

She turned and looked at him with that look of, (I guess I'll have to ball you for the part). Danny caught the look, sat back and smiled. "I know what you're thinking, and no, you don't have to do anything for it."

She breathed a sigh of relief. "Thank goodness. I've had my share of POGO's (put out or get out). We'll just play it by ear. Shall we?"

"Good idea. Come on, I'll walk you home. We have a busy day tomorrow." She got up and they headed for the door. They stopped in front of her door. She gave Danny a kiss on the cheek and was gone. On the way back to his room he thought, *"A nice Italian girl."*

Chapter 30

They got to Detroit and checked into the hotel. Johnny and the girls went to the club to set up and rehearse the band. Danny didn't have to go. Johnny would take care of everything. He'd do a sound check before he went to pick Carmen up at the airport. The only thing he had to do was call Louie Caggini, the Capo of Detroit. The Don had set it up. He wanted to make sure Louie and his fiends had complimentary tickets for Danny's show, as well as, the guys from Canada.

After making the call, he got ready to go get Carmen. The Ox and the Weasel were waiting for him. The limo was down stairs waiting. They got off the elevator. Danny hadn't taken three steps when a lady yelled out, "My God. It's Danny Angel." She came running over. That started a flood. The Ox and the Weasel had their hands full. Danny was gracious and signed whatever they had. He even signed one girl's sweater on her chest. They were big. He could have written a small novel on them. They got to the limo and made their escape.

The Ox said to Danny, "I don't think you should go into the airport. If they see you, we may never get to the plane. Those women can get vicious. The Weasel and I don't want to have to pop anyone, especially broads."

Danny thought for a minute. "You're right. The Weasel will stay with me, and you can go get Carmen. I guess we can expect this from now on. We may have to get some local help to control the crowds."

They got to the airport and the Ox went to get Carmen. When she came out she was smiling. Danny got out to meet her and they kissed long and hard. They finally broke apart.

"The Ox tells me that you were mobbed back at the hotel. That's good. You're being recognized."

"I don't know if I like it. I've always been in the shadows. It's going to take some getting used to."

"Yeah, I guess so." They got in the limo and headed back to the hotel. They were close together and Carmen had her hand on the inside of his leg. She whispered in his ear, "I have something special I brought for you."

"Oh, yeah. What is it?"

She squeezed him harder. "I'm sitting on it."

"Well, not for long. Get ready for a marathon. I'm more than ready"

They got to the hotel and there were women everywhere. Danny told the Ox, "Drive around back and we'll go through the kitchen."

They got out and made their way to the room with no mishaps. Once inside, they went at each other like animals. They did everything until they were exhausted. They were lying on the bed covered with perspiration. Carmen rolled towards him. "That was worth waiting for. Let's take a short nap, shower and order some food." That's what they did.

They arrived at the club early so Danny could get a sound check. The dressing room had a bar, two couches, an adjoining shower, and all the amenities awarded to a star. One door led out to a small patio with tables and chairs for outside dining. The view was overlooking the river into Canada.

Danny got dressed while Carmen went out front to make sure that the Capo's and the other wise guys were well taken care of. Danny was just tying his tie when the owner and his son came in to greet him. The owner was a neat well dressed man with an easy smile. His son was like an ex college jock, going to fat and spoiled. Danny took an instant dislike to him. They introduced themselves as John and his son, Terry. John told him they were having a big party after the second show. The press and friends were all invited. Danny thanked him and they left.

The shows were both sold out and Danny tipped them over at both shows. They were screaming for more. After the second show, Danny showered and put on clean clothes. When he got out front, the party was in full swing. They started to applaud and whistle as he walked in. Danny was all over the place, shaking hands and signing programs. He saw Carmen talking to the Capo and made his way over. Louie gave him a big hug. "You were absolutely wonderful. Don Angelo didn't tell me you were that good."

"He likes to surprise people."

"Well, he sure surprised me. You're going to do great here and in Canada. A lot of people from this side will go over to see you while you're there. Come on. Let me introduce you to the owners of the Elmwood Casino where you'll be working." Danny kissed Carmen and was led away.

Carmen watched them go and was turning toward the bar when Terry came up and grabbed her arm. He was drunk. He came close to her. "I haven't seen you around here before. Come on, let's get a drink and go to my place." Carmen pulled her arm free. "I don't know who you are, but I belong to Danny and he wouldn't like the fact that you're being rude to his girl."

Terry stood back and looked down at her. "Well, fuck him. I pay him, so I can do what I want. This is my club." He grabbed her again. He had her pinned close to him. Before he could do anything, he was lifted up from behind by the Ox. The look on the Ox's face was terrible. He walked him through a door, and the last thing Carmen saw before the door closed, was the Ox slamming him into the wall.

She went to find Danny and told him what happened. Danny was livid. He grabbed her and they went out the door. The Ox was standing over Terry. He was on the floor blubbering. Danny knelt down next to him. He grabbed his hair so Terry could see him. "Now, see what you did? You made my man mad. You should know better than to fool around with somebody else's girl friend. You're lucky it wasn't me who saw you, or you would be on your way to the hospital now. I don't want any more of this bull shit. Do I make myself clear?" Terry nodded his head and Danny let go. He took Carmen and the Ox back to the party.

"Thanks Ox. I owe you. Keep an eye on her." The Ox nodded. Danny went back to being Mr. Nice guy.

The party broke up around two in the morning. While Carmen was talking to Rosalie, he went back to his dressing room. He opened the door to the patio and stood in the darkness looking across the river. A sound caught his attention. He felt someone coming up behind him. He dropped down and spun to his left on his heel.

A blackjack whistled through the air where his head would have been. The momentum carried the attacker past him. He hit the railing. Danny heard a whoosh as the air went out of him. His legs were dangling in front of him. He stood up, grabbed the legs and threw him over into the river. It was a good ninety feet to the water. Danny watched as Terry hit the water with a splash. He didn't bother to see if he made it or not. He went back inside, locked the door and went to find Carmen. They all went back to the hotel and had a late night drink in Danny's suite.

They were lying in bed when Danny told her what happened. Carmen sat up. "Do you think he's dead?"

"I don't know, nor do I care. He deserved what he got. Hell, we were all at the party. I didn't see anything, did you?"

Carmen started to laugh. "Not me. We'll have to wait to get the news in a few hours. Until then, I have some plans for you. She ducked under the sheets. Danny let out a sigh. "I love your plans."

Chapter 31

They were sitting at the table having coffee in the suite when the news came on. The announcer was standing in front of the club. "Late last night, the manager of the Rooster Tail, Terry Ryan, fell off the terrace and into the river. Luckily, a fishing boat going by heard him hit the water. They got to him very quickly, and called in a police helicopter and boats. He was very fortunate that someone was in the vicinity. The hospital is reporting that he has numerous broken bones and a bad concussion. After checking his blood level it was determined that he was overly intoxicated. His father Pat Ryan, the owner of the Rooster Tail said that his son has had a drinking problem and over did it at a party for their star performer, Danny Angel. We'll update you on his condition at the six o'clock news."

Danny switched off the TV. "He got what he deserved. Maybe this will teach him a lesson, but I doubt it."

Carmen smiled at him. "You should have seen the Ox. He was furious. I thought he was going to kill him."

"He might have, if I hadn't gone out there. Send him some flowers from us. Make it a big one so he'll think about what he tried to do."

Carmen went to get a phone book. The phone rang. It was Louie. "You were terrific last night. The boys across the river can't wait for you to play their club. They're going to go all out for you. By the way, they want you to do a commercial for Canadian Club Whiskey. Their big distributorship is in Windsor. It's big money. Who do they have to contact?"

"She's here with me. You met her last night. My lady,

Carmen. She handles all those things for me."

"Good. How about I pick you up at one o'clock and we go to Canada for lunch and get it settled?"

"OK. We'll be ready. See you."

He hung up as Carmen walked back into the room. "That was Louie. They want me to do a commercial for Canadian Club Whiskey. He said it's big money. He's going to pick us up at one o'clock to go over to Canada, have lunch and talk it over. I told him you handle all that for me."

"I'll take care of it for you, big boy. I know how to negotiate. I learned it from my father. The residuals should be great, but getting that handsome face of yours plastered all over Canada and the U.S. is worth a great deal more."

"Well, maybe they'll throw in a case or two of booze. We could have a hell of a party."

"All in good time. First the commercial. Then we can talk about other clubs in Canada."

Louie picked them up and drove them into Canada to the offices of Canadian Club Whiskey. The conference room was full of executives. Carmen was wonderful. She charmed the pants off of them. She made a great deal for Danny. He would do the commercial while he worked the Elmwood Casino. When the meeting was over, Carmen had sewn up not only Canadian Club Whiskey, but commercials for Pabst Blue Ribbon Beer. It was a million dollar deal.

Danny just sat there and marveled at the way she worked. Her father had taught her well. When it was over and the contracts were signed, the CEO asked Carmen if she would like to work for them. She laughed and told them she appreciated the offer, but Danny was a handful and needed constant attention with all offers coming in from record companies, movies, and night club engagements. They said their goodbyes.

On the way back to Detroit, Louie said to Carmen, "Lady, you got balls as big as grapefruits. I thought you were only going to talk about the whiskey deal. How the hell did you know they had Pabst beer too?"

Carmen smiled, "I called my dad. He does business with the beer companies in and around Toronto and western New York. He called the head man at Pabst and found out that they are a subsidiary of Canadian Whiskey. So, it was easy to tie them together. Of course, a good word from my father didn't hurt."

Danny started to laugh. "You're too much babe. I do believe you could sell a hot plate to an Arab."

"When you have a hot product, it's easy to sell it. And my boy, you are a hot product." She reached over and squeezed Ninja lying along the inside of his leg.

The rest of the contract at the Rooster Tail went great. Every night was standing room only. Rosalie was wonderful. Her numbers with Danny were outstanding and brought the crowds to their feet. Closing night was a mad house. They were oversold, so Danny did an extra show for them. Then came a party for the staff. Tearful goodbyes came from waiters, waitresses and bar tenders who loved his show and, of course, made a lot of money in tips with him performing there.

Back at the hotel Danny had a party in the suite for his people. There were a few wise guys there as well. He called Carmen and Rosalie over to a corner. "I have something I want to discuss with you two. I've been thinking about this for awhile and I would like to have Rosalie open for me. I called Chuck Eddy. He can place Chapter One with a guy from Vegas called Billy Kaye. Billy has a group called The Kings Four. He wants to go out on his own. Chuck said he would add a girl he knows from Vegas and they would back Billy at the Frontier. What do you think?"

Carmen turned to look at Rosalie who was standing there with her mouth open in complete shock. "I think that is one hell of an idea. When do you want to make the change?"

"Right after we finish the Elmwood Casino. That will give the girls a chance to rehearse with Billy. Chuck will fly him up here so they can learn his act. They will open at the Frontier. The Jewish guys from Toledo are handling him." He turned to Rosalie. "Well, what do you think?"

She finally got over the shock and jumped in his arms and

hugged him. "What do I think? I think it is just wonderful and I won't let you down. But what songs will I be singing?"

"I've already discussed this with Johnny. We'll pick out some good songs and he'll write the arrangements for you. All you have to do is sing them."

"That I can do. Thank you, Danny. Can I call my mother and tell her? She will be so happy."

"Sure go on. Tell her hello from Carmen and me." She left. Carmen looked at him. "You know something? You're a pretty nice guy. When this party is over I want to reward you with something you really like." She smacked her lips and walked back to the party.

Chapter 32

Big Louie was pacing around his office. His face was wet with sweat. His clothes hung on his big frame but couldn't hide the fat he carried around. Expensive clothes on him were a waste of money, but he didn't care. He was angry and was shouting at the wise guys that were sitting around his office. "What the fuck do I pay you guys for? How difficult is it to take out one guy? Ritchie has been a thorn in my side for fucking years. I want him dead. Now, you tell me. Why is he still breathing and not sleeping with the fishes?"

A natty little guy in a thousand dollar suite said, "We can't get close to him. He's well protected and doesn't have a regular routine. He changes all the time. Some times he let's it be known that he is going to be someplace at a certain time, but shows up somewhere else."

"I'm surrounded by fucking idiots. I send two of my best guys to take out Don Angelo. One gets killed, and the other is hiding out until things cool down. Do I have to call in a shooter from somewhere else to do this simple job? Now I want you to get together and come up with some kind of a plan to get rid of Ritchie. We got people in Niagara Falls and Buffalo who can help keep track of him. Get a hold of some one in his organization and squeeze him. I don't care how the fuck you do it, but get it done. Do I make my self clear?"

They all nodded. A mean looking guy leaning up against the wall said, "There's one way we can get him to come to us. His daughter. He's nuts about her and she's his only child. We snatch her, and set up a meet. He comes, we kill him, and it's over."

Big Louie looked hard at him. This was his number one hit man since Tony left. His name was Alfonzo. Not only was he a stone killer, he was smart. "OK, so we snatch the daughter. You know he's not going to come alone. He'll have a fucking army with him."

"We tell him to come with just two guys. We set the meet out in the open, at a place of my choosing. I can pop him with a sniper rifle from a good half mile away and take out the other two in the confusion."

Big Louie had no doubts about that. The guy was a crack shot with no feelings whatsoever. "OK, so we take him out. What about the daughter?"

Alfonzo looked at him with those cold eyes. "We won't need her anymore. Do what you want with her. I hear she's a real knock out. Put her in one of your whore houses up north or just kill her and leave her with Ritchie. It's up to you."

All eyes in the room turned to Alfonzo. Now they knew why everyone in the business called him Alf the Icier. He had nothing but ice water in his veins. Big Louie smiled. That's why he hired him. "OK, you guys. Get on it. But this time, I want results. No fucking around. You keep me posted on everything. Meantime you do what Alf says. It's his baby. Now get out of here."

They got up and left. Once outside Alf stopped them. "I want to know all her habits. Where she is now, where she goes, when she goes. Call our people in Buffalo and tell them to get on it. I want the information by tonight."

The little natty guy who looked like Mr. Peepers spoke up. "I do believe we have a guy in their organization. A smalltime hood. He's one of Ritchie's soldiers. I can call him and find out about the daughter."

"Good, do it and let me know. I'll be at Mama Vivie's. Call me there."

They split up and the natty little guy, whose name was Ignacio, went into his office. He was the banker. Whatever money came in, went through him. He picked up the phone and asked the operator to get him a number in Buffalo. He waited. When a guy answered he said, "Would you tell Johnny to call his father." He hung up the phone and waited. That was the code he used to contact the mole. A half hour later his phone rang. Ignacio answered it. It was the mole. "Are you on a clean line?"

"What do you think, I'm stupid.? Of course, it's a clean line. What can I do for you?"

"I need to know everything about Ritchie's daughter. Where she goes, her routines, anything that can help me get a profile on her."

"You mean Carmen? Yeah, I can do that. What's up?"

"You don't need to know that right now. Just get me the info by tonight."

"OK, will do. I'll call you later."

Five hours later Ignacio's phone rang. He picked it up. "Yeah."

"OK, I got your info. She's out of town right now in Detroit with that new singer, Danny Angel. She's like his manager. She won't be back for a couple of weeks. When she's home, she runs errands for her father. She belongs to a couple of women's clubs and goes to meetings once in a while. She goes out to dinner with her family or the girls. I can let you know when. Is that good enough?"

"Yeah, let me know when she gets back." Ignacio hung up, then called Mamma Vivie's and asked for Alfonso. When he came on the line Ignacio relayed what the mole had said, "Good, that gives me a couple of weeks to find a location in Buffalo that will suit my purpose. Keep me informed." Alfonso hung up and went back to his table.

Chapter 33

The front of the Casino looked like a World War II movie. Klieg lights were crisscrossing the sky above the Casino. Limos, Mercedes and Cadillacs were showing up and people dressed to the nines were going into the club. The casino had been sold out for a month. Danny's dressing room was filled with flowers and all kinds of drinks. Food trays and buckets of champagne had just been delivered for after the show. Telegrams lay stacked on the dressing room table. Danny was talking to the Don. Carmen was laying out his tux and shirt. Johnny was going over the music with the girls to make sure they had it right. Danny hung up the phone.

"The Don wishes us luck. But, I don't think we need it. It was a good rehearsal today. Just remember what I always say to you before a show. Have fun. Now get out of here and get ready for a big night." They left in a hail of laughter and joking.

The show went over like gangbusters. The lights, sound and special effects were great. The girls sang their asses off. The number with Danny and Rosalie got a standing ovation. They couldn't get enough if him. Danny did three encores. Then, it was over and they waited in the dressing room for the arrival of the press and other dignitaries. They came in a mob and were all over him. The press was very careful not to take any pictures of the Detroit and Windsor families. The bodyguards made sure of that.

Nick, the owner of the club was ecstatic. He came over to Danny. He was short and handsome with a George Raft look about him. Danny knew all about him from the information the Don had provided. He was a made man. The club was his baby. He grabbed Danny and gave him a hug. "I knew it was going to be good, but I never expected it to be this good. You're the best. This is going to be the best engagement this club ever had. From now on, consider this your home."

Danny smiled down at him. "Thanks Nick. I'll remember that." He was going to say more, but Carmen came over and put her arm through his. "Nick, can I steal him away for a bit? I want to introduce him to the people that have contracted with Danny for a commercial."

"Sure go head. Remember what I said, Danny. Come back anytime."

Carmen directed him to two executive looking guys standing with four knock out ladies. Carmen said, "Danny, this is Carl Warren and Jack Polliard. They're the guys that are going to make you famous across Canada. Gentlemen, say hello to Danny Angel."

Danny shook their hands. "Glad to meet you. I'm looking forward to doing this for you."

Carl motioned for the ladies to come closer. "We're excited ourselves. These lovely ladies will be doing the commercial with you. This is Jill, Jenny, Dorothy and Cherry." The girls shook his hand and gave him the once over.

Carmen broke into his thoughts. "We start in five days. Johnny has the music. I'll get you the script tomorrow so you can go over it. That will give you time to learn the song and the dialog. It'll be shot here in the club."

"That's great." He shook hands with the executives and the ladies. The next five days were hectic. The crowds were super and Danny had to add a second show to accommodate the overflow crowds. This made Nick very happy. Danny spent the afternoons going over the song and rehearsing with the girls. It was going to be a classy commercial, with Danny on stage singing the special material about Canadian Club. At ringside would be the four ladies. He was to come off the stage, sit with them and finish the song. Then they do the dialog. It ends up with Danny saying, "So, if you're going to have a party, invite Canadian Club along. Trust me. You'll be glad you did."

He winks at the camera and the girls while holding up his

glass. While this was going on, his own girls were back in the band room rehearsing with Billy Kaye for his new Vegas act. The girl they brought in from Vegas was an adorable, blonde doll. Her name was Pam. She was a great dancer and singer, but what Danny liked most, was that she was funny. She would break Billy and the girls up with things that were not in the script. Like a Marie Wilson sort of blonde, Billy was smart enough to let her have her head and play off of her.

******

The first two weeks flew by. The commercial was in the can and the club was packed every night. Billy Kaye left with the girls for Vegas. Rosalie was doing just great. Carmen sat in first class, sipping a drink and contemplating all that had gone down. Danny was well on his way to becoming a major star.

His commercial would hit in a week and be shown in Canada as well as the U.S. She was already working on his next album. Velvet would be filled in on all the things going on, so she could handle the finances. With all the money Danny would be making, he needed a financial advisor to help him invest and keep him out of tax trouble. Carmen didn't want the I.R.S. snooping around. She was also worried about her father. Big Louie was pushing hard to get rid of him.

The plane made a smooth landing and taxied to the terminal. Carmen looked out the window and saw Gino, Joey, and little Ernie waiting for her. She deplaned and Gino gave her luggage ticket to Little Ernie. "You get the luggage and meet us at the limo." Ernie nodded and took off. Gino took Carmen's arm and walked her through the terminal. Joey was a step behind. His eyes never stopped moving. Once in the car, he turned to her, "Sorry about all this, but your father is worried about the guys in Toronto so he's just being cautious."

"Yes, I know. He worries about me like I was still a teenager." They made small talk until Ernie returned with her luggage. Her father was waiting for her when she arrived. He hugged her. "You look great. I hear your boy is doing fine and is on his way. I get the reports from the Winsor families. The Pabst beer commercial will be shot in Niagara Falls, so you can be home for awhile."

"That's great dad. It will be nice to spend some time with mom and Velvet." They went into the house and mamma was all over her.

"It's about time you came home. I almost forgot what you look like." She offered more kisses and hugs.

Little Ernie brought the luggage in and set it down. He left and got in his car and drove to a phone booth about mile from the house. He called a number in Toronto. When it was answered he said, "Would you have Alfonzo call his son?" He gave him the number and hung up. Two minutes later the phone rang. He picked up the phone and a voice said, "Talk to me."

"She's back in town. We picked her up at the airport. I'll let you know when she's going out. I gotta be careful."

"You're being paid to take chances. Just let me know when she makes her move. We'll take it from there. Just make sure you're not with her."

"OK. Will do." The line went dead. He drove back to the house.

Alfonzo called Big Louie on his private line. "She's back. I'll let you know when we're ready to move."

"Good, just don't fuck this up. I'm counting on you. I would hate to be disappointed again."

"Don't worry. I'll handle it." He hung up. He thought to himself. *"That fat fuck. He hates to be disappointed. Tough shit. I'll do the job."*

Chapter 34

Carmen had been home for a week and was busy everyday. She spent lots of time with Velvet telling her all about the plans for Danny. She was in contact with agents and record companies getting things ready for Danny's new album. Booking requests were pouring in from top clubs around the country. They wanted him for television shows as well. Everybody wanted Danny Angel.

She did too. She missed him. They talked every night. The crowds were overflowing. Danny's commercial was to be shown that night and she was anxious to see it. Carmen called Don Angelo and told him what time the commercial would be airing. He was excited too. He said he would call the guys and let them know. Ritchie had invited some friends in to watch.

They were all in the big parlor waiting. To get the best exposure, they bought spots on the Ed Sullivan show. Ed was taking an act off named The Vagabonds, which had completely destroyed the audience. Ed turned to the camera and said, "And now a message from our sponsors." Boom. There was Danny. He was singing the special song as he walked off stage. Then he sat down and did the dialog with the girls. The camera came in tight as he did his last line. He was devastating.

When it was over, Ed came back on and said, "That was Danny Angel, the new heartthrob. We're hoping to have him on the show soon." Everybody in the parlor applauded. Momma was overjoyed. "He did so good. What a handsome boy he is."

Carmen hugged her. "You're right momma. He's going to be a big star. You wait and see."

Her father came over and hugged her. "You did a great job

with him. I'm getting calls from New York City and the whole east coast. Everybody wants him."

"Dad, I know with this commercial playing all over the states and Canada, they'll be knocking down the doors to get him. That's why I've set up a recording session here in Buffalo after he finishes Winsor. He can do the Pabst commercial and the album at the same time. Johnny's going over the songs with him, so he should know the arrangements before he gets here."

"Looks like you have everything under control, my dear. There is one thing you must promise me. I don't want you going anywhere alone. You take Gino, Georgie or Joey with you. I don't want to take any chances with the guys from Toronto. I wouldn't put it passed Big Louie to try something stupid. I told Velvet the same thing. No limos when you go out. I bought two plain Buicks to use. They know your car, so we won't use it. When I have to go out, I've been sending the limo out as a decoy. I go out the back way through the woods in one of the Buicks. It's worked so far."

"I really don't have to go anywhere until Danny gets here. I can do everything I have to do by phone."

"That's good, honey. That makes me feel better." He hugged her, then walked over and sat down with everybody having drinks.

Danny was having a good week. He rehearsed the songs with Johnny during the day. The shows were packed every night. He had already gone through Jill, Jenny and Dorothy plus Cherry two more times. Also, he scored two cocktail waitresses and the Mayor's wife. Rosalie was doing just great. They loved her. Danny added two more songs for her. They would have a couple of drinks in Danny's suite after the shows. It had gradually progressed to a hug and a kiss on the lips while saying good night.

Danny was looking forward to recording the new album in Buffalo. His commercial was playing day and night. Carmen had sent him the script for the beer commercial along with the music. This one was in a bowling alley. It called for Danny to sing the song with a ladies bowling team around him. Then came the dialog. The last thing he had to do was say, "So remember, if you want the best for your guests, give them Pabst Blue Ribbon Beer." Then he was to throw a ball down the alley. Thanks to the Don, he had developed into a fairly good bowler. They always held their meetings in a bowling alley, so the F.B.I. couldn't tape their conversations. Danny used to bowl in a league while they talked.

Closing night was a mad house with standing room only for both shows. The after show party was wild. They finally got back to the hotel around 2:30 am. They all went to Danny's suite before calling it a night. Johnny and the boys left at three thirty. Rosalie was half in the bag and curled up at the end of the couch. She had trouble forming her words. Danny walked over and leaned down. "Come on, I'll take you home."

Rosalie reached up and grabbed him around the neck and pulled his head down and kissed him hard on the mouth. Her tongue was working and she was breathing hard. Danny pulled her to her feet and they stood locked in a tight embrace. Her hands found Ninja, causing her eyes to open wide. She stopped kissing him and said, "Damn, I don't think I can take all of this, but I'm willing to try."

She smiled at him and went limp in his arms. He picked her up and carried her into the guest bedroom. He laid her down and took her shoes off. He sat her up and pulled the gown over her head. She lay there in her bra and panties. He thought to himself, *"What a body this kid has. Under any other circumstances I'd screw her brains out."* He covered her up and left.

The next morning he was having coffee when she came to the guest room door. She looked like hell. She was wearing one of his tee shirts that came down to her knees, and was holding her head. Danny came over to her and led her to a chair. He poured her some coffee and tomato juice. Getting two aspirins, he made her take them with tomato juice. "There's vitamin B in the tomato juice that will help your hangover."

She took the pills. She was ashamed to look at him. "Danny, I'm so terribly sorry. I don't know what came over me. I never drink that much. You must think I'm a loose woman, but the truth is, I have only been laid four times in my life by the same guy, and we were engaged."

He put his hand on hers. "I know that. Don't let that worry you. It has nothing to do with our relationship. One thing though, you do have a dynamite body." Rosalie actually blushed. "I enjoyed undressing you. That was good enough for me."

"Thank you for understanding." They ate breakfast. She was feeling better as she grabbed her clothes. She looked out in the hall. No one was there, so she scampered across the hall and into her room.

The phone rang. It was Carmen. "Hey, big boy. You ready to come home?"

"You bet your ass, I am. I'll be on the plane at one o'clock. I should arrive in Buffalo sometime around seven. Do you have rooms reserved for the band and Rosalie?"

"Of course, I do. I got them in the hotel right down the street from the recording studio. They'll have a car to drive if they want to go anywhere."

"You're so good, sweetheart. Johnny wrote some great arrangements. Just wait until you hear them. The beer song really swings."

"Good. I'm looking forward to it. You just get that body home so I can take care of it."

"Will do. See you around seven." He hung up and started to pack.

The plane touched down at seven-thirty. They got off the plane and two limos were waiting on the tarmac. Gino, Georgie and Joey were there along with Carmen. She came running up and kissed him hard. "Boy, I'm glad you're home."

Danny looked at the three bodyguards. "You expecting trouble?"

"It's my father's idea. He's afraid that something might happen to me. You know about the trouble he's having with Big Louie. He says, better safe than sorry. Come on. Joey will take care of the guys and the luggage. You and Rosalie can ride with me."

They got in the limos. Gino headed for the house, while

Joey and the guys went to get the luggage.

When they arrived at the house it was all lit up. Momma had cooked a feast. The table in the main dinning room was set for ten. Carmen had invited Tony Odie to dinner. He was Velvet's date. They walked into the house and momma came running over and grabbed Danny. She was kissing him and crying at the same time. "Oh, my beautiful boy. It's so good to have you home."

Danny hugged her and kissed her on both cheeks. "Do you really think I could stay away from your cavatelli? Nobody makes them like you."

"Oh, so it's my cooking you come home for. You're a rascal." She gave him another hug.

Velvet came over to give him a hug, too. She was absolutely beautiful. "It's good to have you home Danny. You're doing so good. Your commercial is wonderful. Carmen's been going crazy answering all the phone calls with people wanting you."

Tony Odie came over and put out his hand. "It's good to have you back."

To his surprise and every one else's, Danny gave him a hug. "I can't thank you enough for what you've done for me. Now the question is, can you teach me how to tap dance? I didn't know it, but Rosalie is a great tap dancer. I'd like to be able to put it in the show. You know, like an Italian Fred and Ginger."

"Sure I can teach you. I think it's a great idea. It will certainly add another facet to an already great show."

Then Ritchie came over and gave him a hug. "Good to have you back. We'll talk more tomorrow. I think it's time for a drink. As soon as Joey gets here with your guys, we'll eat."

Chapter 35

The Pabst commercial was a breeze. When it came time for him to throw the ball down the alley, they planned to just show him making the approach, then cut to the pins showing the strike. He asked if he could try it. Danny stood to the left of the alley and made his approach. He laid the ball down on the second arrow from the right. The ball headed for the gutter, hooked left and hit between the one and three pin in a classic strike. The producer went nuts. "Can you do that again?" Danny nodded, and it was right on the money again.

Ritchie sent Gino and Georgie along with the Ox and the Weasel to take care of their security. They were in Canada and he was going to take no chances.

They took a couple of days to rest and go over the music for the new album. There were two new songs, "Here She Is" and "You Taught Me how to Feel Again." The studio was on Seneca Street in a quiet neighborhood. Rosalie, Johnny and the boys could walk to it from the hotel. The first two days went fine. They managed to get four songs down and mixed. They worked long hours, but it was worth it.

They were in the kitchen at Ritchie's house having a late night snack. Gino, Georgie and Little Ernie along with the Ox and the Weasel were having a sandwich. Carmen said to Danny, "I won't be going in with you in the morning. I have some work to do here. I'll join you around two."

Ritchie spoke up. "Gino will drive you. Take the green Oldsmobile. Gino, you go out the back way and take Seneca down to the studio." Carmen started to protest but Ritchie cut her short.

"Gino will drive you. That's it."

She knew better than to argue with him. She nodded. "All right dad. Anything you say."

Danny came over and put his arm around her waist. "Your dad's right. We can't be too careful." They said their good nights and headed for the guest house.

Little Ernie couldn't wait to call Alfonzo. He drove to a diner and used the pay phone in the back. He called and left the code. The phone rang a minute later.

"She will be leaving the house tomorrow around two. One guy with her. They will be in a green Oldsmobile and going down Seneca. The street narrows between Twenty-first Street and Fifth Avenue. Parking only on the south side of the street. Most people drive their cars to work, so there shouldn't be any trouble parking. You can block him easy there."

"That's good to know. You did good. We'll be there early and set it up."

"You going to snatch the broad?"

"Yeah, but keep your mouth shut and your eyes open. Let me know when they leave. Call me at this number in Buffalo." He gave him the number and Ernie copied it down.

"You got it." The line went dead.

Alfonzo turned to the wise guys sitting around the room. "OK, it's tomorrow. I want two cars with New York plates. Here's how it's going to come down. They'll be in a green Oldsmobile."

He repeated what Ernie had said about the street and the parking. "Nickie will be in the first car parked on the south side of the street. We'll be parked a few cars back. As soon as you see him pass us, you pull out and block the street. At the same time we'll pull out and block him from backing up. Nickie, you and your boys take out the driver, snatch the broad and get the hell out of there."

"We'll meet in Niagara Falls at the Acme garage, to transfer her to the Frontier Bakery truck. The border guards are used to seeing that truck making deliveries on the Canadian side, so there won't be any trouble. Once on the other side, we put her in the car and bring her here. I've got chloroform, so she'll be out like a light.

Listen to me. I don't want any slip ups. This is a piece of cake. We'll leave here in an hour for Niagara Falls and cross over in the morning. Nickie, get on the phone. Call our guys in Buffalo and get the cars lined up. The rest of you get ready. I have to call Big Louie."

******

It was supposed to be an easy snatch and grab. They got there at noon to make sure of the parking. Ernie was right. Plenty of parking spaces were available. They parked the cars and left. Two cars were waiting to take them to The Anchor Inn to await the call. At one forty-five the call came through from Ernie. They would be leaving in fifteen minutes or so. Alfonso and his boys jumped in the cars and were back on Seneca in no time. They settled in to wait. At ten after two Nickie saw the green Olds coming down the street. He waited until it was two car lengths back and pulled out in front, blocking the street.

Gino saw the move and slammed on the brakes. He caught the movement of a Buick pulling out and blocking his retreat in his rear view mirror. He yelled for Carmen to stay down. Grabbing his gun and the spare one on the seat, he came out of the car. Nickie was opening the door of his car when Gino shot him. The guy in the back seat fired hitting Gino in the shoulder. Gino went down, but not before he killed the guy in the back seat. There was a shot from behind him and a bullet hit him in the side. It was the driver from the Buick.

Carmen came out of the back door with her gun in hand. She saw the shooter and took him out with one shot. Alfonzo was getting out of the passenger door when Carmen fired and knocked him down. The third guy in Alfonzo's car fired twice through the windshield. Both bullets hit Carmen, one in the heart and one next to it. She was dead before she hit the street. Gino saw this and staggered to his feet. The shooter behind him fired and the bullet passed through Gino's arm. Gino spun around and shot the attacker before falling. The other shooter grabbed Alfonzo, pushed him into the front seat of the Buick and backed all the way to the corner before taking off. Gino crawled over to where Carmen was lying. He knew she was dead. He kept saying, "Oh no! oh no!" until he passed out.

Danny was taking a break when he heard the sirens. They were close. He thought it must be a fire somewhere. The door burst open and one of the technicians came rushing in. "There's been a shooting down the street! Bodies are lying everywhere. Even a girl!"

Danny was out the door, running with the Ox and the Weasel right on his heels. He saw the lights of the ambulance and police cars three blocks down. He was running full tilt and slammed through the people who were standing around gawking. Danny saw Carmen lying there. Desperately, he ran over pushing the four paramedics out of the way. Then dropping to his knees, he gently lifted her into his arms, and holding her close to his chest he rocked her back and forth. He looked at her face, so peaceful, then saw the blood and knew she was dead. Like a wave crashing against the shore, the pain and anguish came. A feeling of anger and rage started building inside. He threw back his head and an animal sound came out that shocked the hell out of everybody there.

A photographer from the Buffalo evening newspaper caught that moment on his camera. That was the picture that hit every front page in America. New singing sensation, Danny Angel's fiancée shot down on a Buffalo street. Two detectives came over. They knew who Carmen and Danny were. The chief detective named Ron Battersby, a big Englishmen, said to Danny, "I called Ritchie. He's on his way down here." Danny turned his head toward the detective. He saw him through a fog. "What about Gino?"

"He's hurt real bad. Took three bullets, but he took out four guys in the process. He's on his way to Buffalo General. Danny, can we put Carmen on a stretcher?"

The answer came out like a bark. "No, I'll hold her." Before Ron could respond Ritchie showed up. He walked over to where Danny was standing holding his daughter. The two men stood staring at each other. Finally, Danny said through clenched teeth, "Somebody is going to pay for this. I don't care how long it takes. Somebody is going to suffer."

Ritchie put out his arms and Danny gently handed him his daughter revealing the blood stains on Danny's shirt and the wound in Carmen's chest. Richey stood there looking at the beautiful face of his daughter. The sorrow and grief on his face was indescribable. Within seconds Richey's face transformed becoming hard and brutal. He looked at Danny and said one word, "Vendetta." Taking a deep breath, he slowly walked over where the paramedics had placed the stretcher and gently laid his daughter down on it. "Take her to Lombardi's."

The paramedics looked at Ron. He nodded. "It's on Sycamore and Walnut." He turned to Ritchie. "I can't tell you how sorry I am. We'll do everything we can to get the guys who did this."

Ritchie looked at him. He said in a cold voice, "You do that." He turned and walked away with Danny. When they got out of ear shot he said to Danny, "We both know who did this. It was Big Louie. He just killed the one person that meant everything to me. He's a dead man. I'm going to destroy him."

"No, we're going to destroy him. You're not talking to Danny Angel now. You're talking to Danny Di. You better go home and be with momma. I'm going to the hospital and see if I can talk to Gino and find out exactly what came down. Then I'll come home. Momma's going to need all the support we can give her. We'll talk later." He gave Ritchie a hug and left for the hospital. Gino was in surgery when he got there. He waited.

He decided to call Don Angelo and fill him in. The Don said he would be flying in tomorrow and to expect him. Danny was grateful for that. He had this cold lump inside. He got that when he was angry, real angry. Big Louie was as good as dead. He would handle that personally. And it wasn't going to be a pretty death. He'd make him suffer.

The nurse finally came out and told Danny that Gino was awake. He was in ICU. There were two detectives already there and Danny would have to wait until they finished.

Danny gave the Ox and the Weasel a signal. They grabbed the detectives and slammed them down in chairs. "You two better stay here until Danny comes back." One look at the Ox, and they complied.

Gino was awake when Danny walked in. He was all bandaged up and still dopey from the ether. When he saw Danny, tears came into his eyes. Danny sat down next to him. "I'm sorry, Danny. I tried. There were six of them in two cars. They boxed me in. I got three of them. Carmen came out the back door shooting. She got the driver and wounded the guy coming out the passenger door. The shooter in the back seat shot her through the windshield. My God, how can I face Ritchie? She was my responsibility." He cried silently.

Danny put his hand on Gino's shoulder. Now he was thinking like Danny Di. "I'm wondering how they knew you would be on that street at that exact time. The only ones who knew were you, Georgie, Little Ernie, and my guys. I trust my guys, you and Georgie. So who does that leave? Little Ernie."

"Danny, Little Ernie's from Canada. He use to live in Niagara Falls, but moved to Toronto before coming to Buffalo. Ritchie took him in on a recommendation from Guy Scallize. He runs a book in Niagara Falls. Ernie's his nephew."

"That explains a lot to me. I think we have a mole. I'll find out. Gino, you rest. If you need anything, you let me know. There's detectives outside that want to talk to you. Tell them what you told me. Don't worry. You did your best."

Danny got up and walked out of the room. When he walked out of ICU, there was a neatly dressed gentleman waiting for him. The two detectives were still sitting where he left them. He walked over to Danny and handed him his card. "I'm Walter Green, Gino Sposito's attorney. Mr. Regerio called me. I'll handle it from here." Danny shook his hand and left.

It was real quiet in the car going back to Ritchie's house. Danny was sitting in the back, deep in thought. His insides were tied in knots. He was filled with hate, anger and grief. The Ox and the Wesel let him have his space.

He finally said, "You two are finally going to get your chance. We're going to take Big Louie out. Him and anybody else that gets in our way. Ox, when we get back to the house, I want you to call Bert and tell him I need two of his best shooters. You know the guys, so you pick 'em. Tell him I'll let him know when and where to send them."

The Ox looked at the Weasel, smiled and said, "There is a God."

Chapter 36

Big Louie was pacing back and forth in front of Alfonzo who was lying on the couch with his right arm in a sling. His shoulder was heavily bandaged. "Now, tell me how you fucked up an easy snatch and grab, and get four of my guys killed in the process. You, Mr. Big Shot. You know what this means? Ritchie is going to come down hard on me."

Alfonzo looked at Big Louie. He thought, *"I could kill this fat, fuck right now."* He shifted positions to get comfortable. "First off, our guys weren't carrying any identification. The cars were stolen and had New York plates. It's going to take them awhile to figure out who they are. So until they do, you're off the hook. Make like nothing happened. Send flowers. Make like you know nothing about it."

"Now, about the other thing. When we blocked the car, the driver came out shooting. He took Nickie down with two shots. Tommy managed to hit him and knock him down. As he was going down, he took Tommy out. Milt fired from our car and hit him. Then the back door opened and the broad came out with a gun in her hand. She shot Milt. I was coming out of the car when she hit me. Pete was in the back seat and shot her as she was drawing a bead on him. The guy on the ground shot Gene as he was coming around the back of the other car. That's when Pete grabbed me and pushed me in the car and took off. How was I to know that the driver would come out shooting?"

"Stupidone. Nickie should have shot him the minute he pulled in front of him. I'm surrounded by idiots. You're laid up and useless. I'm out four soldiers, and I got one of the biggest crime bosses in the country going to come after me. I want you to get on the phone and get me some soldiers. I want this place surrounded. I want it so not even a gnat, can get in here without being seen. See if you can do something right for a change."

Alfonzo got up and walked out of the room. He thought to himself, "*Ritchie won't have to kill him. I will.*"

*****

When Danny got to Ritchie's house, the entrance was blocked with people in front of the gates. There were press, TV vans, and police everywhere. The gates were always guarded by Ritchie's soldiers, but today they really had their hands full. Danny told the Ox to go around and come in the back way. That was also guarded, but when they saw who it was, they let them pass.

When Danny walked into the house it was bedlam. Mamma was in the parlor lying on a couch. The doctor was there giving her something to calm her down. Ritchie was with his soldiers and Velvet. His eyes were red from crying. Danny walked over and, without saying a word, grabbed and hugged him.

He had all he could do from busting out crying himself. That would come later when he was alone. Now he had to be strong. He turned Ritchie loose and Velvet came into his arms. Her body was shaking. Danny soothed her by talking to her and holding her. The phones were ringing off the hook.

Danny took Ritchie and walked into the den. "Don Angelo will be here tomorrow. I imagine a lot of people will be coming in. It's going to be a circus. When this is over, we have to have a sit down. That mother fucker took something from us that can never be replaced. He's going to die for it."

Ritchie looked at him with cold eyes. "Yes he is. I should have taken him out a long time ago. But Danny, I don't want you mixed up in this. I know how you feel but this is my call. Carmen made you a star. I don't want anything to jeopardize that."

"That's exactly why I have to do this. For her. Besides, who the hell would suspect me? Danny Di was the best at this kind of thing. Let me work it out. I have some ideas. I'll run it by you after the dust settles. Now it's time to grieve."

*****

Danny stood at the casket looking down on Carmen's face. His insides were torn up with emotion…love, hate, rage, sadness. The last three days were like a fog to him. The nights were the worst because he was alone. He couldn't cry. The church was overflowing. Families came from all over New York, Boston, Cleveland, and Chicago, to name a few. The press had been all over him since that picture had hit the papers.

Flame came with her new boyfriend. A big Italian guy named Carme. The girls from Utica came to pay their respects. News shows all over the country played it up big. Don Angelo had been his constant companion. He knew what was going on inside Danny. It was now time to take Carmen to the Mausoleum. Cars were lined up for blocks. The FBI guys were having a field day taking pictures of license plates, which was stupid since the cars were all rented. Danny rode with Ritchie, Velvet, Don Angelo and momma who desperately held on to him.

The service at the Mausoleum was short. Danny sang the "Ave Maria." That brought tears to the eyes of all that were there. When it was over, Ritchie had a big meal catered at his house. The families were invited. When it was over, Ritchie had the limo take the Don and his bodyguards to the hotel. They would have a meeting tomorrow afternoon. He said his goodnights, then hugged and kissed momma who was still in shock.

Danny went to the guest house. He stood inside and the emotions came. He could still smell her perfume. Her clothes were lying where she had left them. He clenched his fist and had all he could do to stop the anguished yell that was building up inside him. He wanted blood. He wanted to kill, mame, destroy. He paced like a lion, back and forth moaning and shaking his head. The tears would not come. The anger was so great that it blocked out the tears.

For three days he had to hold it in and play the part of a bereaved Danny Angel, a new singing star, who had tragedy befall him. He wasn't used to this. He had never loved anything in his whole life. He never let anybody get close. Carmen came the closest to breaking down the wall he had built up. Now she was gone. All that was left was a cold empty feeling in his stomach and rage. There was a soft knock on the door. He went over and opened it. Velvet was standing there. Her eyes were red from crying. She looked up at him.

"Can I come in?"

Danny stepped back and let her in. She walked to the middle of the room and turned to him. "Would you please hold me?"

Danny stared at her for a moment. He walked over and put his arms around her. He lowered his head so it was next to her face. Then, the tears came.

He woke early. Velvet had left sometime during the night. He lay awake while she slept, thinking about how to get to Big Louie. He remembered Tony Gracci in the Bahamas. If anybody knew how to get close to him, Tony would know. Danny put in a call to Paradise Island. When he got the hotel, he asked for Tony. He had to wait while they located him. Finally, a voice said, "This is Tony."

"Tony, this is the guy who saved your life in Chicago. I told you I may need a favor. Well, now I do. You heard about Ritchie's daughter, Carmen, getting killed in Buffalo? We have reason to believe it was Big Louie's doing. You were his number one guy. I want to know how I can get to him."

"I saw all the coverage. I am truly sorry. Big Louie is a piece of crap. There's a way you can get into the house with out being seen. A secret tunnel leads to his bedroom. It runs under the walls. I found it accidentally. On the north side of his house there is a stand of trees by the dirt road. When you go into the stand, there's a bush. It's fake. Looks real, but under it is a trap door. There's a light switch on the wall at the bottom of a short ladder. It lights up the whole tunnel. At the end of the tunnel is a panel. It slides easy. Just grab the handle and slide it. That takes you into Big Louie's closet. It's big. Like a small room. Right outside is Big Louie's bed. I'd like to come with you. I owe you and I never liked the way he did things. I could be a lot of help."

"Thanks Tony, but I think we can handle it from here. You just sit tight until you hear from me. It'll be worth your while, trust me." He hung up the phone. Now he knew how to do it. They would be expecting them to come from the outside, but he would take them from the inside out. He showered, shaved, got dressed and went to the main house. When he entered the kitchen momma was making breakfast. She still would cry at any moment. He went to her and hugged her and kissed her on both cheeks.

She said, "Now I only have you and Velvet." She bowed her head and broke into tears.

Danny held her. "I know momma. We all miss her." He signaled Velvet to come take her. Velvet came over and took her and sat her down at the table. Danny went to find Ritchie. He was in the den talking on the phone. His eyes were blood shot. Danny waited until he was through talking. "Ritchie, I have a plan. Now, let me finish before you say anything."

He told him what Tony had said, "I can do it with four guys. I'll use the Ox and the Weasel and two of Bert's best guys from New York City. They'll be expecting you to make a move, so you'll be watched like a hawk. They'll never expect anyone to come at them from the inside."

Ritchie looked at him for a minute. "I didn't want you mixed up in this, but you're right. They'll be expecting me not someone else. Tell you what, if Don Angelo says it's OK, I'll go for it. I want that cocksucker dead."

"Call Don Angelo and have him come over."

Ritchie made the call and half hour later, the Don walked into the den. Danny told him everything. When he finished the Don said, "Ritchie, he's the best you're ever going to find. If anyone can take that fat bastard out, it's Danny. He's never failed me in all the years I've known him. I say, let him do it."

Ritchie sat back in his chair. "OK, I give you my blessing.

Just make sure Louie knows who sent you to kill him. And make him suffer."

"Oh I will. Another thing Richie, I think you have a mole here." He told him about Ernie. "He knew when Carmen was leaving and what car she would be in. I trust Gino, Georgie and my guys. He's the only one that could have tipped them off. If it's all right with you I want the Ox to question him. He has ways. It'll tell us for sure, that what came down, was from Toronto."

"Go ahead. Let me know what he has to say. After that, he's yours."

Chapter 37

It didn't take a lot of persuasion from the Ox to make Ernie sing like a bird. He told them everything. Then he went for a swim in Lake Erie wearing cement swim fins. Danny filled Ritchie in. Ritchie sent Georgie and Joey to Canada and Guy Scallize had an unfortunate accident soon thereafter. Danny called Bert and made arrangements for the two shooters to come to Buffalo.

They were all in Ritchie's den; the Ox, the Weasel, and the two guys from New York City. Ritchie sat behind his desk and listened to Danny lay out the plan. The Don was right. He knew what he was doing. Danny called Tony again. He got the layout of the house, where the guards were posted, where they slept, and how many there were. Tony also told him that Big Louie would be on guard and that he, most certainly, would beef up his soldiers. But, they both knew that when you cut the head off a snake, the body dies with it.

That was Danny's intention. Take Big Louie out first. Then work his way down through the ranks. He had given Ritchie a list of things he needed. Silencers, Thompson sub machine guns, a 12 gauge sawed-off shotgun with double aught buckshot, duct tape and a two foot piece of rebar were all on the list. Danny had a black Ninja type outfit with a hood, so he could not be recognized. He briefed the guys on what they were supposed to do. He went over the layout of the house with them. They were ready.

They left Buffalo and drove to Lockport to pick up highway nineteen to Niagara Falls. They would cross into Canada and drive the ninety miles to Toronto. They timed it so they would get there after midnight. It was a clear night. They found the road and, with the lights off, drove until they saw the stand of trees. They parked the van off the road, and then found the trapdoor with little trouble. The Ox went first to make sure it was alright.

Once in the tunnel, they started for the house. The tunnel was high, wide well lit and sloped upward. When they got to the sliding door, Danny turned off the lights throwing the tunnel into complete blackness. With guns at the ready, he slid the door open and stepped into the closet. The others followed. With a small pen light Danny found the door leading into the bedroom. He opened the door just far enough, so he could peek into the bedroom.

There on an oversized bed lay Big Louie. He looked like a beached whale. Sleeping beside him was a young girl. Danny whispered in the Weasels ear. "When I grab Big Louie, you take the girl. Make sure she doesn't holler."

The Weasel nodded. They crept into the bedroom. Danny went to the side of the bed that Big Louie was sleeping on. The Weasel went to the right. Donny and Jake, the shooters from the city, went to the bedroom door to guard against anybody coming in. The Ox and Danny stood over the sleeping figures.

With a signal from Danny, they both reached down and covered the mouths of the sleeping figures. Big Louie's eyes shot open. All he saw was a figure dressed in black, a covered face and eyes that scared the hell out of him. Cold hate filled eyes were staring down at him.

The girl started to scream, but the Weasel held his hand over her mouth and told her to be quiet, if she didn't want to be hurt. She nodded and started to cry softly.

Danny came close to Big Louie's ear. "You utter one sound you fat son-of-a-bitch, and I'll drive this ice pick straight up your nose." He pricked him with it to show him he meant it. There was a soft ripping sound as the Ox tore off a piece of duct tape. At Danny's signal, the Ox replaced Danny's hand with the duct tape. He grabbed Big Louie by the hair and pulled his head up. Danny took the roll of tape and wound it around his head three or four times. Big Louie, for once in his life, was speechless. Danny gave the roll back to the Ox. The Ox taped Big Louie's feet and hands.

He was wrapped up like a Thanksgiving Day turkey.

The girl was trying to talk to the Weasel. Danny came around the bed and got close to her. "I'm not going to hurt you. If he takes his hand away, you won't scream will you?" She shook her head, no. "OK, do it." The Weasel took his hand off her mouth.

"Please get me away from him. He's kept me here for weeks. He's done terrible things to me and made me do nasty things to him. I'm only thirteen."

Danny calmed her down. "You're safe now. He won't ever touch you again. Here's what I want you to do. Get dressed. The Weasel is going to show you a tunnel. You go though the tunnel to the end. It's well lit, so don't be afraid. Once you get to the end, climb the short ladder and push the top open. There's a van parked across the road in some bushes. You get in the van and wait for us. Understand?"

She nodded. Danny walked around the bed and stood over Big Louie. "You're going to suffer. Not only did you have my girlfriend killed, it seems you also rape little girls." Big Louie's eyes opened up wide. Danny got close to him. "That's right, you killed Ritchie's daughter. As soon as that little girl is gone, we are going to have some fun." He turned and watched as the Weasel led her into the closet and started her through the tunnel. Danny turned back to Big Louie.

He took the hood off and leaned down. "You recognize the face? Yeah, it's Danny Angel, but what you don't know, is that under this face is the face of Danny Di. You sent two guys to kill Don Angelo. I gave you a pass on that one. But, not this one. I want you to hurt."

He motioned to the Ox who was standing behind him with the rebar in his hand. The Ox stepped around him and swung the rebar down breaking both ankles. Big Louie tried to scream but nothing came out. Danny glared and said, "Hurts, doesn't it?" He nodded and the Ox broke his shins, then his knees. Big Louie was thrashing around in pain. Danny smirked. "You're going to beg me to kill you." Once again, the Ox wielded the rebar breaking Big Louie's ribs, wrists, and finally, both arms. Big Louie passed out.

Danny took some smelling salts out of his pocket and put them under his nose. Immediately, he revived and was once again in excruciating pain. Then Danny said, "I want you awake to feel the rest of it. Bam, the shoulders and collar bones went.

Danny got close to him. Now, I want to give you something from Ritchie and me." He took the ice pick and put it in Big Louie's nostril. "Go straight to hell you fat mother fucker." He drove the ice pick right up into his brain. Big Louie stiffened and died. Danny left the pick where it was.

He stood up and put the hood back on. "Let's get the rest done." He walked to the bedroom door. Danny had his pistol with the silencer on at the ready. He cracked the door and took out the two bodyguards in the hall. They split up and went from room to room quietly killing whoever was in them.

Danny went into the end bedroom. Sitting in a chair was Alfonzo. Danny knew him. When Alfonzo saw Danny, he reached for the gun on the table. Before he could grab it with his left hand, Danny was there. He picked up the gun and aimed it at Alfonzo. "Before you die, there's something I want to know. Who killed my girlfriend? Was it you?"

Alfonzo knew he was going to die. "No, she's the one who shot me. It was suppose to be a snatch and grab but it went wrong. She killed the driver and was aiming at Pete who was in the back seat of the car. He shot her before she could get him. I'm sorry about that. If I'm going to die, I'd like to see who's doing it."

Danny took off his hood. Alfonzo stared at him. "Wait a minute, aren't you Danny Angel? What the hell do you have to do with this?"

"Everything. You remember the job you did in Calgary and got in a jackpot. Who pulled you out of that mess?"

"Wait a minute. There's only one guy who knew about that and he's dead."

"Really, Alf? The face has changed, but Danny Di is still under it."

Alfonzo sat back in his chair. "I'll be a son-of-a-bitch. It is you."

"Yes it is. And you remember that nobody fucks with me or mine. You did." He moved the gun in his right hand. Alfonzo's eyes followed it. While he was staring at that gun, Danny shot him with the silenced pistol he had in his left hand. He put his hood back on and left him where he was. The boys had cleaned out the upstairs. Now, it was time to do the downstairs. Armed to the teeth, they went into the big room that housed the guards and soldiers.

They never got a chance to reach for their guns. The Tommy guns and the shotgun took out the whole bunch. The noise brought the two guards in from the front of the house, only to be cut down by the Ox and the Weasel. That left the guard at the front gate and a couple patrolling the grounds. The four of them went out to take care of the rest while Danny stayed in the house to make sure everyone was dead. Hot blood was coursing through his veins, just like in Korea during the heat of battle. He heard gunshots from outside then silence. Ten minutes later the four of them came back inside. The Ox walked over to Danny. "It's done."

"Good. Now let's get back in the tunnel and get the hell out of here. I'm going to call the cops and tell them to get out here. By the time they arrive, we'll be long gone." They went up to the bedroom and Danny made the call. They returned to the tunnel, closing the closet door behind them. Without the need for silence, they made good time. They arrived at the van, and found the little girl asleep in the back. The Weasel started the van and took off down the dirt road away from the house. As they approached the main road, they could hear the sirens. The girl woke up with a start.

Danny put his hands on her shoulder to calm her. "It's all right. You're safe now. What's your name and where do you come from?"

She sat up. "My name is Ginger and I'm from Yellow Knife."

"How did Big Louie get a hold of you?"

"My mother works in one of his houses in Yellow knife. The guy that runs it is the one who gets young girls for Big Louie. I'm not the first one. When he gets tired of one he just throws her out and gets another. I don't want to go back there."

the desk. Ritchie motioned him to take the chair in front.

When he was seated Richie said, "I've been doing a lot of thinking and I want to ask you something. How would you like Velvet to handle you like Carmen did?"

Both of them jumped. It was a complete shock to Velvet. Before they could say anything Ritchie continued, "She knows all about the contracts and everything that has to do with you. Carmen told her, in case she couldn't do it. I trust her completely. She is already keeping your finances up to date, taxes paid, and employees paid. You're going to be getting a lot of money from now on and you need her to keep things straight. What do you think?"

Danny looked at Velvet. "I think it's a hell of an idea. Carmen would have approved it in a second. Welcome aboard." He leaned over and kissed her on the cheek. She actually blushed.

"I don't know what to say. I'd love to do it."

"It's done." He took a piece of paper out of his pocket and handed it to Ritchie. "That's Tony's number in Toronto. He's there now. You can call him and get things straightened out. Velvet, you come with me. We have business to discuss."

Chapter 39

The new album went gold in a week. Offers were pouring in. Velvet had her hands full. She turned the guest house into her office. She had to hire a secretary to keep up with the correspondence. Ginger was helping her prepare promotional packages to send out. Velvet put her on salary. Danny was playing the Copa in New York City and doing a landslide business. He would soon be playing the east coast from Boston to Miami.

Las Vegas was coming up in the near future. The boys wanted him out there. Movies and TV were in the making. Danny had driven himself to exhaustion every night to get ready. He would come home hot and sweaty, shower, eat something and go to bed. The new stuff he put in the act was dynamite. Rosalie was perfect for him. The dance numbers were getting standing ovations.

The only thing that worried Velvet was Danny's moods. He was having a tough time getting over Carmen. He was fine around people, but when he was alone he brooded and paced. He would workout on the punching bag and pound it unmercifully, trying to take out all his anger on it, as though killing Big Louie wasn't enough. Velvet would stand outside the workout room unseen and watch him.

She wanted to try to help him. She would wait until the right moment. Ritchie and she would be flying up to Boston to catch Danny's opening at Blinstrums in two weeks. Mike O'Bannion, the owner of the club from Chicago was going to be there also. It should be a great opening.

Danny had just come off stage after his second show. The front row was all mob guys. They were having a ball. They had invited him and Rosalie to a party at a Fifth Avenue penthouse. He didn't really want to go, but they were friends of the Don's and, of course, they wanted to meet him.

They left the car with the doorman and took the elevator up. When they arrived at the penthouse they heard the noise. The party was in full swing. He was greeted like a star. They couldn't do enough for him. He told the Weasel to look after Rosalie and took the Ox with him. People were coming up and hugging him, and congratulating him on his show. He was standing having his first drink, when a voice behind him said, "I don't mind you using my guys, but do you have to spoil them by overpaying them?"

Danny spun around and there stood Bert with a big smile on his face. "You son-of-a-bitch. I've been here a week and a half and you finally get around to seeing me." He gave him a playful punch.

"Hey, you know the doors swing both ways."

"Yeah, but how would it look for a big star like me to be seen going into your building. I have to think of my reputation." He tried to keep a straight face but couldn't. They both hugged and laughed. Bert said, "I guess my boys did a good job for you. They told me you're one tough mother fucker. I'm glad you got rid of that prick. A lot of people wanted him dead, but nobody wanted to pay the price for it."

They heard a ruckus and looked over. The Weasel was holding a drunk wanna-be wise guy who was hassling Rosalie. Bert headed that way with Danny and the Ox right on his tail. When Bert got to the Weasel, he pushed him aside and grabbed the drunk. He pulled him close so they were nose to nose. When the drunk realized who it was, his knees started to buckle. He knew he was in deep shit.

Bert said to him in a quiet voice, "There's a door over there. Use it and I don't ever want to lay eyes on you again. I don't think New York is good for you." He shoved him toward the door.

The guy practically ran out the door. The host came over and apologized for the trouble. Bert acknowledged him and said it was nothing. He turned to Rosalie and took her hand. "You, my dear, are wonderful. Anybody who can make Danny look good is my friend forever." He bowed and kissed her hand.

Rosalie smiled at him. "And anybody with a line of bullshit like yours is my friend." That broke them up. They all went to the bar for drinks. The party broke up around four in the morning

*****

They closed the show and got ready to fly to Boston. They had lunch with Bert before leaving. He was taken with Rosalie. He was coming up to Boston to spend some time with them. Johnny and the guys were driving up with the music and instruments. Danny had bought them a nice van to drive. Velvet said it was a write off.

When they got off the plane in Boston, there were two or three hundred people waiting for him. They screamed when they saw Danny get off the plane. He waved to them. The Ox and Weasel flanked him and Rosalie. The Boston police department was there to keep order. They got into the limo without too much trouble. The women were wild. They were holding up cards with their telephone numbers on them. Some also had bra sizes written on the card. That made Rosalie chuckle.

At the hotel and there were women everywhere. The police had formed a lane for them to walk through. When they saw Danny they went nuts. He stopped and shook hands, signed things and was just as gracious as could be. They checked in and went up to the suite. The Ox and Weasel were next door. There was a connecting door to Danny's suite. Rosalie had one bedroom in the suite. Velvet had booked all the suites on that wing of the hotel. There was a security elevator that could only be activated by a special key. With Ritchie and his bodyguards, Mike O'Bannion and his body guards, Bert with his guys, plus Danny's band and Velvet, it was going to be quite a crowd.

Monday was a busy day. Rosalie and Johnny went to rehearse the house band. Danny waited for all the people to arrive. Ritchie and Velvet showed up first, once they were checked into their suites. Velvet was stunning. Danny forgot how beautiful she

Danny was fuming inside. "No, you're not going back there. You're coming with us. I'll take care of you." He gave her a hug. "You're one of us now. We're your new family."

The boys all gave her a hug and they chatted all the way back to Buffalo.

Chapter 38

It was morning when they got back to Ritchie's house. They went inside. Momma was cooking breakfast. She turned as they came in. Danny walked over and gave her a kiss. Ritchie and Velvet were sitting at the table having coffee. Momma saw the girl. She was standing behind Danny peeking out at her. "And who is this?"

Danny pulled Ginger out from behind him. "Her name is Ginger. She's had a real rough time, but right now, I think she's hungry."

Momma took charge. "Come here, sweetheart. Sit down."

Danny motioned for Ritchie to follow him. They went into the den. When Ritchie was seated Danny said, "It's done. Nobody was left alive in the house. I made sure Big Louie knew who killed him. Now, I want to ask you something. The other families in Canada are going to wonder about this and where they stand. I'm sure they'll understand why you did this. According to Tony, who used to be Louie's number one man, he wasn't that well liked. What I'm getting at is this. The guy who told me how to get to Big Louie is in the Bahamas." He told him the quick story. "I know this guy. He's a stand up guy. If Tony was to take over the Toronto family, you would have no more trouble."

Ritchie sat back. "You trust this guy? That's good enough for me. I'll make it known in Canada that this is my wish. That, if this happens, there will be peace."

"That's great. I'll call him."

"So, what's with the little girl? Where did she come from?"

Danny filled him in on her story. Ritchie was furious.

"That porko. That dirty bastard. I wish we could kill him all over again. What are you going to do with her?"

"Hell, I don't know. Find her a home somewhere." He looked at Ritchie and Ritchie smiled.

"You're a sneaky bastard. You know that? I know what you're thinking. My wife needs something to take her mind off Carmen. It might work. But we have to make it her idea. Let's go back in the kitchen and you tell her the story."

When they got to the kitchen, Ginger was sitting down and momma and Velvet were all over her, making sure she had enough to eat and drink. Danny and Ritchie sat down at the table. Momma looked at Danny. "So, you got something to tell me about this girl?"

Danny told them the story. Momma started to cry and Velvet put her arm around Ginger. "So you see, she can't go back to Canada because she has no family. I guess I'll have to put her in an orphanage or something."

He sat back and waited. Momma stood up and put her hands on her hips. "The hell you will. She's been through enough. She stays here. I'll take care of her." She looked at Ritchie. "Well, what do you have to say?"

Ritchie threw up his hands. "Not a thing. I think it's a great idea."

"Good. Velvet, take Ginger upstairs and get her cleaned up. Then you and I are going to take her shopping for clothes. Ritchie, have Georgie bring the limo around in an hour." She was back in charge. Ritchie looked at Danny and gave him the OK sign with his fingers. Mission accomplished.

Danny excused himself and went to the guesthouse out back. He showered and shaved and was relaxing when Velvet knocked on the door. He went to the door and opened it. She came into his arms and kissed him.

"You are one incredible guy. You know that? That little girl is just what momma needed. I have to go. It's shopping time." When she was gone, Danny called Johnny and told him that they would be back to work tomorrow. He called Tony Odie and told him the same thing. He needed to lose himself in his work.

He then called Tony in the Bahamas. When he picked up the phone Tony said, "Jesus, you were mad at him weren't you? It's all over the news here. Nobody left alive."

"Listen, I talked to Ritchie. He wants you to take over the Toronto family. He's contacting all the other families in Canada to tell them that's what he wants. You will step into Big Louie's shoes. Can you handle it?"

"Wow, this is a surprise. Yeah, I can handle it. I know everything he was doing. I was his right hand, remember? You had something to do with this, didn't you? You saved me from getting killed in Chicago and put me here. Now you want me to be the head Capo in Toronto. I don't even know your name. So, why me?"

"Let's just say it's professional courtesy. One day, I'll tell you why. Now, how fast can you get to Toronto?"

"I can be there tonight. Let me give you a number where I can be reached." He gave Danny the number.

"OK, I'll call you tomorrow." He hung up. He needed to rest, so he lay down and took a much needed nap.

The next day he was at the studio hard at work. Rosalie kept looking at him until he finally told her, "Hey, I'm all right. Let's get this down." After that she was fine. The TV was full of the story of the massacre in Toronto. They were playing it up big. Momma had come home with enough clothes for Ginger to clothe an entire girl scout troop.

When they finished recording for the day, Danny and Rosalie drove over to Tony Odie's studio. He put him through the basics. Rosalie helped him. He was light on his feet and shifted his weight easily. They worked up a good sweat. Finally, they called it a night. Danny dropped Rosalie at her hotel and drove back to the house. He needed a shower.

When he got out of the shower, the phone rang. It was Ritchie asking him to come to the house. As he passed through the kitchen, momma had Ginger at the stove teaching her how to cook Italian. They were laughing. Momma said to Danny, "I'm teaching her how to cook Italian and speak it. She's doing good." Danny waved and went into the den. Velvet was sitting in a chair next to was. She had a list of things for them to do. Radio, TV spots, interviews with local TV shows, and an album signing at a prominent music store. They were having drinks when Mike O'Bannion showed up. He had Mary Ann with him. Danny noticed she had a big diamond engagement ring and a wedding band to match. After hugging her, he raised up her left hand and said to Mike, "OK, who made an honest person out of who?"

Mary Ann laughed, "I think it was mutual. Mike just said one day, "Let's slip in to Reno and get married. So we did."

"I think it's wonderful. Let's have a drink on it." They had drinks all around. Finally, Velvet had to get Danny aside and discuss business. The others left to get ready for the show. She was very efficient. She was close to Danny explaining all the things he had to do. Her perfume was getting to him. He looked at this beautiful lady and realized he wanted her. He'd have to play his cards right.

He remembered an old saying, *"Never shit where you eat."* It worked with Carmen, but would it work with Velvet? He'd find out in time.

The shows that night were both smashes. There were standing ovations all through the shows. Danny was pleased. They were in the dressing room celebrating the opening. Mob guys from Boston and the surrounding areas were there with their comares. Bert showed up and immediately took charge of Rosalie. Danny was glad of that. If he wanted to get close to Velvet, he had to have a clear field. Two hours into the party Rosalie came over and whispered in his ear. "Danny, is it all right if I go with Bert? He wants to go someplace quiet and talk."

Danny hugged her. "Sweetheart, go with my blessings. Bert is a hell of a guy and we have no ties. Go, have fun." She smiled and skipped away. Bert gave him the OK sign and they left.

Mike came over. "You did a hell of a job for me. This is your home now. Anytime you want to come back, you just call me."

"Expect it. This is a wonderful club. Would you do me a favor when you get back to Chicago?"

"Sure. Anything."

"Would you call the Don and tell him I missed him being here?"

"I will do that gladly."

Velvet came over and brought him a drink. "I thought you could use this. You were really wonderful tonight. The show is outstanding. We have a busy day tomorrow, but it's all in the afternoon, so you can sleep late."

"I thank you for that. Let's end this and get out of here." He thanked them all for coming, but had to beg off as he had a busy day tomorrow doing things for the club. They left and the Ox drove them back to the hotel. They went to Danny's suite and got comfortable. Velvet took off her jacket and shoes and curled up on one corner of the couch.

Danny sat across from her on a chair. They made polite talk for a while, both staring at each other over their drinks. Finally, Velvet put her drink down, stood up and walked to where Danny was sitting. She stood in front of him. He looked up and saw the look on her face. He opened his arms and she knelt down and leaned inside them. They held each other tight, not saying a word. Velvet slid her head along his until she found his mouth and clamped on it. He responded immediately. They were animals kissing, clutching, and feeling.

Finally, Velvet broke away and sat back. She was breathing hard and flushed. She placed her hands on Danny's knees. "I've been wanting to do that for a long, long time but never could due to the circumstances. Danny, I fell in love with you the first day you came into the hospital to see me. Oh, I know it was crazy, but I couldn't help it. Then Carmen came and I was happy for you. I loved her like a sister. I was happy just to sit back and watch you two. I never thought we would ever get together, and I don't know why I'm babbling like this."

Danny leaned forward and looked into her eyes. He reached out and started to unbutton her blouse. She sat perfectly still. He pulled her blouse way from her shoulders and it dropped to the floor. He pulled her close and put his mouth on hers while he the desk. Ritchie motioned him to take the chair in front.

When he was seated Richie said, "I've been doing a lot of thinking and I want to ask you something. How would you like Velvet to handle you like Carmen did?"

Both of them jumped. It was a complete shock to Velvet. Before they could say anything Ritchie continued, "She knows all about the contracts and everything that has to do with you. Carmen told her, in case she couldn't do it. I trust her completely. She is already keeping your finances up to date, taxes paid, and employees paid. You're going to be getting a lot of money from now on and you need her to keep things straight. What do you think?"

Danny looked at Velvet. "I think it's a hell of an idea. Carmen would have approved it in a second. Welcome aboard." He leaned over and kissed her on the cheek. She actually blushed.

"I don't know what to say. I'd love to do it."

"It's done." He took a piece of paper out of his pocket and handed it to Ritchie. "That's Tony's number in Toronto. He's there now. You can call him and get things straightened out. Velvet, you come with me. We have business to discuss."

Chapter 39

The new album went gold in a week. Offers were pouring in. Velvet had her hands full. She turned the guest house into her office. She had to hire a secretary to keep up with the correspondence. Ginger was helping her prepare promotional packages to send out. Velvet put her on salary. Danny was playing the Copa in New York City and doing a landslide business. He would soon be playing the east coast from Boston to Miami.

Las Vegas was coming up in the near future. The boys wanted him out there. Movies and TV were in the making. Danny had driven himself to exhaustion every night to get ready. He would come home hot and sweaty, shower, eat something and go to bed. The new stuff he put in the act was dynamite. Rosalie was perfect for him. The dance numbers were getting standing ovations.

The only thing that worried Velvet was Danny's moods. He was having a tough time getting over Carmen. He was fine around people, but when he was alone he brooded and paced. He would workout on the punching bag and pound it unmercifully, trying to take out all his anger on it, as though killing Big Louie wasn't enough. Velvet would stand outside the workout room unseen and watch him.

She wanted to try to help him. She would wait until the right moment. Ritchie and she would be flying up to Boston to catch Danny's opening at Blinstrums in two weeks. Mike O'Bannion, the owner of the club from Chicago was going to be there also. It should be a great opening.

Danny had just come off stage after his second show. The front row was all mob guys. They were having a ball. They had invited him and Rosalie to a party at a Fifth Avenue penthouse. He didn't really want to go, but they were friends of the Don's and, of course, they wanted to meet him.

They left the car with the doorman and took the elevator up. When they arrived at the penthouse they heard the noise. The party was in full swing. He was greeted like a star. They couldn't do enough for him. He told the Weasel to look after Rosalie and took the Ox with him. People were coming up and hugging him, and congratulating him on his show. He was standing having his first drink, when a voice behind him said, "I don't mind you using my guys, but do you have to spoil them by overpaying them?"

Danny spun around and there stood Bert with a big smile on his face. "You son-of-a-bitch. I've been here a week and a half and you finally get around to seeing me." He gave him a playful punch.

"Hey, you know the doors swing both ways."

"Yeah, but how would it look for a big star like me to be seen going into your building. I have to think of my reputation." He tried to keep a straight face but couldn't. They both hugged and laughed. Bert said, "I guess my boys did a good job for you. They told me you're one tough mother fucker. I'm glad you got rid of that prick. A lot of people wanted him dead, but nobody wanted to pay the price for it."

They heard a ruckus and looked over. The Weasel was holding a drunk wanna-be wise guy who was hassling Rosalie. Bert headed that way with Danny and the Ox right on his tail. When Bert got to the Weasel, he pushed him aside and grabbed the drunk. He pulled him close so they were nose to nose. When the drunk realized who it was, his knees started to buckle. He knew he was in deep shit.

Bert said to him in a quiet voice, "There's a door over there. Use it and I don't ever want to lay eyes on you again. I don't think New York is good for you." He shoved him toward the door.

The guy practically ran out the door. The host came over and apologized for the trouble. Bert acknowledged him and said it was nothing. He turned to Rosalie and took her hand. "You, my dear, are wonderful. Anybody who can make Danny look good is my friend forever." He bowed and kissed her hand.

Rosalie smiled at him. "And anybody with a line of bullshit like yours is my friend." That broke them up. They all went to the bar for drinks. The party broke up around four in the morning

*****

They closed the show and got ready to fly to Boston. They had lunch with Bert before leaving. He was taken with Rosalie. He was coming up to Boston to spend some time with them. Johnny and the guys were driving up with the music and instruments. Danny had bought them a nice van to drive. Velvet said it was a write off.

When they got off the plane in Boston, there were two or three hundred people waiting for him. They screamed when they saw Danny get off the plane. He waved to them. The Ox and Weasel flanked him and Rosalie. The Boston police department was there to keep order. They got into the limo without too much trouble. The women were wild. They were holding up cards with their telephone numbers on them. Some also had bra sizes written on the card. That made Rosalie chuckle.

At the hotel and there were women everywhere. The police had formed a lane for them to walk through. When they saw Danny they went nuts. He stopped and shook hands, signed things and was just as gracious as could be. They checked in and went up to the suite. The Ox and Weasel were next door. There was a connecting door to Danny's suite. Rosalie had one bedroom in the suite. Velvet had booked all the suites on that wing of the hotel. There was a security elevator that could only be activated by a special key. With Ritchie and his bodyguards, Mike O'Bannion and his body guards, Bert with his guys, plus Danny's band and Velvet, it was going to be quite a crowd.

Monday was a busy day. Rosalie and Johnny went to rehearse the house band. Danny waited for all the people to arrive. Ritchie and Velvet showed up first, once they were checked into their suites. Velvet was stunning. Danny forgot how beautiful she reached around and unsnapped her bra. It fell between them. He leaned back and looked at her body. It was perfect. Her breasts stood straight out with nice pink areolas. The nipples were hard. He fondled them and leaned down and kissed and licked them. She shuddered and pushed forward to help him enjoy them. In one fluid motion he stood up and took her with him. Holding her close to his body, his lips on hers, he walked her into the master bedroom.

He kicked the door closed with his foot. Then carrying her over to the bed, he sat her down, stood back and slowly undressed. As the shirt came off she saw the scars. The body was rock hard and the muscles well defined. She leaned forward a little to see him. She watched his hands undo his belt and unzip his fly. He let the pants fall and she took an involuntary breath. His erection came slowly up to greet her. Ninja was standing straight out.. It was beautiful.

Danny lifted her up and stood her in front of him on the bed. He unzipped her skirt and slid it down, panties and all. She was standing naked and beautiful. He pushed her down on the bed. He did all the tricks he had learned, and they worked to perfection. She came hard and often. She was begging for Ninja.

. They did it every way they knew how until they were completely spent. Velvet said to him, "That's the first time I've been laid since Cheech put me in the hospital. Before that, it was just a job. I never climaxed." She chuckled. "Of course you know that I'll be sore as hell tomorrow. I feel like I was riding a horse."

Danny smiled at her. "You'll get use to it, Babe. We have a lot of time together and we'll make the best of it." She turned her back to him. He reached around her, cupped her breast and pulled her close. They finally slept.

Chapter 40

They were having breakfast in the hotel dining room when Ritchie arrived. Ritchie began by telling Danny that Ginger was doing just great and momma loved her. He said they planned to adopt her and make her Ginger Regerio. Danny was pleased that Ginger was also helping Velvet and was getting a salary.

"She's a real go-getter. She's been through a lot, but she's not bitter about it. She's putting it all behind her. Ginger is filling a big void for the both of us. That Tony is quite a guy, too. And, by the way, the Toronto gang is really coming around. Now we are doing things the way they were meant to be. Thanks, Danny."

"I'm glad it worked out." They saw Velvet approaching. She came to the table and sat down real gingerly. Danny had to laugh and Velvet actually blushed.

Before Danny could say anything, Bert and Rosalie came to the table and sat down. They both looked like kids who were caught with their fingers in the cookie jar. The fact that Rosalie didn't sleep in her bed last night was a good indication that they were playing hide the weenie. Danny was glad. "So Bert, are you going to hang around a few days?"

Bert looked at Rosalie. "Yeah, I thought I'd do that. There's nothing pressing me in New York that I can't handle by phone. Besides, it gives us time to hang out a bit."

"Good, Ritchie has to get back to Buffalo. Velvet and I have some TV things and an album signing to do, but we'll still have time to have some fun.

And that's the way it was for the rest of the week. Danny and Velvet did all their things during the day, and at night after the shows, they all went out and partied. On Sunday Bert and Velvet had to leave. They took one limo to the airport. Bert and his bodyguards went one way, and Danny escorted Velvet the other. The Ox and the Weasel had to keep the people back because they wanted Danny to sign things and just get close to him. Rosalie was waiting by the limo when they got back. She sat next to Danny on the way back to the hotel.

"Danny, can I ask you something?"

"Of course. What's up?"

"I really care for Bert. And I know he cares for me. He wants to get engaged. I don't know what to do?"

"I think that's just great. Bert is a stand up guy and I'll be your best man any time you say. So go for it. The brass ring doesn't come around very often. Grab it while you can."

She hugged him and kissed him on the cheek.

The second week was bigger than the first. People were lined up for blocks to get in to see the show. Danny was irresistible on stage as well as off stage. He managed to score four broads along the way, and his album went platinum.

Velvet and Chuck were busy setting his schedule for the rest of the year… The Latin Quarter in New York, Palumbo's in Philly, The Copa in Pittsburg, The Twin Coaches and Diplomat Hotel in Miami, The Cave in Vancouver, then back to the Chez in Chicago. Then came Eddie's in Kansas City, The Twenty's in Omaha, followed by Carnegie Hall for a grand concert. TV shows included the Ed Sullivan show, The Milton Beryl show, and the Hallmark Theater. Vegas was crying for him, but the boys held off. They knew exactly when to put him there.

Hollywood now wanted him for movies. The mob guys who ran the studios, knew they had a major star and were going to use him to the best advantage they could. Velvet managed to be with him as often as she could. Bert spent as much time with Rosalie as he could. They were getting married soon with a big wedding in Rochester.

Danny had Chuck book him at The Embers, a big mob joint on the lake owned by Rosalie's father. The reception would be held there. Ritchie was coming over with momma, Ginger and Velvet. The wedding was a once in a lifetime affair. The church was mobbed. Danny and Velvet were in the wedding party.

The ride to the club looked like a mafia caravan. Limos, Caddies, Mercedes, and two Rolls Royces headed up the procession. All that was missing was a hearse. Danny had hired musicians from the Eastman School of Music for the reception. He had Johnny rehearse them at the school. They were excited about working with a major star. They played a couple dance sets, and then Danny went up. The kids were good.

One trumpet player was outstanding. A young Italian guy from New Jersey named Peter Valorino. He had Vegas chops already. The show was wild and the crowd loved it. After the reception Danny said to Johnny, "I want that trumpet player to go with us. See if he's interested. I don't think he can learn much more here. Seems to have it all already."

Johnny went to talk to Peter and Danny left to be with Ritchie and the family.

The shows at the club were right on. The band smoked and the crowds were ready to party. Only one thing happened. One night a bunch of motorcycle guys came in. They were rowdy and troublesome. The Embers is situated on the shore of Lake Ontario. When you walk into the club you are on the second floor where the showroom is located. The dinning room is down stairs. There used to be stairs going down to the water where the boats were docked.

Through the years, the stairs and dock disappeared leaving only the door leading to nowhere. Danny was in the middle of the show and they started to heckle him and call him a fag.

Danny turned to Johnny. Play my song. Johnny went into the Friday night Gillette fight song. The Ox and the Weasel were on the move along with Rocky, the bouncer at the club. They converged on the bikers and fists flew. The bikers didn't have a chance. Danny yelled at a waiter to open the back door. They took them one by one and threw them out the door and into the lake. It was a long drop, and after a big splash, they did not return. The door slammed shut, and Danny walked back on stage. Johnny picked it up right where he left off before the fun and games started.

The rest of the engagement went off with out a hitch. They left to go back on the road with an extra player in the band.

The year flew by. Danny did two more albums that both went platinum. He had his own jet plane with a pilot, copilot, a flight attendant. He also hired a few more bodyguards that the Ox had chosen.

Then it was time for Hollywood. The Don had called him. It seems that there was a part in a movie just made for him. The guys wanted him to do it, so off to Hollywood they went.

Rosalie went to New York to stay with her husband. Danny arrived in Hollywood and checked into the hotel, reserved for him and his people. The studio had sent extra guards for protection. That didn't set very well with the Ox and the Weasel. They let it be known that if trouble started, the Hollywood boys were to get the hell out of the way. They arrived at the studio early to talk to the producer and director.

The producer was enthusiastic about the movie, but as luck would have it, the director wasn't too happy. He wanted Dean Martin for the part, but was told that he was to use Danny Angel. No ifs, ands or buts. The script was about a night club singer who gets involved with some strange people. It contained singing, drugs, sex, fights and general mayhem. It was a meaty roll for him, even though he was third on the star list. Danny had done enough television shows to get by. He was a natural, and this guy in the script was him all the way, even if the director didn't know it.

They handed him the script and told him they would be shooting in two weeks. To help Danny, they were sending over an acting coach to help him go through the script. Also, he would be working with Sylvia Silvers, the hottest star in the studio. She was blonde and gorgeous. He was wondering if they would have any love scenes together. He'd read the script tonight.

The day came to start shooting the movie. Danny got there early. He had a little trouble at the gate. It seemed the guard wasn't going to let the Ox and the Weasel in. One phone call and they were on their way. His trailer was next to Silvia's. Hers looked like a mansion on wheels next to his. He had yet to meet her. Word had gotten back to Danny that she wanted Dean too, but was stuck with him. Too bad. He was here to stay. There was a knock on the trailer door. The Ox answered it, and scared the hell out of a little natty guy standing there with a clipboard. He regained his composure and said, "There is a cast meeting on sound stage three. I'm to take you there."

"Whatever you say. Come on guys." They got outside to find a golf cart waiting. The little guy looked at Danny and the Ox. The Weasel was no trouble, but these two were. "I don't know if I can get all three of you in the cart."

Danny smiled at him. "That's no problem. The Ox drives, I sit next to him and you and the Weasel stand on the back where the golf clubs go. Simple." Before he could say anything the Ox was behind the wheel with Danny next to him. The Weasel took the little guy's arm and helped him on the back of the cart. The Ox said, "OK, where to?" He was directed to a sound stage. When they got there, people were standing around talking. They saw Danny coming and it grew quiet. They watched this strange spectacle approaching. The Ox stopped right in front of the crowd and got out. The little guy ran around and waited for Danny to get out. With the Ox and the Weasel along side of him they made their way to where the people were gathered.

A man with a cap that read "A.D." came running over. "Hi, I'm George Meek, the assistant director. They're waiting for you inside." Danny started to follow with the Ox and the Weasel behind. The A.D. saw the three of them following and said, "Oh, I'm afraid your friends will have to stay out here. They're not allowed in."

Danny gave him a look that made him step back. "Let's get one thing straight from the start. These men are my personal bodyguards. Where I go, they go. There is no discussion."

The A.D. looked like he was going to cry. "Well, OK, let's go inside and see what the director has to say."

He turned on his heels and entered the building. It was made to look like a big nightclub, bandstand and all. Everyone was seated around a long table. Danny spotted Sylvia right off. It wasn't hard to find a platinum blonde in a dimly lit room. Sitting next to her was Brett Favor, the star of the movie. The director was sitting at the head of the table. He frowned when Danny came in. The A.D. ran over and whispered in his ear.

The director stood up. "Ladies and gentlemen, I'd like you to meet Danny Angel. He will be costarring in this movie." Heads turned. Sylvia took one look and her mouth dropped open. The director went on to introduce him to all the people there.

When he was through with the introductions, the director said to Danny, "It's nice of you to be here, but I'm afraid this is a closed set and your friends will have to leave."

Danny knew this was the time to get things straight. After all, this guy was just an employee. He had the sanctions of the mob guys that ran Hollywood and could break this guy in a second. "I really don't think so. These are my personal bodyguards. If you'll read the contract, you'll find out that where ever I go or am, they're with me. They won't get in your way."

The director's face started to turn red. Danny had him and he knew it, but to be put down in front of his stars was a little too much. He had been told that he was to bring this movie in on time and to make Danny a movie star. He sputtered something unintelligible and motioned for Danny to be seated across from Sylvia. She was looking at him with admiration. He gave her the look that said, "I want to tear off your clothes and fuck you." She gave him the look back that said, "Any time big boy."

The director continued about the next day's shooting. They would shoot Danny singing with the big band, and his first scene with Sylvia. He was to rehearse the band that afternoon. The meeting broke up. Everybody came over and shook Danny's hand and told him how much they enjoyed his music and welcomed him aboard. Brett was charming and Danny liked him. Sylvia hung back for a bit then approached him. He took her hand and kissed it. "I've been a fan of yours for a long time. I never thought I'd ever be this close to you or working with you."

She gave him her famous smile. "You know you made an

enemy today. Nobody has ever talked to Cid that way. He's like a spoiled child. I'd watch my back if I were you."

Danny smiled at her. "You see those two guys over there. They watch my back. I'd rather watch you."

She let out a laugh. "Boy, you are an Italian smoothie. I can't wait for our love scenes." She caught his look. "Oh yes, we have a couple of torrid love scenes. You don't mind getting naked in front of a camera do you?"

"Hell no. Who's going to be looking at me with you there?"

Sylvia laughed again and said, "They may be looking at me, but I'll be looking at you." She gave him a wink and walked away.

Chapter 41

The band was super. They kicked the hell out of the songs. Danny had already been to wardrobe and make up. The nightclub was full of extras. There were guys hanging all over the scaffolding with lights, cameras, and sound booms. His name in the movie was Danny Dante. The A.D. called for silence. Everybody was ready. Cid yelled, "Action."

The band went into the intro for his song, then the announcement and he was on stage. He sang and moved and did Danny Angel. When he was through he heard Cid yell, "Cut. Do it again. Take two."

After the forth time Danny knew what was going on. He was punishing him. Danny got that feeling in his stomach. He waited for the first break and walked over to Cid. "I'd like to talk to you, if I may?"

Cid looked at him and started to walk away. Danny grabbed his arm and hustled him into the makeup room. He told the people in there to get out. The Ox was told that nobody was to bother him. Danny grabbed Cid by the throat and pinned him against the wall. It took all his willpower not to hit him.

He got close to his face. "Listen to me very carefully. I know what you're doing and it's bull shit. I'm here to do a job and you're here to see that I do it right. I'll do anything you tell me, because you're the one in the know. I'm here to learn from you. You're the teacher, I'm the pupil. But don't fuck with me. If I'm wrong, you tell me and I'll change it. But don't fuck with me. I know you didn't want me in this movie, but were forced to take me. I didn't want to be in this movie, but was forced to take it. So you see we're in the same boat. We answer to the same people. The only difference is they'll kill you! They can't kill me. I'm too big a star. Now I'm going to let you go. You can walk out of here and try to get me fired, or we can work together and make something out of this."

He let go and stood back. Cid massaged his throat. Nobody had ever dared to do this to him, but the kid was right. His life and career was in the balance and he knew it. He also knew that his life wasn't worth a plug nickel if he blew this one.

He looked at Danny. "I hate to admit it, but you're right. We are in the same boat. OK. I'll direct this movie and I'll drive you hard. I'll get the best out of you I can. Now, let's see if you can act. We'll walk out of here like old friends, laughing and joking. We're running late. I suggest that we get back to work." And that's what they did.

Cid drove him hard and Danny learned. The scenes came and went and Danny was right there on top of things. The crew and extras loved him. He was charming to them all and Sylvia was smitten with him. She couldn't wait for the day they would do their first love scene together.

Danny was sitting in a chair in the make up room. He was wearing a robe with just boxer shorts under it. He was worried. He'd have to show his body with all the scars. He turned to the makeup lady and said, "Can you get Cid in here? I have to talk to him." She nodded and left. A few minutes later, Cid showed up.

"What's the trouble Danny?"

Danny stood up and opened the robe. Cid stared at the rock hard body and the scars. "Jesus, what did you do, go through a meat grinder?"

"Let's just say, I wasn't always an alter boy. What can we do about it?"

Cid smiled, "This is Hollywood. We can fix anything." He turned to Martha, the make up lady. "You know what to do. I'm going to be shooting him from the rear mostly. So concentrate on that first, I'll be using low lighting so he'll blend right in." He said to Danny, "See, all fixed. We'll see you in an hour."

When Danny got to the set it was dimly lit. It was Sylvia's bedroom. The crew was making last minute adjustments to lights and sound. When everything was to Cid's satisfaction, he ordered everybody out except the camera and sound guys. That was Sylvia's demands. She came on the set wearing a beautiful dressing gown. She looked gorgeous. Danny couldn't wait to see all of her when she dropped the gown. When everything was ready, Sylvia's maid held the gown, while she slipped in bed under the sheets. Nobody saw anything. Danny was to come into the bedroom, start kissing her, then stand up and take off his clothes with his back to the camera.

He came in and laid down along side her. The dialog went smoothly. He started to kiss her. Her tongue was all over the inside of his mouth. She finally said, "I want to see all of you. Take off your clothes." He stood up and took off his shirt. She saw that big hard muscled body and shivered. She kept her eyes on his hands as he undid his belt and unzipped his trousers. She wasn't ready for what was about to happen. He dropped the pants and she got a look at Ninja. It was el dente, half hard and growing. With his back to the camera, they couldn't see it, but she could. She held up the covers and he slid in next to her. She was like silk with creamy breasts and pink nipples.

They continued the scene. She reached down unseen and grabbed him. He rolled on top of her. The lines came fast and breathless. Danny moved forward just enough so that the head slid inside her. She was trying to get more but he held back.

They finished the scene and Cid yelled, "Cut."

Sylvia looked at him over Danny's shoulder. "Cid, leave us alone for a while, will you?"

Cid gathered the crew and left. As soon as they were gone, Sylvia said, "Let's finish it. I want all of that." And that's what she got. After that, it was sex anytime, anywhere. She was insatiable. Danny didn't mind. He loved it. Here he was, balling the biggest star in Hollywood, finishing his first picture, and doing a big concert at the Hollywood palladium. Las Vegas was coming up after he was through with the picture. Life was good.

*****

They decided to premier the movie in Chicago while Danny was there playing the Chez Paree. The Don had seen to that. He wanted Danny home. The time was right to put his plan into operation.

The opening at Caesar's Palace was strictly Las Vegas. Spotlights out front were crisscrossing the sky. Stars were arriving from the other hotels in limos. Everybody was dressed to the nine's. The crowd was four deep from the showroom door all the way outside, waiting to get in to see Danny. The stars and VIPs were let in first, then the crowds. The showroom was packed to the rafters and no amount of money could get you down front. The thirty-six piece band was on the stand waiting to start the show.

Danny's dressing room looked like a florist shop. There were flowers from Frank, Sammy, Dean, Rickles, Sophie Tucker, and Nat King Cole, to name a few. Sylvia was there to cheer him on. According to the tabloids, they were an item. Danny had to explain to Velvet that it was for publicity reasons. She understood, after all, she was coming to Vegas to stay with him for awhile.

The show opened with Danny coming out singing. The crowd went wild. The orchestra was smoking and driving him to the limits. Rosalie had them eating out of the palm of her hand. The numbers they did together got standing ovations. An hour and forty-five minutes later, it came to an end. Danny stood on stage and thanked them all for coming. He did some shtick with the stars that were ringside and introduced Sylvia. The lights dimmed as the orchestra went into the intro to "Somebody Loves You."

Danny stood there and tenderly sang the song, touching every heart in the room. The last note he held while the orchestra swelled around him. The applause was deafening. He stood there with his arms outstretched and acknowledged the crowd as the curtain came down.

He thanked the orchestra and went to his dressing room to get ready for the crowd. There was a full bar set up with a bartender. Food was buffet style with cocktail waitresses ready to serve. They came in a bunch. It looked like the who's who of Vegas stars. Don Rickles came over and gave Danny a hug, "I knew you were going to be a big star, but I never expected you to be this big. Now, I gotta open for you. Now, I ask you again, "Who's going to be looking at me?" He gave Danny a playful punch and wandered away. Sylvia was charming and had a crowd around her.

Frank, Sammy and Dean came over. They offered some laughs and good humor kidding. The Vegas mob was present. They were gracious, giving him compliments on the show. It was a special evening. The party lasted until two o'clock in the morning. Danny and Sylvia went to the suite and celebrated by wearing each other out until they fell asleep.

Chapter 42

Both shows were sold out every night. During the day Danny played golf with Freddie Bell and Buddy Greco. Both were working the Sands down the street. Dean would make up the foursome. Once in a while, Sonny King, who was working with Jimmy Durante at the Desert Inn, would join them. The Desert Inn golf course was the place to be. For all of them, it was free golf.

Every night after the second show it was party time in the dressing room. Stars came from all the other hotels to have some drinks and laughs. Velvet flew in and Danny was glad to have her around. She was a smart schmoozer. Aside from being gorgeous, she was on top of things. She made more deals in the dressing room than the guys did on golf courses. When they found out they couldn't lay her, they'd get down to business.

Danny decided to buy a house in Vegas, where the action was. He bought an impressive house on the Desert Inn golf course, two doors down from Freddie Bell. It had a guest cottage that Danny used for the Ox and the Weasel. There were a lot of stars that had homes there. Velvet furnished it tastefully. He got his Nevada drivers license and Sheriff's card. Danny had to have the boys get that for him. They used The Don's nephew's fingerprints.

Danny and Velvet settled into a star's life in the desert, full of work and parties. Velvet had already booked him back in Vegas after Chicago. The Frontier wanted him next. The boys from Toledo wanted their turn. He would be spending a lot of time in Vegas. The Don came to visit and stayed in Danny's home. He loved it. Danny suggested the Don give his bodyguards a break. He would protect him.

The Ox and the Weasel met him at the airport as he stepped off the plane. Danny was waiting for him in the limo. They had champagne on the way to the house. After getting him settled, they had lunch on the patio. The Don said, "You've come a long way Danny. You don't know how proud I am. I'm getting calls from everybody. They all want you. In a few days the guys are coming in for sit down. A couple of them are in the black book, so we gotta be careful."

Danny replied, "We could have the meeting here. Nobody would expect it. We can bring them in quietly in different cars. No limos. Drop them off and come back later to pick them up."

"The FBI will be watching the guys in the black book closely. How do we get them here?"

"No problem. They can come by golf cart. Their clubs can be rented at the clubhouse. I'm on the third fairway, so they can just stop in here. People do it all the time."

"That's a great idea. I'll get the word out. Now about Chicago, it's going to be the biggest opening the town has ever seen. The guys at the Chez have added to the room so it seats more people. The premiere will be shown at the downtown theater, red carpet and all. Those Hollywood guys are handling it. They're flying Sylvia and Brett in to be seated with you. The usual political assholes will be there too, including the Governor, the Mayor and his ass kissers. Of course, the Police Chief isn't too happy about it. He has to supply the protection for the whole affair. Every time I think about it, I have to laugh. If he only knew who he was protecting." He broke into laughter.

That night he sat ringside with Velvet and the owners of the hotel. After the shows, there was a special party in his dressing room for invited guests only. A white haired, distinguished looking gentlemen, was introduced to him as Bill Fanning. Danny asked one of the owners and was told that he was the head of the FBI office in Vegas. Danny liked him immediately. They chatted for awhile and promised to have lunch one day soon.

The meeting came off without a hitch. The black listed guys came by golf cart, sat in on the meeting, then finished the front nine like nothing had happened. After the meeting, when everybody was gone, the Don said to Danny, "When you come to Chicago there's something very important that I have to discuss with you. Don't worry about it now. It'll keep until you get there. Capisci?"

"I understand. I'm looking forward to coming home. We'll have the suites at the Palmer House, but I want to spend some time at the house with you and momma. I miss her cooking."

"She'll like that. She misses you too."

The Don went back to Chicago, Danny finished up at Caesar's Palace, and Velvet flew back to Buffalo to get ready to move her office to Vegas. Danny got ready for Chicago. There would be the four guys from the band, Rosalie, Danny and four bodyguards traveling with him. The next morning they were at the airport. The Lear was waiting for them. They boarded and took off. Half way into the flight, Rosalie leaned over to Danny and said, "I have to tell you something and I hope it doesn't make you mad."

Danny looked at her, "You mean about getting pregnant?"

Rosalie's mouth dropped open. "Did Bert tell you?"

"No, I just saw the signs. Your breasts got bigger and your tummy's starting to pooch out. I think it's wonderful."

"Oh, I'm so glad. Bert was worried."

"Well, he needn't be. You work until you think it's time to quit. I'll get some nice maternity dresses made for you that will hide the little one. After the baby is born you can make up your mind what you want to do. You can come back with me, go out on your own, or just be a housewife. What ever you decide I'll help you with. But there's no hurry. Take your time."

Rosalie reached over and kissed him on the cheek, "You're the best."

*****

Chicago went wild. When the plane landed at O'Hare, there were more than three hundred people waiting for Danny along with the TV cameras and the press. He stopped and did a short interview thanking the people of Chicago for coming out and greeting him. They cheered and hollered as he made his way through a cordon of Chicago's finest to the waiting limos. It was like a parade. The streets were lined almost all the way to the hotel. When they got to the Palmer House it was mobbed with people. Danny waved and smiled all the way into the hotel.

They had reserved the whole top floor. It took a special key to get the elevators to go there. Four of the suites were reserved for Ritchie, Carlo, Patsy, and Tomasso. Two others were reserved for Sylvia and Brett. Danny was curious to see how they acted surrounded by mafia bosses. It should be interesting to say the least. The bodyguards would be staying in rooms close by. Danny settled into his suite. Velvet called to inform him that Ritchie was bringing momma and Ginger to the premier. She was setting up the move to Vegas and would be coming up later.

The Don called and informed him that there would be a party at his house in the evening. He was to bring the band and Rosalie. Momma was making a special dinner for him. He'd send the limo at seven. Danny called Johnny and Rosalie to let them know.

The limo was there promptly at seven. When they arrived, there were cars parked all over the compound. Inside they were greeted with applause and laughter. Momma came over and hugged and kissed him. "Welcome home my beautiful boy. I missed you. This is your party."

The whole family was there plus some of the Chicago families. Mike O'Bannion and Mary Ann were the only non Italians there. Momma had outdone herself. She had cocktail waitresses serving drinks, and waiters ready to serve dinner. The Don had a piano, bass and drums set up along with a sound system. It was going to be a real bash. Danny was everywhere, hugging, kissing, and laughing. Momma took charge of Rosalie when she found out she was pregnant. They laughed and chatted in Italian.

The boys were playing Italian music. It was home. The meal was superb, and the wine flowed like water. Danny got up with his guys and did an impromptu show, with Rosalie joining him and the people loved it. When they sat down, Peter Valorino got up and went to the mic. He was half in the bag from too much wine.

He said, "I would like to do a song for all my Italian friends here." He turned to Johnny, "My-ass-tro, if you please." Johnny was laughing. He went into "The Dark Town Strutter's Ball" ala Lou Monte. Peter sang it in Italian and English. He went into a comedy routine that had every one laughing until tears came. He finally said, "And now for a closer, I would like to do a number on my trumpet. The song I have chosen to play is Malaguena, which was stolen from the Italian people. Its real name is Mala Guinnie." Danny almost fell out of his chair with laughter. Peter put the horn to his lips and played. It was absolutely beautiful. He finished to a standing ovation. They all came over and hugged and congratulated him. He was standing there smiling when Danny came over. "Peter, I knew you could play the horn, but I never knew you were so funny. You killed me. Thanks"

Peter shook his hand. "I just wanted to contribute something to the party. It's like being back in Jersey with my family."

Danny gave him a hug. He motioned for Johnny to come with him. They walked away from the crowd. "I want you to write a big arrangement for that song. I've got an idea, so keep it to yourself." Johnny nodded and walked away. The party broke up at midnight.

The next day everybody arrived. Danny had seen to their protection. Ritchie left his boys home, because Danny said he didn't need them here. The other bosses had their own guys. Don Angelo had some of his soldiers in the hotel to block any trouble. It looked like an armed camp. When Ritchie's limo pulled up to the hotel, Danny was waiting to greet him and momma. Ritchie got out first and gave Danny a hug. Then momma got out. She was teary eyed as she hugged and kissed him on both cheeks. When, Ginger stepped out, Danny was flabbergasted. She was absolutely beautiful. Dressed to the nines, she was a real little lady. Danny hugged her and said, "You look just gorgeous. You're going to be my date tonight for dinner."

She smiled up at him. "I'd love to, but you'd better check

with my dad. He doesn't like me to go out with strangers."

Danny, Ritchie and momma burst out laughing. Ritchie said, "She's a killer. Keeps us laughing all the time. It's OK honey. I'll be there to chaperone." She took Danny's arm and said, "OK big boy, let's go." Danny was taken back a little. That was Carmen's phrase. He shook it off and they went into the hotel.

Sylvia and Brett arrived in a flurry of press, TV, and Hollywood movie people. Silvia even brought her hair dresser, valet, and makeup people. You'd think she was doing a film. As she left the elevator with her entourage, she was met by six mean looking Italian bodyguards belonging to Carlo, Patsy and Tomasso. Danny had to come out and tell them it was alright. Brett took it all in good humor. Sylvia came over and grabbed him and kissed him. "I can't wait for tonight. I want that salami of yours."

Danny pulled back, "Oh, you're going to get it. But let's get through dinner first." She laughed and walked away.

They had reserved a table for twelve for dinner and show. Tony Bennett was performing that week. Danny had met him on several occasions. The bodyguards would be at an adjoining table. The Don and momma came up to the suite for drinks and introductions. Ritchie's wife and the Don's wife hit it off immediately. Sylvia and Brett arrived and met everybody. Carlo, Patsy and Tomasso were all over Sylvia, like Great Danes trying to put the make on a poodle. She was flattered and a little bit scared.

When it came time to go to dinner, it was like moving an army. The bodyguards went down first to be ready to escort them to the showroom. They piled in an elevator and went down. When the doors opened, the lobby was full of people waiting to get a look at them. They were cheering and waving. The boys had all they could do to hold people back. They got to the showroom and were seated. Ginger sat next to Danny and the Don was on his right. Sylvia was sandwiched in between Carlo and Tomasso. Carlo was a tall, handsome, distinguished looking charmer. Tomasso looked like a wrestler, big and beefy. The dinner was great. The bodyguards had to block a few people from coming over.

Then it was show time. The lights went down and the

orchestra started playing. Tony walked out with no introduction and started singing. It was magical. He did an hour and a half. At the end he introduced Sylvia and Brett, but when he introduced Danny, the people started hollering for a song. Tony waved him up on stage. Danny walked up, gave him a hug and turned to the crowd.

"Tony is one of the greatest singers you will ever hear. I hope one day to be as good." The crowd loved it. Danny called out a song and the orchestra went into a swing version of "Blue Skies." Tony joined him at the bridge and they ended the song together. The crowd went wild. After the show Tony joined them at the table. Danny invited him to the premier opening of the movie. He graciously accepted. Then it was drinks and laughs until time to go. They got to the elevators. Danny did a head count and came up four short. Sylvia, Carlo, and his two bodyguards were nowhere to be found. Danny smiled to himself and thought. *"Good, I'm off the hook. Better him than me."*

Chapter 43

The premier was right out of Hollywood. Big spot lights crisscrossed the sky in front of the theatre with a red carpet running from the door to the curb. TV trucks, newspaper photographers, magazine and tabloid people along with huge crowds lined the streets and the front of the theatre. The limos started showing up with the Governor and his entourage, the Mayor, Chief of Police, and city councilmen. A huge roar went up as Sylvia and Brett's limo pulled up. The limo stopped at the red carpet, and the bodyguard opened the door. They walked to the microphone that was set up, said a few words and went into the theatre. Danny's limo pulled up and the women went wild. He stepped out and they screamed. He helped Don Angelo and momma out, then Ritchie, his wife and Ginger.

The police that were there had a hard time holding back the surging line. Danny got to the mic. He raised his arms for silence. It took a minute for them to quiet down. He said, "I want to thank you all for coming. I hope you enjoy the movie. I had fun making it. I'm glad we're premiering it here in Chicago, my favorite town." Another roar went up as he waved and went inside. A section was cordoned off for dignitaries. Carlo, Patsy and Tomasso were already there. Mike O'Bannion was seated next to them. The Don's seats were right in front. Sylvia and Bret were seated along side Danny. Sylvia leaned over to whisper in Danny's ear. "I'm sorry about last night, but Carlo wanted to take me out on the town."

"Don't worry about it. Have fun. He's a nice guy." She patted his hand and sat back.

The movie was great and Danny came across like a star. He

was a natural for the part. After the movie ended, the Governor and Mayor got up to make a speech. Sylvia said some words as did Brett. Danny got up and closed out the proceedings. They walked through the cheering crows to the limos. They had decided to go to the Chez Paree to see Jimmy Durante. It was his closing night. They had reserved ringside tables.

The show started and Jimmy came out with Eddie Jackson and Sonny King. They sang, Eddie danced, and Sonny sang so high only dogs could hear him. At the end of the show Jimmy introduced Danny. The crowd went crazy. Danny got up on stage and the three of them did an impromptu comedy and song routine. Eddie Jackson just sat down front and watched. It was magic. They seemed to know what the other was going to do. The crowd loved it. After the show they went backstage to the dressing rooms and continued the party.

Jimmy was talking to Danny. "I gotta tell ya, I love working with you. When you get back to Vegas we gotta hang out. We'll go to the Leaning Tower of Pizza or the Copa Lounge and have some fun."

"Yeah, I'd like that. Sonny and I play golf every once in a while. You should join us."

"Not with a shnoze like this. It could get sunburned. It sticks out farther than my hat. When I look down, I can't see the ball. Birds stay under my nose for shade. I'll stick to piano playing." He laughed and took Danny over to meet some people.

Danny's opening at the Chez was huge. They came from everywhere. The showroom was packed to the rafters. Sylvia had stayed over to be at the opening and to be with Carlo. They were an item. The dressing room after the second show was jammed with people. The Governor was rubbing elbows with Tomasso and Patsy. Little did he know they could snuff him out with just a look to one of their bodyguards. The boys from Milwaukee were trying to get him to play the Italian Festival. The Don had already set it up.

Sheila was there looking gorgeous. Don Angelo came over and gave him a hug. "You were beautiful tonight. Just when I think you can't get any better, you fool me. I want you to come to my office tomorrow afternoon at two o'clock. There's something important that I want to discuss with you."

"I'll be there. He gave the Don a hug. Momma came walking over. Danny hugged her. "Well momma, did I do you proud?"

"Better than that, you made me all warm inside. It's still strange to hear that voice coming out of Ferdinando's mouth. All the years I knew you as my other Danny, I never expected you to have a voice like that. God gave you a wonderful gift and you're sharing it."

"I know. I'm blessed momma. I want you to come to Vegas and spend some time with Velvet and me. I have a big kitchen."

"Then I'll come. How could I turn down a big kitchen?" The Don started to chuckle. "Me, I could never get her to go anywhere. I never thought about a kitchen. We'll come and stay with you when you're back in Vegas." Now, go have some fun."

When Danny walked into the Don's office the next day they were all there; Carlo, Patsy, and Tomasso. The only one missing was Ritchie. The Don greeted him with a hug. "Come in Danny. Sit here." Danny sat down. The Don sat behind his desk. "Well, we accomplished what we set out to do. We made you a superstar. The money is great. We're getting our share and have no complaints. But, what if I told you that there were millions to be made over the top of what you're making now?"

Before Danny could answer the Don continued, "You went to Peoria and to Toronto to handle some things that needed to be done. Nobody suspected you. You did the job. Now, I've been working on a thing for over two years with some people. There's a lot of big shots around the world that need someone to do a certain job for them, even here in this country. They need some people killed and will pay big money for it. I'm not talking chicken feed here. I'm talking millions. That's where you come in. Who would ever suspect a superstar? When a contract comes in, we book you in that country or state. These people will all be in your circle, so it should be easy to get to them. How you do it is up to you. We'll give you anything you need. So, what do you say?"

Danny sat there stunned. This was too much. He came all this way only to have to kill again! He also knew that this was not a request. His answer could seal his fate. They made him and they could break him. He remembered the code. "Nothing personal, strictly business." And, he loved the Don.

He looked at the four of them and said, "This comes as quite a shock. You'll have to give me a minute to digest this. You do have a strong point. Who would ever suspect me? And you all know I would do anything for the Don. OK, I'm in."

The Don slapped the desk. "Didn't I tell you? He's my boy. Now, we work out the details. Danny, you don't worry about anything. When we get it together we'll let you know. Meantime, just go on like before."

Danny got up and shook hands all around. "OK, you let me know what's going on. Don, can we meet at your restaurant around five o'clock? I will have some questions."

"Of course, I'll meet you there. Anything you want."

Danny took his leave. When he was gone the Don said to his friends, "I knew he'd do it. He likes killing too much to turn this down. It's the excitement. He misses that. As you know, there's a congressman from Wisconsin that is causing problems with some of our people there. He'll be at the Italian Festival as an honoree. Danny will be there too. That will be his first assignment. This is only a hundred thousand dollar hit, but I took it to see how well Danny does with it. Then we'll go for the big money."

Danny needed some time to think. This came out of the clear blue and he wasn't prepared for it. He thought he'd left that life behind him. The Don must have been thinking about this for a long time. That's why he let him do those jobs in Peoria and Toronto. He was setting him up, testing him. He should be mad that he was taken for a patsy, but deep down he was getting that old feeling. He did miss that adrenalin rush that came with the killing. The stalking, the execution, watching them die and knowing that his face was the last thing they would see.

Yes, this was a challenge and, like the Don said, who would

suspect a superstar of murder? The idea of getting away with murder was intriguing. To be able to kill people and not be suspected or dragged in for a line up. He had a lot of questions for the Don. He told the Ox and Weasel drive him around until it was time to go to the restaurant. He needed to think.

When he walked into the Don's office, he was sitting behind his desk. He motioned for Danny to sit across from him. When he was seated, the Don spoke. "I know you have a lot of questions, but before you ask them, let me tell you some things first. I've been waiting over two years for you to become a big star. We did that for you. I had a meeting a couple of years ago with some very powerful people. They're not our people. I'm talking about governments, here and overseas, and our own CIA. There are big shots that they want taken down. I'm talking ambassadors, heads of countries, and people like that. And, they'll pay a lot of money to have it done."

"You are the best I've ever seen at this. When you asked me to go to Peoria and Toronto to take care of things, I let you go. I had people who could have done that for me, but I wanted to see if you were suspected in any way. You see, that's the beauty of this whole thing. Nobody will suspect you, because you are a superstar and beyond suspicion. I know deep down you miss it. Danny Di is still inside you. I could tell that by the people you punched out in the last two years and the two jobs you did. Now, what kind of questions do you have for me?"

Danny leaned forwards, "First off, you're right. Danny Di is still under the surface and I do miss the excitement. I thought about this since you told me at your office what you want of me. I can do the jobs, but how much time will I have to set it up? You know I have to learn their habits, where they go, what they do and so forth."

"You're not going to have that much time. We book you in the town where the mark is. We'll get as much information as we can from the people there. You have to pick the time and place. Whatever you need will be supplied by the people who want the job done. How you do it is up to you."

"Well that answers some questions. Have you got a target date to start this thing?"

"Yes. When you close the Chez, you're going to Milwaukee to do the Italian Festival there. There's a congressman who needs to be whacked. I have all the information here in this envelope. He's one of the grand marshals of the fest, so he'll be there every day. Twenty thousand dollars will be sent to your account in that Swiss bank we use. This one is a cheap one. The rest will be a lot better."

He handed Danny the envelope across the desk. "By the way, the boys from the fest are coming in tonight to see you. I'll be there too."

Danny took the envelope. "OK. I'll get it done. Can I ask you one more question?"

"Sure, what is it?"

"If I had said no, what would have happened?

The Don gave him a long hard look. "You know I love you like a son, but you also know our code. Nothing personal, strictly business."

"I thought as much." He stood up. "I have to go to the airport to pick Velvet up. I'll see you later tonight." He walked around the desk. The Don stood up and they hugged. Danny took his leave.

The Don sat down and picked up the phone to call the hotel where the boys from Milwaukee were staying.

Chapter 44

The Weasel came out of the air terminal with Velvet. She looked just beautiful. Danny got out of the limo to greet her. She ran into his arms and they kissed. The flash bulbs went off. The press came out of nowhere and wanted pictures and interviews on the spot. Danny made a quick statement then ducked back into the limo. The Ox took off. Velvet sat next to him with her hand on the inside of his right leg. "I've missed you Danny. I got all the things sent to Vegas. Ginger is going to be taking over all your fan mail and fan club mailings. I'm keeping her on salary. She'll send out your pictures and take care of the correspondence. She's quite a young lady considering all she's been through. Momma is so happy. She moved her into Carmen's room."

At the mention of Carmen's name, Danny got a cold lonely feeling which passed as quickly as it came. He often thought of Carmen. It brought back a warm feeling, but along with that came hate and anger for what had happened to her. He reached over and squeezed Velvet's knee. "I'm glad everything worked out, especially you taking over handling my career. You're doing a bang up job. I think you need to be rewarded for it. When we get to the suite, I'll give you the first installment."

Velvet got close to his ear. "And I'll give you the best piece of ass you ever had."

When they got to the hotel they went immediately to the suite. Once inside clothes flew everywhere. Danny still marveled at her body. It was absolute perfection. She stood there naked and he just looked at her. She came to him, took his hand and led him into the bedroom. She pushed him down on his back and started kissing and licking him all over. She started to nibble and tongue him until he was ready to explode.

She knew all the tricks. She got on top of him and eased Ninja inside. She could feel it pulsing. He was ready. She climaxed with him. She leaned forward and rested on his chest. She finally caught her breath. "You are the greatest. I never enjoyed sex until you came along."

Danny smiled down at her. "Then we have a lot of making up to do."

"True. And we will. Let's take a shower. I have some things to discuss with you." They took a shower together and fooled around. They dried off and were sitting on the couch having coffee. Velvet had her briefcase out and said, "When you finish here, you're booked in Miami at the Fontainebleau Hotel." Before she could go on, Danny interrupted her.

"No, I'm going to the Italian Fest in Milwaukee. You'll have to move that date ahead."

"Wait a minute. I just can't do that! We have a contract with those people."

Danny took her hand. "Listen to me. The Don booked me at the Fest. He has a reason. You can tell the people in Florida that it's at Don Angelo's request, that I have to postpone the date. You won't have any trouble. Trust me. This will happen from time to time so be ready and don't worry. It's all in the family. You just keep my finances and my dick straight and you'll be fine." He kissed her on the nose.

"I can do that. I just have to get used to people doing things out of the ordinary. I got a taste of that at Richie's. Speaking of things out of the ordinary, what ever happened to my pimp in Utica? Knowing him, I can't understand him just leaving all the girls. We were making him lots of money. Not that I care. He was a real son-of-a-bitch."

Danny smiled at her. "Let's just say he took a long one way trip. Utica wasn't good for his health."

She looked at him funny. She knew under that handsome face there was a violent person lurking. She had seen it a few times and was shocked by it. There was a lot about Danny that she suspected, but felt it best to kept her mouth shut. The time he went to Toronto, finding Ginger, tearing up the diner on their way to Buffalo, numerous fights with pushy photographers, jealous boyfriends, husbands and wanna-bes were all clues. She smiled back at him. "Well good riddance. He was a real schmuck."

"Yeah, now let's get ready to go. Gotta big night ahead. Some people from Milwaukee are coming in to see the show. You can talk business with them afterwards. Get everything straight on the Fest. Don't worry about a contract, this is a handshake deal."

The month at the Chez flew by. Danny was on. The crowds loved him. Rosalie was getting bigger every week. Danny told her that, after the Fest, he would send her home to Bert. He decided that he would use Peter Valorino to open for him. He'd try him out at the Fest.

He read the dossier on Congressman Beale. It appeared that the best place to take him out was at the Fest. He still had his spare ice pick. He'd work out the details when he got to Milwaukee. Velvet was terrific. She not only took care of him sexually, she was wheeling and dealing on movies, commercials, and personal appearances. She was a tough negotiator, but she had a valuable product and they all knew it.

They arrived in Milwaukee, and the crowds at the airport were tremendous. The Mayor gave a speech, and Danny thanked them all for coming. The Congressman was there to make an appearance and glom on to Danny. They got into their convertibles, with the Congressman in Danny's car. They drove to the hotel through streets lined with Italians waving Italian and American flags. It was a very festive atmosphere. At the hotel they had suites on the top floor. Congressman Beale's suite was four doors down from Danny's. Louis Prima and Keely Smith, Jerry Vale, Dick Contino, Sergio Franchi, and the greatest Italian singer around, Jimmy Roselli, were also on the same floor. Danny was in good company.

A dinner was planned for them that night at Capazzoli's, one of the biggest Italian restaurants in town. When they left the hotel to go to dinner, it was like a parade of limos with police everywhere. Motorcycle cops were leading and following the limos. Danny had the only personal bodyguards there. There were a few security people. The Congressman had his rent-a-cops with him. All in all, it was a small army.

Dinner was exceptional. The food and wine were top of the line. The laughs and jokes flew like shrapnel. Danny noticed the Congressman drinking heavily. He was already slurring his words. He had a beautiful call girl with him, compliments of the Fest. When they were ready to leave, it took two security guys to get him into the limo. Once back at the hotel, it took the same two guys to get him up to his suite. Danny said to the call girl, "Looks like you're going to have an easy night."

She looked at him and smiled, "What are you doing later? Maybe it won't be a totally wasted evening. As soon as he's tucked in, I'm gone."

Velvet overheard the conversation. She came over. "He's already booked my dear. But, you do have good taste." She took Danny by the arm and got in the elevator. Once in the room, Danny opened the doors leading out to the balcony. He looked both ways and determined that the balconies were not that far apart. It would be easy to get to the Congressman's suite and back again without anybody knowing.

A plan started to form in his mind. He could do it tonight. It would be an unfortunate accident. Everybody knew how drunk he was. A case could be made that he was drunk enough to fall off his balcony. Yeah, he liked it. He'd have to wait until everybody was asleep. Velvet was a sound sleeper, so he could slip out and back and she wouldn't know. The security guards were in the hall sitting by his door. That would be no problem. He took Velvet to bed. She was asleep in minutes.

He lay there waiting. At three o'clock he got up quietly and put on his sneakers and dark clothes. He went to the balcony doors and opened them. It was dark and quiet. He looked at the three balconies next to him. The shades were drawn. The maids did that because the balconies faced East, and the morning sun would shine through the windows. He looked down. Nothing was stirring.

Carefully he made his way over until he was on the Congressman's balcony. He tried the door. It was locked, but he expected that. Using a slim knife, he eased it in the door and slid the lock up and out of the way. Quietly, Danny entered the bedroom. The girl was gone and the Congressman was snoring loudly. He went over to the bed. He took his right hand and clamped it down over his mouth and nose.

The Congressman woke up with a start and began to struggle. Danny lifted him up with his left hand and snapped his neck, killing him instantly. He then dragged him outside onto the balcony. One last look around. Nobody was anywhere to be seen.

He bent the Congressman over the balcony railing, flipped his legs up, and sent him plunging downward. As soon as he did this, he was over the balconies and back into his room within seconds of the body hitting the ground. He undressed and got into bed. He lay there waiting for the excitement to begin. It wasn't long.

There was noise in the hall and people talking loudly. Danny's phone rang. It was the hotel's night manager telling him that there had been a terrible accident. The Congressman had fallen off his balcony! The police were on the scene and would be talking to everyone.

Danny replied that he would get dressed and be waiting. He ordered some coffee and pastries from room service. The food got there as the detectives were arriving. The Ox ushered them in. He and the Weasel sat on the couch and had coffee. The taller of the detectives said, "We really hate to bother you, but as you know, Congressman Beale apparently fell off his balcony. According to the other people on the floor, he was really intoxicated when he got back from the restaurant last night."

Danny shook his head. "I'd say he was drunk on his ass. It took two security guards to get him to his room. They half carried him."

"I have to ask you a question. I hope you don't mind, but it's standard procedure."

"Not at all. Go ahead. Shoot."

"Did you see or hear anything suspicious, or notice anybody who wasn't supposed to be on this floor?"

"I didn't hear or see anything. We were in bed. My guys here can tell you. Maybe they saw something? One of them was outside my door at all times. I thought you had two security guys in front of the Congressman's door. You don't suspect foul play do you?"

"Oh no, it's just that we have to ask these questions. I'm sorry we bothered you."

"No problem. Hey, sit down and have some coffee."

The two detectives looked at each other. The shorter one said, "My wife is never going to believe this. I'm having coffee with Danny Angel!" They both sat down and for the next half hour had the time of their lives. When they left, they had autographed pictures, signed albums, and backstage passes for the Fest to take home to their wives.

The phone rang in Danny's ear just before nine o'clock in the morning. It was Paulie from the Fest. He was all excited.

"Did you hear what happened to Congressman Beale? He's dead! Fell off his balcony. This puts us in a real bind. He was our Grand Marshall. Danny, I hate to ask, but could you take his place? The people would love it."

"Sure I'll do it. Just let me know when, and I'll be there. I don't perform until the day after tomorrow, so I'm wide open."

"Oh Jesus, Danny. You're a life saver. I'll be in touch." He hung up. Danny looked at Velvet who was just waking up. "Guess what? You're going to be a Grand Marshalette in the big parade."

She yawned and cuddled up next to him. "But, I'm not Italian."

"You are by injection, my dear. Besides you'll add a lot of beauty to the occasion." He was about to kiss her when the phone rang again. He picked it up and said, "Hello." The Don said, "I just saw the terrible news on TV. The poor Congressman fell off his balcony. If I've said it once, I've said it a hundred times. You are the best ever. I'll be there tonight. We can talk."

"Good. You can stay with me in my suite. I'll have the Weasel pick you up. What time is your plane getting in?"

"Seven o'clock. I'll have Johnny and Georgie with me."

"No problem. They can stay with my guys in the suite next door. There's plenty of room."

"Good. See you tonight." He hung up.

Chapter 45

They were sitting in the parlor of the suite, just Danny and the Don. Velvet was off doing something. The bodyguards were in their suite. The Don was talking. "That has to be a record for hits. The first day you're here, and the job is history."

Danny smiled at him. "The opportunity was there, so I took it. It was a piece of cake." He told the Don how he did it. The Don started to laugh. "That's beautiful, just beautiful. And nobody suspected anything. See, I told you it would work. I'm working on a big one. This one pays big. It's in Africa. When I get it all worked out, I'll let you know."

"Africa? Who the hell am I going to whack? A Watusi? A Ubangi?"

"No, some big shot from Nairobi. Don't worry about it. When the time comes, I'll let you know."

"Fair enough. Tomorrow is the big parade and the opening of Festa Italiana. It should be fun."

And fun it was. You could smell the garlic for fifteen miles. There were over one hundred thousand Italians and non Italians there eating everything in sight. When Danny arrived the screams could be heard for miles. He made a speech opening the Festa. Then they went around sampling the food from the booths that were set up everywhere. The nine stages were going strong. Louie and Keely along with Sam Butera were killing them. Dick Contino, Jerry Vale and Sergio had them in the palm of their hands. The other stages had lesser known Italian entertainers.

Danny, they were saving for the last day of the Festa. He would be on the big stage. Johnny would rehearse the band the morning of his show. He already had Peter's music written without his knowledge.

This will be his big opening. It's the break that entertainers would give a left testicle for. Opening for a star of Danny Angel's magnitude, and in front of thousands of Italians, would be a dream come true. It would be like throwing pepperoni to a starving Italian. Danny hadn't told Peter about the Festa or opening for him in Las Vegas. He decided to tell him tonight back at the hotel.

He was sad about one thing though. It would be Rosalie's last show. He had a party planned for her at Capazzoli's after the Fest was over. Velvet took care of that for him.

When they got back to the hotel, they all went up to Danny's suite. Velvet had called ahead and refreshments were waiting for them. When they were settled, Danny said, "I have an announcement to make. As you all know, our dear Roslalie is leaving us to go back to New York to have her baby. The Fest will be her last performance. We will miss her very much. So, I have decided to hire a new opening act."

He was watching Peter. Peter had just taken a big sip of coffee. "I decided that Peter here should fill that spot." Peter, upon hearing this, blew coffee out of both nostrils. He was choking and trying to say something to the amusement of everyone there. Everybody was laughing. He finally collected himself. "Danny, are you crazy? I can't do that. I have no charts. I have no act."

Danny held up a hand for him to stop. "First off Peter, you're a funny man, can comment off the wall, and make fun of the situations around you. I've heard you do that in the band room. I had Johnny here write some charts and you'll rehearse them the day of the Fest. I want you to do around thirty minutes. We have the show laid out for you, and all you have to do is be funny. You'll be working in front of our people, and the fact that you're opening for me, already gives you a big edge."

Peter looked like a deer caught in the headlights. "Wait a minute. I'm opening for you at the Fest? Oh shit!"

Danny came over and put his arm around Peter's shoulder. "Tomorrow the Weasel is going to take you to a tailor. You'll get a new tux, shoes and all that goes with it. Then back here to the beauty parlor downstairs for a haircut and manicure. You're going to be beautiful."

Peter fell back on the couch. "At least, if I die I'll be dressed for it." They roared. Everybody gave him a hug and wished him well. The Don came over to Danny. "He'll do fine. If he's half as funny as when he did that thing at my house, they'll love him."

"I know. I can't wait to see their reaction when he plays his horn on the last number."

The day flew by. Danny had to go to the Fest, Peter to the tailor, and Velvet to get the table set up for all the merchandise to sell. Then it was back to the hotel. Velvet, Danny, the Don and Rosalie were in Danny's suite having drinks when they heard a knock on the door. The Ox went to see who it was. He opened the door and Bert strolled in. Rosalie squealed, came off the couch and jumped into his arms hugging him and kissing him. Danny came over and hugged the both of them. "What the hell are you doing here?"

Bert smiled and gave Rosalie a kiss on her forehead. "You didn't think I would miss my wife's last performance did you? In addition to that, I didn't want her to have to fly by herself. I wanted to take her home."

Danny replied, "Well, I didn't know that you were so gallant. I'll phone downstairs and get you a suite."

"Don't bother. I have one. Seems some Congressman thought he could fly. I guess he was doing fine until he hit the ground. So I have his suite."

Danny started to laugh. "Just stay off the balcony. Did you bring your guys with you?"

"Yeah, they're out in the hall with the Weasel."

"They can bunk next door with my guys and the Don's. There's plenty of room."

The Don came over and gave Bert a hug. "It's good to see you old friend. Tomorrow the three of us will have a sit down. But don't think about that now. Enjoy your wife."

"Thanks Don Angelo. Now I'm going to take my wife to our suite. I'll see you for breakfast." He took Rosalie's arm and guided her out the door.

Danny said to the Don, "I never thought any woman could tame him. I'm really happy for both of them."

******

It was Fest Day. Johnny rehearsed the orchestra. He rehearsed Peter's charts and had Peter play them so he knew the arrangement. He was absolutely thrilled. He never played in front of so big an orchestra. Danny arrived with the Don and Bert. Show time was nearing and people were coming from every corner of the fest to get a good seat or a place to stand. There had to be ten thousand people waiting for the show.

Peter was so nervous he was shaking like a leaf. If you had put a cocktail shaker in his hand, he could have mixed a martini. The orchestra was on the stage, and the lights came on. Danny walked over to Peter. He put his arm around his shoulder. "I want you to remember these two words when you go out on stage. Have fun. This is your night, so let it all hang out." He slapped him on the shoulder.

He heard a drum roll, and then an off stage announcement. "Ladies and gentlemen, Festa Italiana is proud to present the one and only Danny Angel." The crowd went wild. The announcer continued. "And now, to open our show, here's Danny Angel's favorite comedian, Peter Valorino." The orchestra went into his opening number. He hit the stage running, right into the opener, "When You're Smiling."

The song ended and Peter started in on everybody and everything around him. He had them screaming. He did an Italian routine that had thousands howling. He went into "Dark Town Stutters Ball." Ten thousand people were clapping and singing along with him. Then came the moment Danny had been waiting for, the closing number.

Peter picked up his horn and walked to the microphone. He

stood there until the crowd quieted down. "Ladies and Gentlemen, I want to thank you for the wonderful applause and the love you have shown me. Now I would like to close with a wonderful song, Malaguena, which was stolen from us Italians. It really is called Mala-guinne." The crowd went wild. They laughed, hooted, and hollered.

Peter put the horn to his lips. The orchestra went into the intro. When he played the first notes the crowd went deathly quite. He filled the grounds with beautiful tones and intonations. He swelled up and quieted down. It was like they were listening to Gabriel blowing his horn. He got to the end of the song. He hit the last note and held it long, pure and sweet. The music died. He stood there with the horn still on his lips. The crowd went crazy. Ten thousand people screaming and whistling. He took his bow. The orchestra went into his bow music, "When You're Smiling." He walked off to thunderous applause. Danny was waiting for him in the wings. "Now, tell me you can't do it."

Peter had tears in his eyes. "I have to tell you the truth. I didn't know I was that funny. Surprised the hell out of me. Danny, those charts are wonderful. Thank you so much."

Before Danny could answer, the announcer said, "And now ladies and gentlemen, the moment you have been waiting for. Here he is, our very own, Danny Angel." The music started and he walked out to absolute pandemonium. He was half way through the first number before they heard him. He did it all. For an hour and a half he and Rosalie completely destroyed the crowd. They had to do two encores.

Then, it was over. Danny was soaking wet from perspiration as was Rosalie. Their dressing room was a big house trailer. Danny went in and showered. Rosalie did the same. People were waiting, so he had the Ox let them in. Bert and the Don sat on the couch and greeted all comers.

The party was beautiful. Johnny and the boys took over the bandstand and the music and jokes flew. Danny and Rosalie got up and did an impromptu duet together. Peter got up and did some funny shtick on the people there. All in all, it was a great night.

They got back to the hotel. The Don asked Bert to come to Danny's suite after he put Roslalie to bed. Velvet went into their bedroom and got ready for bed. It wasn't long before Bert arrived. They sat around the table in the breakfast nook. The Don started, "First off Danny, Bert knows what we're doing. I brought him into this thing because he's a paison and I wanted him to have a piece of the pie. He's going to help me set things up. He's got good connections and knows what I need."

Danny looked at Bert. "I'm glad Bert. Be like old times."

Bert reached over and shook hands with Danny. "I want to thank you for getting rid of the Congressman. I wouldn't have had a suite here. They were booked solid." That brought a laugh. The Don said, "OK, let's get down to business."

Chapter 46

From Milwaukee, Danny took a short job in the Bahamas via Miami. Danny and Velvet were looking forward to a few days of warm, sandy beaches. Velvet deserved some time off. After four nights at the Fontainebleau, they flew to Freeport, Grand Bahamas to do the Kings Inn. It was there that Danny had a run in with the leader of the black mafia, Scarbu. He was big, black, ugly and liked to carry a club up his sleeve. He ran Freeport, or so he thought. One night after the show they were all in the lounge having drinks. Scarbu started to hit on Velvet. Danny reminded him that she was his girl.

That didn't set too well with Scarbu, so he brought out the club. Before he could do anything, the Ox had him by the neck and was putting a choker hold on him. His bodyguards started to move, but the Weasel stood up. They found themselves looking down the barrel of a gun. Danny came over and took the club out of Scarbu's hand. He nodded to the Ox and he let him go.

Danny got real close to his ugly face. "I'm only going to say this once, so pay close attention. While I'm here, you don't fuck with me or any of my people. If you do, you're going swimming with the fishes. Do I make myself clear?" Scarbu was looking into his eyes and didn't like what he saw.

"Now get your ass out of here." Scarbu got up and motioned his guys to follow him out. The Ox said to Danny, "You know he might just try to come after you. You embarrassed him in front of everybody."

Danny agreed. "How would you and the Weasel like to earn a little bonus?" The Ox smiled at him. Danny continued, "Why don't you see if he can swim."

The Ox nodded. "Consider it done." Two days later they found him floating in the bay with several rounds of lead in him. The British were glad to be rid of him, so there was no investigation to speak of. The next day they were all on their way back to Vegas, where Danny could relax and enjoy his new lifestyle.

Danny loved his home and valued his time off. He was playing lots of golf with Freddie Bell, Sonny King and Bill Fanning. It was quite a foursome with three Italians and a WASP who was FBI!

Danny was giving a lot of thought as to how to whack somebody in a hurry. The Congressman was one of the easiest hits he'd ever done. He was watching TV one night about the Pygmies of New Guinea, and how they brought down big game with darts or arrows tipped in curare poison. He decided to read up on it. It was just what he needed, but how was he to administer it? He couldn't walk around with a blow gun or a bow and arrows. It had to be something small and able to fit in the palm of his hand.

He remembered the knife he had made. It had a heavy duty spring held down by a notch. There was a little knob sticking up. One move of the knob and the spring loaded blade would shoot out with lots of force. Force enough to kill. You had to pull the knob back down to get the blade back inside and set the spring again. He needed something that could flick out and back like a snakes tongue. Just squeeze the side to activate it. A jeweler could do it. He'd make a rough sketch and get somebody to make it for him. In the meantime, he would be doing the New Frontier for the Jewish guys from Toledo and cutting a new album.

Two weeks into the Frontier gig, he got a phone call from Don Angelo telling him he would be going to Sun City Resorts in South Africa when he finished the Frontier. He was mailing him an envelope with all the information needed for the job. He expected that Danny would be gone a month. The mark spent his vacations in Sun City, so he would be where Danny would have easy access to him. This was a big money job. A hundred thousand would be deposited in Danny's Swiss account.

He thought to himself, *"They must really want this guy whacked to pay him that kind of money."* He wondered what the Don and Bert were getting for this job. He didn't really care.

His next step was getting some curare poison. He called a druggist friend from Chicago and asked him about it. He wanted wild aconitum. The druggist said, "Jesus Danny, that's powerful stuff. What the hell do you want that for?"

"Hey, I live in the desert and have all kinds of critters around me. I got this blow gun from a guy who went to New Guinea. I've been practicing and I'm pretty good. I can get rid of some of these pests. My neighbors are not too crazy about guns. So what do you say?"

"OK, I'll get it and send it to you. But, you don't remember where you got it. Capisci?"

"I understand and thanks." He gave the druggist his mailing address. "I'll need it as soon as possible. I'm leaving in two weeks. I'll see that some money is dropped off for you. And if you ever want to come to Vegas, it's on me."

"Thanks, Danny. I'll be in touch."

Danny sat back and thought to himself, *"Now all I need is somebody to make me the little goodie."* He decided he would get it made in South Africa. That way somebody would have to go a long way to find out who made it.

*****

The plane made a lazy turn on its approach to the Cape Town airport. Danny had been studying up on the guy he was to take out. He was a real bad ass named Hadi Macumba, a self proclaimed dictator who wanted to take over Kenya. He had already killed thousands of people who got in his way. The United States would like him to disappear, but as always, they were too chicken shit to get it done. Macumba would be staying at Sun City along with his bodyguards and, according to the folder, he traveled with a small army. This was going to be a real challenge.

They changed planes in Cape Town and boarded a plane for

Johannesburg's Tambo airport. When they arrived, they were met by a committee from the hotel. They had beautiful South African girls, all over six feet tall, dressed in native garb with arms full of flowers. African police were standing by to escort him to the Cascades Hotel. There were two or three hundred people waiting outside the terminal to greet him.

When they saw Danny, they cheered and waved to him. He waved back, smiled and was hustled to a waiting limo. It looked like a parade. There were cars and motorcycles in front and in back of him with sirens blasting. Once out of the airport, they shut off the sirens. The drive to Sun City was spectacular. The scenery in Pilanesberg National Forest was breathtaking.

They got to the hotel and were shown to the suites. Five black soldiers were standing guard outside the door at the end of the hallway. The hotel manager explained that it was the Presidential Suite and was occupied by Hadi Macuba from Nairobi. Danny's suite, a few doors down, was spacious and well appointed. The Ox and the Weasel had adjoining rooms. The band was one floor below.

Danny asked to see were he would be entertaining. The hotel manager took him down and out of the hotel to a large building. They came through the loading area and onto the stage. It was huge. The room sat six thousand people. The hotel hired a thirty six piece orchestra from Johannesburg to back him. He was told he would be doing one show on Friday and Saturday only.

That night they were having dinner in the tropical dining room. Johnny, Vinnie, Sal, the Ox and the Weasel were with him. In the middle of dinner, Danny looked up and saw a big black man approaching his table. He was wearing the traditional African Barriga garb. With him were three soldiers and one of the most beautiful black girls Danny had ever laid eyes on.

She was just over six feet tall, and willowy with a long elegant neck. The princess kaftan she wore didn't conceal the body under it. Danny stood up as they approached. The black man said, "Pardon the interruption of your dinner, but I just had to meet you. I am, how you say, a big fan of yours. My name is Hadi Macuba, and this is Candelario." He held out his hand and Danny shook it. He smiled at Candelario, took her hand and kissed it. She lowered her eyes. She was so black that Danny didn't know if she was blushing or not. "It's nice to meet you. Won't you join us?"

Before anybody could say anything, two waiters showed up with chairs and made room at the table. That put them across from Danny. He couldn't keep his eyes off of Candelario. When she caught him looking at her, she smiled and the whole room lit up. She had the whitest teeth, but framed by her black face, it became all the more startling. He had to take his eyes off her when he heard Hadi talking to him.

"I must tell you Mr. Angel that I have all your albums. And I've seen your movies. You are the best."

"Well thank you, but please call me Danny. Mr. Angel sounds too formal."

"Good, then you can call me Hadi. I have already made reservations for all your shows. I have many people here that want to see and hear you."

"I'm glad. So you're going to be here a month?"

"Yes. I want to relax and have fun. I'm having a party tomorrow night at eight o'clock in my suite. I would be honored if you could come."

"I'll be there Hadi. I wouldn't miss it."

The rest of the evening was small talk, gambling, and a walk in the gardens. Danny learned that Candelario was Ethiopian, from the Hammer tribe. She kept looking at him when Hadi was looking elsewhere. Danny decided that, as soon as he dispatched Hadi, she would be his.

The next morning, Danny was on his way to Johannesburg. He had learned from Hadi that there was a jeweler that could make any kind of jewelry he wanted. He found the shop. The Ox and the Weasel stayed with the limo. Danny walked into this quaint little jewelry store. The jeweler looked like Peter Lori. Danny explained what he wanted and showed him a rough sketch. The little jeweler studied it and made some changes in the design. "I can make this, but it will be expensive with the pearl, the gold lettering and the spring mechanism."

"I don't care how much it costs. I trust you. When can I have it?"

The jeweler considered it a moment and made some notes. "Next Monday afternoon."

Danny thanked him, left a deposit and went back to the hotel to get ready for the party. He gave the Ox and the Weasel the night off. He would be protected by Hadi's army. All he had to do was walk down the hall.

At seven-thirty the elevator started dinging every few minutes. People were arriving. Danny got there at eight fifteen. When he was let in, Hadi ran over and greeted him. He took him by the arm and introduced him to everybody. He was the only white person there. Candelario brought him a drink. When she handed it to him, she made sure she touched him. She looked at him with those black eyes. It was like a black leopard eyeing its prey. Danny smiled and winked at her. She smiled and walked away. She didn't really walk, it was more like she glided. Danny sat at the bar talking to whomever came up. He got the distinct impression that this was the black mafia and Hadi was the Capo. Even the women there were comares, not wives. Hadi announced that tomorrow they would be going on a picture taking safari through the Pilanesberg National Park. He said to Danny, "Danny, I hope you are coming too."

Danny got off the bar stool and walked over to Hadi. "I'd love to. What time do we meet?"

"Tomorrow morning at nine in front of the hotel. Why don't you meet me in the restaurant for breakfast at eight o'clock?"

"You've got a deal. I think I'll call it a night. It's been a long day." He said his good nights. Candelario took his arm and escorted him to the door. She looked down at him and smiled. "You are a very handsome man. I've never had a white lover before."

"That can be arranged, my dear. Just hold on for a little while." He kissed her hand and was gone.

Chapter 47

The week flew by with Safari's, dances, gambling, and parties every night. He was getting real close to Hadi. He did manage to cop a feel or two along the way from Candelario, and he liked what he felt. Friday came. The room was sold out. Danny rehearsed the orchestra in the afternoon. He would be doing almost two hours. When he got to his dressing room that evening, it looked like a florist shop. There were all kinds of flowers and sitting in a big silver bucket, was a magnum of champagne from Hadi. He had reserved the first two rows in the middle section. The lights came down. The orchestra went into its first song, "Way Marie." The offstage announcer made his introduction. When he mentioned Danny's name, six thousand people screamed and applauded.

He hit the stage right into his opener, "I'm Gonna Live 'Till I Die." From then on it was magic. For two hours he held them in the palm of his hand. When it was over, the applause was deafening. He took three curtain calls. When he got to the dressing room he was exhausted. He took a quick shower and changed into casual attire. When he walked out of the bathroom area into his dressing room, it was packed with people. Hadi saw him and came running over and hugged him. "That was the greatest show I have ever seen. You were magnificent. My friends all love you."

He took Danny over to a crowd of people. The men were all tall and dressed in African garb. While he was talking to them Candelario came over and handed him a glass of champagne. "I think you need this." She turned and glided away. Danny charmed them all. Finally, he said to Hadi, "Let's go to my suite and have a drink. It'll be nice and quiet. I'll have some food sent up."

Hadi nodded. "Good. I will say goodnight to my guests and meet you there. Oh, could you take Candelario with you?"

"Sure, I can do that. I'll have everything ready by the time you get there. See you in a little while." Candelario was talking to three women. He walked in her direction and motioned her over.

"You're to come with me to my suite and wait for Hadi. He'll be along shortly." She nodded and followed him out to the waiting limo. Once inside, she got close to him. Just having her this close gave him a raging hard on. She looked down and saw the bulge along the inside of his thigh. She reached down with her left hand and squeezed it gently. Danny had all he could do to control it from coming. She said in his ear, "Can you hold it until we reach your suite?"

"Not if you keep doing that," he responded. She gave him that dazzling smile and let go. When they got to the suite, Danny told the Ox to stand in the hall and let him know when Hadi showed up. Once inside they wasted no time. In one fluid motion the kaftan fell away from her body. She wasn't wearing anything under it. Danny had never seen such a body. It was magnificent. She was tall and willowy without an ounce of fat. She looked like an ebony statue. Her breasts stood straight out. He was out of his clothes and came to her. She bent her head down and kissed him. She spread her legs and with her right hand guided him inside her. It was heaven. She took her mouth off of his, leaned back, grabbed him by the ass and started to move straight in and out. Her long legs supported her as she drove Ninja all the way inside. Her pace quickened and she started to moan. Faster and faster she drove him. She gazed into his eyes. "Come with me." He did.

They exploded together. She kept pumping until she climaxed a second time. Danny's knees were so weak that they sunk slowly to the floor. Their breathing was ragged and fast. They sat looking at each other. She was still sitting on him. Her long legs stretched out behind him. "That was wonderful. Now, I must go get cleaned up before Hadi gets here. We'll do this again soon."

Little did she know how soon it would be. Danny let her slide away. She picked up her kaftan and headed for the bathroom.

Danny went into the other bathroom and cleaned himself up. He called room service and ordered food. When Hadi got there, the Ox and Weasel were sitting, talking to Candelario. Danny was behind the bar mixing drinks. Room service had delivered the food. They ate, drank and had some laughs. When they left, Candelario gave him a warm knowing look. Yes, it would be soon.

Saturday was sold out. Danny outdid himself. Sunday they went to Johannesburg to an outdoor concert, had dinner in a beautiful restaurant, then returned to Sun City.

Monday Danny was back in Johannesburg in the little jewelry shop. The little jeweler was showing Danny his new toy. It was a lovely piece of pearl with Danny Angel inlaid in gold on both sides. Danny squeezed the pearl, a small needle flicked out and back in within a split second. "This is fine. You do excellent work. What do I owe you?"

As the jeweler went to get the bill, Danny opened the vial of curare and flicked the little blade in it. When the jeweler was explaining the bill, Danny flicked him in the thigh with the blade. The jeweler gave a jerk. He stepped back and rubbed the spot where the needle went in. Before he had a chance to say anything, he started to gasp for breath.

Danny watched as he slid to the floor and died. He took the bill and slipped it into his pocket. He said to the dead jeweler, "Too bad you couldn't stick around to see how good it worked." He left the store, got in the limo and went back to Sun City.

On his return, he was figuring out where and when to get rid of Hadi. He didn't have to think very hard. Hadi called him and told him that the hotel was having a big African party at the pool the next night. Everybody was to dress in African attire. Hadi had ordered a Barriga kaftan for him. It would be sent up that afternoon. Perfect. Lots of people dancing, drinking, and having fun would be the perfect setting. And, most would admit, a nice atmosphere for leaving this world.

That evening they had dinner and then went to the casino to gamble. It was a more subdued evening. They sat in a lounge and quietly listened to music then retired.

The next day Danny made his plans. Sometime during the evening's festivities, he would have the chance to pop him with the needle. He'd have to pick the right moment, but that was no problem. At a party, opportunities would be all around him. He told Johnny to have the boys at the party, so he could sing a couple of songs if needed. He also told him to get some African clothes from one of the shops at the hotel and charge it to him.

He told the Ox and Weasel the same thing. He had to laugh. What would the Ox look like in a kaftan? When the time came, he got dressed. He looked at himself in the big bathroom mirror and said to himself, *"You do look great my man. An Afro-Italian lady killer."* He flicked the needle into the curare twice. He put it in the right hand pocket of the Kaftan, then walked into the parlor. There stood the Ox and Weasel. It was all he could do to keep from busting out laughing. The Weasel looked like John Carradine in a dress. The Ox looked like a male version of Kate Smith in drag.

When they arrived at the pool, the crowd gave him a wild ovation. Hadi came running over and escorted him to all his black mafia guys. They complimented him on his kaftan. Drinks flowed like water and Hadi was well on his way to getting sloshed. There were native dancers, drumming, African music, and a fashion show. Candelario modeled four or five outfits. She was the picture of grace and poise.

The entertainment director from the hotel came over and asked Danny if he would grace his people with a song or two. Danny agreed and signaled John to get up on the bandstand. Hadi was standing nearby holding on to one of his soldiers to keep standing up. When the announcer mentioned Danny's name, Hadi broke loose from his leaning post and came stumbling over. Danny saw his chance. As Hadi bumped into him, he popped him on the thigh with the needle. He was so drunk he didn't feel a thing.

Danny gave him back to the soldier and headed for the bandstand. He was half way through the first song, when there was a commotion in the back of the crowd. Soldiers started running around and hollering for a doctor. Four soldiers picked Hadi up and carried him into the hotel's infirmary. Hardly anybody heard or saw anything down front. They were hollering for more so Danny did a couple of extra numbers.

When he came off stage the Ox said, "Your boy is in bad shape. Looks like he had a heart attack. He's in the infirmary." Danny ran over and found the hotel manager standing inside the door. He took Danny to where they had Hadi. The doctor was talking to Candelario and the soldiers. Danny walked up. The doctor looked at him and said, "I'm sorry, but you're too late. Mr. Macuba has expired."

Danny gave him his sorrowful look. "What the hell happened? He was fine. A little drunk, but fine."

"It was a coronary. He had a history of heart trouble."

"So what happens now?"

"His bodyguards are taking him to a funeral parlor. They'll embalm him and ship him home. Once again I'm really sorry."

Danny reached out for Candelario. She came to him. He gave her a hug. "I'm really sorry about this. Is there anything I can do to help you?"

"She whispered in his ear. "I'll come to you after I take him to the funeral parlor. There will be a lot of press over this. He had a wife and children and it wouldn't be good for them to find out that I was here with him. I came to see your shows. We're good friends."

"I'll handle it. Don't worry. I'll see you in a little while." He shook hands with the doctor and went up to his suite. He poured a glass of wine, picked up the phone and asked the operator to connect him to a number in Chicago. He asked her to call him in his suite when she had the number. Five minutes later the phone rang. Danny picked it up. It was the Don. "So how's it going there?"

"Great. I took care of the little problem. The shows are sold out. I'm having a wonderful time."

"That's my boy. Momma says to tell you she misses you."

"I miss you and momma, too. I'll be in touch. Watch the news tomorrow. It should be interesting."

The Don laughed and hung up. Danny sat and thought about how good his invention had worked. Even if the undertaker looked the body over, he wasn't going to find anything. A pin prick on a black body doesn't show. He heard a commotion in the hall. The Weasel came in and told him that the press was in the hallway and wanted to interview him.

The Ox let them in. They all started talking at once. Flash bulbs were going off, TV cameras were rolling, and guys with microphones were looking for interviews. Danny held up his hands for silence. When they quieted down he said, "Tonight I lost a new friend. I only knew Mr. Macuba for a short time, but he was always the epitome of graciousness. Africa has lost a great man. I'm truly sorry for their loss. I really don't know what more I can say." They asked a few questions and left. Danny was mixing himself a drink when Candelario was shown in by the Ox. She came to the bar and sat on a stool.

Danny mixed her a drink. "I'm truly sorry for your loss."

She sipped her drink. "Don't be. He was a pig. I'm glad he's dead. Now I'm free."

"What kind of hold did he have on you?"

"My family. My father opposed him and what he stood for. To keep them from being killed, I agreed to stay with him. Now my father can take over and run the government like it should be."

"Good for him. Now, what about you? What are you going to do?"

"First, I'm going to stay with you until you leave, if you'll have me."

"Done deal, sweetheart. Then what?"

"I'm going back to modeling. He made me quit. I was one of the top models in Africa and Europe."

"If there's anything I can do to help you, let me know. I have some great contacts and know some people that can help you."

"Thank you. If I need any assistance I will call on you. Right now I would like to go to bed with you and have you hold me."

"Now, that's something I do very well. One thing though. May I call you Candy? Candelario is so formal."

"I like that. Candy. Yes, Candy it is. Now take me to bed."

And that's what he did.

Chapter 48

The three weeks were heaven for Danny. Candy was insatiable. They made love day and night. Hadi's funeral was lavish, and then he was forgotten. Candy's father took over and ousted the black mafia guys. Some he had jailed, while others met with unfortunate accidents. The shows were sellouts. Danny had made some calls to New York and, when she was ready, Candy would be brought over and set up with a big modeling agency. He wanted to keep her a plane ride away. He thought he was going back to Vegas, but the Don called and his plans were suddenly changed.

He was going to London to do the Palladium. The Queen would be at one of his performances. The mark was in the British Parliament, a Lord Thomas Crittendale Esq. There would be an envelope waiting for him when he got to London.

Candy's last night with Danny was a memorable one. They didn't get much sleep. They ran through the Kama Sutra book of sexual positions and invented some of their own. They had a tearful parting at the airport. She was off to Nairobi, and he to London.

*****

London was frantic. There were hundreds of people waiting at the airport. The women screamed, trying to get to him. It was all the Bobbies could do to keep them back. The Ox was like a linebacker. He bulled his way to the limo with Danny in tow. The Weasel brought up the rear. They arrived at their suites in the Mayfair Hotel. Danny was pouring himself a drink when he heard a knock on the door. The assistant hotel manager, a tall beautiful lady named Bridget, handed him an envelope. "I'm sorry to disturb you, but my orders were to see that you got this as soon as you arrived."

Danny took the envelope. "Well, Bridget, you did your duty. Come in and have a drink with me."

"Oh I can't. I'm on duty sir. Hotel policy and all."

"I can fix that." He escorted her into the suite. "Sit here my dear, while I fix this little problem." He picked up the phone and asked for the hotel manager. When he came on, Danny explained to him that he'd like to have Bridget show him the amenities of the hotel and where to go for fun.

The hotel manager said it would be an honor. "Mr. Angel, she is at your service. Keep her as long as needed." Danny hung up the phone. "Bridget, my dear, you're mine for as long as I need you. Why don't you take off your jacket while I fix you a drink?"

Danny got a look at what was under the jacket. He liked what he saw. She said, "Tell me, do you always get what you want?"

"If I want it bad enough. I noticed there's no ring on your finger, so I take it you're not married. You have got to have a boyfriend. Somebody that looks as good as you wouldn't be alone."

She smiled at him. "Thanks for the compliment, but I am alone. I just got out of a messy relationship. How about that drink?" The drinks led to dinner in the suite. Kissing and heavy breathing followed. She left the suite at eleven o'clock that night.

Danny went over the information in the envelope. This guy was a piece of work. He was anti-everything, and caused lots of trouble in Parliament. He liked to flex his muscle, step on the wrong toes, and rub it in because he was in the favor of the Royal Family. According to the information, he would be at the premier performance with the Queen and her entourage. A party was to follow with VIP guests only. Perfect. What better a place to take him out? There will be lots of pomp and bullshit going on. He decided to take Bridget with him as arm candy.

The week went by quickly. Danny was the toast of London. His shows were sold out every night. Bridget was spending the nights with him in the suite. Then came Saturday, and his show for the Royal Family. They got to the Palladium early. Danny made sure the Ox took care of Bridget. She was stunning. The gown she wore fit her like a glove.

He peeked through the curtain at the Royal Box. There sat the Queen, with Lord Crittendale just behind her. He had a look on his face as though he was smelling something bad. Sitting next to him was Lady Crittendale. One look at her and Danny knew why Lord Crittendale had that expression. She was butt ugly. All the fancy clothes and the jewelry in the world couldn't hide the fact that she had a face like a horse. He'd probably welcome death, just to be rid of her.

The show started and Danny was really on. They loved him. He did over an hour and a half. The Queen was all smiles as he acknowledged her. Then dedicating his last song to her, he did a kick ass version of "Foggy Day." He changed the words to fit the occasion. They went crazy.

He was escorted to the mini ballroom where the Queen was holding a reception. The Ox brought Bridget over to him. The Queen was most gracious, complementing him on his show. Danny was all charm. They chatted for a few moments, then he moved on so she could receive her other guests. He noticed Lord Crittendale staring daggers at Bridget. She in turn, was avoiding his eyes. Danny put his arm around her and led her over to the punch bowl. "Is it my imagination, or is this Lord Crittendale, the messy situation you just got out of?"

"I didn't know he was going to be here. I'm sorry."

"It's not your fault. Don't worry about it." The string quartet started to play. People started to come over and congratulate Danny. Lord Crittendale came over and walked straight to where Bridget was standing. He was talking down to her and making her uncomfortable. Danny saw his chance. He walked over and put his left arm around Bridget's waist.

People came over to them to talk. They crowded around Danny. Lord Crittendale got pissed and turned to stomp away. That's when Danny popped him in the ass with the needle. It was so fast that nobody saw anything. Lord Crittendale jumped a little. He looked behind him and rubbed the spot where the needle went in. He glared at Danny and went over to his wife.

Danny watched him while talking to the guests. It wasn't long before Lord Crittendale started to gasp for air. His wife became hysterical and called for help. Before anyone could get to him, he was dead. Everybody crowded around. The Queen's doctor came over and pronounced him dead. The wife began screaming and crying. People were trying to console her. The body was taken to an ambulance the moment it arrived. Bridget was confused at all the commotion, and stayed close to Danny. The Queen took her leave and the party broke up.

Danny got Bridget to the limo. "I'm sorry about your boyfriend."

"You needn't be. He was a real wanker. He was mean and a control freak. All he wanted from me was sex, and he wasn't that good at it. He never would take me anywhere and was always afraid we would run into somebody he knew."

"Well, he's gone and we're here. We have the whole night to ourselves. Let's make the best of it. And they did.

When Danny got to the airport, he was exhausted. He slept most of the way back to New York. He decided to spend a couple of days with Bert and Rosalie, so he could see the new baby boy. She named him Bertram Daniel. They wanted Danny to be his godfather. He called the Don from the airport in New York.

The Don was happy to hear from him. "I still say it. You're the best. I don't know how the hell you're doing it, but keep up the good work. You're going back to Vegas to do the Sands. I want you to relax and have fun for awhile. Say hello to Albert for me."

After the baptismal mass at the church, Danny and Bert went to his office. Once inside Bert said, "OK. You get rid of two guys in a crowd of people and one in front of the Queen of England! I saw both stories on TV. Two guys die of heart attacks. What did you do, scare them to death?"

"They didn't die of natural causes. That's for sure. They died from curare poison. It just looks like a heart attack."

"Son of a bitch. How the hell did you think of something like that?"

Danny explained it to him. He took the pearl out of his pocket. "Check this out." He squeezed the pearl and the needle flicked out and back. He did it again. Bert exclaimed, "Son of a bitch, that's beautiful! And it works."

"You bet your ass it does. One thing Bert, you're the only one who knows this. The people putting out the contracts may think the same thing, a heart attack. You have to tell them different, or they may not want to pay. It's not how it's done, but rather it was your man that did it."

"I can handle that. I'll let the Don know when the next contract comes in. Now, let's go to the house. Rosalie is cooking linguini with matzo balls. Hey, don't laugh. The other night I had gefilte fish marinara." That got a laugh out of both of them.

Chapter 49

Velvet met him at the airport. She was as beautiful as ever. They necked on the way to the house. Once inside they spent the rest of the day in bed. That night Velvet brought him up to speed on his bookings. Some TV shows, another movie, and a new album of Italian songs. He was going to be a busy boy. The Sands opening was sold out and most of the stars in Vegas would be there. The Rat Pack was closing on Saturday and would be at his opening on Monday. Peter would be his opening act.

He expected the opening to be a wild night, but it was way beyond his expectations. He opened to a packed house. Peter did great. Then it was his turn. He came on stage and kicked the hell out of them for thirty minutes. In the middle of singing one of Frank's songs the Rat pack showed up. They walked on stage pushing the booze cart. The crowd went wild. Danny was smart enough to let them have the stage. They came at him and he held his own. With songs, jokes, and parodies, they ran the gauntlet. Frank was in the middle of a song when Sonny King and Shecky Greene came on stage. They took the mic away from him and did a ten minute bit that killed the crowd. Rickles showed up and zinged everybody. It was like a parade of Vegas acts.

Two hours into the show Frank called for quiet. "As you know, our paison, Danny Angel opened tonight. We gave him a Sands welcome. Now it's time for him to entertain us." The stagehands showed up on cue with folding chairs. They placed them in half circle in front of Danny. The other acts came and sat in the chairs leaving the center one for Frank. "And now it gives me great pleasure to introduce the one and only, Danny Angel."

Danny came forward and took the mic from Frank, kissed him on the cheek, and patted him on the ass as he went to sit down. He finished in a blaze of glory. They all joined in on his closing number.

The party in the dressing room was wild. People just kept showing up including Juliet Prowse, Ann Margret, Robert Goulet, and Joe Williams. It was like a who's who of stars. Velvet fit right in. She was gorgeous and could hold her own against anybody. The party lasted until four in the morning.

Danny was busy. He flew to Los Angeles to record his album, then back to do his shows. He did a part in a movie which was filmed in Vegas. He managed to get in some golf with Freddie Bell, Buddy Greco and Bill Fanning. He was getting real tight with Bill. The three months really flew by.

*****

He was sitting in his den when Don Angelo called. "Bert just called me. He wants you to go to Hot Springs, Arkansas."

"Isn't that the place where Owny Madden has a joint? The big boys go there for sit downs."

"That's right. They've got gambling and a race track."

"So what's the problem?"

"There's a Senator trying to close the town down. He wants the casinos and the track shut down. He's making a lot of noise."

"So, why doesn't Owny have him whacked?"

"He is. He called Bert and asked for the best guy to do the job. He wants to be out of town and far away when the guy goes down. I'm sending you an envelope. You'll be working the Southern Club for a week, then the Vapors for two weeks. There are lot of wise guys there. You may know some of them. I have one suggestion for you. While you're there, take the baths. They're wonderful."

"I'll do that. Give my love to momma." He hung up the phone.

They landed at the small Hot Springs airport. A limo was

waiting to take them to the Majestic Hotel. After they checked in, Johnny and the boys went to the club to rehearse the band. Danny, with the Ox and Weasel, did a tour of Central Avenue. On one side of the street were big beautiful bath houses. Small quaint shops lined the other side. On the corner was a strip club called The Black Orchid. They dropped in for a drink. It was dark inside. Guys sat around, sipping beer and watching the girls dance. A good looking dancer sitting at the end of the bar spotted them and came over to their table.

She was built like a brick, chicken coop. She was going to say something, but stopped when she saw Danny. Her mouth dropped open. Before she could say anything, Danny reached out, took her arm and pulled her down in the chair next to him. He whispered in her ear, "Yes, it's Danny Angel. But don't say anything. This way you have me all to yourself."

She looked at him. "I can't believe you're here. My God you're beautiful. Aren't you opening tonight at the Southern Club?"

"Yes, I am. I'll be in town for three weeks. What time does your shift end?"

"Eight o'clock tonight. But, I can take off when I want to."

"Good. Come to the club after work. Tell the pit boss, I'm expecting you. What's your name?"

"Phyllis, but they call me Phil."

"OK, Phil, see you tonight." He gave her a kiss and slipped a fifty dollar bill in her hand. "That's for being so nice." They left and went back to the hotel.

The crowds were great with lots of horse people and cowboys. Owny was all charm and made sure that Danny had anything he wanted. It was fun to watch the straight people hob knobbing with the mob guys. Danny knew them all but not as Danny Angel.

Phil showed up looking great. She was wearing a gown that showed her off to perfection. Danny sent the Ox to get her. A lot of heads turned on her way over to him. Owny had set up the dining room so they could all sit and have fun. The jokes were flying fast and furious. One of the boys from Cleveland was drunk and loud.

Danny knew him. His name was Pete Quomo, AKA Bruto. He was an enforcer, and liked to hurt people. He didn't care if they were male or female. Danny never liked him. He spotted Phil and came over. He moved the guy sitting next to her and sat down. He started to talk to her while grabbing a cheap feel.

Danny leaned over to him. "Excuse me, but that's my lady you're messing with. Please keep your fucking hands to yourself."

Bruto jumped up. "Who the fuck you talking to, pretty boy? I'll smash that pretty face of yours."

The Ox was on his feet and moving. Before the Ox could get to Bruto, Owny Madden stepped in front of him and slammed his finger into Bruto's chest. Now Owny was small, no bigger than Sammy Davis. He had to reach up to do it. "Listen to me. You get your ass out of here and cool off. Don't you ever insult one of my guests again or the next time will be your last time." He gave him a shove. Bruto shot daggers at Danny and walked away.

Owny was all apologetic. Danny watched a few minutes until Bruto went into the men's room. He excused himself and followed him. They were the only two in there. Danny waited until Bruto finished. He turned around and Danny was standing right in front of him. Before he had a chance to react, Danny hit him with a sledge hammer blow that knocked him back against the wall. His head hit the wall with a resounding bang. He was almost out on his feet. Danny held him up against the wall hitting him with punishing blows. He dragged him over to one of the stalls and shoved him in.

Danny felt great. The blood was coursing through his veins. Now he wanted to get laid. He walked back to the table and resumed the conversation like nothing happened. The Ox gave him a look of, "What happened in there?" Danny just smiled at him. A half hour later Danny saw two security guards go into the men's room. It wasn't long before the rescue squad showed up and took Bruto out on a gurney to the waiting ambulance.

Owny came over. "How about that? Somebody knocked the shit out of Pete. I don't know who did it, but he deserves a medal."

Danny knew that Pete wouldn't say who did the job on him.

For one thing, who'd believe him if he said it was Danny? Second, it wasn't in the code to rat on somebody. He'd just take it and wait for his chance to get even. Danny knew this and fingered the pearl in his pocket. He may have to do a freebee. But now it was time to take Phil to the hotel.

When they got to the suite Danny pealed her like a grape. She had a hard tight muscled body with natural breasts. He wasted no time.

Chapter 50

The week at The Southern club flew by. Danny had time to work out a plan to get the Senator to Hot Springs. He had the owner of the Vapors send out special invitations for Danny's opening night there. It would be followed by a special party for VIP guests in the showroom. That's when he'd make his move.

Bruto was out of the hospital. Seems he had a concussion along with a lot of bruises. Danny told the Ox and Weasel to watch his back. He knew he would be coming after him. The Ox suggested that, to make matters simple, he and the Weasel should take care of it for him. Danny gave them the green light. He hated looking over his shoulder.

Phil was a permanent fixture for night time fun and games. She would strip for him and invent all kinds of erotic games. She had a great imagination.

Danny was in his dressing room when Dane Harris, the owner of the club, brought Senator John Summer and his wife, Shirley, backstage to meet him. The Senator was a cocky, five foot seven inch, know it all. Danny disliked him immediately. His wife was adorable; the epitome of a southern lady. She was tall, sophisticated and had the sweetest southern drawl. Danny liked her right off. She looked at him under her lashes and actually blushed.

The jerk Senator was telling Danny that he was only there to see the show. He didn't abide with gambling at all. He wouldn't be caught dead in a gambling establishment. Danny had all he could do to keep from laughing. Little did the jerk know, that within a couple of hours, he would be caught dead. Dane took the Senator and Shirley out to the showroom and gave them his booth. Then, it was show time. The room was filled to capacity with horse owners, trainers, jockeys, race fans, touts, and regular people.

Danny had them in the palm of his hand. The Senator's wife never took her eyes off of him. She had that look that women have when they want to get laid. Danny played to her. The crowd loved him. He looked stage left and there sat Bruto, staring daggers at him. Standing, with his back to the wall behind Bruto, was the Ox watching him. Danny did an hour and a half, took two encores and left the stage. He showered and changed clothes. They were setting up the room for the party when he went out front. Bruto was talking to some wise guys when he spotted Danny. He started toward him. The Ox made a move but Danny gave him the sign to wait. Bruto came right in his face. "You're a dead mother fucker. Nobody does that to me and lives."

Danny smiled at him. "If you weren't such a prick, nobody would have to do anything to you. Now, we can go at it right now in front of your boss, which I don't think he would like, or we can go out back after the party and settle this. Either way you're going back in the hospital. So, what's it going to be?" Danny stepped back and turned slightly to his right. The Ox caught the move and got between them. He put his hand on Bruto's shoulder.

"I don't think it's wise to start any trouble in here. I'd hate to have to kick your ass in front of your boss and the other wise guys. And, you know I can do it, so why don't you go back to where you came from, and leave my friend alone."

Bruto gave Danny a look. "This ain't over pretty boy." He turned and left the showroom. The Ox said to Danny, "He won't be bothering you any more. He's going on a long trip soon." He smiled and walked away.

They let the people in. The band cranked up and the booze flowed like water. People were all over Danny. The Senator and his wife came over and were all smiles. They congratulated him on the show. The jerk got on his soap box, telling Danny how he was going to shut down the town and run the mob out of Hot Springs. His wife was looking down at him with this disgusting look on her face. But when she looked at Danny she was all charm and want.

People came over to talk to the Senator. Danny asked Shirley if she would like to dance. She took his hand and they went to the dance floor. She melted into his arms. She was a good dancer. She leaned back and pushed her pelvis against him. "My, my, you are a big boy. I'd like to take care of that, if you have an afternoon free."

Danny smiled at her. "What about the crusader?"

"That piss ant. He's too busy trying to make a name for himself. He thinks he's Elliot Ness. Don't worry about him."

"Oh I won't. We'll set something up." He ground his crotch against her. She shuddered. He took her back to the crowd around Senator Summer. He was still expounding on what he was going to do. Danny saw his chance. He turned his back to him and started to talk to Shirley and two other women. Reaching behind, he popped the Senator in the ass with the needle. The Senator jumped and rubbed the spot. He looked around. Danny strolled to the bar with the two women and Shirley.

They were having drinks when Senator Summer started gasping for breath. Someone sat him in a chair and another ran to call a doctor. Shirley ran over, took his handkerchief and wiped the sweat from his face and brow. She was talking to him when the light in his eyes went out. She sat back in horror with people crowded around and everybody talking. The paramedics showed up, but there was nothing they could do. He was gone. Danny came over and put his arm around her shoulder. "I'm so sorry. Is there anything I can do? Anything?"

She was crying softly. "No, not right now. I need a little time."

The next morning the phone rang. Danny picked it up. It was Bert. "You son-of-a-bitch. You're just beautiful. I just got a call from you know who. He is beside himself. Asked all kinds of questions. I told him that my guy was the best. No questions, just the money."

"It was easy. I would have done it for nothing. He was a malendrino, a mamaluke."

"Enjoy the rest of your stay. I'll be in touch." He hung up.

They had a nice funeral for Senator Summer. People said

nice things about him. Shirley was dressed in black with a veil covering her face. She had her head down, and Danny was sure she was trying to cover up a smile.

The week went by. Pete, the Brute, disappeared with out a trace. Somewhere in a well on a deserted farm in rural Arkansas, Bruto took a dry dive. Saturday, Shirley called and asked if they could get together on Sunday. She wanted to meet in Benton where she had a home. She gave Danny the address.

Sunday, Danny had the Ox drive him to Benton. He found the house and sent the Ox back to Hot Springs. She opened the door wearing a beautiful silk robe. Danny knew there was nothing under it. She pulled him inside and locked her mouth on his. Danny could feel her body through the silk. It was soft and smooth. He stepped back and opened her robe. She was beautiful with long legs, and small perky breasts. She pulled him into the bedroom. Shedding the robe, she lay down on the bed.

Danny undressed slowly. She never took her eyes off him. She saw the hard body, and the scars, but when he dropped his pants, she stared at Ninja in awe. "I've never seen one that big." She slid over the edge of the bed and took it in both hands. "Am I ever going to enjoy this." All afternoon and into the evening she had her fill.

The last week at The Vapors went great with packed houses for every show. Phil was there every night. In addition, a Jayne Mansfield look alike alternated with the hostess at the hotel as Danny's private matinee performances.

They flew back to Vegas on Sunday and opened at the Desert Inn the next day.

Chapter 51

It was business as usual. Packed shows every night, golf every day weather permitting, and impromptu parties at the house. The heads of families from all over the country came for a visit. Some stayed at the house. Velvet was the perfect hostess. She was also the perfect lover. Then came the call from Bert. He was setting up a tour through Europe. He had contracts from Italy, France, Germany, Denmark, Spain, Portugal, and Norway to name a few. Danny would be gone three months. Danny decided to take Velvet with him. He was becoming real fond of her, and she would be good arm candy.

The tour started in Italy. The Mayor of Florence had a sudden heart attack and died at a state dinner. A high ranking Don from Palermo, Sicily was found with an ice pick stuck in his ear. This one was done to spark a war between rival families. It worked. The Governor of Niece, France was found in the men's room with a snapped neck. Danny didn't like him. He came on to Velvet and wouldn't leave her alone. The Chancellor of Germany's right hand man met with an untimely death. The Queen of Denmark's financial advisor was found dead in his car.

The biggest Promoter of bull fights in Madrid was found dead of a heart attack immediately following a huge fiesta. Portugal's Ambassador to the U.S. died at a concert. In Norway, the head of the commerce board died of a freak accident. He was sitting on a balcony during a party, when he fell over backwards into the swimming pool. They surmised he was dead before he hit the water of cardiac arrest.

The money kept growing in Danny's Swiss account and,

nobody suspected him of anything. He was the toast of Europe.

They came back to Vegas and rested up for a couple of weeks. Don Angelo came out and spent a few days with them. Danny's next contract was in Australia. The Don brought all the information with him. The guy he was to take out was a big shot industrialist. Seems his partner wanted to take over the business, and according to the Don, take over his wife, as well. He was paying a fortune to get it done. Danny knew that the wife was in on it. She had to be.

It was a long flight to Sidney. Danny went over some new tunes with Johnny. When they landed, the tarmac looked like a sea of women. They were yelling and screaming as he got off the plane. The Mayor was there with the press. They had a microphone set up on a small stage. Danny made a nice speech which was mostly drowned out by the women screaming. Then it was off to the hotel. That night they had a big party for him in the hotel ballroom. He met the movers and shakers in Sidney.

The mark was there with his wife, a real looker. He came over and introduced himself. "I'm Jack Patterson, and this is my wife, Debra. It's a pleasure to have you down under to entertain us. We have been looking forward to this for weeks."

"Well, I'm glad to be here. I've heard so much about the wonderful audiences from fellow performers. Now I get a chance to see for myself."

Debra was giving him the once over without her husband noticing. "You'll have to come out to the ranch and relax and have some fun. We'll have a cook out."

"I'd like that." He was going to say something else, but was interrupted by a slick looking guy with an attitude. He reminded Danny of a gigolo. He barged right in and took over the conversation. "Hi mate. I'm Steven Frost, Jack's partner."

"Pleasure to meet you." Danny shook his hand.

"Good to have you here. Oh, I have to borrow Debra for a few minutes. Some of her guests want to have a chat." With that he took her arm and they were gone. Danny caught the look on Jack's face. It was a look of frustration and pain.

Danny felt sorry for him. He took Jack's arm and said, "Come on, I'll buy you a drink." They went to the bar and immediately were surrounded by women. Jack held his own. He was actually having a good time. Danny kept glancing at Debra and Steve, who were engrossed in heavy conversation. He kept Jack from seeing them by blocking his view.

Debra saw all the women around the two men and came over to protect her investment. She managed to brush up against Danny a few times so he could feel her breast through her dress. The party lasted until midnight. Danny promised to see them after the show tomorrow. They would be in a box seat on stage right.

The opera house was packed to capacity. Danny was using the Sidney Symphony Orchestra to back the show, all forty of them. The sound was magnificent. He sang, did his jokes, and did the tap dance. The crowd was going wild. He did a two hour show, then begged off after three encores. In the dressing room, he showered and changed clothes. When he came out the room was packed with people. They gave him more applause.

Jack was standing with Debra. The gigolo was hanging around her. People were coming over and talking and fawning all over him. Debra gave him a hug and a kiss on the cheek. That pissed the gigolo off to no end. Jack just laughed and patted him on the shoulder.

The week went by in a flurry of parties and sightseeing. Jack and Debra took him everywhere. The gigolo tried to horn in, but they never told him where they were going. Debra kept giving Danny all the signs. She wanted him and made it known. Sunday was the day of the big cook out. Jack had invited lots of people. They had half a steer on a rotisserie. The aroma was wonderful. A band was hired for listening and dancing pleasure.

When the band took a break, Danny had Johnny and the boys take over the bandstand. He went up and did an impromptu show for the people. They went crazy. Jack was overjoyed. He couldn't thank Danny enough. Debra took his arm and led him away from the crowd. "That was wonderful. Are you that good at everything you do?"

"Depends on the woman."

"Well, then we'd have a hell of a time. I'm real good at what I do."

Before Danny could respond, the gigolo showed up. He had fire in his eyes. He glared at Danny. Danny gave him a look that would make most men run. The gigolo backed away.

"Debra, you're wanted to help carve the steer." She gave Steve a look of distain and walked back to the party. The gigolo said to Danny, "If you know what's good for you, you'll stay away from Debra. You're not in the States now. Consider this a warning."

Danny came up to his face. "Listen you little prick. You get in my way and I'll step on you like a bug. Now get the fuck away from me." Steve saw the look on his face and hurried back to the party.

The rest of the day was great. Danny got back to the hotel and called Don Angelo. It was morning there. "Don, I have to ask you a question. Is the money already in the bank for this job?"

"Yes, of course. Why do you ask?"

"Just wondering. I'll take care of it next week. Give my love to mamma."

Chapter 52

The second week was bigger than the first one. Danny was doing some TV shows during the day when he wasn't out with Jack and Debra. Friday afternoon he was in the suite when the door bell rang. He opened it to see Debra standing there. She smiled, "Well, are you going to ask me in?"

Danny stepped back and let her in. "Where's Jack?"

"He had some big meeting today with Steve. He'll be along later." She took off her jacket and sat on the couch. "Aren't you going to offer a lady a drink?"

Danny went to the bar. "What will you have?"

"A gin and tonic would be fine. Why don't you bring it over and sit next to me?"

Danny mixed the drinks. He came over, gave her the drink and sat on a chair opposite her.

"What's the matter? Are you afraid of me?"

Danny smiled. "I'm afraid of nothing, my dear. I was just wondering what your boyfriend would say about it."

She jerked upright. "My boyfriend? What boyfriend?"

"Let's not play games. You know who I'm talking about. That gigolo, pantywaist partner, your husband has. I'm not blind my dear. Neither is your husband. I don't know what you see in him. He's as phony as a three dollar bill."

"I didn't come here to be insulted."

"No, you came here to get laid. You want some of this." He stood up and unzipped his pants and pulled out Ninja. Her mouth dropped open. She couldn't take her eyes off of it. Danny put it away. "But you're not going to get it. I like your husband. He's a nice decent guy. Go get your kicks somewhere else."

She got up off the couch, put on her jacket and headed for the door. Before she left, she said, "I'll see you and Jack after the show. This never happened." She went out and closed the door.

The phone rang. It was Bert. "Danny, you're not going to believe this. The Australian guy who contracted with us called a little while ago. He wanted to know how much more it would cost to have you killed. I almost shit. He said you're stepping on his toes. He wants you out of the way."

Danny started to laugh. "Bert, this guy is a piece of crap. How much did he offer?"

"An extra two hundred thousand."

"Take it, and let me know when the money is in the bank."

"Are you crazy? You're going to kill yourself?"

"Trust me on this Bert. I'll explain later. You're going to love this."

"OK. I'll let you know." Danny hung up the phone and broke into laughter. This was just too beautiful for words.

Sunday they were at Jack's ranch. Debra was her usual friendly self. It was like nothing had changed. Danny paid more attention to her and she responded. Steve saw all of this and was steaming. Danny wanted to make him mad and it was succeeding. While they were talking to Jack, Danny put his arm around Debra.

Jack was on the other side and didn't see Danny put his hand on Debra's ass. Steve did and his face grew red. Danny moved his hand back and forth. Debra reached back and held his hand there.

This was too much for Steve. He came stomping over to them. "I have to get back to the city. I'll call you later." He turned and stomped off. Danny excused himself and followed him to his car. Steve jumped in and started the engine. Danny leaned in the window. "I just want you to know that she's a great piece of ass." Steve yelled something and slammed the car into gear.

Before he took off, Danny popped him in the arm with the needle. Steve was so mad he just floored the car and left in a cloud of dust. Danny walked back to where Jack and Debra were sitting. He looked at Debra.

"Steve was in a hurry. He said he'd call later." Debra dropped her eyes. Jack ordered more drinks for them. They were making small talk when they heard an explosion in the distance. A black column of smoke rose up. They all jumped to their feet.

Jack said, "Let's go check that out." They got in to the Land Rover and took off. When they got close they could see it was a car on fire. It had flipped over and over. Debra screamed, "It's Steve's car! Oh, my God, he's still in there! Get him out. Get him out."

Danny and Jack got close to the car, but the heat and flames made it impossible to get to him. They could see he was dead. He was a charred corpse. Debra was crying and blubbering. Jack went to console her. They drove back to the house and Jack called the police and told them what had happened. They left Debra in the hands of the maid and went back to the car. A fire truck arrived about the same time and extinguished the fire. It took awhile to get Steve out. He was burned to a crisp.

After they took him away, Jack and Danny went back to the house. Debra was red eyed and weepy. Jack said to her, "It looks like he was speeding and missed the turn. There was nothing anybody could do. We need to notify his next of kin. Debra, do you feel well enough to take Danny to the hotel and stay with him until I get things straightened out? I don't want to leave you here alone at a time like this."

She nodded. "That's very kind of you. I'll get my coat." She was back in a minute. They drove to town. Nothing much was said until they arrived at the funeral home. Jack got out and helped Debra into the driver's seat. He kissed her lightly and went inside. She drove Danny to the hotel. Once inside the suite, she started to cry.

Danny walked over and put his arms around her. She snuggled in. He said, "I'm sorry about your boyfriend."

She tried to pull back, but he held her tight. "He's not worth your tears. He was a conniving, back stabbing, son-of-a-bitch. Do you think he wanted you for your love or for your percentage in the business? How long do you think you would last once he got control?"

She pulled her head back and looked up at him. "I don't know what you're talking about."

"Oh, yes you do. I have a lot of connections, and they tell me that Steve put out a contract on your husband. He wanted Jack dead so he could get the whole enchilada; you, the business, and all the amenities that go with it. Too bad he killed himself before that happened. And my dear, you knew all about it."

She started to protest. "Save it lady. No sense in denying it. I'm not going to rat out on you. From now on you're going to be the perfect wife. I can call the people who have the contract on your husband and call it off. But, if you step out of line, they'll come for you. It's already paid for. There's no statute of limitations on a hit"

She never took her eyes off him while he was talking. She knew she was trapped. "You're pretty smart for an entertainer. OK, I'll play your game. It may sound funny to you, but I do love my husband. The thing with Steve got out of hand. It was exciting at the time, sneaking around and all. But he was a jealous, manipulative person. I saw that by the way he looked at you when you talked to me. Please call it off."

"It's as good as done. He'll never know how close he came to dying. You will though."

*****

Bert was laughing so hard he couldn't talk. Danny waited. Finally he said, "That's the funniest thing I've ever heard. You whacked the guy who paid to have you whacked. That's just beautiful. I don't think that's ever been done before."

"He was a real low life. Besides, I liked the guy who I was supposed to pop. Everything worked out all right. We got paid double. Nothing wrong with that. And, who's going to complain? "

"You're one of a kind. Now, you're back at Caesar's Palace for awhile. If anything comes up I'll call."

Danny was sitting on his sun porch having coffee. He waved to the golfers going by. Bill Fanning came by and drove his gold cart up to Danny's house. "You got a drink for a hot thirsty golfer?"

"Park that thing and get in here. It's a hell of a lot cooler in here than outside." Bill came in the door. "Ah, that's nice." He sat down and wiped his brow. Velvet came out with a pitcher of ice tea. She greeted him and poured him a big glass. She put the pitcher down and left. "Now that's what I call the perfect hostess. So, how was Australia?"

"It was great. Sold out every night. Now I'm staying home for awhile."

"Good, we can play some golf and do the town. I'll be at your opening. I have some friends from Washington in town. OK, if I bring them back stage after the show?"

"Of course. Be my guest. There's nothing like having a bunch of feds mixing with the local mob!" They laughed. Bill went out and resumed his game. Danny walked into his bedroom. Velvet was standing by the dresser holding something in her hand. She waved it at Danny.

"I don't remember this." She was holding the little pearl switchblade in her hand. Danny froze.

He said in a calm voice, "That's a gift from the owners of Sun City for doing such a good job." He walked over and took it out of her hand breathing a sigh of relief. He'd have to be more careful in the future. He put it in his pocket.

"How about you and I taking a little nap?"

"And, if I'm not sleepy?"

"Then, we'll think of something else to do."

******

The opening was wonderful and completely sold out. It was a real Vegas opening with Klieg lights and all. Stars were dressed to the nines. The press set up in the back.

Peter opened and had them laughing right off. Danny came on and did an hour and a half. He had to beg off after two encores. Back in the dressing room, he showered and cleaned up. He came out into the main dressing room. The usual people were there. Bill introduced Danny to his FBI pals and their wives. He signed some albums for them and posed for pictures.

Bill was standing with his back to the band members. He overheard Johnny's comment to Vinnie and Sal. "I don't know guys, but I think we're some kind of a jinx. Wherever we play, some big shot dies, or gets whacked. It's really spooky."

Bill turned and joined the conversation. "I couldn't help but hear your comment. Johnny, I hadn't heard about any of that. Do you think it's your playing?"

Johnny smiled at him. "It's true. Wherever we go, some big shot dies. Right guys?" They nodded in unison. Before he could ask any more questions, Bill was called back to his friends. He kept it in the back of his mind. It would be interesting to look into.

The next day he got out Danny's itinerary of bookings that Velvet had given him. He back tracked to the dates of the engagements. Using the FBI computer, he checked the local newspaper in that town to see if there were any murders or deaths of big shots. He came up empty until he got to the Italian Fest in Milwaukee. A congressman fell off his balcony. He dug deeper. In South Africa, England, France, Italy, Spain, Norway, Germany, some big shot died or was murdered. Could this be a coincidence?

Everywhere Danny played there was a death. He decided to check out the people around Danny. He ran them through the FBI files. He came up empty with the band. Nothing. They were like choir boys. He ran the Ox and the Weasel, they both had rap sheets with everything from assault and battery to stealing cars. Most arrests were when they were juveniles, but no convictions. As of nineteen fifty, they were clean.

Just for fun, he ran Danny through the system. Ferdinando Dominico Bello. Hell, this kid was a choir boy. Nothing. He traced him all the way back to Italy. True, he was the nephew of the top Capo di Capi in Chicago, but he was completely clean. He saw where the Chicago FBI had run a make on him, too. And they also came up empty. All these things must be coincidences. He shut down the computer and left.

Chapter 53

It was in the third week of the engagement that Bert called. "Danny, I need you to go to Vancouver, Canada two weeks from now. We got Tony Bennett to fill in for you. The brother of a good friend got whacked in the office of his night club. His brother is afraid he's next. The rival family wants to take over his territory. The guy's name is Guido Cappono. He's a ruthless bastard. He shot his own brother over a broad. He's tough to get to and surrounds himself with lots of muscle and shooters. That's why I have to send you. He loves to hang out with stars. You're going to be doing a charity telethon for the Variety Club. By the way, I'm paying you for this one."

"No you're not. Let's just say it's a charity hit. Besides, I am the godfather of your son, so that makes us family."

"I can't argue that. I'll mail you all the stuff I have on Guido." He hung up.

Danny wasted no time calling Tony in Toronto. "Tony, how's it going?"

"Well, this is a surprise. A voice from my past. It's been a long time. What can I do for you?"

"That's what I like about you. Cut right to the chase. How well do you know Guido Cappono from Vancouver?"

"That piece of shit. I know him. He's worse than Big Louie. He's caused me some problems. Why do you want to know?"

"He whacked the brother of a friend of mine."

"Yeah I know. He was a friend of mine too."

"I have something I want to discuss with you. Can you meet

me in Vancouver in two weeks?"

"Does this mean we're finally going to meet?"

"Yes. I'll call you and let you know, when I'm getting there and where I'll be staying."

"Let me know and I'll be there." They said their goodbyes and hung up.

They checked into the Fairmont hotel. Danny found out that all the acts were on the same floor. Tony's suite was next to his. He had Velvet set everything up. Tony would be getting in that evening. They had a briefing in the hotel's ballroom for all the acts. Danny was the main star. There were a lot of local acts to fill in the blank spots, when the big acts were not working. Sitting around a big table were, Eartha Kitt, Jamie Farr, Pete Barbutti, Gloria Loring, Alan Thick and Carme. Danny came over and gave Carme a hug. "It's good to see you. How's Flame?"

"You can ask her yourself. She's upstairs in the suite. When she knew you were going to be here, wild horses couldn't keep her away. Oh, we're going to be in Vegas for a while. I'm opening at the Thunderbird in a show called "Pardon My Can Can." Flame is the exotic in the show."

"That's great. Then we can hang out. Come on, let's go up and surprise her." And surprise her they did. When she saw Danny she squealed and jumped into his arms. He gave her a big hug and kiss then set her down. "You look terrific. You're even more beautiful than I remembered. Living with that big Italian must be good for you."

Carme smiled. "She's a handful. I have to be good to her. She still carries that little pop gun in her purse."

Danny laughed, "I saw her pull it one time and she was ready to use it. Nothing more scary than a woman with a gun."

Flame came over and put her arm around Carme's waist. "I use it to protect this big Dago from all the little groupies hanging around."

"It's true. She's knocking the hell out of my Rudolf Vaselino image."

"Good for her. Look, I have to meet somebody on business.

I'll call you later." He gave them a hug and left.

Tony arrived at seven-thirty. The Ox let him into the suite. Danny was standing with his back to the door. He turned around and Tony gave a start. "Hey, you're Danny Angel."

"Right you are. How about a drink? Are you still drinking scotch and Pepsi cola?"

"How the hell did you know that?"

Danny thought for a moment. He trusted Tony to keep a secret. "Before I tell you that, do you still have a starburst on your right shoulder?"

"Yes, I do. You seem to know an awful lot about me."

"What I know, I know from personal experience. You got that starburst in North Korea after the Chinese came into the war. Somebody carried you back to an aid station to get you patched up. It was freezing, remember? The cold sealed the wound and stopped the bleeding."

Tony stood up. He looked at Danny. "Only one guy would know that, and that's Danny Di, and he's dead."

Danny came around the bar and stood in front of Tony. He handed him the drink and looked into his eyes. Tony stared into Danny's eyes. Then, his facial expression changed, and the recognition hit him. Tony shook his head in disbelief. "There's only one guy I know with eyes like that, and that's Danny Di."

He got closer and stared into Danny's eyes. "Shit, it is you! Son-of-a-bitch." He grabbed Danny and hugged him.

Danny smiled, "Well, I'm not dead. I have a new face. The Don had me blown up in a car, so I would be dead and off the police blotter. I know it's hard to believe. Wait, look at this." He opened his shirt and showed Tony the scars.

"So that's why it was so easy to get rid of Big Louie."

"Yeah, thanks to you." He sat Tony down and told him the whole story. Danny said, "The reason I wanted you here, is that I'm going to whack Guido. I've got to get close to him. I figured with you here, maybe we could have a dinner and you could talk a little business. You know, schmooze him a little."

"Wait a minute. You're a superstar and you're still in the

business? I know you don't need the money, so what's the deal?"

Danny explained it to him. When he was through he said, "So you see I'm still in, like it or not. The only difference is, the money is big and who would suspect me?"

"True, but Guido travels with a small army. How do you expect to whack him and live?"

"You let me worry about that. Have we got a deal?"

"You bet your ass. This, I've got to see." They broke up laughing and went to the bar and got a drink.

Chapter 54

The Telethon was great. They raised over two million dollars. Tony brought Guido around to see him. He was bigger than Big Louie. He waddled when he walked. He was enthralled being around Danny. He had some cute looking girls with him. They looked to be under age. All he could think of was Ginger and it made his blood run hot. They decided to have a big dinner at the Penthouse. It was a three story club. The first floor was a deli, the second floor was a strip club and the third floor was a beautiful Italian restaurant.

Tony had called Ross and had everything set up. Tony and Danny arrived first and were drinking wine when Guido and his entourage showed up. He took the little elevator up and it was all the elevator could do to get him up to the third floor. They practically had to grease him to get him out. He brought some dynamite chicks along. The strippers from downstairs were invited to join the party. Guido was sitting at the head of the table shoveling food in his mouth. He would wash down the food with big gulps of wine. He was sweating like a pig.

Danny was seated at his right and Tony was across from him. Tony kept looking at Danny like, "Well?" Danny had dipped the needle in the poison three times to really make it potent. There was a lot of fat to go through. One of the strippers came over and tried to sit in his lap, but he was so fat, he didn't have a lap. She slid off onto the floor. Guido tried to catch her, and that's when Danny popped him in the leg twice. Guido swore and rubbed his leg. He thought the girl pricked him. He pushed her away and continued talking and eating.

It wasn't long before he turned pale and started to gasp for breath. He shot out of the chair and staggered around grabbing at his chest. They tried to grab him, but he was like a bull in a china shop. He wheeled around and headed for the elevator. He missed it and fell down three flights of stairs. The building shook. He landed at the bottom in a heap. It scared the hell out of the hat check girls. His bodyguards ran down the stairs and managed to roll him over. He was dead. They called for an ambulance. It took all of them to get him on a gurney and into the ambulance.

Danny and Tony stood at the top of the stairs watching. Tony kept looking at him sideways. Finally he said, "OK, how'd you do it?"

Danny gave him an innocent look. "Do what? The man died of a heart attack."

******

Bill Fanning was sitting in his office reading the paper. On the second page was a big article, "Crime Boss Dies of Heart Attack." It went on to tell all about the dinner and Danny being there with Tony the crime boss of Toronto. He sat back. Could this be another coincidence? Danny was right there when he died.

He contacted the FBI office in Washington. When the operator came on, he asked for Dick Paige. "Dick," he said, "This is Bill Fanning from our Las Vegas office. I need a favor."

"Sure Bill, how can we help you?"

"I just read that Guido Cappono died. Can you check and see what really killed him."

"Yeah, we have connections in Vancouver. What's up Bill?"

"Just a hunch, Dick."

"Well, who ever is responsible, needs to get a medal. We're glad to get rid of him. He was a bad ass. Caused us lots of headaches. I'll check it out and get back to you."

"I appreciate it. I owe you one." They hung up. He said to himself, *"This has got to be a coincidence. He died in a room full of people."* He would have to wait to get the results from Dick.

Danny flew home and resumed his shows at Caesar's. Bert called and thanked him. "I still say you're the best there ever was. What was Tony doing there?"

Danny told him the whole story. Bert understood and knew that Tony wouldn't say anything. "You have fun and enjoy yourself." He hung up. It wasn't five minutes and the phone rang again. He answered.

"Danny, it's Bill. How about some golf tomorrow?"

"I'd love it. Get a tee time and let me know. I'll meet you at the clubhouse."

When he got to the clubhouse the next day, Freddie Bell and Sonny King were waiting for him along with Bill. They got to the first tee. Before they teed off, Sonny said, "Now listen, we're playing golf with the FBI so there's a few things we can't say. We can't say, "Nice Hit, I whacked that one, or I buried that one in the sand." They had to wait to tee off because everyone was laughing so hard they couldn't hit the ball.

On the fifth tee, they had to wait for the foursome in front of them. Bill was riding with Danny. He said, "That must have been quite a shock in Vancouver to be there when Guido Cappono died."

"Yeah it was. I was sitting right next to him. He was way overweight and sweating like a pig. He kept shoveling food in his mouth and gulping vino. I guess it caught up to him."

"Yeah, I guess it would. That's happened before hasn't it?"

Warning bells went off in Danny head. Why was he asking these questions? "Yes, a couple of times. But at least I wasn't sitting next to them."

"That's funny. I was just wondering."

"Well, wonder later Mr. Hoover. Right now it's your turn on the tee. Try to keep it in our fairway."

They finished the round amid laughs and playful insults. No more was said about people dying. Danny thought that maybe he was being a bit paranoid. He'd wait and see.

Bill was thinking on the way home, *"I must be crazy. Danny never batted an eye when I brought the subject up about people dying. What the hell was I thinking? I've been an agent too long. He's a superstar for Christ's sake. He was checked out and came up clean."* He shook his head and pulled into his driveway.

Things were going fine. Work every night and play every day. Vegas was swinging. Carme's show at the Thunderbird was a great success. Two and four in the afternoon and it was packed every day. Velvet and Flame got along like sisters. Flame couldn't believe how good she looked after Cheech destroyed her face. She was happy for her and Danny. Danny and Carme got along like brothers. Both were big Italians. Both had big voices. They became golfing buddies. Things were good.

Chapter 55

Danny had closed Caesar's Palace and was taking some time off. He was sunning himself by the pool when the phone rang. It was Bert. "So you're taking some time off, huh? Well, I got a quickie for you in San Juan, Puerto Rico. They're having a big communication strike down there. The union leader is becoming very annoying to the big money people. He's disrupting their financial flow. They figure if you cut off the head of the snake, the body dies with it. His name is Julio Pacheco. He's staying at the El San Juan hotel. He's friends with Tito Puente and Humberto Morales. They're working in the big lounge there. Pacheco is there every night."

"I know those guys. I did a show with them in New York. Here's what I'll do. I'll take Velvet on a vacation. We can fly down in my plane and spend a week. I'll have her make the reservations. Consider it done."

"Hey, I never had any doubts. I'll over night the info. Have fun."

Danny called Velvet in. She came over and sat on his lap. He liked that. She would cuddle up like a little kitten. "And what can I do for you?" She slid her hand along the inside of his thigh.

He laughed. "Well, besides that, I want you to make reservations at the El San Juan Hotel in Puerto Rico. I'm taking you on a vacation."

She squealed. "Really? A real vacation?"

"Yes. A real a vacation. I think we deserve one."

"W certainly do. I'll go make the reservations. When do you want to go?"

"Three days from today. Make it for a week. If we want to stay longer, we can."

She kissed him, jumped off his lap and went to make the reservations. Danny lay back and stretched. It would be nice to wander around Old Town and take in the sights. The last time he was there at the Americana Hotel, he didn't get much of a chance to sight see. This time he would take the time to see San Juan like a tourist.

The info arrived the next day and he read it twice. The guy was a bad ass. His picture should have been in the post office. He looked like Poncho Via with out the sombrero. Danny was deep in thought when the phone rang. It was Carme. "Hey Danny, guess what. They're moving the show from the lounge into the main room. Seems we're doing so much business that we're blocking the casino. People have been standing outside, looking in. We have a couple of weeks off so they can make new scenery. I'm adding four more dancers and two nudes. They're going all out for me."

"That's great news. You deserve it. Wait a minute. Can you get away for a week? You and Flame?"

"Sure, what do you have in mind?"

"Velvet and I are going to San Juan for a week of fun and games. We're flying down in my plane. Be nice if you could join us."

"You bet. When are we leaving?"

"In three days. Why don't you and Flame join us for dinner tonight at eight o'clock so we can make plans."

"We'll be there." He hung up. Danny told Velvet what the plans were. She loved it. She'd have somebody to shop with.

******

Danny's plane landed in the private sector of the airport. A limo was waiting to take them to the hotel. There were no screaming women. Nobody but the authorities knew he was coming. He wanted it that way. He sent the plane back to Vegas. The Ox and Weasel were the only security with him. Besides, with the two girls along, who would be looking at them. They had suites overlooking the pool area, with the ocean beyond and big balconies with tables and chairs, if they wanted to eat outside. Also, there were lounge chairs to sunbathe and the balconies were close together.

Danny found out that Julio Pacheco was on the same floor, four doors down from him. He looked down at the pool. From the twenty fifth floor, it looked like a blue band aid. He wondered if Julio was a good diver. They changed into bathing suits and spent the afternoon in the ocean and the pool. The girls were getting the once over from the local Don Juans. One of them started over, but ran when the Ox stood up and headed towards him. Danny and Carme had a good laugh at that.

Danny called Tito and Humberto and extended an invitation to dinner. They were delighted. Velvet had reserved a table for eight. The Ox and Weasel would be joining them.

They were seated at the table when Tito and Humberto showed up. With them was a beautiful girl with black hair hanging down to her waist. It was as black and silky as a raven's wing. She was wearing a Chinese dress that was slit up both sides to her upper thighs. She had a body as good as Flame's and Velvet's. The boys stood to greet them and Danny introduced the girls and Carme. Tito grabbed Carme and hugged him. "Where have you been amigo? It's been a long time."

"Too long." Carme hugged Humberto, grabbed the girl, picked her up and hugged her. He looked at the group. "And this beautiful lady is Lolita Vargas, a great singer and dancer. We worked together in Atlanta at Club Peachtree."

She smiled. "Carme was responsible for me getting to work with these two great guys."

Danny took her hand and kissed it. "You can tell us all about it over dinner, my dear."

Dinner was fun and laughs. They headed for the big lounge. Tito got them ringside tables. Danny glanced around the room. Sitting in a booth was Julio surrounded by ladies of question and other unsavory looking characters. It looked like the cast of a D movie. They were already drunk and noisy. Tito hit the stage and for the next three hours rocked the place. He got Danny up to sing and was joined by Carme. They did an Italian version of Sadler and Young. While they were up on stage, some of the local Don Juans came to the table, but the Ox ran them off. One guy was belligerent until the Weasel pulled his coat back and showed him a very intimidating forty-five he had in his shoulder holster.

When it was over, Tito, Humberto and Lolita came to the table for some drinks and laughs. In the middle of their party, Julio decided to join them. He was drunk and obnoxious. Tito tried to calm him down, but he was too far gone. He saw Velvet and Flame and immediately tried to hit on them.

Danny got up along with Carme and the Ox. The Weasel slid around behind Julio. The guys with him backed off a little when they saw the show of force. Julio was too drunk to notice.

Danny came around the table and stood in front of him. "I don't know who you are, but this is a private party. You must be a friend of Tito's. If you'd like to join us, you're more than welcome, but you leave the ladies alone. They belong to me and that other big Italian over there. They are ladies, not putas. Do I make myself clear?"

He was staring into Julio's eyes. Julio looked into Danny's eyes and stepped back. As drunk as he was, he recognized danger when he saw it. He finally looked around and saw that he was boxed in. The Ox had come around the table and was standing within arm's reach. He turned his head and the Weasel showed him the forty-five under his jacket. He gave a fake laugh and said to Tito, "Amigo, I'll see you manana. I've got to get some sleep. Busy day tomorrow."

With that he staggered away. Tito watched him go. "I'm really sorry about that, Danny. He's a union organizer and I think the power has gone to his head."

"No apologies necessary. There's usually one in every crowd. Let's have a nightcap." They finished their drinks and called it a night.

Once in his suite Danny began pacing and thinking. *"This is one hit I'm going to enjoy. I'm going to get rid of that loud mouth son of a bitch. But how? How do I kill him? I'd like to throw him off the balcony into the pool, or catch him somewhere and snap his neck. I still have the ice pick in the secret compartment of my luggage along with the pistol and silencer. I have six more days to figure it out. Meantime, I'm going to enjoy myself."*

For the next five days it was swimming, sunning, eating, shopping and dancing. Every night they spent with Tito and Humberto. Julio was there too. During the day he was out on the street with people on strike causing trouble. At night he would come to the club and drink himself into a stupor.

After watching him for a couple of nights, Danny knew that it wasn't just alcohol. He was high on something else. He would hear him staggering down the hall to his suite. His goons would make sure he was tucked in and then leave. He had a couple of putas one night. Standing on his balcony, Danny could hear them. He finally figured out what he was going to do, so let him have his fun.

The last night before they had to go back was a big party. They rocked the lounge until two in the morning. Julio was drunk as usual. Danny counted on that. They went to the suite and Velvet turned in. Danny heard Julio going down the hall talking to his guys. Danny peaked through the security hole in the door. There were three guys holding Julio up. They tucked him in and left. Danny watched to make sure that the three guys had left. He didn't want any surprises. He waited until four. Slipping outside, he jumped three balconies, and ended up on Julio's. The door was locked so he slid the thin blade of his pocket knife in the slot and opened it. He had tried it on his own door earlier in the week, so he knew it would work. He could hear Julio snoring loudly. He cracked the curtain to make sure he was alone.

Danny slipped into the room and stood over him. He had the pearl in his left hand. He slammed his right hand down over Julio's mouth. He eyes shot open, but he couldn't move. Danny had him pinned.

He leaned down close to his ear. "I want you awake so you

would know what's going to happen to you. You've been a bad boy. You're causing a lot of people problems. I'm going to make them go away. You are going to die of a heart attack. All that booze and drugs are going to catch up to you."

    He popped him twice in the hairy part of his chest. Julio started to squirm. Danny used both hands to keep him pinned to the bed. Julio started to convulse. Danny held him down. He looked in his eyes. "Die you son of a bitch." His eyes glazed over and he was gone. Danny took his hands off his mouth.

    He went to the door and peeked out. Nobody was in the hall. He put the do not disturb sign on the outside of the door. Danny locked and bolted the door and put the safety chain on. He went to the door leading to the balcony and peeked out. Nobody was anywhere to be seen. He slipped out. Using the knife, he let the latch slip back down on the inside of the door, locking it. He was back in his suite in a flash. He got into bed and curled up next to Velvet and went to sleep.

    They were at the airport at eight o'clock the next morning. At eight fifteen they were in the air headed back to Vegas. It was a fun flight. When they got home, Carme and Flame went to the Thunderbird where they were staying. Danny and Velvet went to the house. He mixed himself a drink and turned on the TV.

    The story was all over the news. Julio Pacheco was found dead in his hotel room of a heart attack. The announcer was reporting, "When Mr. Pacheco didn't answer his phone or the door, the hotel security broke in and found him dead. According to reliable sources, Mr. Pacheco was drunk and drugged up before he went to bed. The coroner's office stated that he died of a coronary. Funeral services are pending." The announcer went on to tell about his involvement with the unions and such. Velvet was standing behind him. "Isn't that the nasty drunk we met?"

    "Yes it is. Guess all that booze caught up with him."

Chapter 56

Bill Fanning was on the phone to San Juan. He saw the news broadcast and knew Danny had stayed at the El San Juan hotel. It just couldn't be another coincidence.

He got the chief of detectives on the line. "Hello, my name is Bill Fanning. I'm with the FBI here in Las Vegas. Who am I speaking to?"

"This is detective Martinez. How can I help you?"

"I'm calling about Julio Pacheco. I see where he died. Did you, by chance, have anything to do with the investigation?"

"There was no real investigation. He was in his hotel room. All the doors were locked from the inside. There was no indication of foul play. The man had a reputation for drugs and alcohol. Do you think otherwise?"

"No, I was just curious. Thank you so much for your help."

"Por nada. Any time." He hung up.

Bill sat there for a moment. He said to himself, *"Shit, it's got to be a coincidence. I mean people die every day. You got to quit thinking like a G man."* He sat back in his chair and turned the TV to a sports channel.

Danny was on the phone with Don Angelo. "I don't know how you're doing this, but what ever you're doing, keep it up. Oh, by the way. I got a call from Don Bannacci in Utica. He wants you to call him." He gave Danny the number. "He said it was important."

"OK, I'll call him now. Talk to you soon." He hung up and called the Don. "Don Bannacci, it's Danny Angel."

"Danny, how are you? It's been a long time."

"Too long. What can I do for you?"

"It's not for me. It's for Cheech. I sold him the club and it was doing fine for awhile. He changed it. Put the stage against the back wall and did it up nice. But now he's going under. What he needs is a shot in the arm. Do you think you could help him out?"

"Hey, all you people were there for me when I needed you. Of course, I'll help. I'll call Cheech and set up a date to come there and perform. Charge them plenty at the door. Be good to see you again. Besides, your nephew can spend some time with you. He's been a God send."

"I can't thank you enough. Oh, don't forget to bring my song." He laughed and hung up.

Danny called Velvet. She came into the den. "How would you like to go back to Utica and see your friends?"

"You mean it? I'd love to. What's up?"

He told her. "I want you to call Cheech and set up a date. Tell him the sooner the better. He can advertise the hell out of it. Charge a hundred or better at the door. Tell him I'm working for nothing to help out a friend."

"That's wonderful, Danny. I'll get right on it."

Danny called Johnny. "Hey, were going back to the Plush Horse for a week or so. I want a good band."

"How many pieces? That stage is sort of small."

"He redid it. Moved it to the back wall. I think three trumpets, four saxes, two bones and four rhythm should do it. Can you handle that?"

"Sure, might cost a little more. They have to drive there."

"I don't care about the cost. I'll put them up at the hotel across the street. Room and board too."

"Wait a minute, are you paying for this? What's going on?"

Danny explained it to him. "So, I'm paying back a friend. Besides, your uncle wants to spend some time with you."

"Yeah, that sounds good. I'll get right on it."

Danny called Peter and told him that they were going to Utica.

******

Danny's plane, "The Velvet Touch," landed in Utica. There were hundreds of people waiting for them including the press, the Mayor, and the Lieutenant Governor. They deplaned and the Mayor greeted them. They had a small stage set up with a microphone. The Mayor made a speech. Then Danny stepped up to the mic. "I can't tell you how much I looked forward to coming back here. This is where it all began. I hope to see you all at the shows tomorrow night. Once again, thank you."

He got off the stage and into the limo with Velvet and his entourage. They went to the club first. When they walked in they stopped and stared. The club was beautiful. Cheech had outdone himself. Cheech came running over. He grabbed Danny and hugged him. "You don't know what this means to me. I don't know how I can ever thank you enough."

"Well for starters, how about a drink?" They laughed all the way to the bar. Danny asked him, "What happened, Cheech? You were doing so well."

"I got upside down. Cost me a bundle to remodel, then they laid off a whole bunch of people at the Maxwell House coffee plant. I just need to get this paid off. Then I can breathe again."

"Well, start breathing. We'll get it done." He told him Johnny would be in tomorrow afternoon with the band. Cheech said he had a good sound and light man. They had a drink then went across the street to the hotel. When Lois saw him she ran around the desk and hugged him. "You look wonderful. When I got the call that you would be staying here, I couldn't believe it. I thought you'd be staying at a five star hotel."

"Hey, sweet cheeks, to me this is a five star hotel. The band should be in by tonight." He leaned in and said in her ear, "These are all young guys, so you should have a hell of a week." She smiled at him. They got their room keys and went upstairs. The bellhop brought the luggage up. Velvet went to the big window and looked across the street. The whole front of the club was a big marquee. It said, "HE'S BACK! The one, the only, Danny Angel."

She turned to him. "You do know that Cheech didn't recognize me. Do you think we should tell him?"

"Naw, let's just enjoy the week and have fun. He'd be embarrassed. He's had enough to worry about." The phone rang. It was Don Bannacci. "I just called to tell you I reserved the whole ringside for my people. Got some big shots from out of town, so I thought I would treat them. I can't wait to see you."

"It's going to be fun. I brought a real funny Italian comedian with me. You're gonna love him. See you tonight." He hung up and the phone rang again. It was Clarise. "Danny, it's Clarise. I can't wait to see you. I bought a whole row of seats for me and the girls. They're so excited."

"Hold on a second. Somebody wants to talk to you." Danny handed the phone to Velvet. "It's Clarise."

She grabbed the phone. "Hey, girl. You still making a living on your back?" Danny could hear the screams all the way across the room. "Velvet, My God! What are you doing here? I thought you were in Buffalo. I can't wait to see you."

"For your information my dear, I am the other half of Danny Angel. We've been together for over a year. We have a week to catch up on everything. I'll see you tonight." She hung up. Yep, she thought, it's going to be a great week.

The club was packed to the rafters. There was standing room only. Johnny had set the bandstand up and it looked great. He had tweaked the sound and lights. Everything was ready. Velvet had gone out front for a tearful reunion with the girls. She would be sitting with them. The Ox was watching out for her. The Weasel was back stage. Danny peeked through the curtain. Yep, there were the two blonde bimbo's sitting with two nice looking wise guys. He looked for Darleen but she wasn't there. The Don's friends were all down front.

He turned to Peter. "You're going to kill them. Just go out there and have fun. The little guy in the front row with the pinstripe suite is the Capo de Capi. He's got a great sense of humor. He's going to love you."

"And if he don't?"

"It's been nice knowing you." They hung on to each other laughing.

The show started. Peter went out and destroyed them. He had them screaming. When he played Granada you could hear a pin drop. He left to a standing ovation.

Danny hit the stage and for an hour and a half he had them in the palm of his hand. He left to a thunderous standing ovation. He came out front and the people mobbed him. He was gracious and charming. The blonde bimbos came over and he hugged and kissed him. The Don's people were hanging on him. Danny excused himself and went over to where Velvet was sitting with the girls. He spread his arms and Clarise came running into them. Danny kissed her and hugged her. She looked like a successful business woman. The girls she had with her were dressed to the nines.

Danny said to her, "I want you and the girls to join Velvet and me for lunch tomorrow. Be at the hotel at noon." She agreed. Danny took Velvet over to sit with the Don. The Don was like a little boy. He was jumping up and down. When Danny did his song for him, he laughed and applauded. He had motioned Danny over and put a hundred dollar bill in his tux pocket. He said, "For old times."

Lunch was a real treat. Danny felt like a sheik with a harem. He was the envy of every guy that came into the restaurant. They didn't come over because the Ox and Weasel discouraged them. However some ladies were allowed the privilege.

Danny got a call from Cheech to tell him they were way oversold. People were still wanting to get in. Danny told him he would do two shows; seven and ten-thirty. Give them time to clear the room and set up for the second show. He thought Cheech was going to cry.

Wednesday, Danny was in the hotel bar talking to the bartender when he got a call. He picked up the phone. A tiny voice said, "Danny, it's Darleen. I hate to bother you, but I'm in trouble. Bad trouble. Can you possibly come to see me?"

"Just tell me where you are."

"I'm in a motel on the outskirts of town. The Utica Inn, room seventeen."

"You just hold on, I'll be there shortly. He grabbed the Ox and Weasel and jumped in the car Cheech had for him. When he got to the motel, the boys stayed outside. Danny knocked on the door. "Darleen, it's me."

The door opened and he stepped inside. She came into his arms crying hysterically. Danny held her at arms length. He was shocked. She was covered with blood and her face was swollen twice its size. She could hardly see. Anger took over. He wanted to kill somebody. He said in a gentle voice, "Who did this to you?"

Gradually, she stopped crying. "My husband. You remember the guy you put in the hospital? Well, I married him. He was alright at first. Then he started to beat me. He'd come home drunk, rape me, and force me to do all kinds of terrible things. I don't know what to do. Nobody will help me. They're all afraid of him and what he might do."

Danny held her close. The anger was coursing through his body. "He's not going to hurt you any more. You're coming with me. Get your things."

She packed her things into a single suit case. They went outside. When the Ox and Weasel saw her, they looked at Danny. He said, "I've got a job for the two of you. I'll tell you later. Right now we have to get this girl some medical help." The Ox drove the car and took them to a clinic. They cleaned her up and bandaged her. It took stitches to close a couple of the cuts. Danny took Darlene back to the hotel and got her a room next to his. He asked her where her husband worked. Danny was also told his normal routine. He tucked her in and sent down for some food and hot tea.

Danny left the Weasel with her so she'd feel safe, then he took the Ox into his room. "I want that son of a bitch gone. I want you to hurt him real bad before you whack him. Let him know, it was me that ordered it. Then get rid of him so nobody finds him. I'll ask Cheech for a good place. And, oh by the way, I'll make it worth your while."

The Ox looked at him. "No, you won't. This one is on the

house. I hate wife beaters. You can buy me a drink sometime."

Danny shook his hand. "Anytime, my friend, anytime."

They set it up for the next night. Cheech told Danny of a good place to get rid of the body. Velvet insisted on taking care of Darleen. She was furious. She asked Danny, "Can you do something about her husband? He deserves to be in jail or have the shit kicked out of him."

Danny held her close. "It's all taken care of my dear. So don't worry your pretty little head about it."

The next night, Velvet stayed with Darleen. Danny did two shows to packed houses. The Ox and the Weasel took care of business. They caught him on his way home from work after leaving a pub. He was drunk. They got him in the car and headed out into the country. After beating him, they broke bones until he passed out from the pain. They woke him up. They wanted him to know what was coming. The Ox snapped his neck like a twig. They threw him down an old, boarded up well, then reset the boards and left. Danny was at the bar with Cheech and some customers when the boys returned to the club. When they walked in, the Ox nodded. Danny called them over and bought them drinks.

The rest of the week flew by. Darleen was healing nicely. Peter was spending time with her, making her laugh. Danny decided to take her back to Vegas with them. Velvet was all for it. She said she could help her with the promo stuff.

The newspaper and the TV were full of stories about a missing man. Nobody had seen him for four days. Darleen was questioned by the police, but Danny said she was with them all week. She kept looking at Danny like she wanted to ask him something. Danny took her aside.

"I want you to come to Vegas with us when we leave. There's nothing for you here. Your husband is not coming back, so don't worry about that. You have to trust me on this."

"Oh thank God. I trust you. I never thought I would ever be free of him. Of course I'll come."

"Good. You don't have to take anything with you. You can start fresh. I'll handle the cops. Don't worry about that."

When they closed on Saturday, Cheech had made up most of the money he had spent remodeling. Danny made up the rest. He had enough money wired from his Swiss account to cover the costs and to give him a buffer for hiring some follow up acts. He called Chuck Eddy and told him to put some good acts in the club. He said he wanted The Goofers, The Treniers, The Vagabonds, The Characters and a few more.

Sunday they had a big party at the Don's house with great food, wine, music and laughter. Darleen was thrilled. Peter took responsibility for her care and saw to it that she had everything she needed. Danny and Velvet both had the same idea. This could be the start of a great romance.

Danny got Don Bannacci aside. "I have a small favor to ask of you."

"Anything you want. What is it?"

"A guy disappeared a couple of days ago. It was Darleen's husband. Not a very nice guy. The police are checking into it. Can you make it go away?"

"Consider it done. It will be my pleasure."

"Thanks. I'm taking Darleen back to Vegas with me. If any questions come up, you know where she is."

"There will be no questions."

Danny knew that. They partied until five o'clock. Afterward, the Don had his limo take them to the airport where the plane was waiting.

Chapter 57

Things were going well. Darleen moved in with Peter and Velvet hired her to take care of the Danny's fan mail. Danny did a TV special, two benefits and then returned to Caesar's Palace. Golfing with his buddies during the day, Bill Fanning became a constant companion.

Every once in a while he'd mention something about people dying around Danny. Danny would laugh it off and joke about it. Don Angelo called, "Danny, I got a special job for you right there in Vegas. It's important. There's a Senator causing all kinds of trouble for some people. Not only in Vegas but Washington as well. He needs to be stopped. They're having a big thirty year party at the Stardust a week from today and he'll be there. You're going to entertain them, so you'll be Johnny on the spot. If you miss him there, we'll have to come up with another plan.

"I won't miss him Don, trust me. Just send me the stuff on him."

"It's already in the mail. You take care of yourself." He hung up.

Danny sat for a while thinking. He had a wild idea. He called Bill Fanning. "Bill, it's Danny. I'm entertaining next week at the Stardust for some kind of thirty year party. You want to go with me?"

"You bet. I just got the invitation yesterday. It's a get together of people who have lived here for thirty years. It will be lots of fun. There's usually a big turn out. They'll love you. I'll see you tonight after the show."

"Sounds good to me." He hung up the phone. What better

alibi than having the head of the FBI in Vegas with you when the guy dies? That should dispel any doubts Bill had about him. He liked the idea.

The night of the show came. Danny, Velvet, and Bill were seated at the entertainer's table. Peter was emceeing the show so, Darleen was sitting with them too. The place was mobbed. Danny looked around and spotted the Senator. He was sitting with the Mayor and some city officials. He would bide his time. The entertainment was great. Wayne Newton, Robert Goulet, Pete Barbutti, Sonny King and Freddie Bell were appearing. The joint was rocking. Danny got up and tore the place apart.

It was one of those magical nights that only happens to show people. The end of the evening was drawing to a close. Danny and Bill made the rounds saying hello and schmoozing the crowd. Senator Friedman was getting ready to leave. Danny maneuvered Bill over to where he was standing. They exchanged small talk and some laughs. Danny waited until he was ready to go. Senator Friedman said his goodbyes and turned to go. Bill was on his left and Danny on the right. As he turned to make his exit, Danny popped him. Bill never saw the move. Senator Freidman rubbed the spot where the needle went in.

He headed for the door. Danny and Bill went back to their table and sat down with the other entertainers. Laughs and jokes were flying. When they were ready to leave they headed for the door. As they were walking out of the ballroom, they noticed an ambulance outside the casino. People were milling around. Bill grabbed a security guard. "What happened?"

The security guard said, "Senator Friedman had a heart attack. The paramedics couldn't revive him. He's in the ambulance."

"That's too bad. He looked all right inside. We were just talking to him."

Danny came up along side him. "What's going on Bill?"

"Senator Friedman had a heart attack. He's gone. They're taking him to the funeral home."

"Damn, he was fine when he left. Maybe he over did the

booze and food. How old was he? Did he have a heart condition?"

Bill shrugged his shoulders. His mind was spinning, trying to reconstruct the evening's events. He was thinking, *"Now Danny was with me all night. We were never separated, and Friedman died outside. I must have been nuts to think Danny had anything to do with it. I'm thinking too much like an agent. Coincidence, that's all it is."* They got into the limos and went to Château Vegas to finish off the night.

Danny was on the phone to the Don the next morning. "OK, now you tell me. How in the hell did you manage to whack the guy in a room full of people?"

Danny laughed. "I also had the head of the FBI here in Vegas with me. Is this a secure line?"

"Yes. I have it checked every day."

"OK, here's how I do it." He explained everything to the Don. When Danny finished, the Don said, "I'll be a son-of-a-bitch. How the hell did you ever come up with that idea? It's beautiful. And right under the FBI's nose! You got balls as big as grapefruits."

"You might say that. Give Bert my love. I'll talk to you soon." He hung up the phone. Velvet was swimming in the pool. She was wearing a small bikini. Danny got up and walked to the edge of the pool. He dropped his robe and stood naked in front of her. She looked up. "Well big guy, you going to use that thing or wave it at the passing golf carts."

He dropped into the water and grabbed her. "You better hang on to the side of the pool. I'm going to cause a tidal wave." And he did.

Three days later the Don called. He was furious. "That son of a bitch that contracted us to get rid of Senator Friedman is making noises. He says that he wants his money back. He says that he don't pay for heart attacks. I tried to tell him it was a hit but he wouldn't listen. He says he and his partners won't pay the other half of the money."

"Who are these people?"

"There's five guys. They own a big investment company.

They also own five cat houses in Nevada. Friedman was trying to shut them down along with blocking a big land deal for these guys worth millions."

"I need the names and where they are. I want the phone number of the jerk who called you. I'll take care of this for you."

"We'll take care of you on this one."

"No, this one is on me. From now on if anybody questions us on anything, we can refer them to the other four partners."

"That's brilliant. I say it again, you're the best. I'll get that stuff out to you today." He hung up.

Danny sat back in the lounge chair. He was thinking, *"This one is going to be interesting. I'll pick one of the five guys, but make them sweat and worry about which one it will be. They'll never know where or when it will take place. I can drive them crazy and have them jumping at shadows."*

The information came two days later. Danny went into the den and shut the door. He opened the big envelope and took out the pictures of the five men. One of the five he knew by the name of Jim Carson. He owned a big construction company in Vegas. He was a loud mouthed, know it all, obnoxious drunk. Danny had met him at a few parties. He avoided him when ever possible.

The other four were scattered around the state. He'd already made up his mind, and knew who was going to die. Jim had to go. He'd be doing the town a favor. His wife was a showgirl in the Follies Bergere at the Tropicana Hotel. Renee was a beautiful, tall, big breasted, lovely lady that Jim treated like shit. Yep, he had to go. Danny waited until seven o'clock to call Carson. When he knew he would be home, Danny called him on his private line. As he answered, Danny said, "Mr. Carson, it has come to my attention that you were unhappy with the unfortunate death of Senator Friedman. Let me assure you it was not a heart attack. I was told that you refuse to pay the other half of the money you owe. So to prove to you and your four other partners that it was a legitimate contract, one of you will die of an apparent heart attack in the very near future."

"Wait a minute. Who the fuck is this and who do you think

you're talking to, some little, know nothing schmuck?"

"I'm talking to a walking corpse. You don't fuck with us. Nobody does and lives to tell about it. So, tell your partners to make out their wills and get things in order. One of you is going to die, and soon."

Danny hung up and immediately called the Don. "Now let's see what he does. I just got a hold of the guy who lives here. He most likely will be calling you and screaming. He may want to make a deal. Tell him it's too late. You can't stop what's coming. Tell him it's out of your hands."

"OK, I know how to handle him. I'll keep you informed." He hung up.

Two days later the Don called. "You got him shitting his pants. At first he tried to be tough. But, when I told him that I couldn't stop it from happening, he started to back peddle. Even offered more money! I told him he had made a mistake and one of them was going to pay for it. I thought he was going to cry. He's sending the other half of the money. I told him it didn't make any difference now."

"Good. I'll let them sweat awhile. He's the one going down. If the town knew it was me that got rid of him, they'd give me the key to the city. I'll be in touch."

Chapter 58

They were all in Jim's office. The other four had flown in for this meeting. Jim was pacing back and forth. Finally, he stopped and said, "We've got a problem." He told them what was coming down. They all reacted the same way, pure disbelief. Harry from Reno said, "They can't do that. You sent them the other half of the money."

"It makes no difference. We fucked up. We questioned them."

John from Carson City spoke up. "You're the one that fucked up. You're the one that questioned them. We were content that the son-of-a-bitch was dead. That's what we wanted and it came about. Now, we're all going to worry about which one of us will pay the price for it."

Before Jim could answer, George from Lake Tahoe spoke up. "Before we get all upset about this, let's look at the facts. We are all wealthy men. Everything has a price. We find out what that price is, and we pay it. No ifs, ands or butts."

Larry from Wendover said, "Do you think that will work? According to Jim, they said it would do no good."

Jim jumped in. "It's worth a try. What have we got to loose except money? It's better than the alternative. I'll call my contact. He picked up the phone and got hold of the Don. "This is Jim from Vegas. I have my partners here and we have something to discuss with you. We are prepared to pay whatever price you want to settle this issue."

The Don smiled. He loved this. "I'm sorry. No amount of money can undo what you started. You made a mistake, now one of you will pay for it. Don't call here again." He hung up leaving Jim to stare at the phone. The four of them waited. Finally Jim said, "It's no good. He won't call it off."

Harry stood up. "Can we go to the cops and ask for police protection?"

George spoke up. "And tell them what? We need protection because we questioned the mob about a contract we put out to have someone killed? That's stupid and you know it."

They all started to shout at the same time. Finally, John shouted them down. "It's no use shouting at each other. What's done is done. I suggest we all return home and get our affairs in order."

It was deathly quiet as they stared at one another. They couldn't understand this. They were the richest men in Nevada and, for the first time, their money was no good. There was nobody they could call to handle this. The reality set in. One of them was doomed. Without a word spoken, they left and went out of Jim's office. A cab took them back to the airport.

Across the street, Danny watched them leave. He had the Weasel keeping an eye on Jim's office. He called Danny when the four showed up. From their expressions, he could see the terror and disbelief. Good. They would sweat and be jumping at shadows. Maybe it would make better human beings out of them, but he doubted it. He had the Ox drive him back to the house.

He let them sweat for a month. He was waiting for the big gala party at the Tropicana. They were premiering the new Follies show. It was to be a star studded evening. Danny made sure that Jim was going to be there. His wife was the lead nude showgirl in the new show. Danny had invited Peter, Darleen, Carme and Flame. There was to be a big party in the ballroom after the show.

When they got to the ballroom, things were swinging. Bobby Milano and his band were knocking out some great music. Danny had a table right next to Jim and his wife. The other people at his table were his ass kissers. He was already on his way to getting drunk. His wife was sitting next to him. People kept coming over, hugging and congratulating her, which pissed Jim off to no end. He started to get nasty to her.

Danny excused himself and walked over to the table. He said hello to Jim, then he took his wife's hand and kissed it. "Renee, you were wonderful tonight. You alone are worth the price of the ticket."

Jim stood up. "You're God damned right she is. She's the best. I'm glad somebody here knows it. Coming from you, it's the very best compliment she can get." He gave Danny a playful punch on the left shoulder. Danny gave him one back then went back to his table.

They danced, ate and had laughs. Danny kept an eye on Jim's table. He had to go to the bathroom sometime. Half way through the party he got up and headed for the john. The one off the ballroom was down a short hallway. Danny excused himself and followed. When he got in the bathroom, Jim was standing at the urinal. There was nobody else in there. Danny checked the stalls. They were empty. Jim saw him. "Hey, come on over. Standing room only." He laughed at his own joke. He finished and zipped up.

That's when Danny made his move. In a flash he had Jim in a choker hold. His eyes bulged and he started kicking. He pulled him into a stall and kicked the door shut. Jim was starting to black out. Danny was at his ear. "So you think you can fuck with the mob and get away with it. Well, Jim boy, you're going to pay the tab." Jim slumped to the floor. Danny kept the pressure on to be sure that he was out cold. He sat him on the toilet, and popped him with the pearl. About the time he would be waking up, the poison would hit. He walked out of the bathroom. Nobody was in the hall. He went back to the table and joined in the fun.

It wasn't until Renee got worried about her husband that they went looking for him. It took awhile. They thought he was in the casino gambling. When they found him in the men's room, he was long dead. They called the paramedics, but nothing could be done for him. Danny was standing with Velvet, Carme and Flame when Renee came down the hall. Danny went over and gave her a hug. "If there's anything I can do for you, please call me. Any time my dear."

She pulled back a little. "Count on it," and she left. Danny had to smile. Yep, she was going to be all right. She was a beautiful lady with lots of money and no abusive husband. It was perfect.

They had a big funeral at Palm Mortuary for him. His partners showed up looking relieved. They smiled and chatted among themselves. Renee looked gorgeous in black. When Danny paid his respects, she hugged him and pushed her pelvis against him. The look in her eyes said it all.

After the ceremony they moved to the grave site. One of the funeral directors handed Jim's partner, George an envelope. He opened it, read it and looked around. He handed it to the other three guys to read. Danny had written them a note that said. "The debt is paid in full. If anybody should ever call you and want to know about heart attacks, you know what to tell them." They all gave a sigh of relief.

Bill Fanning was sitting in his den reading about the death of Jim Carson. He knew him slightly and really didn't like him. They had investigated him on several occasions for different things, but could never get anything on him that was tangible. So, he thought, *"Good riddance."* He noticed that Danny and a number of stars were at the party and the funeral. He said himself. *"Another coincidence? Stop that. You're doing it again."* He finished the paper and turned on the TV.

Chapter 59

It had been three weeks since the funeral. Danny was sitting by the pool when he got a call from Renee. She wanted to see him about something important. Danny got dressed and drove over to her house at El Rancho Bella Vista, a development of real exclusive homes of the rich and perverted. She opened the door wearing a silk robe, and from what he could see, she was naked under it.

"I'm so glad you could come. Please come into the parlor." She sort of floated into the adjoining room. Renee sat across from him. "I wanted to see you for two reasons. The first reason is I'm having a big problem with Jim's partners. They're trying to get rid of me and take over the whole business. They offered me a fraction of what its worth. All Jim's assets are tied up in the partnership. I have the insurance money from his death, but the big money is in the company. I don't know what to do."

Danny sat back. "Don't do anything. I'll handle it. You just leave everything to me. I'll have my lawyers look into it and we'll go from there. Now what's the other thing?"

She stood up and in one move the robe floated down and landed at her feet. She was magnificent. Her very large boobs hung just right and dipped when she moved. She walked over to the couch where he was sitting and stood in front of him. He reached up and felt those big breasts. He pulled her down on the couch and kissed her. She was trying to get him out of his clothes. He stood up in front of her and took off his shirt. He unzipped his trousers and let them fall.

When she saw Ninja, she almost fainted. "My God, That's beautiful. I want every bit of it."

Danny waved it in front of her face. "And that's what you're going to get." He left four hours later.

Danny was furious as he thought to himself, *"I gave those mother fuckers a pass and now, they do this. Well, it's time to show them the error of their ways."* When he got back to his house he called George at his office.

He disguised his voice. "George, do you know who this is? I'm the guy that gave you a new lease on life. Now, I find out that you're trying to cheat Jim's wife out of her share of the business. That's not nice. I thought maybe you had learned a lesson, but I see you're just a greedy bunch of guys taking advantage of a helpless female. So, one of you is going to die a very violent death. That should make the other three give her what she rightly deserves. If I find out that it isn't done, I'll take out the other three. Nobody takes advantage of Renee when I'm around. And it's no good calling her, because she knows nothing about this. I'm what you may call a distant admirer. She has never met me nor will she. So, if you know how to pray, I'd get at it."

Danny hung up before George could answer. He called the Ox and Weasel into the den. "I got a job for you. There's a guy in Carson City, Nevada that needs to be taught a lesson. I want you to make it a violent death. I'll give you all the details. You can drive up, so you don't leave a paper trail. Cash all the way. After that you can take a little vacation in Lake Tahoe at the Cal-Neva Lodge, complements of the management. You deserve it. I'm giving you ten grand apiece for this little jaunt. You can leave at the end of the week. I'll have Velvet set up security for me until you get back."

The Ox looked at the Weasel. "Like old times. Huh, little buddy?" He looked at Danny. "Get us the info and we'll lay it out. It may take a couple of days to see where he goes and what he does, but we'll take him out."

"Take your time. I know you'll be fine. After all, you're the best in the business. Bert said so." They got a good laugh out of that.

The next day Renee called. "Danny, you're not going to believe this, but George called me today and told me that I'm to be a full partner in the business and take over where Jim left off. He sounded strange, like he was scared or something. Danny, I don't know anything about finances and stuff like that."

"I'll handle that. I'm coming over so get ready. We'll talk after we have some fun and games."

"I'll be ready. Hurry up."

They were lying naked in bed when Danny said to her, "Now, down to business. I want you to hire my girlfriend Velvet to be your assistant. She knows all about big business and I trust her enough to handle my finances. She'll teach you what you have to know and what to look for. She's nobody's fool."

"OK, I'll do that. George said they're having a board meeting next week in Vegas. He wants me there."

"Good, you take Velvet with you. Let her ask the questions. She's used to handling good ole boys. Besides, with her busy you can enjoy more of this. He raised his big cock and shook it."

She took it in her hand. "Good, I can start now." And she did.

When Danny got home he called Velvet into the den. He explained to her what was going on with Renee. "So I want you to run interference for her. If I know these guys, she'll be just a figure head with no say in anything. This is a chance for you to really show your stuff. Darleen can handle things around here. You will still handle the big things."

"I take it that you want me to do the same thing that I did for Ritchie. I can do that. It will be an interesting challenge. They think we are just tits and no brains. Well, Renee has the big tits, and I have the big brain."

Danny laughed. "That's my girl. Why don't you and Renee have lunch tomorrow and hash a few things out."

"Good idea. I'll call her and set it up." She left the den.

*****

The Ox and the Weasel pulled into Lake Tahoe and checked into the Cal-Neva Lodge. They had lunch then drove to Carson

City. They found the office of Carson Land Management and Construction. It was a big building with lots of employees. The Ox sent the Weasel in to check things out. He was dressed in a business suit carrying a briefcase.

Except for the slight bulge under his left arm, he could have been just another suit. He found John Moody's office and saw him sitting behind a desk in a heated argument with somebody on the phone. The Weasel kept walking until he reached the elevators. He took it down, went across the street to the car and got in. "He's in there. He was screaming at someone on the phone. Must be one of his partners."

"Good, we wait. Let's see where he goes when he comes out."

An hour later, John came out of the building. He had two burly security guys with him. They got into a limo and headed to Lake Tahoe. The Ox followed them until they got to Harvey's Wagon Wheel. They went in. The Ox parked the car. Inside they found him in the coffee shop at a table in the back. The two security guys were sitting at the counter having coffee.

John was in a serious conversation with another man. The Ox and the Weasel got a table close by and ordered coffee. They knew who the man was. Danny had shown them pictures of the four partners. They talked for half an hour, got up and left. The Ox and Weasel followed them outside. Their limo pulled up and they got in. The Ox got the car and they followed. John's limo drove to a big house on the outskirts of town and went in. The Ox and Weasel parked close by and waited.

Four hours later John and the other man came out in a huff, stomped over to the limo and got in. The limo headed back to Carson City along a twisty and narrow road with steep drop-offs. The Ox said to the Weasel, "I think this is the easiest ten grand we have ever made."

"How so?"

"That limo is going to have a bad accident." They were coming around a sharp curve with an eighteen hundred foot cliff on the left. The Ox accelerated and got on the inside of the limo. He cranked the steering wheel to the left and put his bumper on the inside bumper of the limo. He gunned it, throwing the limo into a tail spin. The limo hit the guardrail and went over. The Ox stopped and looked past the guardrail as the limo hit the side of the mountain and burst into flames.

It continued rolling down the mountain in a big fireball. The twisted mass of metal hit the bottom and lay there burning. The Ox got back in the car, turned it around and headed back to Tahoe. "Easiest ten grand ever." They laughed all the way back to the lodge.

Danny picked up the phone. "Danny, did you hear about the terrible accident on the road to Carson City from Lake Tahoe? Seems a limo with four guys in it went over a guardrail and burst into flames. One of the guys was John Moody, a big land developer. I expect it to be on tonight's news. People should be more careful driving those mountain roads."

Danny laughed. "You're right. Now, I want you and the Weasel to have some fun. Frank is in the main room and Freddie Bell is in the lounge. I set it up so you can see Frank's show and hang out with him after. He usually goes into the lounge and watches Freddie's show. Make sure you say hello to Freddie for me. Oh, you'll have some female company to take along. You enjoy yourselves."

Danny had made arrangements for two hookers to spend time with them until they left. That was the least he could do.

The news was filled with accounts about the accident. It showed the limo, or what was left of it. The bodies were burned so badly, it was hard to identify them. The only way would be through the use of dental records.

Danny called George. When he answered Danny said, "I hope you learned something from this. You'd better walk the straight and narrow and don't fuck with Renee. All the money in the world can't protect you from me."

Danny hung up. George sat there with the dead phone in his hand. He was visibly shaken. He had his secretary put in a conference call to Harry and Larry. When they came on he said,

"Who ever this guy is, he's crazy. He just called me again and told me we had better not fuck with Renee. What the hell are we going to do?"

Larry said, "She doesn't know anything about our business. We make her a figure head. She can take over as Chairmen of the Board, Jim's old position. She'll sign anything we put in front of her."

Harry piped in. "He's right. This time we won't have to deal with that ass hole Jim. We make it look good to who ever this guy is. As for me, I'm tired of jumping at shadows. I spent a fortune on a security system that a gnat can't get through. The only problem is, it makes me a prisoner in my own home."

"John had a security system and two security guards. It didn't do him any good. We'll wait for the board meeting next week and work things out. Meanwhile, Jim's treasurer is handling things there."

They hung up. Each one was left to his own thoughts. When the girls walked into the board room, all heads turned, and mouths dropped open. They stood there, two beautiful women, one tall and statuesque, the other small and petite. George got up and came around the table to greet them. "Renee, how good to see you." He looked at Velvet. "And who is this lovely lady?"

Renee smiled at him. They had rehearsed this. "This is Velvet Morrison, my new company manager." It had the reaction they were expecting. George's face turned red. The other men in the room were all talking at once. Renee went to the head of the table. She motioned for the guy sitting on her right to move down one. She sat down with Velvet at her right. Curt Jenkins, the treasurer, jumped up. "I don't know what's going on here, but I won't work under a woman. I'll resign."

Velvet stood up. "That's your prerogative, but before you go we have to audit the books. I want to see every transaction made in the last five years." They were stunned and silent. Finally, Curt sat down and hung his head. He knew he was out classed. From the looks on the faces of everybody in the room, they knew they were fucked and there was nothing they could do about it. The meeting lasted four hours.

When Velvet got home she was flying high. "Danny you should have been there. It was great. Renee was just wonderful and remembered everything I taught her. She is now the Chairman of the Board for Carson Enterprises, and I am the new Manager of Carson Enterprises. I set my own salary and will start tomorrow. I want to go over all the books and familiarize myself with what's going on. Those good old board members didn't fight me on anything. They didn't like it, but went along with it."

Danny laughed, "It must have been your cute ways and dynamite body that made them go along with everything. You enjoy yourself. You love this kind of challenge. I saw that, when you worked for Ritchie."

She came over and cuddled up in his lap. "You're right. I can do that and still take care of you." She reached down and squeezed his cock.

So, that's how it went. Velvet went to work every day and ran Carson Enterprises, and Danny balled the Chairman of the Board of Carson Enterprises every day.

Things couldn't be better. His shows were complete sellout's everywhere he went on the strip. He was due to close at the Frontier Hotel in two weeks and take a much needed break, but that was not to be.

Bert called. "Danny, my man, I have got a good one for you. This one pays over a million dollars American."

"Shit, you want me to kill Kennedy?"

Bert burst out laughing. "No, this job is in Bogota, Columbia. There's a drug lord down there that needs to be eliminated. He's causing the government lots of grief not to mention the rival drug lords. They want him gone without starting a drug war. Who better to do that, than you? You'll be working at one of the top clubs in Bogota. The guy frequents the place almost every night. He's heavily guarded, but I know you can get around that."

"Thanks for the confidence. Send me the stuff. Hey, how's my god child?

"He's growing like a weed. Stop in on your way back and spend a few days."

"I can do that. Give the kid and Roz a hug for me."

Danny hung up then had a great thought. He called Renee. "Hey, sweetheart. Have you ever been to Columbia?"

"No, why?"

"How would you like to go with me? I'm doing a gig down there in two weeks. It'll be fun."

"Good. Count me in. I still have my passport."

"Great, I'll make all the travel arrangements and let you know. Meantime, I still want that body."

"Well, it's here. Come and get some."

"Be right over." Danny was thinking. *"Nothing like a tall, beautiful, blonde with big breasts to make a drug lord come sniffing around."*

The envelope came two days later. Danny opened it. He read through the contents. This guy, Carlos Muretta, was a real bad ass, but a real handsome ladies man. The folder read like a movie script with murder, drugs, prostitution, extortion, kidnapping, and sadism. He liked to torture his victims before he killed them!

No wonder getting rid of him was worth so much money. According to the file, he was heavily guarded. He would be staying at the Bogota Plaza Hotel, right down the street from where Danny was working. The hotel had a big, beautiful lounge with live bands playing at night. It was the local hot spot. Danny decided to use his private plane, which would be a lot more comfortable to fly accompanied by Renee.

Danny closed the Frontier and took a couple of days off. Velvet was engrossed in her new enterprise. She found a whole bunch of discrepancies. The books were a mess, and filled with entries which suggested that Jim was stealing from his own company. His partners were no better. They had a lot of shady deals going with kickbacks and bribes. Velvet began restructuring and fired a lot of dead weight personnel. She was a tough boss and the real workers in the company loved her. Renee gave her full rein. She was content to sit around and enjoy her money, which was considerable.

The day came when Danny was to leave. Renee met Danny at the private airport on Las Vegas Blvd. She looked stunning. They took off and headed south on the beginning of a long flight, refueling in Miami, then on to Columbia. When they got to the Bogota airport, there was a big welcoming committee. It was a carnival atmosphere, with a band playing and people dancing. Danny made a small speech using his rusty Spanish which the people found very entertaining. They proceeded to the hotel and a beautiful suite on the top floor. The Ox and Weasel had an adjoining room. The pilot and co-pilot had rooms down stairs.

At the end of the hall there was a desk set up with armed guards sitting around. Danny knew that it belonged to Carlos. The balcony outside was actually a walkway. It ran all the way down to the end. Sitting in a chair at the end was another guard. He was carrying an AK47. Carlos took no chances. This was going to be a real challenge.

The show was jam packed. People were standing in the back. Carlos had a big table down front. Rene was sitting with the Ox and the Weasel. Carlos kept looking over at her, but knew that she had her own bodyguards. Danny was watching him through a hole in the curtain. He was thinking, *"Look all you want you greasy bastard, but don't touch."*

The show was great and the audience wouldn't let him off the stage. He finally bowed out. Back in the dressing room, he showered and changed. Renee was waiting along with Carlos and all his people when Danny came out. His army was scattered around the room watching the doors and the hallway. The Ox and Weasel were with Renee.

When Renee saw Danny she got up and kissed him. "That was a wonderful show. You really had them going."
About that time Carlos came over. "You were sensational. My name is Carlos." He held out his hand and Danny shook it.

"Nice to meet you. Oh, this is Renee." Carlos took her hand and kissed it. He looked into her eyes. "I have never seen such beauty here in Columbia. You have captured my heart." All this was said in a very charming accent. Renee looked him in the eyes. "I bet you say that to all the beautiful girls you meet."

Carlos laughed. He reminded Danny of Gilbert Roland, mustache and all. They went to the bar that was set up in the dressing room and had a drink. Carlos was on Renee like a bird on a June bug. She was use to handling guys like this, and did it in a way, so as not to offend. Finally, Danny stepped in and took her by the arm. He said to Carlos, "It's time to take the little lady home. How about a nice, leisurely breakfast in the morning?"

Carlos smiled and showed those white perfect teeth. "It will be my pleasure. Say nine o'clock?"

"Nine it is." They left and went to the hotel. In the elevator, Renee said, "What a charming man. I can see that he's a real lady killer. He says, he has a beautiful place in the jungle he'd like to show me, but by the looks of him, all I would be seeing is ceiling."

"I'd say that would be a safe bet. But listen, this is a vacation for you. If you want to have some fun with him, it's OK."

She looked at him. "Really? You don't mind? Boy what a difference between you and Jim. Jim would have slapped the hell out of me for just saying he was a charming man. You know he was insanely jealous."

"You don't have to worry about that with me. We have no strings. You just do what ever the hell you want. It's time you had some fun and excitement in your life. That's why I brought you here. I want you to have fun."

At nine o'clock sharp Carlos showed up in the restaurant. He had his usual goons with him, and a beautiful Columbian girl, with gleaming, black hair and sparkling, black eyes. At five foot two, she had finely chiseled features, a tight little body and moved like a cat.

Carlos kissed Renee's hand. "How wonderful you look so early in the morning." He shook Danny's hand. "I would like you to meet Louisa Catalina Morales. Her father runs my business here in Bogota."

She looked up at him with those fantastic, dark eyes as Danny took her hand. A message passed between them. "It's a pleasure to meet you, my dear. Please sit here." He pulled a chair out for her, which put Carlos next to Renee. They took their time with breakfast, talking and laughing for more than an hour.

Finally Carlos said, "Danny, if it's all right with you, I would like to show Renee my beautiful Bogota. There are some wonderful places here. I promise to have her back this afternoon."

Danny looked at Renee. The look on her face told him she wanted to go. "That's fine with me. Maybe Louisa can show me old town. I read somewhere that it's worth seeing." She gave him a sideways look. Carlos said, "I'm sure she would love to do that. Why don't we meet back here for cocktails at four o'clock?"

Danny smiled and stood up. "Good. Sounds like a plan." He helped Louisa to her feet and they went outside. Danny had to laugh. There was Carlos and Renee with his small army. So much for intimacy. They split up. Renee was in Carlos's amour plated Cadillac, and Danny with Louisa on foot. She had spoken but a few words since they met. Danny gently offered her his arm. "OK, my dear. Where would you like to take me first?"

She looked up at him. "You're really Danny Angel! I never thought we would ever meet. I have all your albums and have seen all your movies. You're much more handsome in person."

"I'll take that as quite a compliment coming from such an attractive lady." They started walking. Danny took her hand. She gave him a slight squeeze. They made small talk on the way to old town. She was a good guide and told him all about her country and what she did for a living. She owned a large travel agency, booking tours and cruises. They stopped on a crowded street in front of a restaurant described as an Italian Columbian trattoria. It had a nice outside patio facing the street.

They sat down, ordered drinks and were enjoying the casual setting. Across the street sitting at a table were four men dressed in suits. Danny glanced down the street and noticed a moped approaching with two guys wearing helmets. Danny turned to the Ox and Weasel. "I think we are about to witness a drive by shooting. Check out the moped. They're wearing helmets. Nobody else is. The guy in the back is the shooter." Louisa looked at him.

"How do you know this? They could also be wearing them for protection."

"I doubt it. They're too hot. See how they've stopped." She glanced down the street. The moped was sitting there waiting. Slowly it started to move. The Ox and Weasel reached for their pieces, but Danny stopped them. "It's not our fight."

The moped picked up speed. When it got close to the four guys in suits, the driver ran the moped up onto the sidewalk. As it sped by the four men, shots rang out. The guy in the middle took all three rounds right in the chest and the impact forced his body through a plate glass window. Before anybody could move, the moped was gone. Screams and confusion broke out. Louisa sat there frozen, then turned pale. "It has to be drugs. There's so much killing over drugs."

Louisa was visibly shaken. Danny paid the tab. They hailed a cab and went back to the hotel. He took her up to the suite. She was shaking like a leaf. He laid her down on the couch and got a cold cloth for her forehead. He was sitting next to her when she took his hand. "I have never seen anybody killed before," she said in a trembling voice. "Would you please hold me?"

Danny put his arms around her and held her closely. Her face was next to his. She turned her head and their lips met. It was a tender kiss. She pulled back and looked in his eyes longingly. She felt safe and was moved by his gentleness and compassion. Then the fireworks started. He was absolutely irresistible. She asked, "Do you find me attractive?" Danny smiled, "Absolutely." She couldn't believe her good fortune. Her breathing and heart rate increased and she was putty in his arms. He picked her up and took her into the bedroom. He stood her up, slowly undressing her. She had a body like Flame's, with perfect breasts and not an ounce of fat. She began groping for him, as he sat her down and undressed himself.

When she saw Ninja, she started to rub her legs together while arching her back. She reached out with both hands and caressed it. She tried to get it in her mouth, but it was much too big. Danny laid her on her back. Very carefully he slid inside her. She was so tight that he almost came. She winced and he knew he was hurting her. He started to back off, but she grabbed his buttocks. "No, please don't stop. Go easy. I want to feel it all."

He started to move in and out gently. He only gave her half of it for now. She was bucking like a horse, moaning and thrashing around. She came multiple times. He couldn't hold it any more and came with her on her last climax. It was heaven. He was going to take it out but she said, "No, leave it in. It feels so good. I want to be able to take all of it before you go."

"We can work on that. But right now, let's shower and cool off."

At four o'clock they were sitting at the bar when Carlos and Renee showed up. By the looks on their faces, they had a good afternoon. Rene was all excited and chattering like a magpie. Louisa told Carlos about the shooting. His face got dark for a minute. He said to her, "Unfortunately, that happens here, but I'm glad both of you are alright."

He turned to Danny. "Renee tells me that you are not, how you say, emotionally involved. I would like to take her to my hacienda for a few days. We will be back on Saturday, if that's all right with you."

"Hey, it's her call. If she wants to go it's fine with me. She's a big girl."

Renee hugged him. "Oh thanks, Danny. This is so exciting. I'll go up and pack a few things. I'll be right back." She left. Danny looked at Carlos. "She's had a rough time recently. This will be good for her."

Carlos shook his hand. "I'll take good care of her." Renee came bouncing back into the bar carrying a small suit case. They said their goodbyes and left. Danny turned to Louisa. "Now we can work on you getting all of this." He grabbed Ninja through his pants. Her eyes lit up. "Can we start tonight?"

The week flew by. There were full houses for his show every night and Louisa was insatiable. It took two more sessions before she managed to take it all. After that it was all the time.

Danny had come up with a plan. He would put it into effect

when Carlos and Renee got back. He needed the Ox on this one. He asked the Ox to get real friendly with the guard positioned on the balcony. They'd have drinks together with the Weasel. With Carlos gone, the guard had all kinds of time on his hands.

Carlos and Renee returned Saturday afternoon. They acted like two kids caught with their hands in a cookie jar. Renee was all bubbly. She told Danny all about the hacienda, the animals, and the helicopter ride to and from. Finally she wound down.

Carlos said, "It was delightful to have her on my hacienda. It added some sunshine. Now I must go tend to a few things. I will see you tonight at the show." And he was gone. Renee said to Danny, "What a charmer. He's a good lover, too. Not as good as you, but different. I really had a good time."

"I'm glad you did. And I'm glad you came down here with me. You would have never known any of this stuck in Vegas." He felt sort of guilty having to burst her bubble by killing him, but it was nothing personal. It was strictly business. She'd get over it.

He decided on Sunday night. They were dark on Sunday, so they all went to dinner then found a great place for dancing. Louisa was a marvelous dancer.

Danny had put a mickey in a bottle of Tequila for the Ox to give to the balcony guard. Danny needed him asleep. He laced a bottle of good champagne also.

They got back to the suite. Renee was getting into something more comfortable before joining Carlos's in his suite. Danny said to her as she was getting ready to leave, "Here babe, I got a special bottle of champagne for you and Carlos. I want you to have some drinks on me. It will help your love making. Trust me."

"You're so sweet. I'll do that. I want to thank you for being so understanding."

"Hey, what are friends for?" She took the bottle and went down the hall. The guards gave her the eye as she went into the suite. Danny called the Ox in. I want you to take this bottle to your buddy, the guard at the end of the balcony. But don't you drink any. Just him."

The Ox looked at him. "You know, Bert says you're the best

he's ever seen. I believe him. The Weasel and I can't hold a candle to you."

Danny looked at him. "You know?"

"Of course we know. Bert told us from the get go. I don't know how you're doing it, but whatever it is, it's freaking brilliant. I'll make sure the guard goes out, even if I have to throw him off the balcony."

"That won't be necessary if he drinks this. It would knock an elephant on its ass." He gave the Ox the bottle and he sauntered down the balcony and said hello to the guard. He took the bottle out from under his shirt and gave it to him. The guy hid it under his chair. The Ox talked to him a bit then came back. They used a mirror to watch him. He looked around, took the bottle out from under the chair and took a big swig. He waited a minute and took another. He put the bottle under the chair again and sat back. Ten minutes later he was out like a light.

Danny waited until everything got quiet. He walked down the balcony to where the guard was sleeping. Very carefully, he opened the door to the suite. Nobody was moving. He got to the bedroom and peeked in. They were sprawled on the bed naked. Both were out cold. He went to the side of the bed. He really hated to do this but, he hit Carlos twice with the needle. Picking up the bottle of champagne, he poured the remaining contents down the bathroom sink. He grabbed the bottle of Tequila as he passed by the guard. One last look around, and he was back in his suite having a drink.

It wasn't until eleven thirty that all hell broke loose. He could hear Renee screaming all the way down the hall. Everybody rushed out to see what was wrong. The guards were running around in circles.

Danny came out of his room and grabbed Renee. "What the hell's wrong?"

She was sobbing and crying. "He's dead! He died in bed with me. He was fine last night. Now he's dead."

Danny stepped back with her as the emergency team came rushing down the hall dragging a gurney. They went into the room.

The guards held everybody back. Danny took Renee back to his suite. He had to give her a drink to calm her down. It wasn't long before there was a knock on the door. It was hotel security. With them was a very mean looking guy who flashed his badge. "I'm detective Santiago. I would like to ask the lady some questions."

"Come in. She's pretty shook up, but I'm sure she can answer any questions you may have." He went over to the couch where Renee was sitting. "I know this is a shock to you, but I have to ask you some questions." She nodded. "Can you tell me what happened?"

Renee blew her nose. "We were having some drinks before going to bed. We made love and fell asleep. I don't remember anything until I woke up and saw him next to me. I thought he was sleeping, but I couldn't wake him up. That's when I realized that he was dead!"

Santiago wrote something in his little book. "I guess that about covers it. I'm sorry to have bothered you at a time like this. Please forgive me." He turned and let himself out. The Ox and the Weasel were looking at Danny. The Ox smiled and shook his head. He mouthed, "You're the best"

Danny got a phone call from Bert the next day. "How is everything there? I read all about the untimely death of Carlos Muretta. That's a shame. Did a detective Santiago come to see you?"

"Yeah, how did you know that?"

"He's one of the guys that hired you. He had to make it look good. Now finish up and get the hell out of there."

Chapter 60

The plane landed in Vegas at noon. They took a limo to Renee's house. She was still upset about the death of Carlos. He was feeling a little guilty for using her in such a way. She kept saying that she thought she was like a black widow. He told her that her thoughts were pure nonsense.

"You just need a little rest. It has been a long and tiring flight. I'll see you in the next few days to see how you are doing. When you are feeling better, we'll get together with some friends and go out for a few laughs. Trust me, you'll be fine."

When he got home, a note from Velvet was waiting. She requested that he call her at once. When Velvet came to the phone she said, "Danny, I got trouble."

"What kind of trouble, honey?"

"Remember that old boy friend of mine that you threw out of the hospital? Well, he called me a couple of days ago. The newspaper had a big write up and there was also some TV coverage about me running Carson Enterprises. He read the article and wants money or he'll call the press and tell them I use to be a hooker. I stalled him, buying time until you got back."

The blood was pounding in his veins. "Where is this son of a bitch?"

"He's staying at Motel Eight on Tropicana. He wants to meet me tonight and I'm supposed to have the money with me. He knows you're out of town. I told him you weren't due back until next week."

"Good. Come on home. I'll handle it."

"I knew you would. I'm on my way."

Danny called the Ox and Weasel in. "We have a job to do tonight. We'll need the van, so get it ready." He told them what was coming down. They both grinned. The Ox said, "I take it that this won't be a heart attack?"

Danny scowled. "Definitely not. I gave that son of a bitch a pass once. This time he's going to pay in pain. Lots of pain."

Velvet came into the house. She saw Danny and ran into his arms. She started to cry. "Oh Danny, I tried so hard to make something good of myself and erase my past. Now this happens."

Danny held her at arms length. "You have nothing to worry about. I'll take care of it. Here's what were going to do." He told her the plan.

That night the Ox and Danny arrived just before Velvet. She showed up at Motel Eight at exactly nine o'clock. His room was at the end of the complex. Sitting in the corner of the parking lot was a dark van. Velvet pulled up in front of his room. She got out. Danny and the Ox were standing on both sides of the door. When he opened the door and saw Velvet standing there with a briefcase, he said, "I see you got smart. Come on in here. I want the money and a nice piece of ass."

That's all he said, 'cause Danny came around the door frame, grabbed him by the throat and pushed him into the room. The Ox followed him in and shut the door. Velvet got into her car and left. Danny had him up against the wall.

"Remember me? I'm the guy that told you to leave Velvet alone. I see you didn't take my advice. Now my man, you're going to suffer for it." He motioned to the Ox to take him. The Ox grabbed him by the neck and squeezed. Danny opened the door. The Weasel had backed the van up to the door. The Ox picked the guy up and threw him into the van. He followed him in and sat on him.

Danny got in front and they drove out of town. They were heading for Searchlight. Danny had done a show there for Frontier Days. He remembered taking a tour of several old mines. Abandoned mine shafts were just what the doctor ordered. The guy was crying and trying to make amends. Everytime he did the Ox would punch him, breaking teeth. They got to the mine shaft. They dragged the guy out. He had wet his pants.

Danny got in front of him. "Look at me, ass hole. I'm the last thing you're ever going to see. He never saw the ice pick until it went in under his ribcage. He died standing up. Danny let him hit the ground. They removed the boards from the shaft. The Ox picked him up and dropped him in. It took awhile before they heard him hit bottom. They replaced the boards and left.

When Danny walked in the house, Velvet was sitting on the couch. Her eyes were red from crying. Danny came over and sat next to her. "You have nothing to worry about, honey. He will never bother you again. Nobody will. That's a promise. You just run your company. I'll take care of the bull shit"

She hugged him. "You're the best. I don't know what I would do without you."

"Hey, you're stuck with me. We're a team. Remember?"

*****

Bill Fanning was sitting in his den with the paper in front of him, reading about the death of Carlos Muretta. Again Danny was there, and on the same floor. It couldn't be him. He had checked him out completely. There wasn't even a parking ticket. Yet his instincts told him something was wrong, but what? What was he missing? Danny was back at Caesar's and opening tonight. He had been invited.

Bill dressed and went to the hotel. As usual the place was sold out. After the show, they had a big party in Danny's dressing room. Everybody was there. The party lasted until two in the morning. Danny and Bill were sitting at the bar having a night cap. They were all alone except for the Ox and Weasel. Velvet was asleep on the couch. Danny went over and woke her up.

"Time to go home, honey." He pulled her to her feet. "I'll see you tomorrow, Bill." They left.

Bill sat there for a minute. Danny's glass was sitting in front of him. With out thinking, he picked it up with his two fingers inside the glass and put it in his pocket. Just for fun he'd run his fingerprints tomorrow.

The next morning he was at the office early. Nobody was in yet. He dusted the glass and carefully lifted off the prints. After photographing them, they went into his computer and on to FBI headquarters in Washington. He waited for the results. He was watching the screen when Danny DiBernardo's face popped up. It shocked him. He read the report. He had died in a car bombing. He read his rap sheet and everything about him. He said to himself, *"It has to be a mistake!"* He ran them again with the same results.

Bill printed the report and erased all the information. He went into his office. He stared at the picture of Danny Di. He reread the reports. He sat back. *How can this be? A superstar who was a hit man for the biggest crime boss in Chicago!* He stared at the picture again. He got up and took the picture off the wall that Danny had signed for him. He put them side by side. His trained eye saw the difference. He had work done on his face.

He needed more before he could make any accusations. He remembered the town in Italy that Danny was supposed to come from. It was in his bio. Perusia. Yeah, that was it. He'd call Interpol and have them check it. In the meantime, he called the Chicago office of the FBI.

He identified himself then asked, "Can you get me a run down on a Danny DiBernardo? He was killed a few years back." They would call him back. When the call came in, he requested a fax. They faxed him everything they had on Danny Di.

He read it all. Medal of honor recipient, marine corps records, arrests, and his mob ties. This was incredible! Who would ever believe this? Questions popped into his mind. *How did he get back into the country with a passport in the name of Ferdinando Bello? You have to be fingerprinted for that. And there was his driver's license. How come nobody checked his fingerprints for that? How did he get a sheriff's card here in Vegas? He'd have to be fingerprinted for that, too.*

Then it came to him. *The mob! The mob can do anything. He worked for the most powerful man in the country. He'd have all kinds of people in his pocket.* The fact that Danny was passing himself off as the Don's nephew raised some questions. *Did the Don have a nephew in Italy?* He'd check back through Danny's life, since he supposedly came back from Italy. He'd start in Chicago and work his way forward.

He knew Danny was a tough guy. He'd seen it first hand on occasion. There was the time when, on the golf course, Danny hit a ball into the foursome ahead of them. It wasn't intentional. He just got into one. The guy came back and got in Danny's face. Danny broke his jaw in front of all his buddies. They had to pull him off the guy. Yeah, he was tough alright.

He put a call through to Interpol. He asked them to check to see if there was a Ferdinando Domanico Bello anywhere in the town of Perusia, in Umbria, Italy. They said it would take awhile. He said he would wait and gave them a fax number. He remembered that Danny was engaged to Carmen Regerio, Ritchie Regerio's daughter. Ritchie was the head Capo in Buffalo. In fact, he was in Buffalo a lot. He'd check on that, too.

Another thought crossed his mind. *How can I prove Danny was doing all these killings? There was no violence. I was with him when Senator Friedman died. He was never out of my sight. Then there was the one in Vancouver. How do you kill a top Capo in a room full of bodyguards? The last one in Columbia had a girl in the room with the victim when he died. This could all be circumstantial.*

What would the media say about it? "Hit man goes straight and becomes a superstar." *Shit, this is the stuff movies are made of. The press would have a ball with it. They'd make a martyr out of him. Then again, what would the mob do to him if they found out he was on to something? His life wouldn't be worth a plug nickel!*

He got on the computer and researched the deaths of people that were around Danny when they died. It took him most of the day. When he had all the information, he sat back and studied it. A pattern started to form. Every one of the people that died was bad. Most of them deserved killing. The crime boss of Toronto ordered the killing of Danny's fiancé. He was wiped out brutally. It was the act of a very angry and violent man. The broken neck of the guy in

France, the brutal killing of the mafia boss in Sicily, the Congressman falling off a balcony in Milwaukee all seemed unrelated. Other than that, no violence, just heart attacks which happened on a daily basis all over the world.

He went over all the information again. He sat back and said to himself, *"If he is doing this, then what I have here is a singing vigilante!"*

Chapter 61

They were lying side by side. Renee was breathing hard as was Danny. They had just completed a marathon love making session. She turned her head and looked at him. "You know something. You're the best ever. I've never had a lover like you."

"You just never had one this big before."

"True. Now that I'm use to it, it gets better every time. Let's go out and swim naked in the pool." They jumped up, ran out the door, and dove into the pool. He had her pinned against the side, her big breasts, floating gently in front of him. She kissed him. "Danny, I want to ask you something."

"What is it?"

"You know that Velvet is doing a wonderful job of running the business. Me, I know nothing at all about what goes on. I'm Chairman of the Board, but if it wasn't for Velvet speaking for me, I wouldn't know what the hell to do. My point is I want out. I have enough money to last me forever and more coming in, thanks to Velvet. I want to take a tour around the world before it's too late. Do it up right with the best hotels. I mean first class all the way. I can afford it and more. Here's what I want to do. I want to make Velvet the Chairman of the Board. She deserves it and I know with her there, she will protect me. What do you think?"

"I think it's a great idea. And she does deserve it. You call a board meeting and tell them that's what you want. I'm sure they'll vote her in. Then you take your tour. I'll make some arrangements with some people I know around the world to show you a good time. I'll get my travel agent to set it all up for you. Planes, hotels, tours, visas, and anything else that you want."

She pulled him close and kissed him hard on the mouth. "I knew I could count on you. You do take good care of me. Danny, I must tell you that I'll miss you and that tool of yours though."

"We'll be here when you get back. Don't worry about that."

When Velvet got home that afternoon, Danny was lying out by the pool. She fixed them a drink and brought it out. "Hey, I thought you might like a drink?"

He sat up and took it from her. She leaned down and kissed him. "Renee called an emergency board meeting for tomorrow. I don't know what it's all about. She wouldn't tell me why, and that's not like her."

"Maybe she wants to surprise you with something. What else can it be?"

"I guess I'll find out tomorrow. I'm uncovering a lot of graft and kickbacks. This company could be the greatest if the partners would stop stealing from it. They're worse than the people that were stealing from Ritchie. I think I'll get into a bathing suit. Be right back."

She went into the house. Danny picked up the phone and made a call. "You know who this is? Tomorrow at the board meeting you will vote Velvet in as Chairman of the Board. If it's not done, then you know what will happen. This time it will be you." He hung up. He said to himself, *"Nothing like having the odds in your favor."*

She came out in a small bikini and dove in the pool. Before she could come up Danny dove in and grabbed her from underneath. He kissed her underwater and pulled her bottoms off. When they surfaced, he made love to her in the shallow end, near the Jacuzzi jets. She clung to him. "Now, this is what I call therapeutic. I need more." And he gave her more. When they had their fill, they got out and lay side by side watching the sun go down over the mountain.

They were all sitting at the boardroom table when Renee walked in. She greeted them and took her place at the head of the table. Velvet noticed that the three partners didn't look too good. They were fidgety and sweating even though the air conditioning was running full blast. Renee called for order. "I called this meeting to tell you that I no longer want to be Chairman of the Board. I'm taking a world tour and don't know when I'll be back. I am appointing Velvet Morrison to take over for me."

She turned to Velvet. "I don't know how this is done. Can you handle it for me?"

Velvet was thoroughly shocked. She paused then replied, "Yes, I have to be voted in by the other board members."

"Oh, well let me see. With a show of hands, how many of you want her as the new chairman?"

Before Velvet could say anything, they all raised their hands. Renee laughed. "See, it's all settled." She got up out of her chair. "I have to go make arrangements for my trip. Velvet will keep me posted weekly on everything."

She left. Velvet looked at the other board members. She could feel the hate coming from them. Well that's just too bad. She got up and sat in the chair at the head of the table. She looked at the other members and said, "All right. Let's get down to business."

Renee called him and told him it was done. She stated that it went very smoothly, with no objections. She wanted to cap off the day with a little sport sex. Danny agreed. He hung up. Got in the car and drove to her house.

Chapter 62

Bill Fanning got off the plane in Vegas. He was exhausted from all the traveling the last few days, including Chicago, Buffalo, and down state New York. His folder was full of evidence. He felt sick inside. He liked Danny. They had become real close. He knew everything. He located Ferdinando in a nursing home in Perusia suffering from a coma. The picture on his passport was Danny's. His identity had been stolen. So, who was it that was blown up in the car? In Buffalo he found out that Ritchie's close friend was a plastic surgeon. It didn't take much leaning on the nurse to get her to reluctantly admit they operated on Danny Di. She recognized an old picture Bill had of him.

It had all come together. *The only thing missing was evidence that Danny was actually killing people! Proof, he had to have proof.* He was torn. He took two Tylenol at the house, sat down on the couch and turned on the TV. *There was only one thing on his mind now. What the hell was he going to do about Danny? As much as he disliked doing it, he would have to confront him.*

He waited until after the show before going backstage to the dressing room. It was full of people as usual. Danny saw him and came over. He gave him a hug. "Boy am I glad you're back. We missed you. Come on, I'll get you a drink." They went to the bar and got two drinks. People were coming up and talking to Danny. This went on for about an hour. Then they started leaving. The only people left were the Ox and the Weasel.

Bill said to Danny, "Can we talk alone? I have something important to discuss with you."

Danny heard bells going off in his head. Bill had been

acting strangely. "Sure, I'll get rid of the boys." He walked over and talked to the guys. They nodded and left. Danny came back to the bar. "OK, Bill, what's on your mind?"

Bill laid the folder on the bar. "Does the name Danny DiBernardo mean anything to you?"

Danny looked at him. "Should it?"

"That's your name, Danny. You're not Ferdinando Bello. That's Don Angelo's nephew's name and he's in a nursing home in Italy in a coma. Just for fun I ran your fingerprints. Twice I came up with the same answer. You're Danny Di. You took the Don's nephew's identity, changed your face, and became him. I found the nurse in Buffalo who was in on the operation. She identified your picture."

Danny took a sip of his drink. "So Danny Di decided to go straight and become a star. What's wrong with that?"

"A lot. Who was in the car that was blown up in Chicago? And, if you were going to go straight, why all the deception?"

"Come on Bill. You know as well as I do, that the law would never leave me alone. They would hound me to the grave. They've tried for years to pin something on me, but couldn't. The only way for me to break free was for Danny Di to die."

"There's another thing that bothers me. It turns out that everywhere you have been performing, here and abroad, somebody of importance has died."

"And you think I did it. Just because of my past. That's not nice, Bill. People do change. Tell me, do you have any proof of this? Any witnesses? Hell, you were with me the night that Senator Friedman died. Did you see me kill him? No. I worked real hard to bury Danny Di and become a superstar. Why would I jeopardize all this? For what? The thrill of killing somebody?"

"I don't know. And, I don't have any proof yet. But the fact still remains, you are a known hit man. Somebody died so you could be somebody else."

"Bill, let me hip you to something. Suppose you go public with this. The press and TV will have a field day. They'll jump on this story in a flash. It's a Cinderella story. Hit man to superstar.

This is the stuff legends are made of. I'll have the sympathy of everybody in the world. The movie alone will set box office records."

"I know, that's why I did it on my own. I couldn't tell anybody in case they let it slip. You don't accuse a superstar of murder without all the facts and the proof. Danny, this is the hardest thing I have ever had to do in my life. I'm torn between friendship and duty. Do I just forget it, and let you go on? Or, do I arrest you, and let the law take its course?"

Danny reached out and put his hand on his shoulder. "Bill, I know this is hard for you. Tell you what. Let's go to my house and hash it out. If you decide to take me in, I'll go gladly. I'll take my chances."

Bill put his hand over Danny's. "Thanks, Danny. That makes it a whole lot easier."

They left the dressing room and headed for the back door. Danny went out first with Bill right behind him. There were a hundred ladies waiting for him. When they saw Danny, they rushed over pushing and screaming. Bill saw them coming and stepped in front of Danny to protect him.

Danny reached into his pocket and brought out the piece of pearl. As Bill was fending off the ladies, Danny popped him in the leg with the pearl. The folder Bill was carrying was ripped from his hand and shredded by the ladies wanting a souvenir.

Danny walked into the crowd of ladies and was swallowed up. He pushed his way to the limo. The Ox and Weasel got out, opened the limo door, and helped him inside. Danny glanced out the tinted window. Sitting on the ground, with his back up against the building, was Bill. He looked at Danny and raised his hand as if to wave. Danny waived back as Bill slowly slumped over, dead.

Danny bowed his head as the limo sped off, recalling the mob motto, "Nothing personal. Strictly business."

The End?